Disney

THE PRINCESS AND THE FROG

Peachtree

Nao Kodaka

Introduction of Main Characters

主要キャラクター紹介

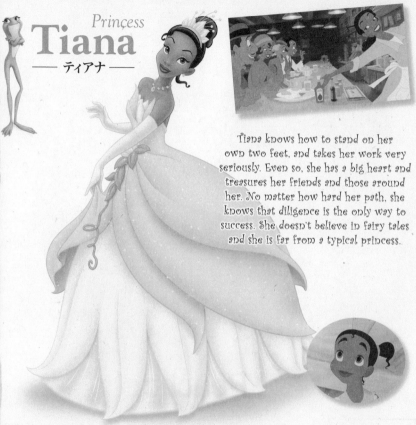

Princess Tiana

―― ティアナ ――

Tiana knows how to stand on her own two feet, and takes her work very seriously. Even so, she has a big heart and treasures her friends and those around her. No matter how hard her path, she knows that diligence is the only way to success. She doesn't believe in fairy tales and she is far from a typical princess.

SUPERVISING ANIMATOR MARK HENN, WHO HELPED CREATE DISNEY HEROINES ARIEL, BELLE, AND JASMINE, FOUND TIANA PARTICULARLY APPEALING. "I THINK YOU CAN EASILY IDENTIFY WITH HER, OR WANT TO CHEER HER ON. OUR ANIMATED LEADING LADIES HAVE EVOLVED OVER THE DECADES, FROM JUST BEING 'PRINCESSES IN PERIL' LIKE SNOW WHITE- CHARACTERS TO WHOM EVENTS HAPPEN-RATHER THAN FIGURES OF ACTION MOTIVATING THEIR OWN STORY. SHE WAS AN EASY CHARACTER TO FALL IN LOVE WITH AND GET IN HER CORNER. TIANA HAS HER OWN MOTIVATING DESIRE, PLUS DECISIONS THAT DRIVE HER AND MAKE HER INTERESTING AND SYMPATHETIC."

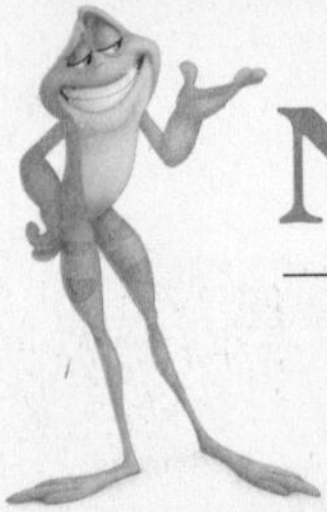

Prince Naveen

—— ナヴィーン ——

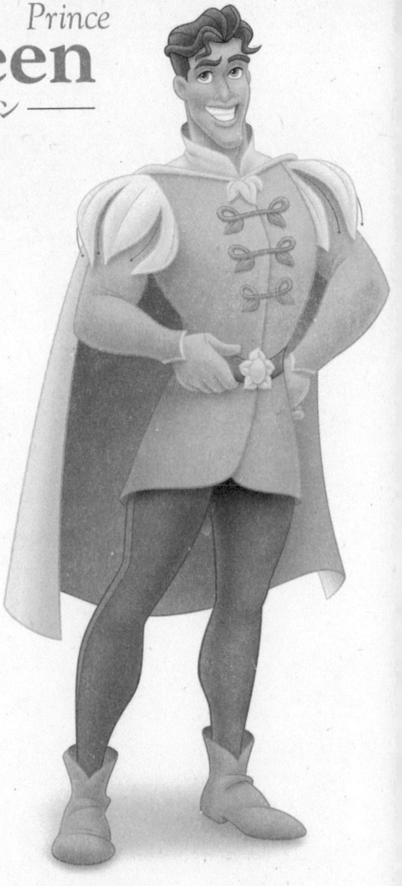

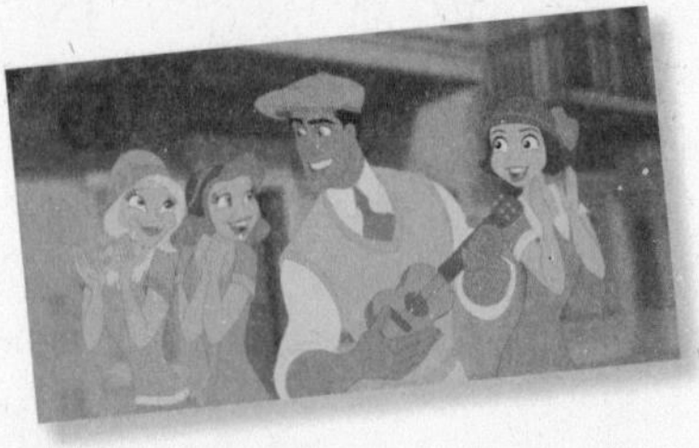

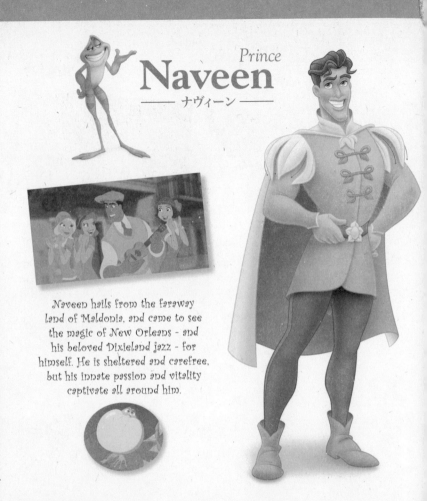

Naveen hails from the faraway land of Maldonia, and came to see the magic of New Orleans - and his beloved Dixieland jazz - for himself. He is sheltered and carefree, but his innate passion and vitality captivate all around him.

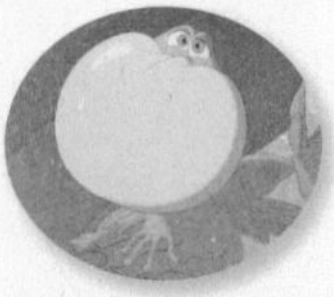

NAVEEN'S SUPERVISING ANIMATOR, RANDY HAYCOCK, HAS ANIMATED CLASSIC DISNEY CHARACTERS, INCLUDING SIMBA AND CHIEF POWHATAN. "DISNEY HAS A LONG TRADITION OF PRINCES, BUT WE'VE NEVER HAD A PRINCE THAT REALLY INFLUENCED A HEROINE," SAYS HAYCOCK. "IT WAS ALWAYS LOVE AT FIRST SIGHT. FOR ONCE WE HAVE A GIRL THAT MEETS A GUY, AND IT FOLLOWS A ROMANTIC-COMEDY IDEA WHERE THE COUPLE MEET AND THEY REALLY DON'T LIKE EACH OTHER."

LIKE ANYONE, NAVEEN'S FLAWS ARE ACTUALLY PART OF HIS VIRTUES. THE HEROINE HAS A FLAW TOO—SHE DOESN'T KNOW HOW TO APPRECIATE LIFE. SHE DOESN'T KNOW HOW TO ENJOY HERSELF. "AND THAT'S WHAT NAVEEN TEACHES HER," HAYCOCK SAYS. "HE TEACHES HER TO SETTLE DOWN ONCE IN A WHILE AND SIMPLY APPRECIATE WHAT'S GOING ON. HAVE SOME FUN, ENJOY, BE HAPPY WITH WHAT YOU HAVE AROUND YOU."

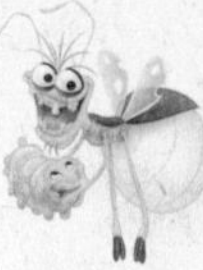

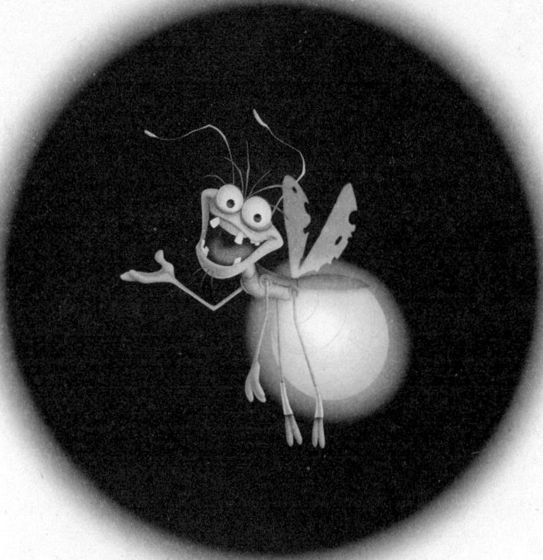

Ray
—レイ—

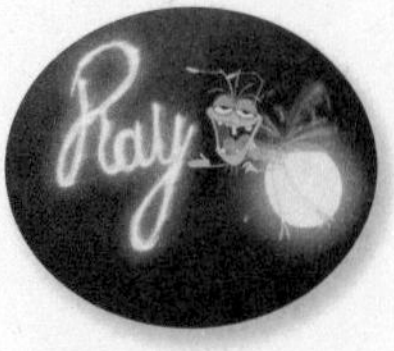
Ray

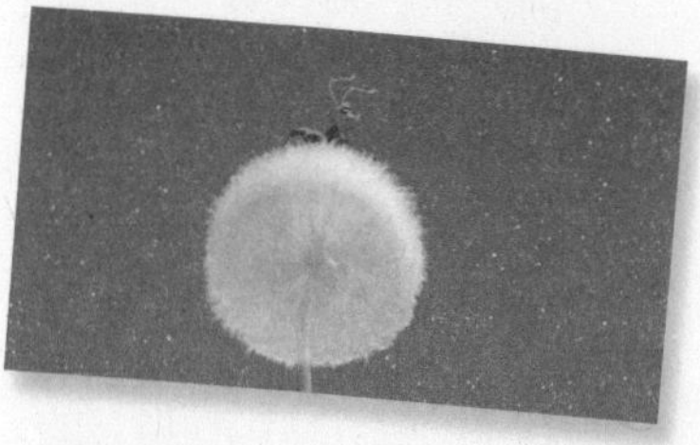

A caregiver at heart, Ray is a firefly in love. He is full of Cajun soul, and his wit and romance burn bright. Ray's heart has been stolen by one Evangeline, the "most beautiful firefly in the world." He doesn't believe in "impossible" -and is fully committed to true love.

SUPERVISING ANIMATOR MIKE SURREY, WHO HAS WORKED ON SUCH LOVABLE CHARACTERS AS *THE LION KING'S* TIMON AND *THE HUNCHBACK OF NOTRE DAME'S* CLOPIN, NOTES THAT RAY IS A CHARACTER WHO DOES WHAT HE HAS TO DO. "HE'S A ROMANTIC GUY. THAT'S NOT TO SAY THAT NAVEEN AND TIANA AREN'T - BUT IN RAY'S CASE, HE'S VERY OPEN ABOUT HIS FEELINGS. HE DOESN'T CARE HOW IT LOOKS TO OTHERS. TIANA AND NAVEEN BOTH FEEL THE SAME WAY ABOUT EACH OTHER, AND WHETHER THEY HAVE REALIZED FOR THEMSELVES OR NOT, RAY KNOWS. HE IS THE BIGGEST PROPONENT OF 'LOVE CONQUERS ALL'. HE SHOULD REALLY GET THOSE TEETH CHECKED OUT THOUGH, HUH?"

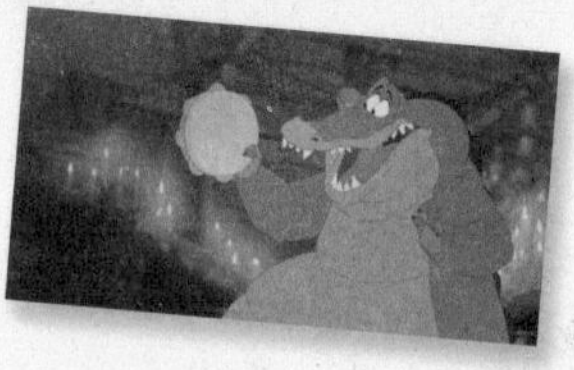

Louis

— ルイス —

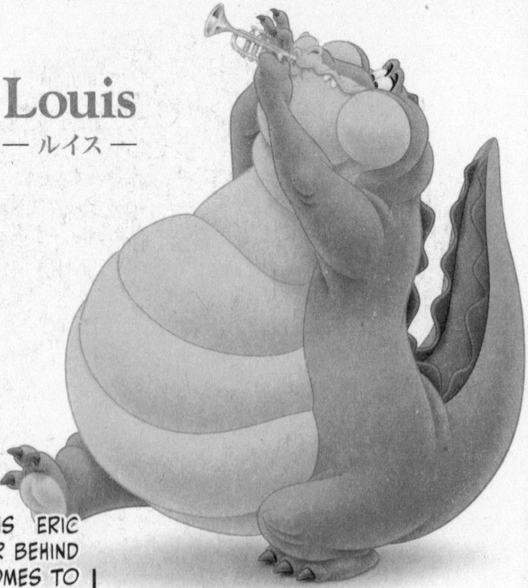

Louis picked up jazz in the marshes, where he first became passionate about the trumpet and performing. He's one charming gator! He makes this Bayou adventure come to life with his charm and humor.

"HE'S STARVED FOR LOVE," EXPLAINS ERIC GOLDBERG, THE SUPERVISING ANIMATOR BEHIND THE GENIE IN *ALADDIN*. "BUT WHEN IT COMES TO JAZZ, HE'S THE REAL DEAL. WHEN LOUIS PLAYS, THAT'S WHO HE REALLY IS."

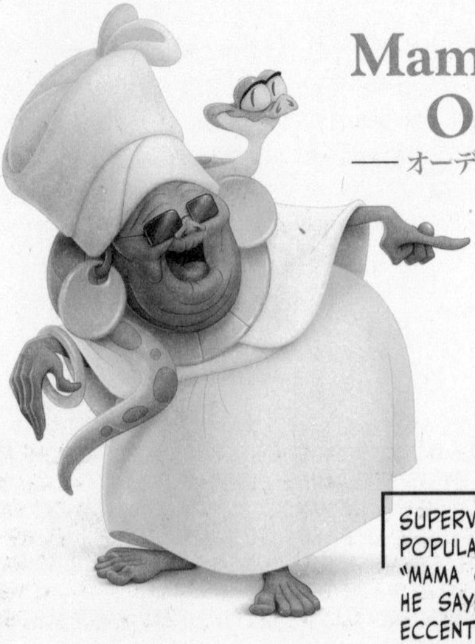

Mama Odie

— オーディ —

You can find Mama Odie in an old fishing boat in a tree deep in the Bayou, where she's been the queen of magic (and quick wit) for 197 years. With nowhere else to turn, Tiana and Naveen come to Mama Odie for help - and she knows just what to do. She, and her snake, Juju, will help you work out any spell you need!

SUPERVISING ANIMATOR ANDREAS DEJA HAS WORKED ON POPULAR CHARACTERS LIKE GASTON, JAFAR, AND LILO. "MAMA ODIE COMPLETELY STOLE MY HEART, THOUGH," HE SAYS. "SHE'S THIS LITTLE OLD BLIND LADY, SHE'S ECCENTRIC, SHE HAS A GUIDE-SNAKE. NOTHING ABOUT HER IS AVERAGE."

Charlotte is a wealthy young heiress. She likes the finer things, and is, a little spoiled - but don't be fooled. Charlotte's not your typical rich girl. Sure, she knows how to get a couture dress or two out of her daddy, but she's got her own dreams, too.

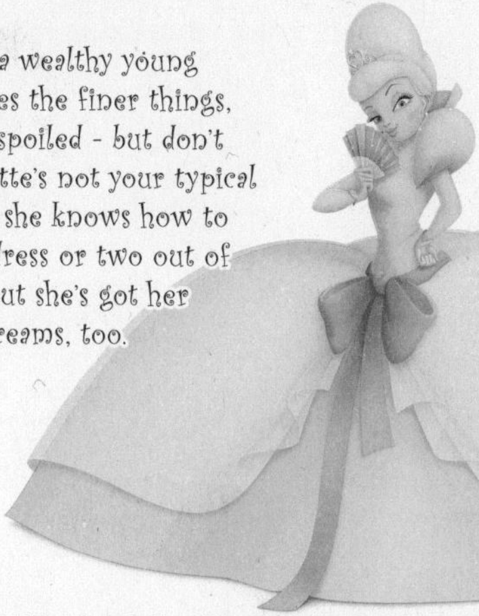

Charlotte

—— シャーロット ——

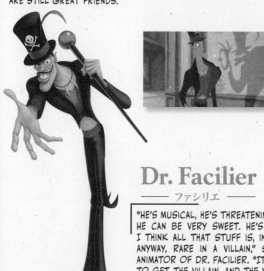

CHARLOTTE AND TIANA MEET AS GIRLS WHEN TIANA'S MOTHER, THE BEST SEAMSTRESS IN NEW ORLEANS, CREATED DRESSES FOR HER. WHEN CHARLOTTE FIRST HEARS THE STORY OF THE FROG, SHE ASSERTS THAT IF SHE GOT TO MARRY A PRINCE, SHE'D BE JUST FINE WITH A KISS. TIANA, OF COURSE, DOESN'T AGREE. BUT THE TWO FORGE A LIFELONG BOND, AND ARE STILL GREAT FRIENDS.

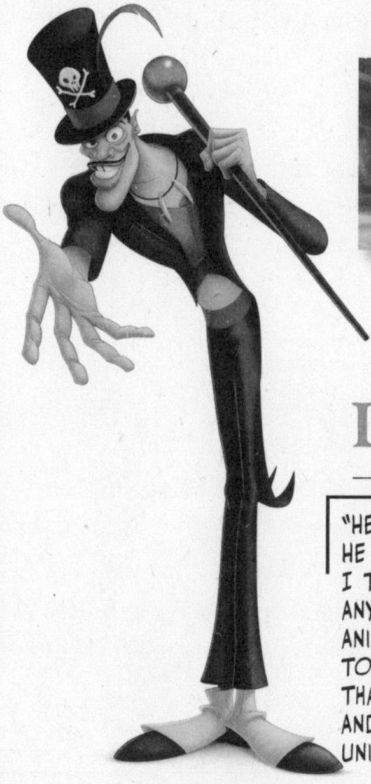

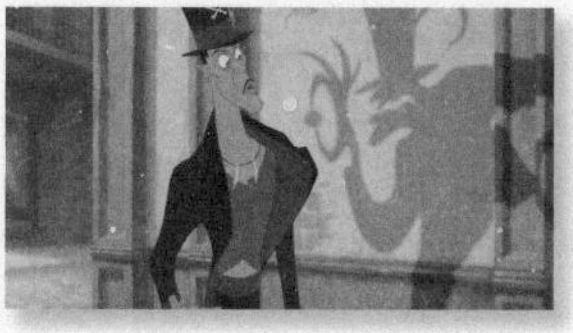

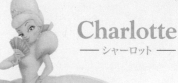

A sneaky man of the shadows, he continuously causes problems for Tiana and Naveen. He's good with a scheme, a bit of magic, and can call in a favor or two from his "friends on the other side." He knows how to use that dangerous charm to get just what he wants.

Dr. Facilier

—— ファシリエ ——

"HE'S MUSICAL, HE'S THREATENING, HE'S TALL, HE'S LEAN, HE'S THIN. HE CAN BE VERY SWEET. HE'S HANDSOME. HE'S GRACEFUL. AND I THINK ALL THAT STUFF IS, IN VERY CONTEMPORARY ANIMATION ANYWAY, RARE IN A VILLAIN," SAYS BRUCE SMITH, SUPERVISING ANIMATOR OF DR. FACILIER. "IT'S ALWAYS GREAT AS AN ANIMATOR TO GET THE VILLAIN, AND THE VILLAIN IS ALWAYS THAT CHARACTER THAT HOLDS UP THE FILM AND KEEPS EVERYTHING INTERESTING AND ON EDGE. LUCKILY, IN THIS CASE, I'VE REALLY GOT A VERY UNIQUE VILLAIN–A GREAT VILLAIN."

Tiana's father
and her inspiration. He instills in
Tiana his strong morals, and teaches
her that sharing food with the people
around you is a lot like love. He tells
her, "Food makes us all the same.
It warms us all up and puts a smile
on our face." Even when he is gone,
his love lives on in Tiana's heart.

James
— ジェームズ —

Tiana's mother.
When Tiana was very little, she
watched her mother build her
own success, and earn the respect
of those around her as a hard-
working woman with her own
business. Whereas James was the
romantic, Eudora was always the
realist. She knows what lies ahead
for Tiana as she begins to come into
her own as a strong, independent
woman, and wants nothing but
the best life for her daughter.

Eudora
— ユードラ —

Charlotte's father,
Mister Eli La Bouff. He is
a charming and sturdy man
of wealth and esteem. He lives
for his daughter, Charlotte, and
would do anything to make
her happy. Charlotte's lifelong
wish is to be a princess, so he
decides to throw her a ball.

Big Daddy
— ビッグ・ダディ —

Garden District
— ガーデン地区 —

The Garden District is New Orleans' oldest suburb. Developed between 1832 and 1900, it is home to many esteemed and historic mansions. These luxurious homes tell the story of the prosperous and wealthy families who came to New Orleans during this period.

The Garden District sets the scene for this American fairy tale. The directors wanted a locale for the film's "royal family" that evoked the same kind of prestige, luxury, and power as the traditional fairy tale castle.

Ian Gooding, art director for the film, said that by adding very exaggerated details to the building design, they were able to imitate some of the stiff, straight lines in the area's architecture, while still keeping the integrity of how these structures appear in real life. The scroll-work, the pillars, ornate decorations, were all exaggerated to liven the scene.

"ONE OF THE UNIQUE THINGS ABOUT THE PRINCESS AND THE FROG —IT'S NOT JUST A FAIRY TALE, IT'S ACTUALLY SET IN A REAL TIME, IN A REAL CITY. THAT'S BEEN REALLY FUN, IT ALLOWED US TO ACTUALLY GO TO THIS PLACE AND RESEARCH, AND A LOT OF ENVIRONMENTS IN THE MOVIE ARE PLACES YOU CAN ACTUALLY VISIT," SAYS JOHN MUSKER, ONE OF THE FILM'S VETERAN DIRECTORS.

The French Quarter is the oldest area of New Orleans, and has become one of the south's greatest spots for tourism. The area boasts many multi-story buildings, all with very brilliantly and ornately decorated balconies and elaborate cast ironwork. Most of these buildings are brick or stucco, painted in vibrant colors, with window and door shutters built to protect against tropical storms. At night, gas lanterns light the small cobblestone streets and open courtyards, and the shadows they create incite a certain sense of romance, imagination, and mystery.

French Quarter
—— フレンチ・クォーター ——

THE ARTISTS USED ALL OF THE ELEMENTS OF THE FRENCH QUARTER TO CREATE A FEELING OF ENCHANTMENT. THE SHADOWS CAST BY THE ELEGANT BALCONY IRONWORK SET A MYSTICAL MOOD; SPACES ARE TALL AND NARROW DOORWAYS HOLD HIDDEN TREASURES. THE STRONG CONTRAST WITH LIGHT AND SHADOW IS UNSETTLING, AND PERPETUATES DR. FACILIER'S HAUNTING YET ENTICING PRESENCE THROUGHOUT.

Bayou
— バイユー —

It's in the Mississippi River Delta that you'll find the marshlands. The winds off the "Big River" blow through the swamps, where the branches sway lazily. Alligators swim through salty waters under grand Palmetto trees, and fireflies light up the shade between the shrubs and oaks covered in Spanish moss. It stirs up a sense of magic, mystery, and romance -the perfect setting for our story.

VISUAL DEVELOPMENT ARTIST SUSAN NICHOLS ADDS, "NEW ORLEANS REALLY IS EMBLEMATIC OF 'AMERICANA,' IN THAT IT'S A MELTING POT OF SO MANY VARIED CULTURES, AND ALWAYS HAS BEEN, WHICH GIVES A FLAVOR TO THE COMMUNITY AND THE ETHNICITY THAT IS INTEGRAL TO THE ENTIRE ENVIRONMENT THERE. IT ADDED A LAYER OF FLAVOR TO THE VISUALS THAT WE HAVEN'T TAPPED INTO BEFORE, AND I LOVED IT."

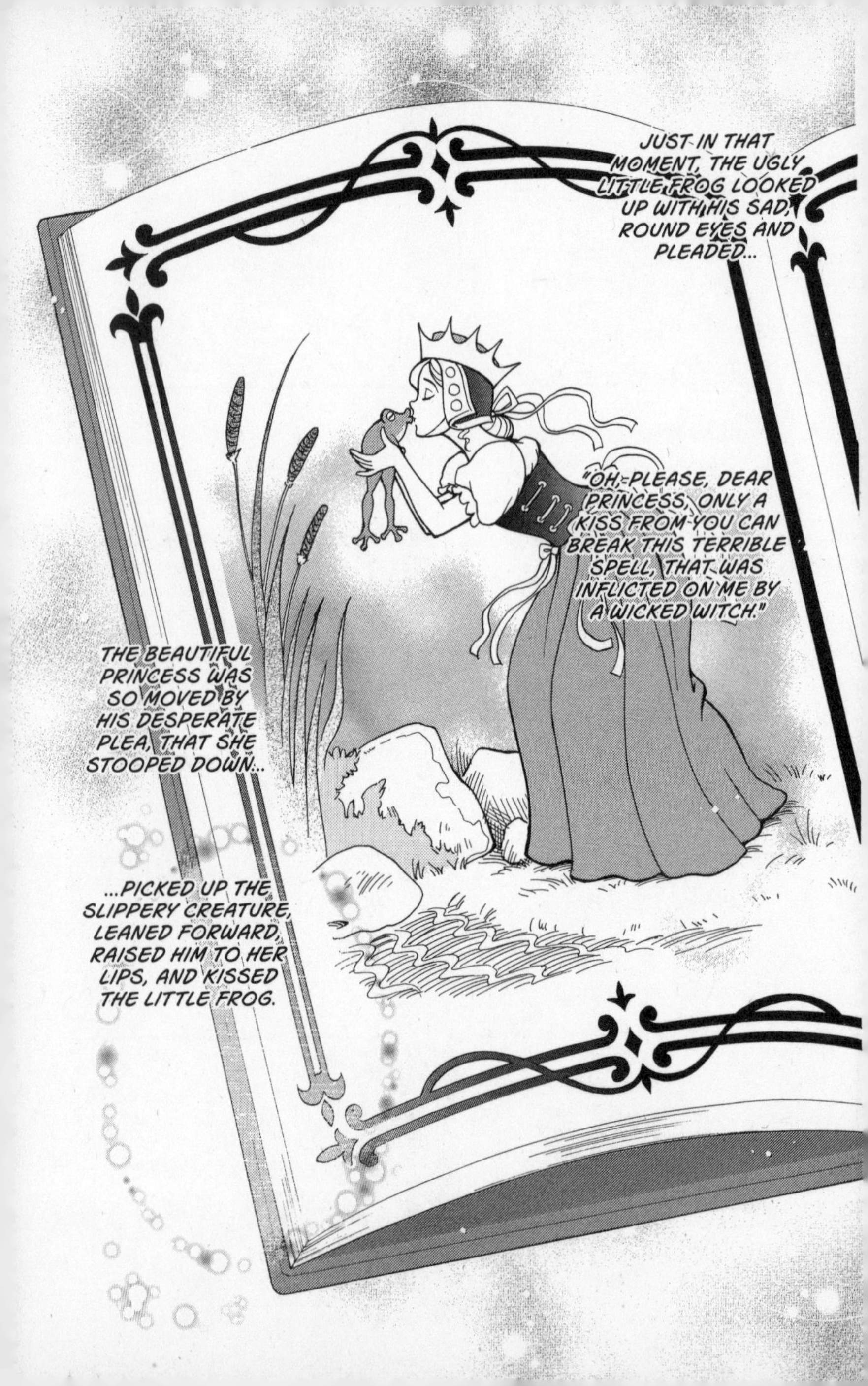
JUST IN THAT MOMENT, THE UGLY LITTLE FROG LOOKED UP WITH HIS SAD, ROUND EYES AND PLEADED...
"OH, PLEASE, DEAR PRINCESS, ONLY A KISS FROM YOU CAN BREAK THIS TERRIBLE SPELL, THAT WAS INFLICTED ON ME BY A WICKED WITCH."
THE BEAUTIFUL PRINCESS WAS SO MOVED BY HIS DESPERATE PLEA, THAT SHE STOOPED DOWN...
...PICKED UP THE SLIPPERY CREATURE, LEANED FORWARD, RAISED HIM TO HER LIPS, AND KISSED THE LITTLE FROG.

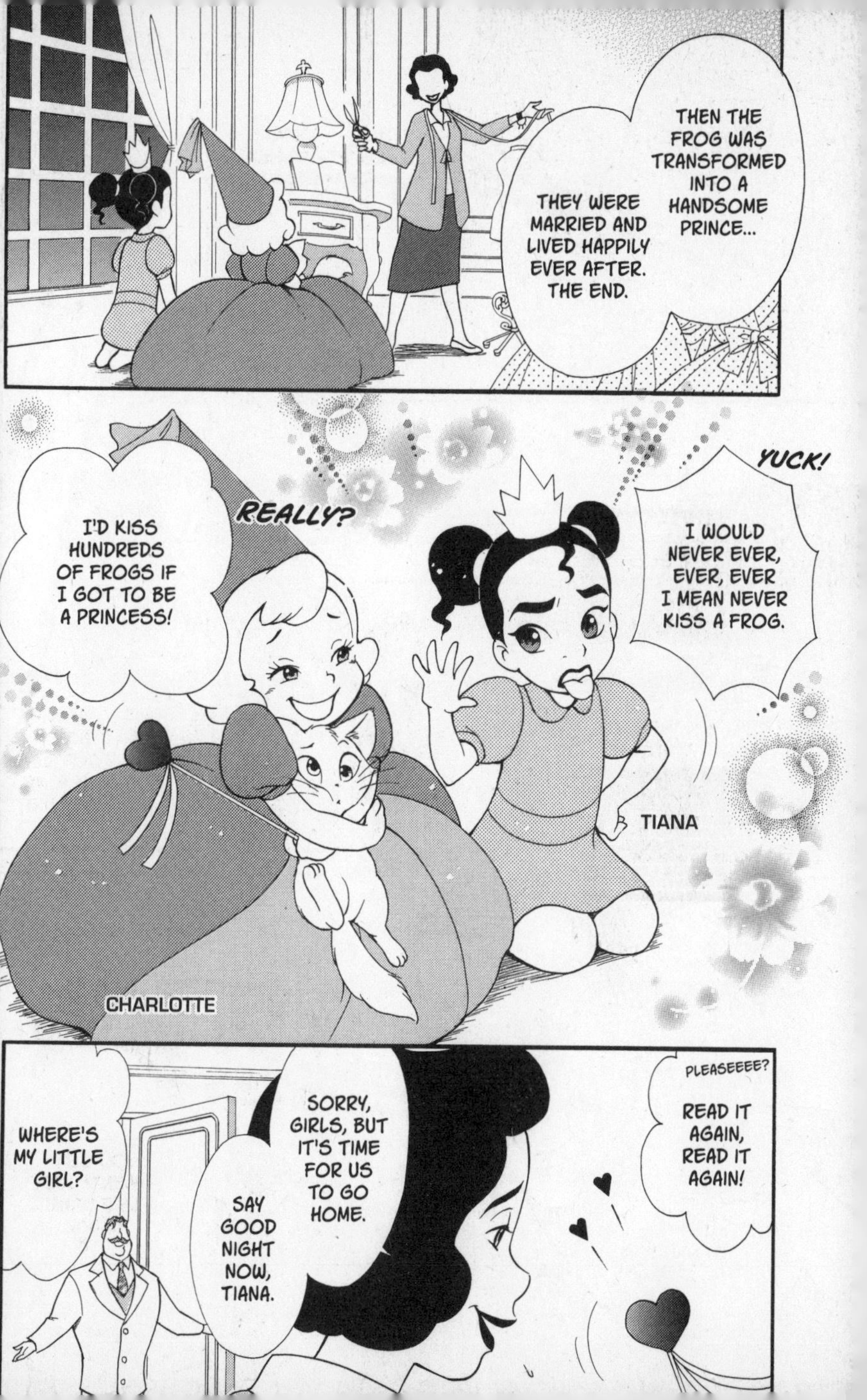
THEN THE FROG WAS TRANSFORMED INTO A HANDSOME PRINCE...
THEY WERE MARRIED AND LIVED HAPPILY EVER AFTER. THE END.
YUCK!
I WOULD NEVER EVER, EVER, EVER I MEAN NEVER KISS A FROG.
TIANA
REALLY?
I'D KISS HUNDREDS OF FROGS IF I GOT TO BE A PRINCESS!
CHARLOTTE
PLEASEEEE?
READ IT AGAIN, READ IT AGAIN!
SORRY, GIRLS, BUT IT'S TIME FOR US TO GO HOME.
SAY GOOD NIGHT NOW, TIANA.
WHERE'S MY LITTLE GIRL?

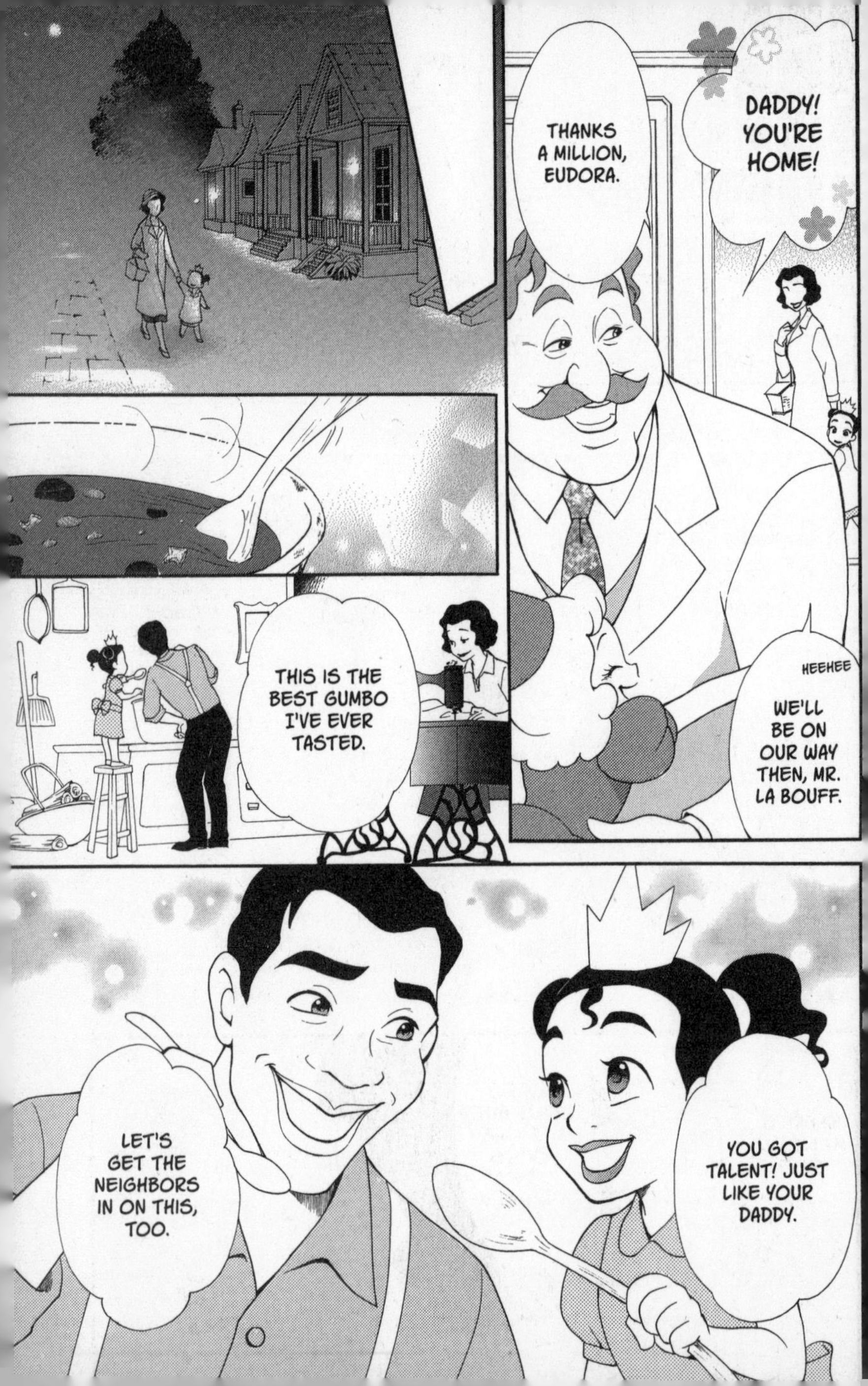
DADDY! YOU'RE HOME!
THANKS A MILLION, EUDORA.
HEEHEE
WE'LL BE ON OUR WAY THEN, MR. LA BOUFF.
THIS IS THE BEST GUMBO I'VE EVER TASTED.
YOU GOT TALENT! JUST LIKE YOUR DADDY.
LET'S GET THE NEIGHBORS IN ON THIS, TOO.

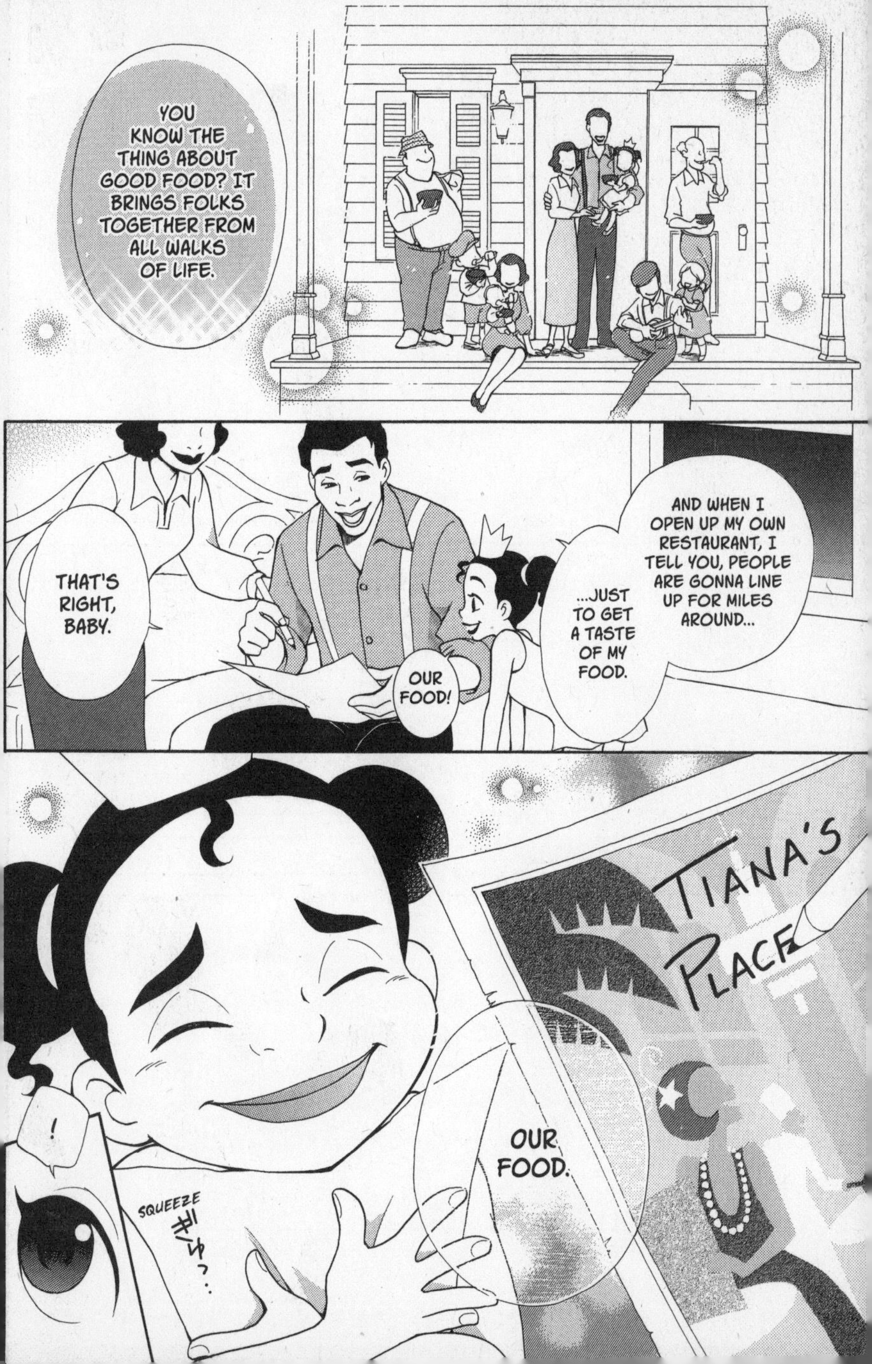
YOU KNOW THE THING ABOUT GOOD FOOD? IT BRINGS FOLKS TOGETHER FROM ALL WALKS OF LIFE.
AND WHEN I OPEN UP MY OWN RESTAURANT, I TELL YOU, PEOPLE ARE GONNA LINE UP FOR MILES AROUND...
...JUST TO GET A TASTE OF MY FOOD.
OUR FOOD!
THAT'S RIGHT, BABY.
TIANA'S PLACE
OUR FOOD.
SQUEEZE
ぎゅっ...

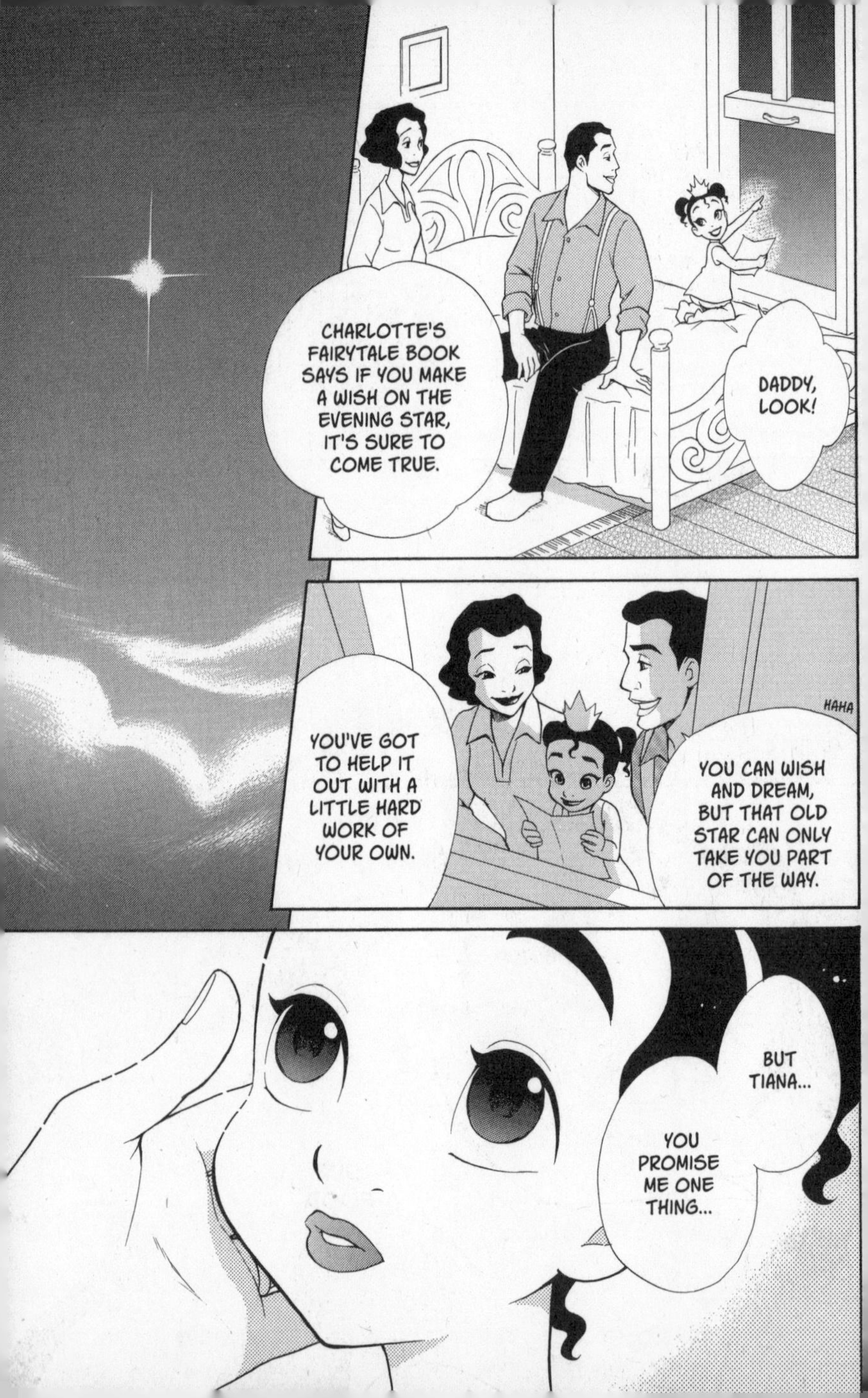
DADDY, LOOK!
CHARLOTTE'S FAIRYTALE BOOK SAYS IF YOU MAKE A WISH ON THE EVENING STAR, IT'S SURE TO COME TRUE.
HAHA
YOU CAN WISH AND DREAM, BUT THAT OLD STAR CAN ONLY TAKE YOU PART OF THE WAY.
YOU'VE GOT TO HELP IT OUT WITH A LITTLE HARD WORK OF YOUR OWN.
BUT TIANA...
YOU PROMISE ME ONE THING...

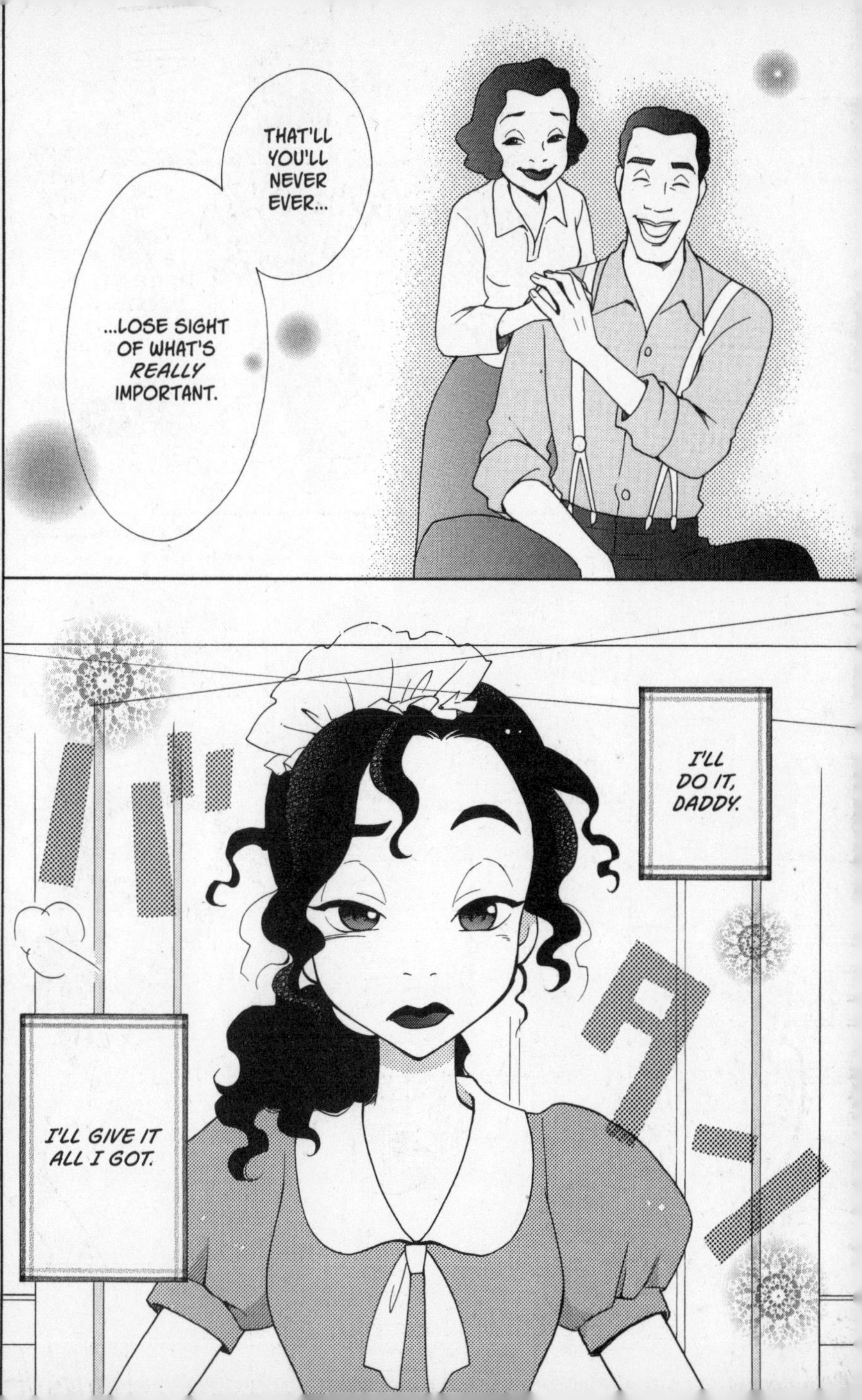
THAT'LL YOU'LL NEVER EVER...
...LOSE SIGHT OF WHAT'S *REALLY* IMPORTANT.
I'LL DO IT, DADDY.
I'LL GIVE IT ALL I GOT.

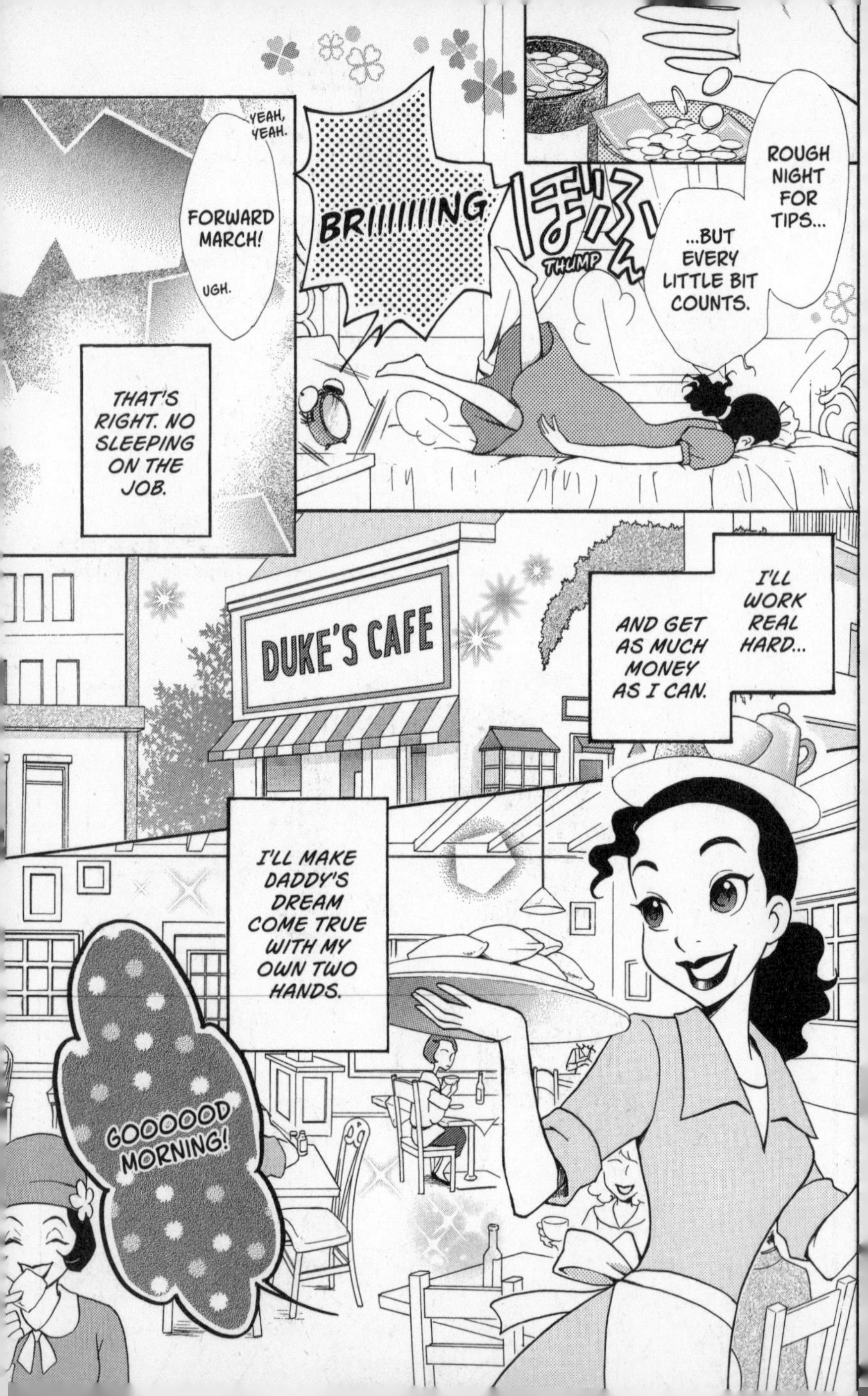
ROUGH NIGHT FOR TIPS...
...BUT EVERY LITTLE BIT COUNTS.
BRIIIIIIING
THUMP
YEAH, YEAH.
FORWARD MARCH!
UGH.
THAT'S RIGHT. NO SLEEPING ON THE JOB.
DUKE'S CAFE
I'LL WORK REAL HARD...
AND GET AS MUCH MONEY AS I CAN.
I'LL MAKE DADDY'S DREAM COME TRUE WITH MY OWN TWO HANDS.
GOOOOOD MORNING!

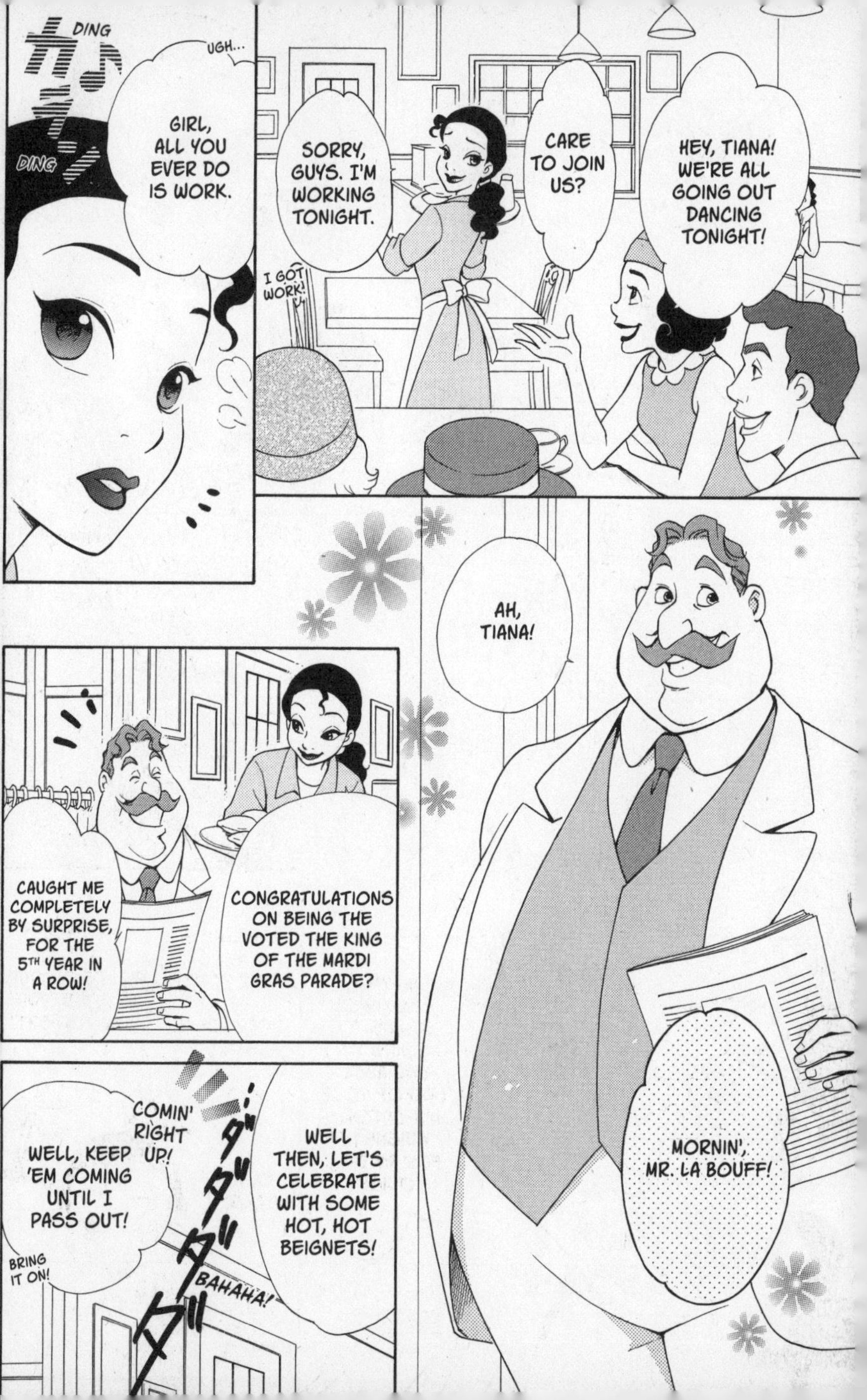
HEY, TIANA! WE'RE ALL GOING OUT DANCING TONIGHT!
CARE TO JOIN US?
SORRY, GUYS. I'M WORKING TONIGHT.
I GOT WORK!
DING
UGH...
GIRL, ALL YOU EVER DO IS WORK.
DING
...
AH, TIANA!
MORNIN', MR. LA BOUFF!
CONGRATULATIONS ON BEING THE VOTED THE KING OF THE MARDI GRAS PARADE?
CAUGHT ME COMPLETELY BY SURPRISE, FOR THE 5TH YEAR IN A ROW!
WELL THEN, LET'S CELEBRATE WITH SOME HOT, HOT BEIGNETS!
COMIN' RIGHT UP!
WELL, KEEP 'EM COMING UNTIL I PASS OUT!
BRING IT ON!
BAHAHA!

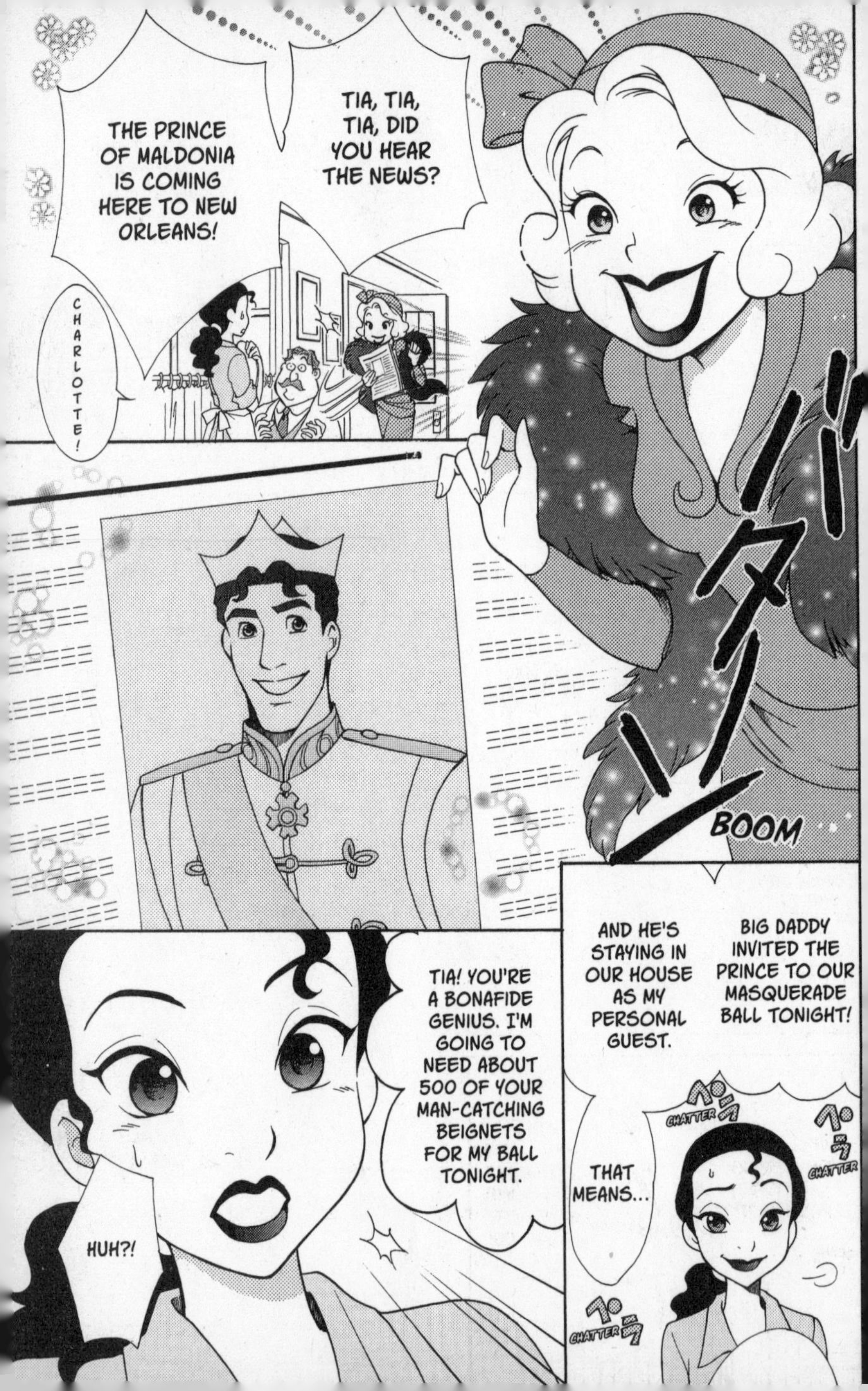
BOOM
TIA, TIA, TIA, DID YOU HEAR THE NEWS?
THE PRINCE OF MALDONIA IS COMING HERE TO NEW ORLEANS!
CHARLOTTE!
BIG DADDY INVITED THE PRINCE TO OUR MASQUERADE BALL TONIGHT!
AND HE'S STAYING IN OUR HOUSE AS MY PERSONAL GUEST.
CHATTER
CHATTER
THAT MEANS...
CHATTER
TIA! YOU'RE A BONAFIDE GENIUS. I'M GOING TO NEED ABOUT 500 OF YOUR MAN-CATCHING BEIGNETS FOR MY BALL TONIGHT.
HUH?!

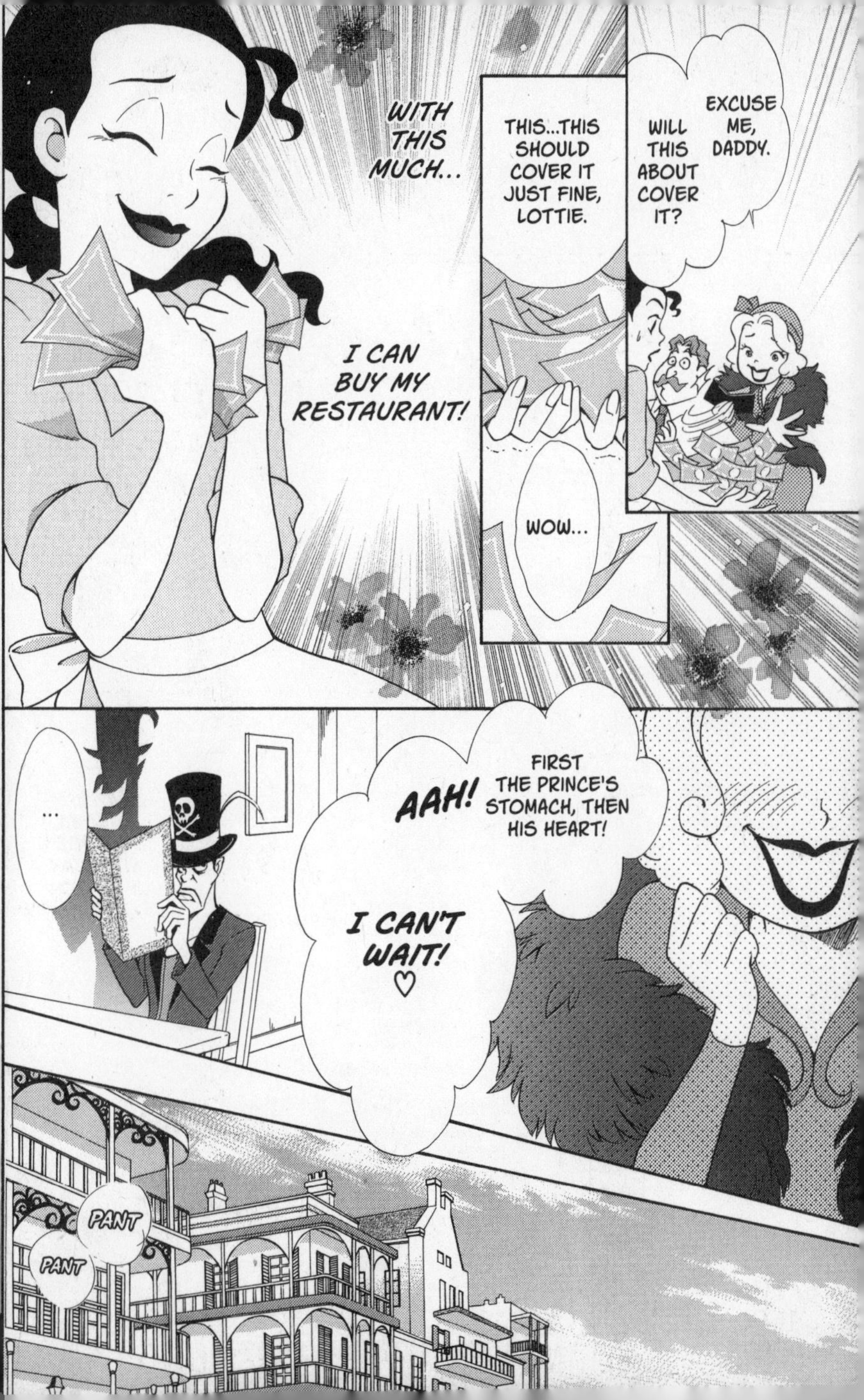

EXCUSE ME, DADDY.
WILL THIS ABOUT COVER IT?
THIS...THIS SHOULD COVER IT JUST FINE, LOTTIE.
WOW...
WITH THIS MUCH...
I CAN BUY MY RESTAURANT!
FIRST THE PRINCE'S STOMACH, THEN HIS HEART!
AAH!
I CAN'T WAIT! ♡
...
PANT
PANT

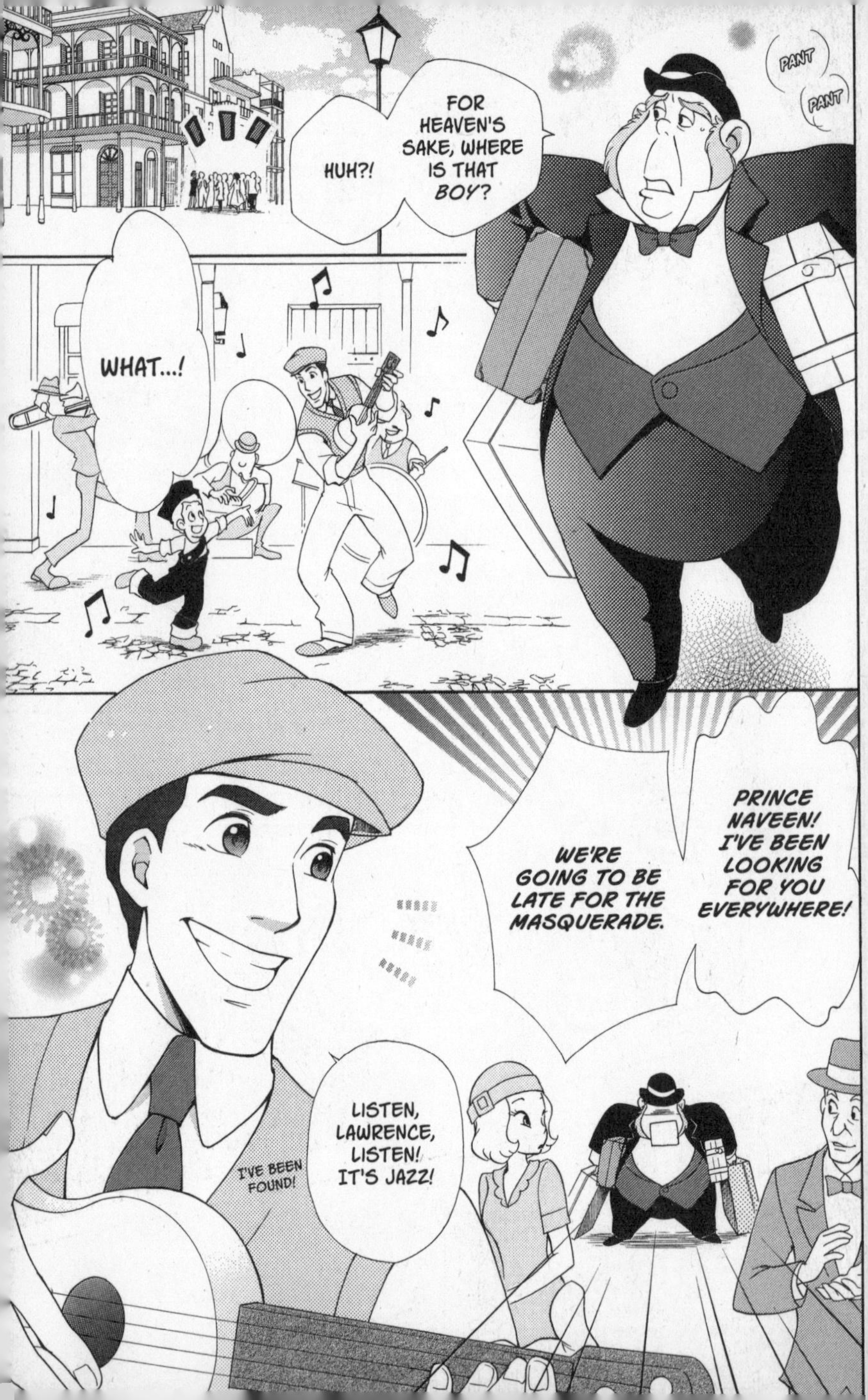
PANT
PANT
FOR HEAVEN'S SAKE, WHERE IS THAT *BOY*?
HUH?!
WHAT...!
PRINCE NAVEEN! I'VE BEEN LOOKING FOR YOU EVERYWHERE!
WE'RE GOING TO BE LATE FOR THE MASQUERADE.
LISTEN, LAWRENCE, LISTEN! IT'S JAZZ!
I'VE BEEN FOUND!

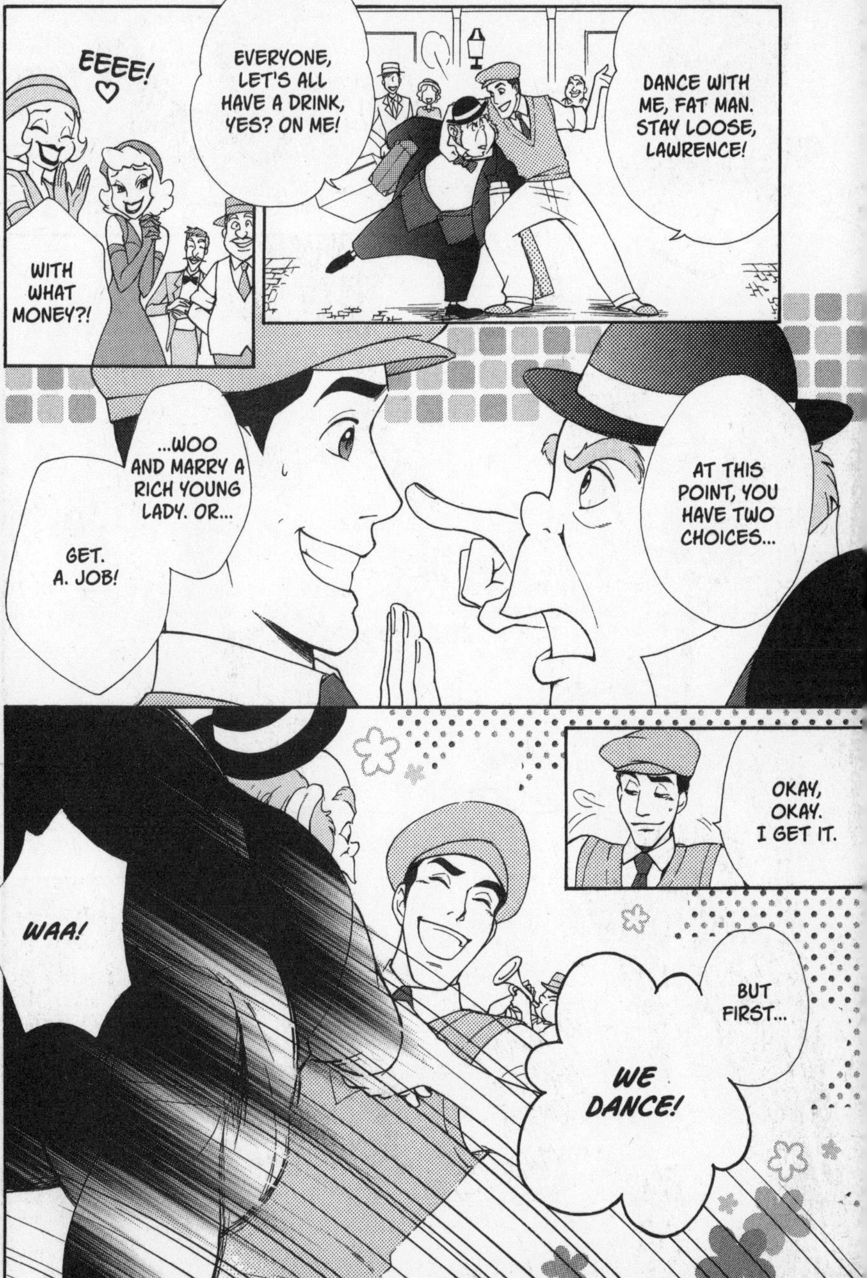
DANCE WITH ME, FAT MAN. STAY LOOSE, LAWRENCE!
EVERYONE, LET'S ALL HAVE A DRINK, YES? ON ME!
EEEE! ♥
WITH WHAT MONEY?!
AT THIS POINT, YOU HAVE TWO CHOICES...
...WOO AND MARRY A RICH YOUNG LADY. OR...
GET. A. JOB!
OKAY, OKAY. I GET IT.
BUT FIRST...
WE DANCE!
WAA!

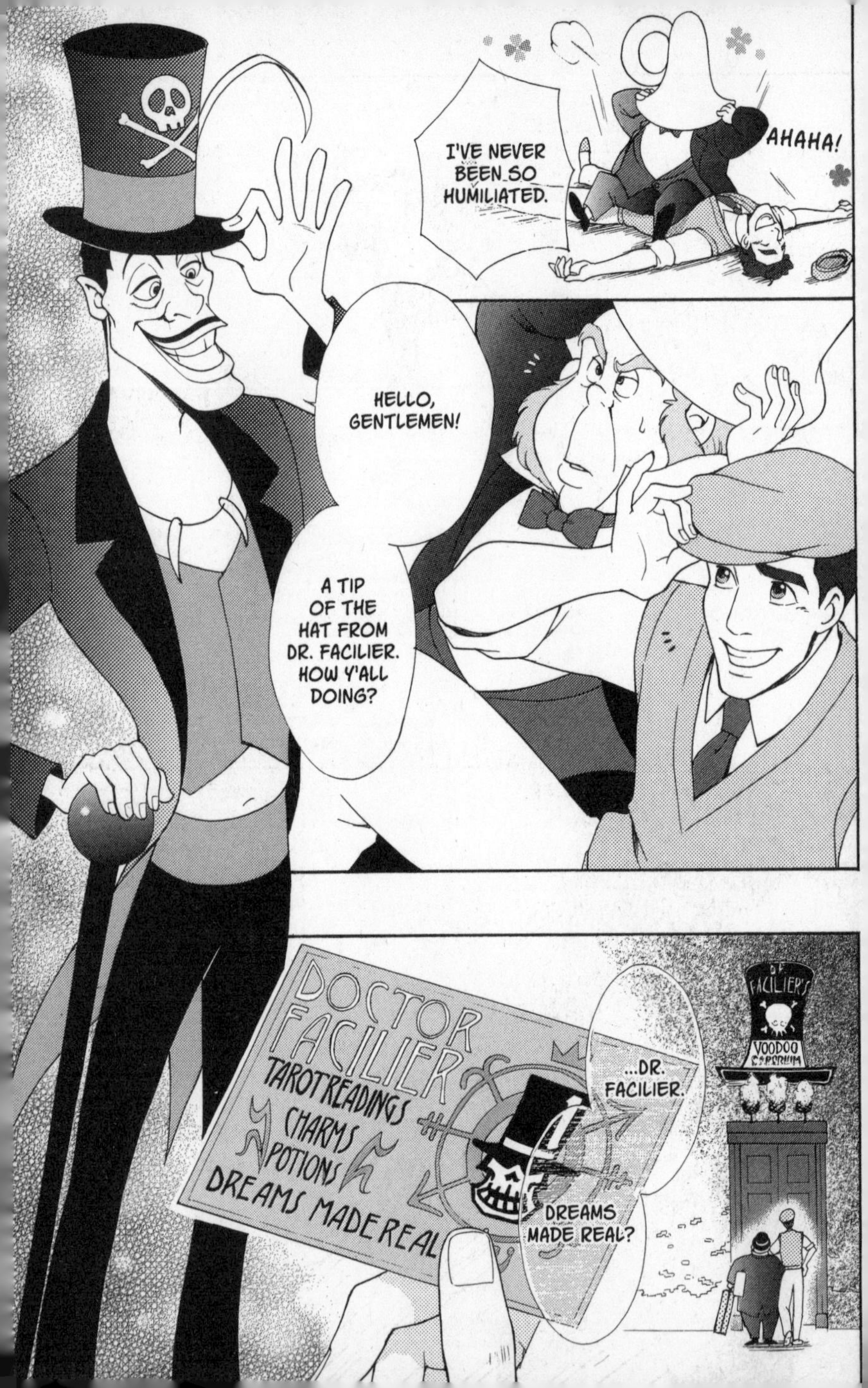
I'VE NEVER BEEN SO HUMILIATED.
AHAHA!
HELLO, GENTLEMEN!
A TIP OF THE HAT FROM DR. FACILIER. HOW Y'ALL DOING?
FACILIER'S
VOODOO
...DR. FACILIER.
DOCTOR FACILIER
TAROT READINGS
CHARMS
POTIONS
DREAMS MADE REAL
DREAMS MADE REAL?

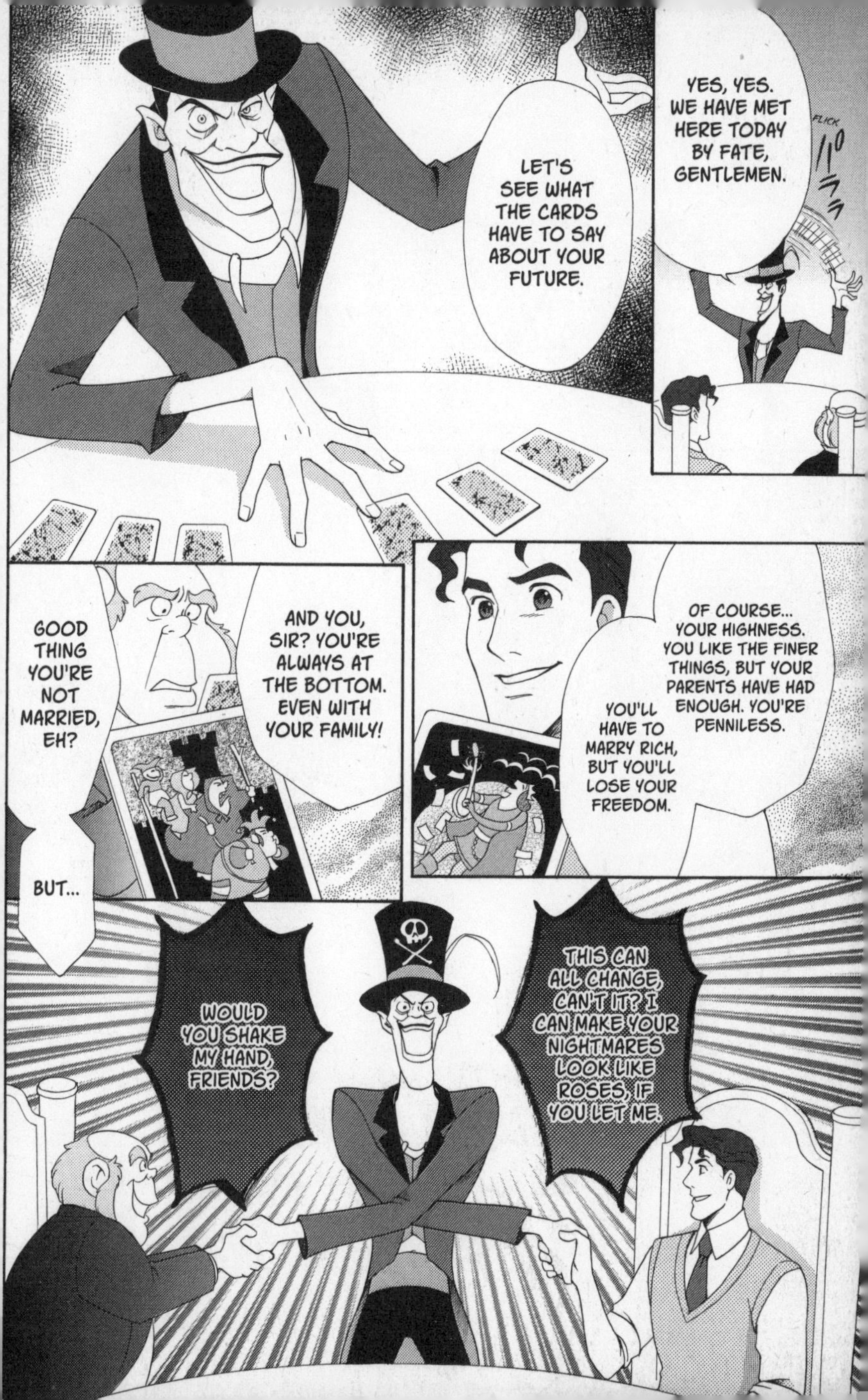
YES, YES. WE HAVE MET HERE TODAY BY FATE, GENTLEMEN.
FLICK
LET'S SEE WHAT THE CARDS HAVE TO SAY ABOUT YOUR FUTURE.
OF COURSE... YOUR HIGHNESS. YOU LIKE THE FINER THINGS, BUT YOUR PARENTS HAVE HAD ENOUGH. YOU'RE PENNILESS.
YOU'LL HAVE TO MARRY RICH, BUT YOU'LL LOSE YOUR FREEDOM.
AND YOU, SIR? YOU'RE ALWAYS AT THE BOTTOM. EVEN WITH YOUR FAMILY!
GOOD THING YOU'RE NOT MARRIED, EH?
BUT...
THIS CAN ALL CHANGE, CAN'T IT? I CAN MAKE YOUR NIGHTMARES LOOK LIKE ROSES, IF YOU LET ME.
WOULD YOU SHAKE MY HAND, FRIENDS?

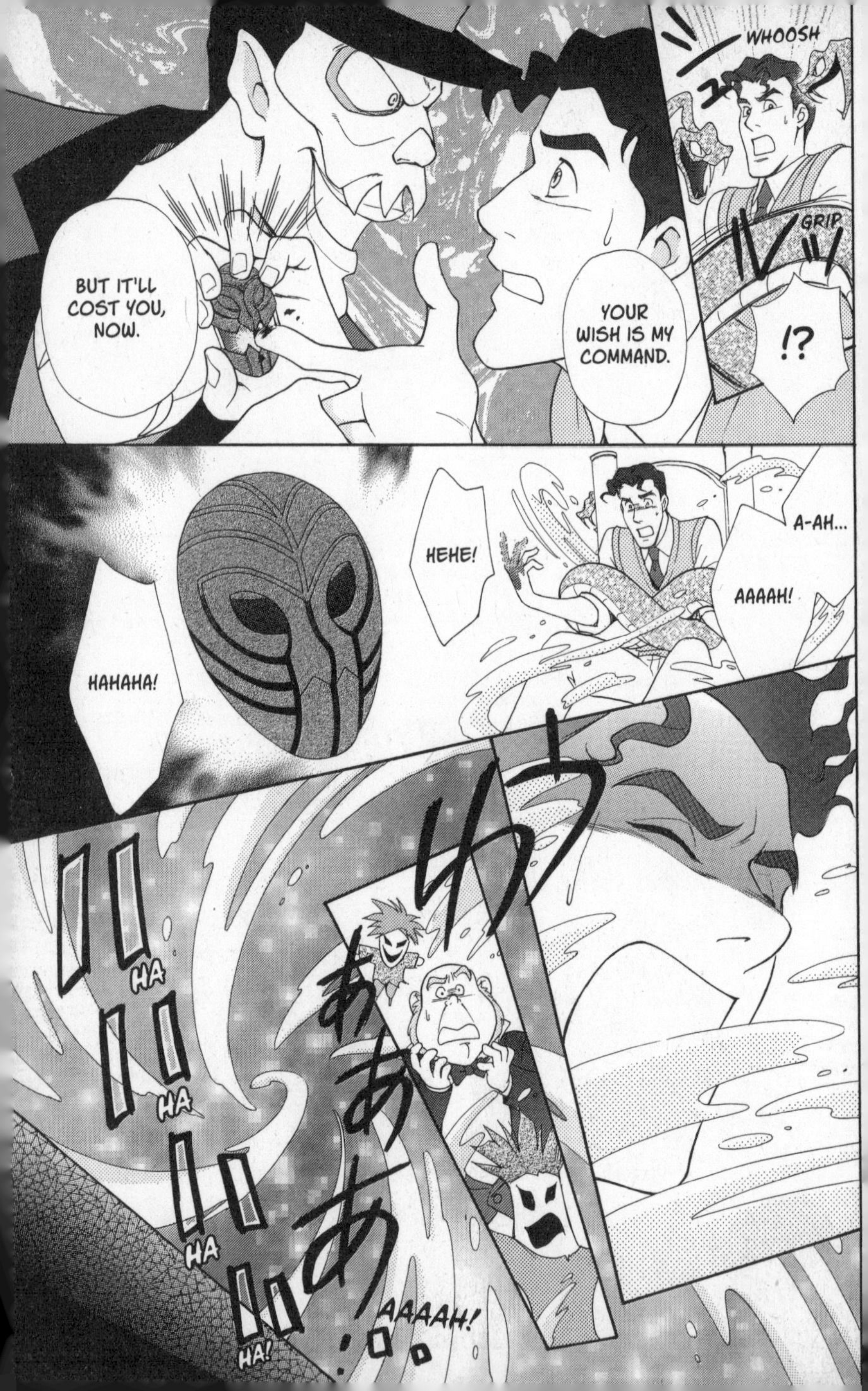
WHOOSH
GRIP
!?
YOUR WISH IS MY COMMAND.
BUT IT'LL COST YOU, NOW.
A-AH...
AAAAH!
HEHE!
HAHAHA!
あああ
AAAAH!
HA
HA
HA
HA!

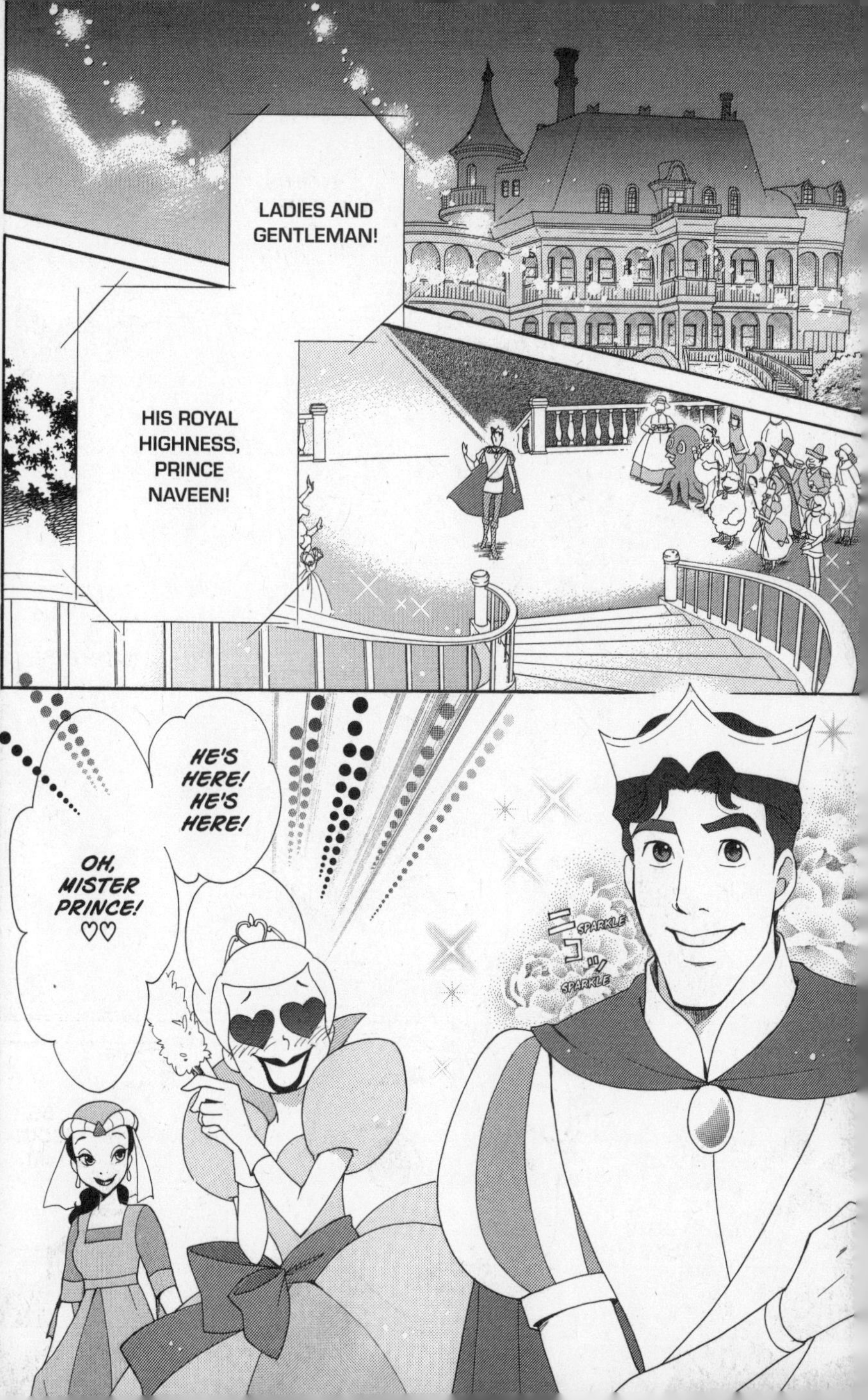
LADIES AND GENTLEMAN!
HIS ROYAL HIGHNESS, PRINCE NAVEEN!
HE'S HERE! HE'S HERE!
OH, MISTER PRINCE! ♡♡
SPARKLE
SPARKLE

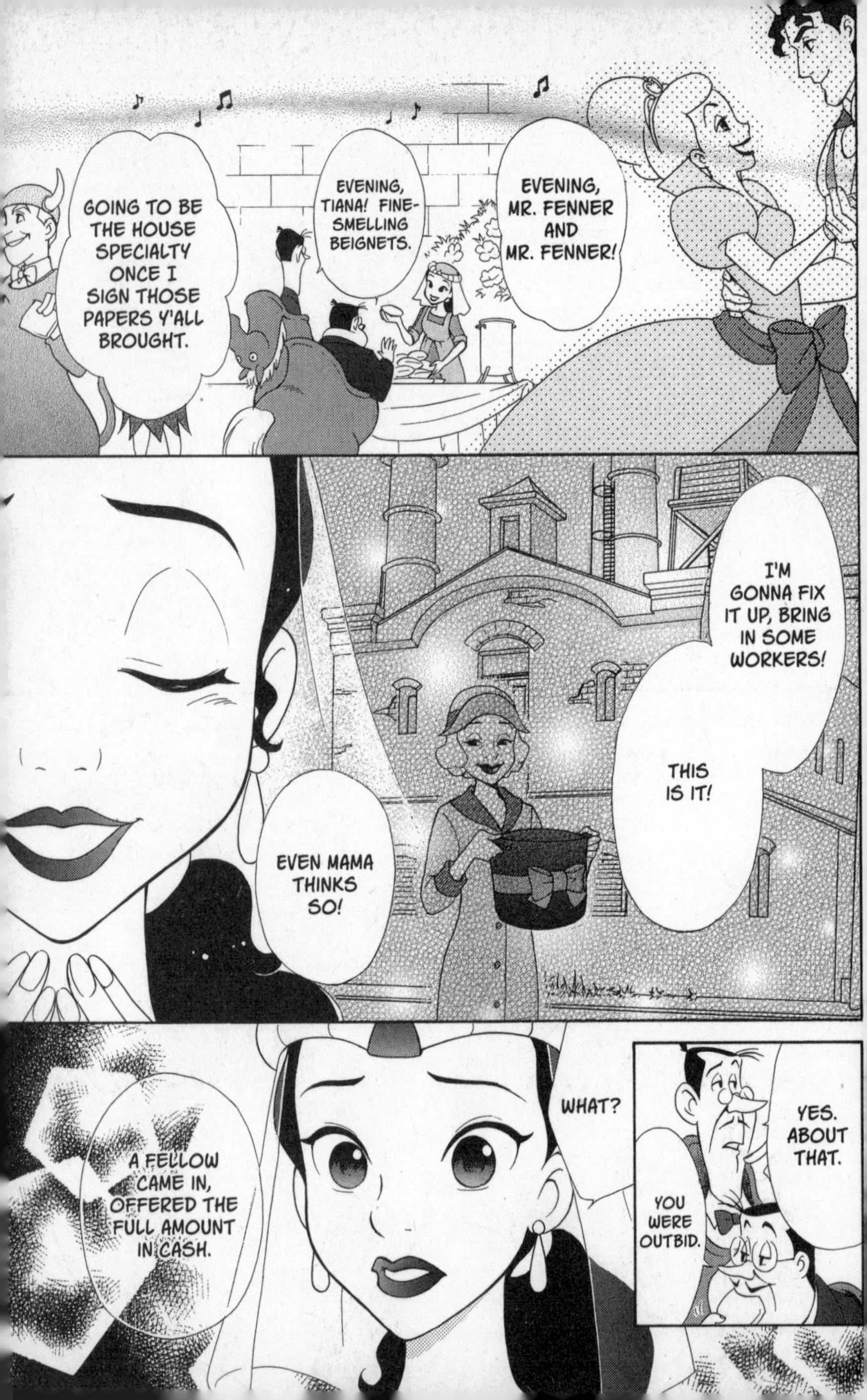
EVENING, MR. FENNER AND MR. FENNER!
EVENING, TIANA! FINE-SMELLING BEIGNETS.
GOING TO BE THE HOUSE SPECIALTY ONCE I SIGN THOSE PAPERS Y'ALL BROUGHT.
I'M GONNA FIX IT UP, BRING IN SOME WORKERS!
THIS IS IT!
EVEN MAMA THINKS SO!
YES. ABOUT THAT.
YOU WERE OUTBID.
WHAT?
A FELLOW CAME IN, OFFERED THE FULL AMOUNT IN CASH.

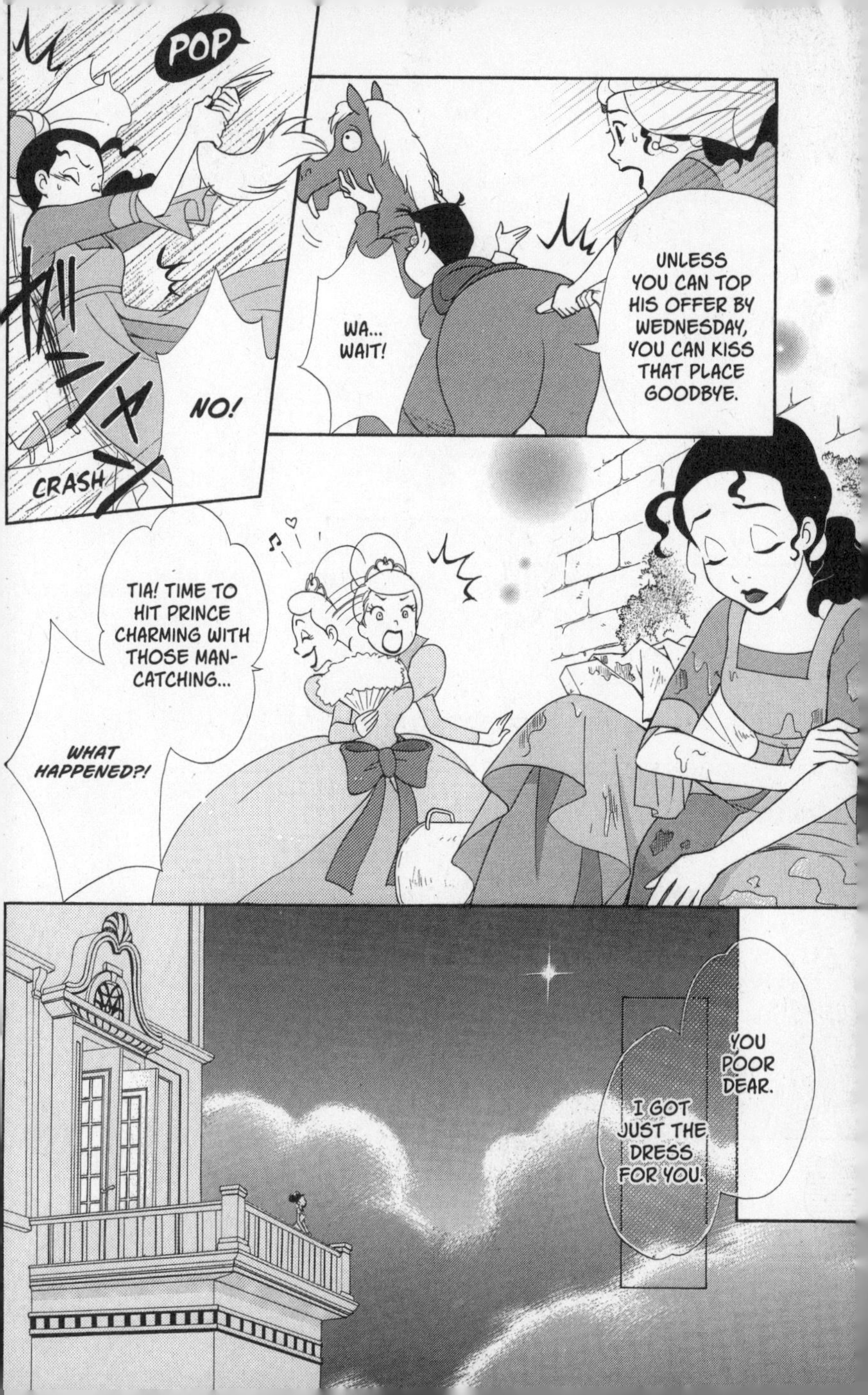
UNLESS YOU CAN TOP HIS OFFER BY WEDNESDAY, YOU CAN KISS THAT PLACE GOODBYE.
WA... WAIT!
POP
NO!
CRASH
TIA! TIME TO HIT PRINCE CHARMING WITH THOSE MAN-CATCHING...
WHAT HAPPENED?!
YOU POOR DEAR.
I GOT JUST THE DRESS FOR YOU.

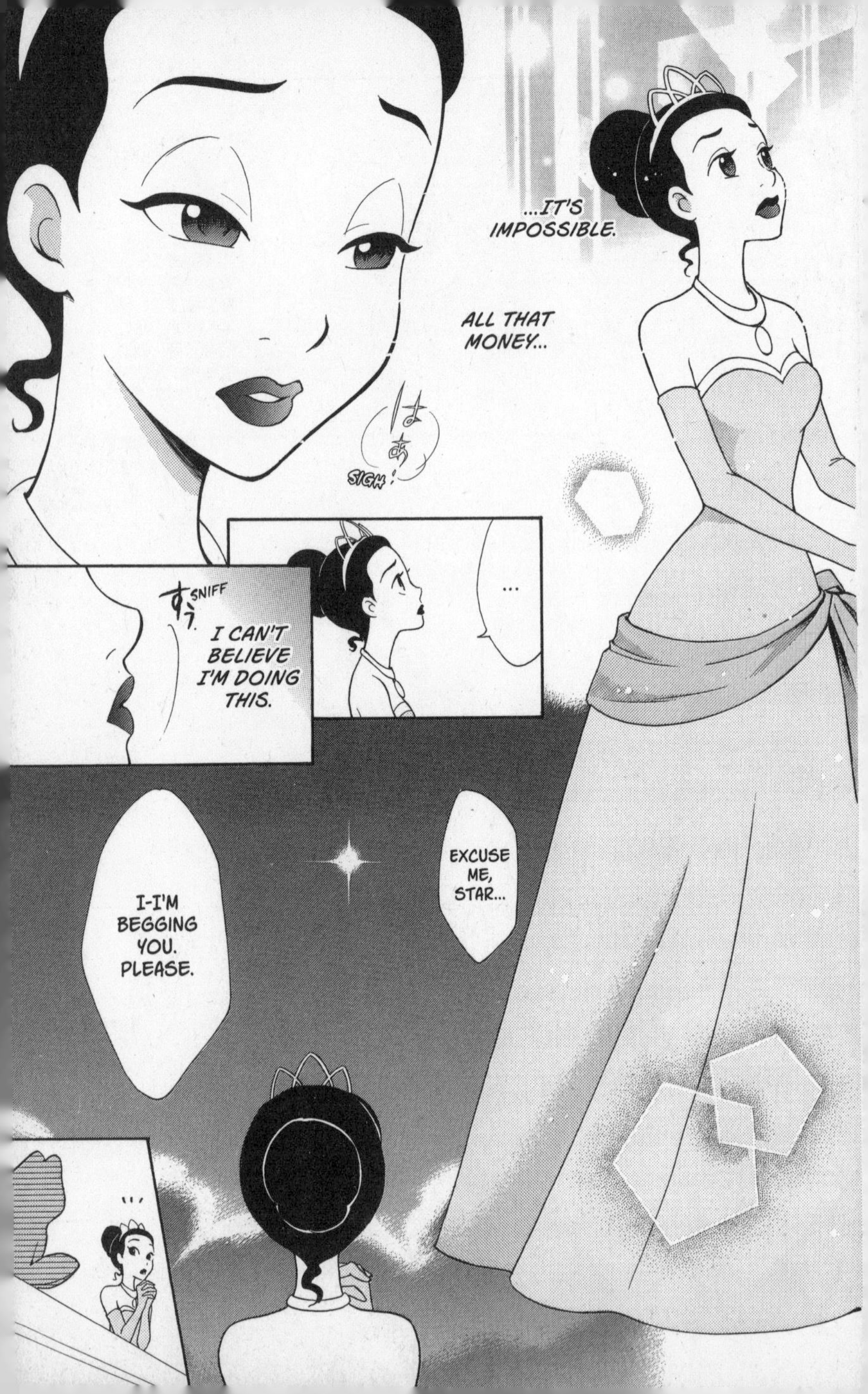
...IT'S IMPOSSIBLE.
ALL THAT MONEY...
SIGH
...
SNIFF
I CAN'T BELIEVE I'M DOING THIS.
EXCUSE ME, STAR...
I-I'M BEGGING YOU. PLEASE.

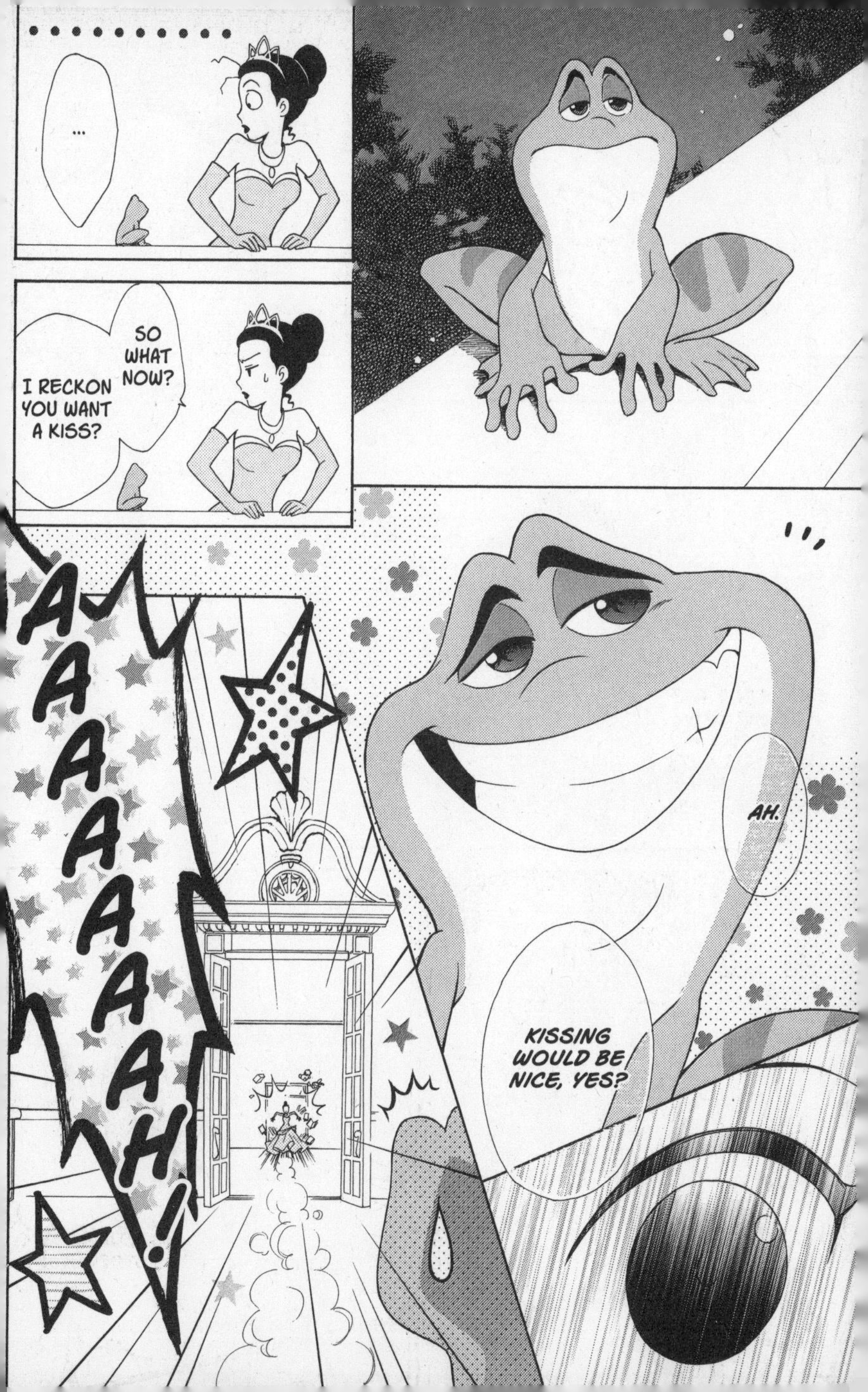
...
SO WHAT NOW?
I RECKON YOU WANT A KISS?
AH.
KISSING WOULD BE NICE, YES?
AAAAAAAAH!

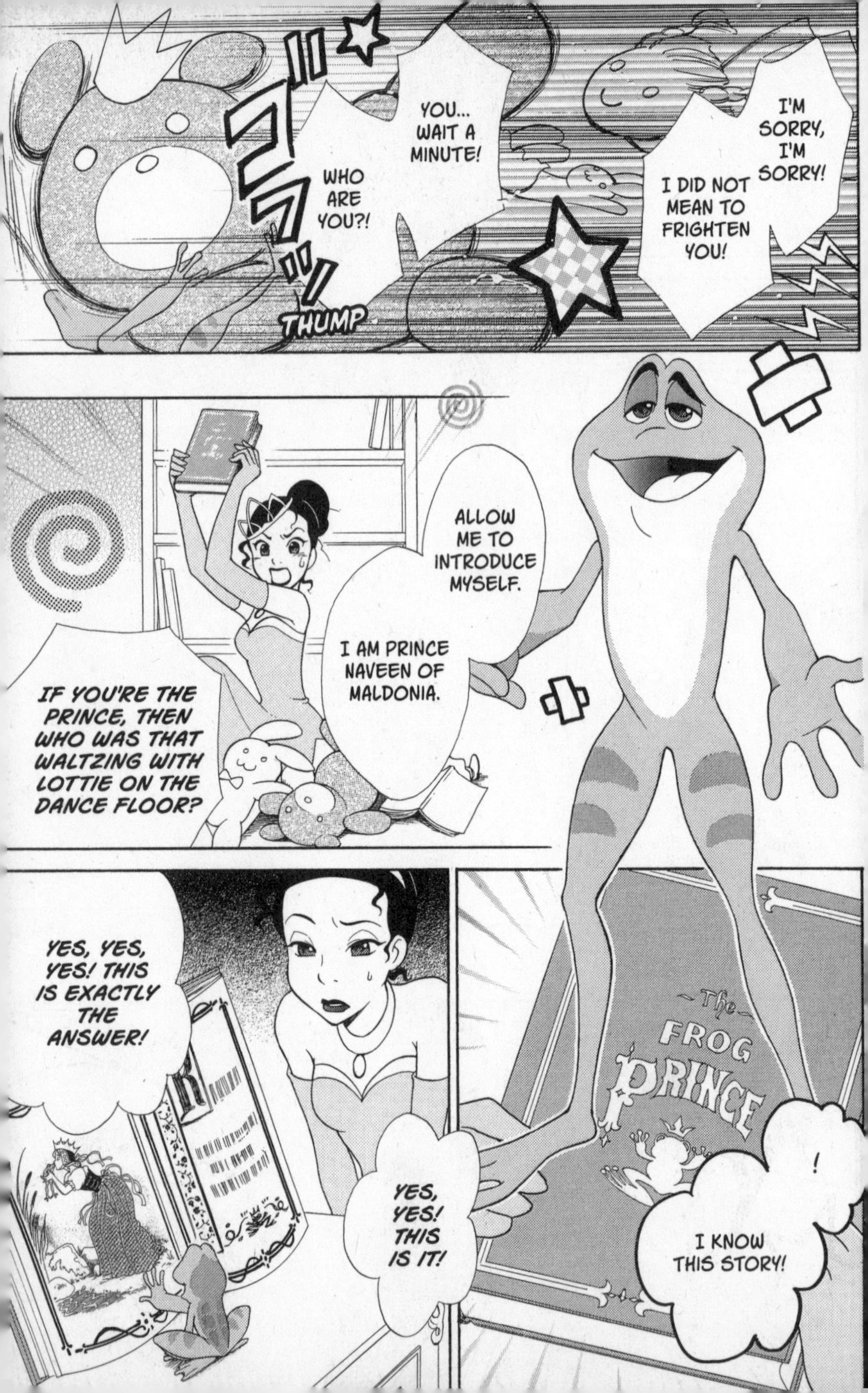
I'M SORRY, I'M SORRY!
I DID NOT MEAN TO FRIGHTEN YOU!
YOU... WAIT A MINUTE!
WHO ARE YOU?!
THUMP
ALLOW ME TO INTRODUCE MYSELF.
I AM PRINCE NAVEEN OF MALDONIA.
IF YOU'RE THE PRINCE, THEN WHO WAS THAT WALTZING WITH LOTTIE ON THE DANCE FLOOR?
The FROG PRINCE
!
I KNOW THIS STORY!
YES, YES! THIS IS IT!
YES, YES, YES! THIS IS EXACTLY THE ANSWER!

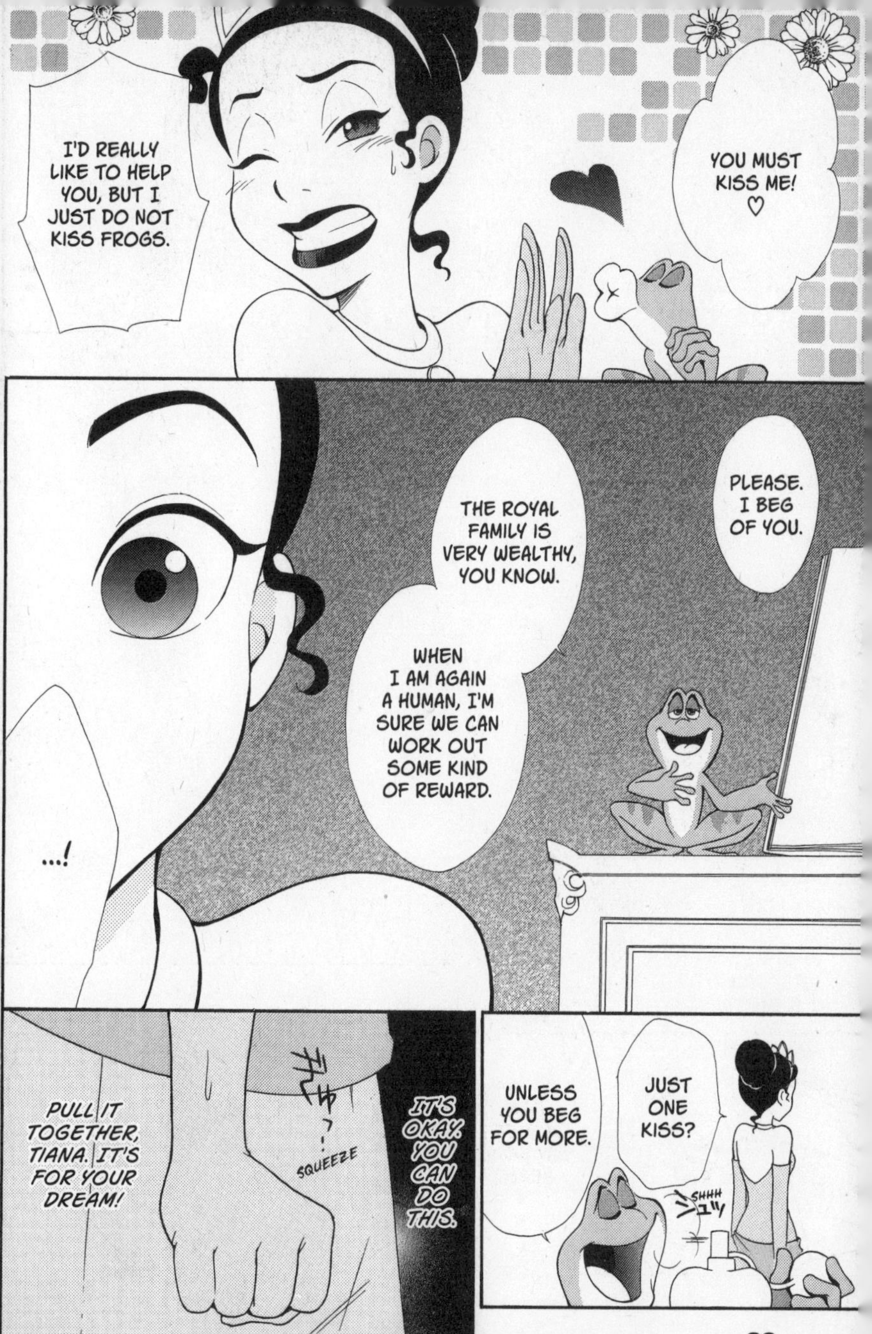
YOU MUST KISS ME! ♡
I'D REALLY LIKE TO HELP YOU, BUT I JUST DO NOT KISS FROGS.
PLEASE. I BEG OF YOU.
THE ROYAL FAMILY IS VERY WEALTHY, YOU KNOW.
WHEN I AM AGAIN A HUMAN, I'M SURE WE CAN WORK OUT SOME KIND OF REWARD.
...!
JUST ONE KISS?
UNLESS YOU BEG FOR MORE.
SHHH
IT'S OKAY. YOU CAN DO THIS.
SQUEEZE
PULL IT TOGETHER, TIANA. IT'S FOR YOUR DREAM!

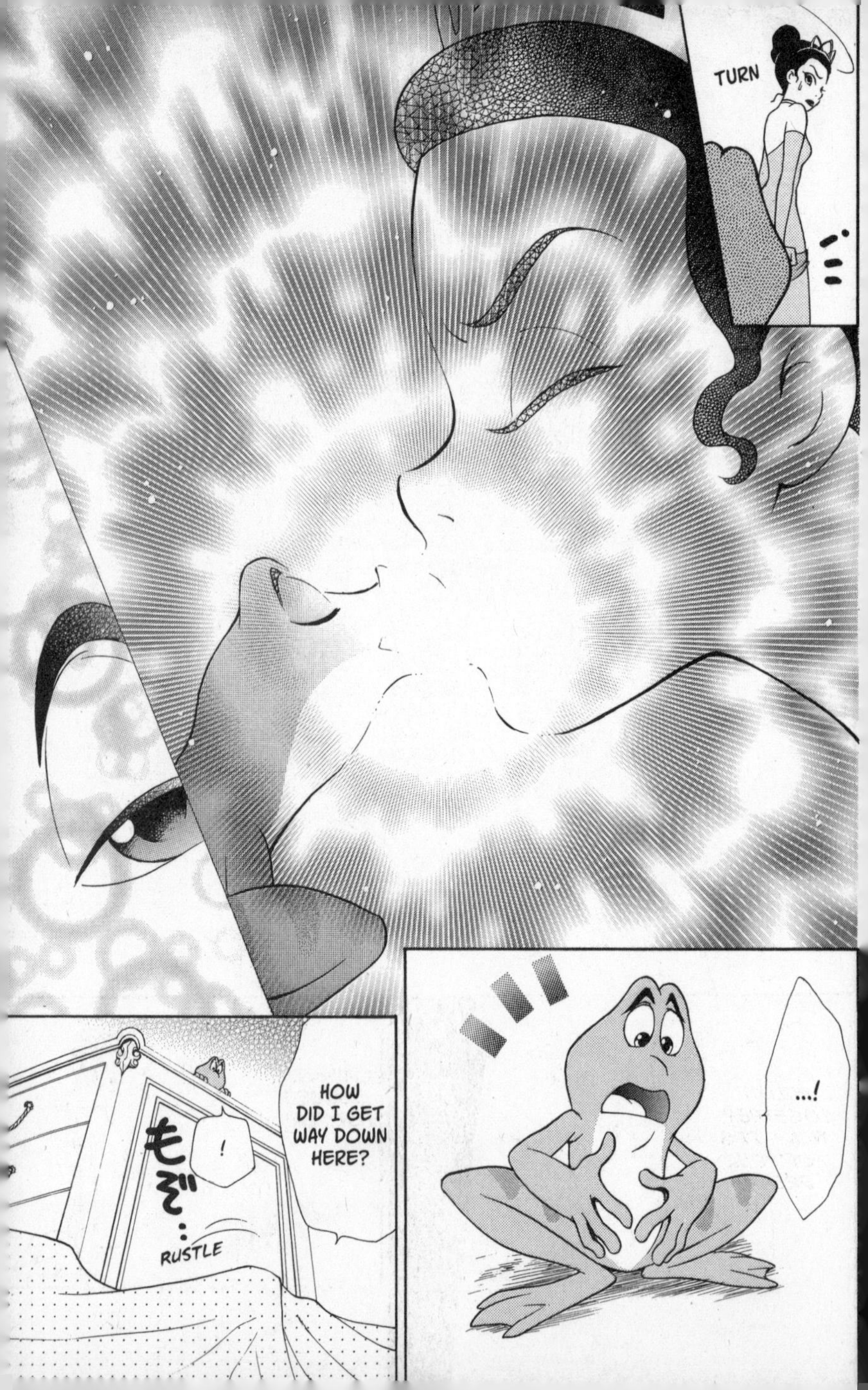
TURN
...
...!
!
HOW DID I GET WAY DOWN HERE?
もぞ…
RUSTLE

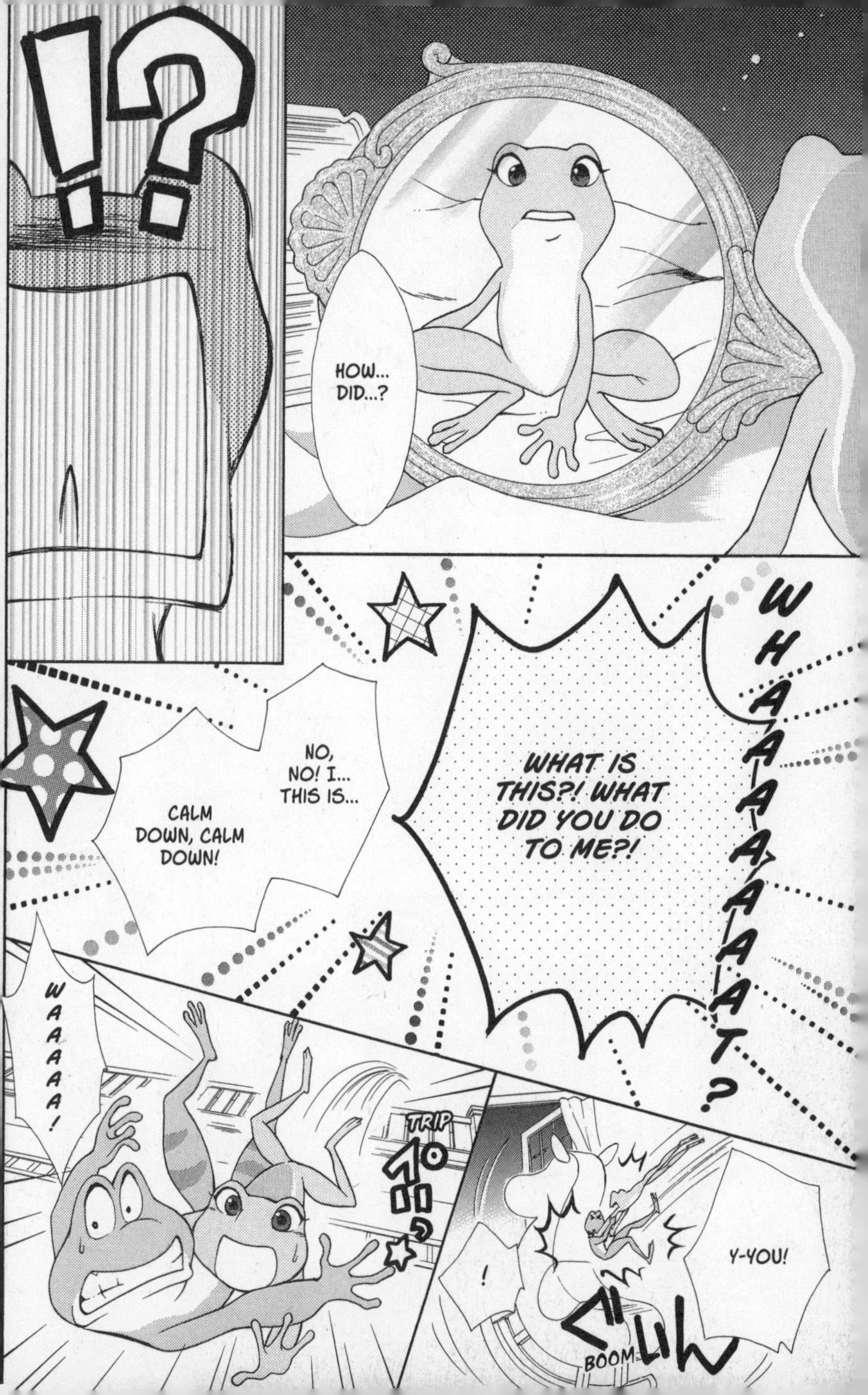
HOW... DID...?
!?
WHAAAAAAAAAAT?
WHAT IS THIS?! WHAT DID YOU DO TO ME?!
NO, NO! I... THIS IS...
CALM DOWN, CALM DOWN!
Y-YOU!
!
BOOM
TRIP
WAAAAAA!

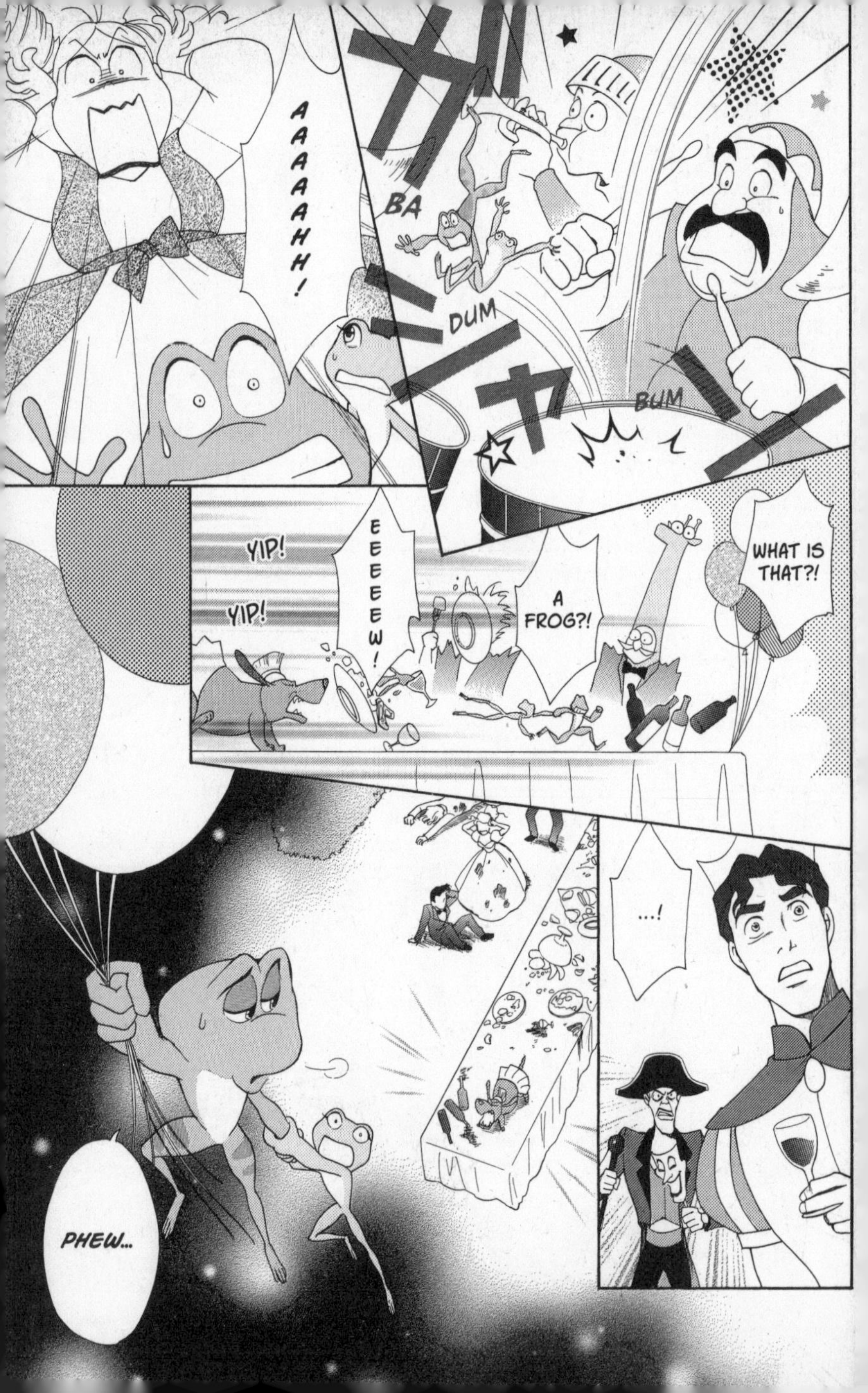

BA
DUM
BUM
AAAAAAHH!
WHAT IS THAT?!
A FROG?!
EEEEEEW!
YIP!
YIP!
...!
PHEW...

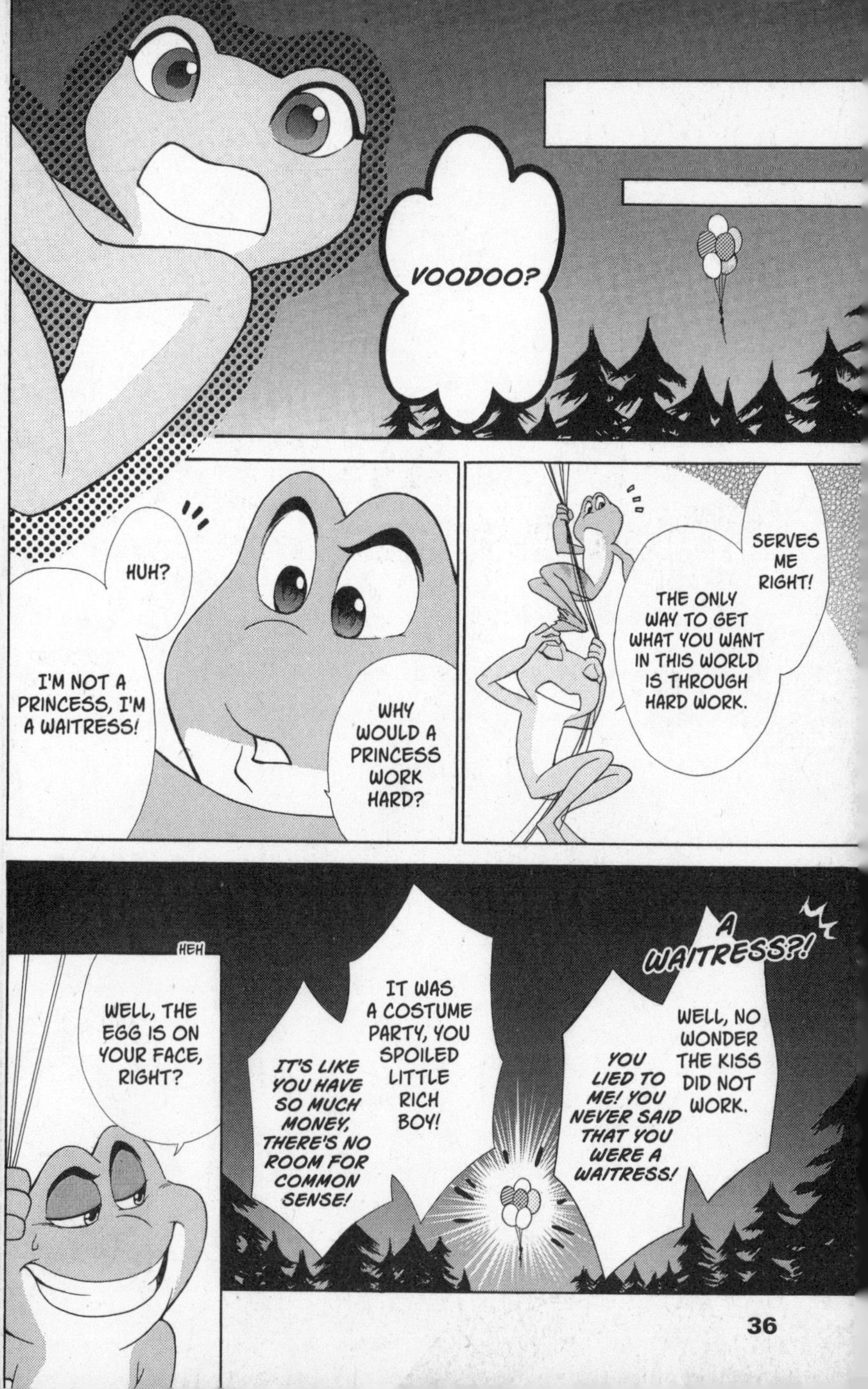
VOODOO?
SERVES ME RIGHT!
THE ONLY WAY TO GET WHAT YOU WANT IN THIS WORLD IS THROUGH HARD WORK.
WHY WOULD A PRINCESS WORK HARD?
HUH?
I'M NOT A PRINCESS, I'M A WAITRESS!
A WAITRESS?!
WELL, NO WONDER THE KISS DID NOT WORK.
YOU LIED TO ME! YOU NEVER SAID THAT YOU WERE A WAITRESS!
IT WAS A COSTUME PARTY, YOU SPOILED LITTLE RICH BOY!
IT'S LIKE YOU HAVE SO MUCH MONEY, THERE'S NO ROOM FOR COMMON SENSE!
HEH
WELL, THE EGG IS ON YOUR FACE, RIGHT?

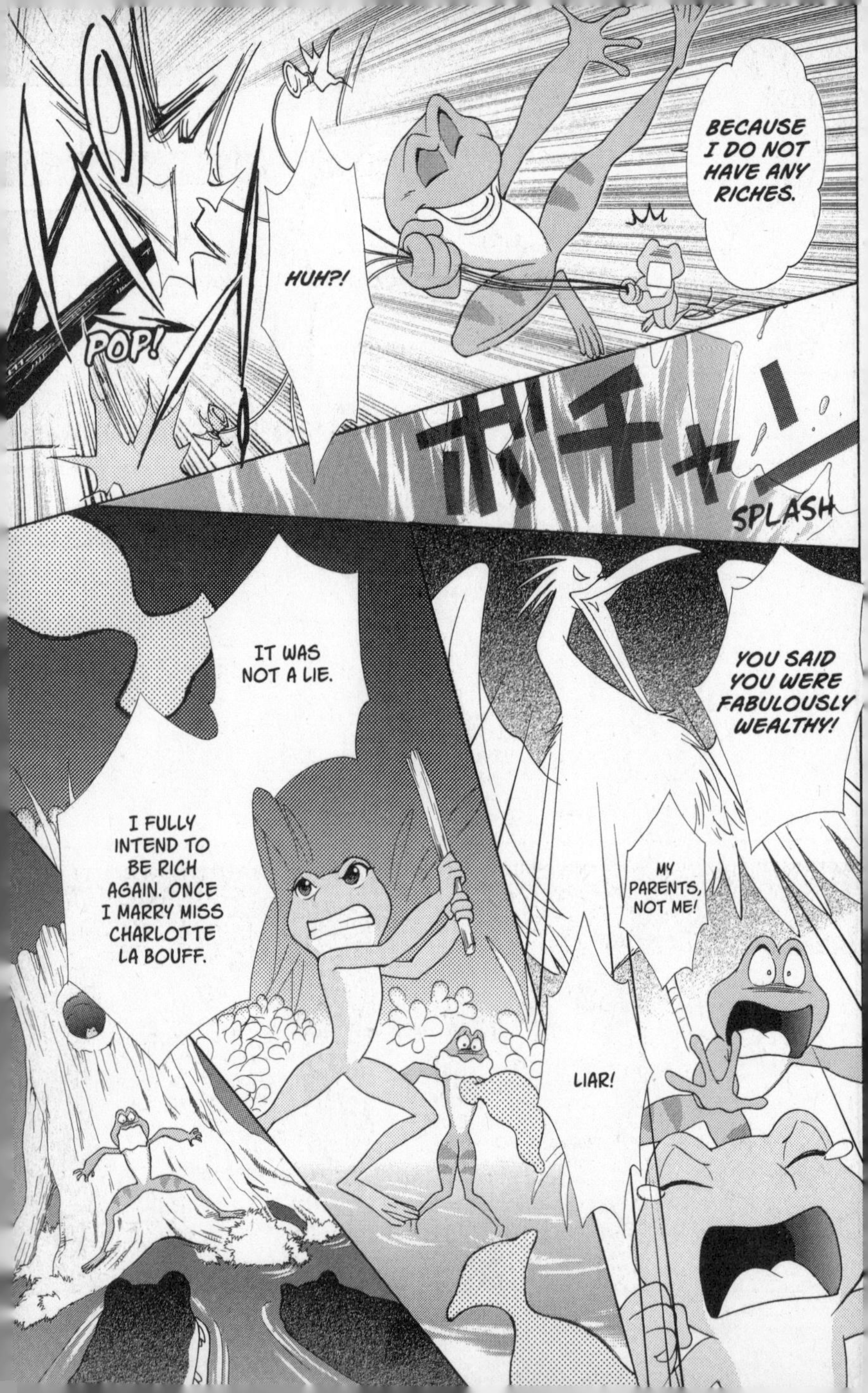
BECAUSE I DO NOT HAVE ANY RICHES.
HUH?!
POP!
ボチャン
SPLASH
YOU SAID YOU WERE FABULOUSLY WEALTHY!
IT WAS NOT A LIE.
MY PARENTS, NOT ME!
I FULLY INTEND TO BE RICH AGAIN. ONCE I MARRY MISS CHARLOTTE LA BOUFF.
LIAR!

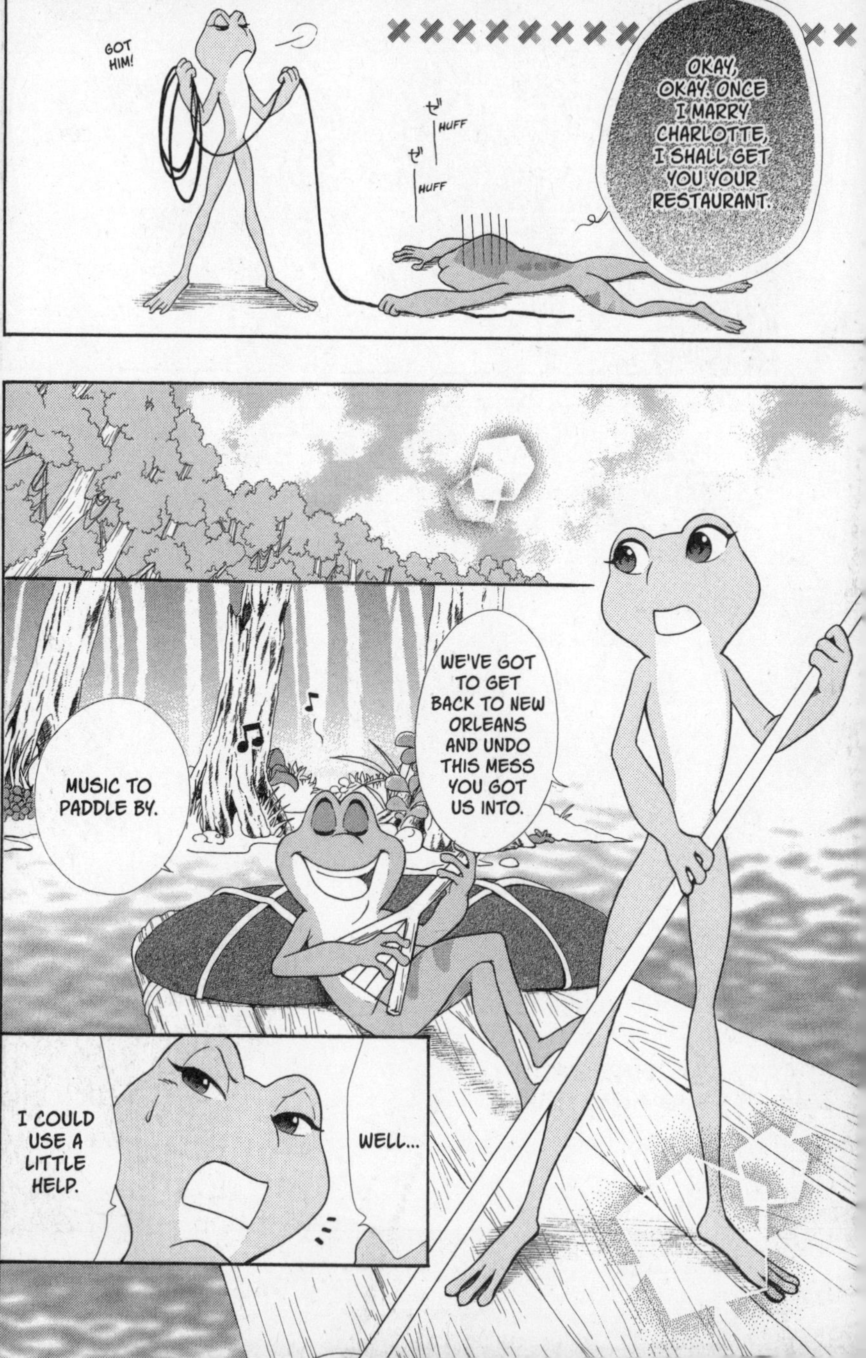
OKAY, OKAY. ONCE I MARRY CHARLOTTE, I SHALL GET YOU YOUR RESTAURANT.
ぜ HUFF
ぜ HUFF
GOT HIM!
WE'VE GOT TO GET BACK TO NEW ORLEANS AND UNDO THIS MESS YOU GOT US INTO.
MUSIC TO PADDLE BY.
WELL...
I COULD USE A LITTLE HELP.

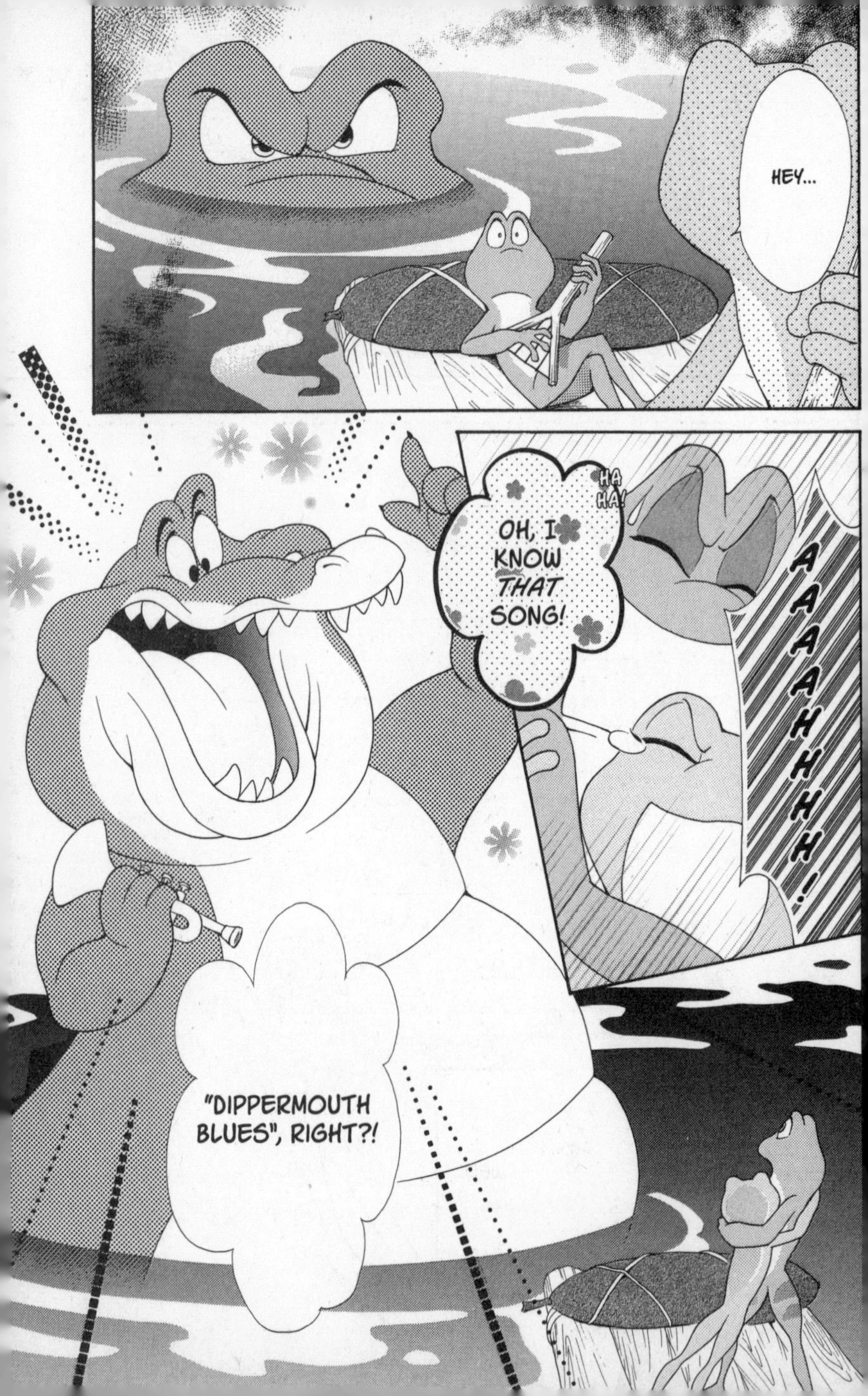
HEY...
AAAAAHHHHH!
HA HA!
OH, I KNOW THAT SONG!
"DIPPERMOUTH BLUES", RIGHT?!

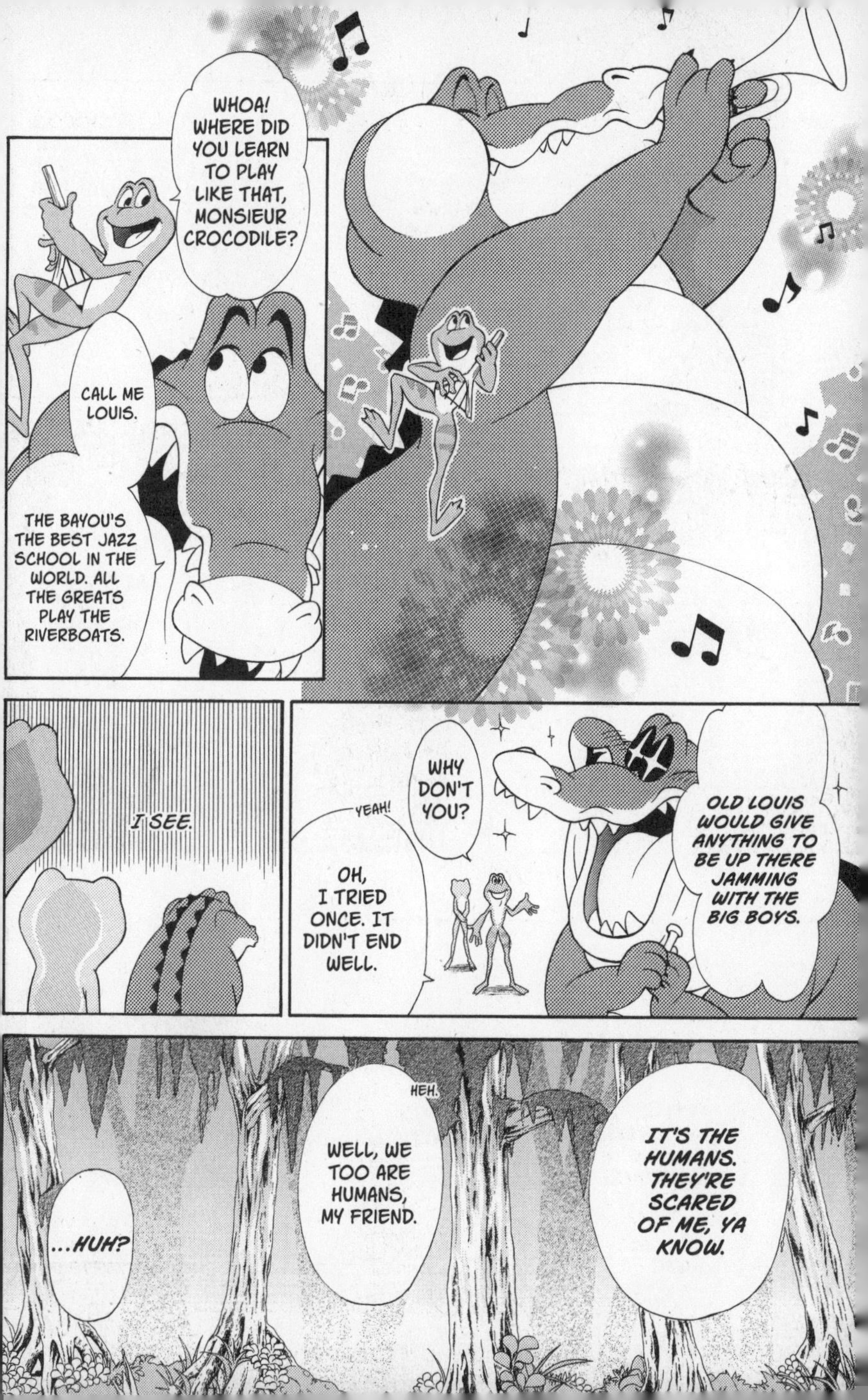
WHOA! WHERE DID YOU LEARN TO PLAY LIKE THAT, MONSIEUR CROCODILE?
CALL ME LOUIS.
THE BAYOU'S THE BEST JAZZ SCHOOL IN THE WORLD. ALL THE GREATS PLAY THE RIVERBOATS.
OLD LOUIS WOULD GIVE ANYTHING TO BE UP THERE JAMMING WITH THE BIG BOYS.
WHY DON'T YOU?
YEAH!
OH, I TRIED ONCE. IT DIDN'T END WELL.
I SEE.
IT'S THE HUMANS. THEY'RE SCARED OF ME, YA KNOW.
HEH.
WELL, WE TOO ARE HUMANS, MY FRIEND.
...HUH?

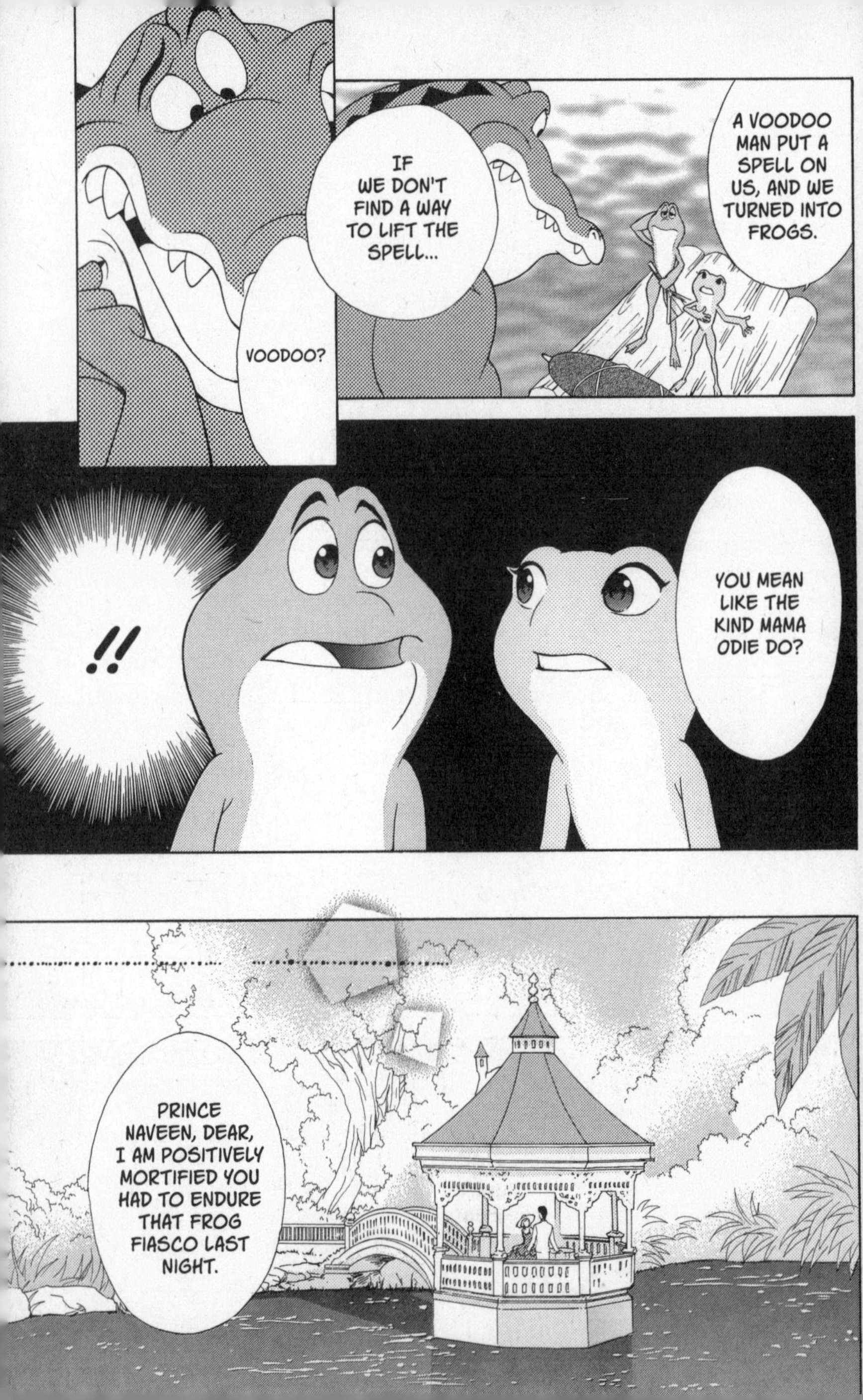
A VOODOO MAN PUT A SPELL ON US, AND WE TURNED INTO FROGS.
IF WE DON'T FIND A WAY TO LIFT THE SPELL...
VOODOO?
YOU MEAN LIKE THE KIND MAMA ODIE DO?
!!
PRINCE NAVEEN, DEAR, I AM POSITIVELY MORTIFIED YOU HAD TO ENDURE THAT FROG FIASCO LAST NIGHT.

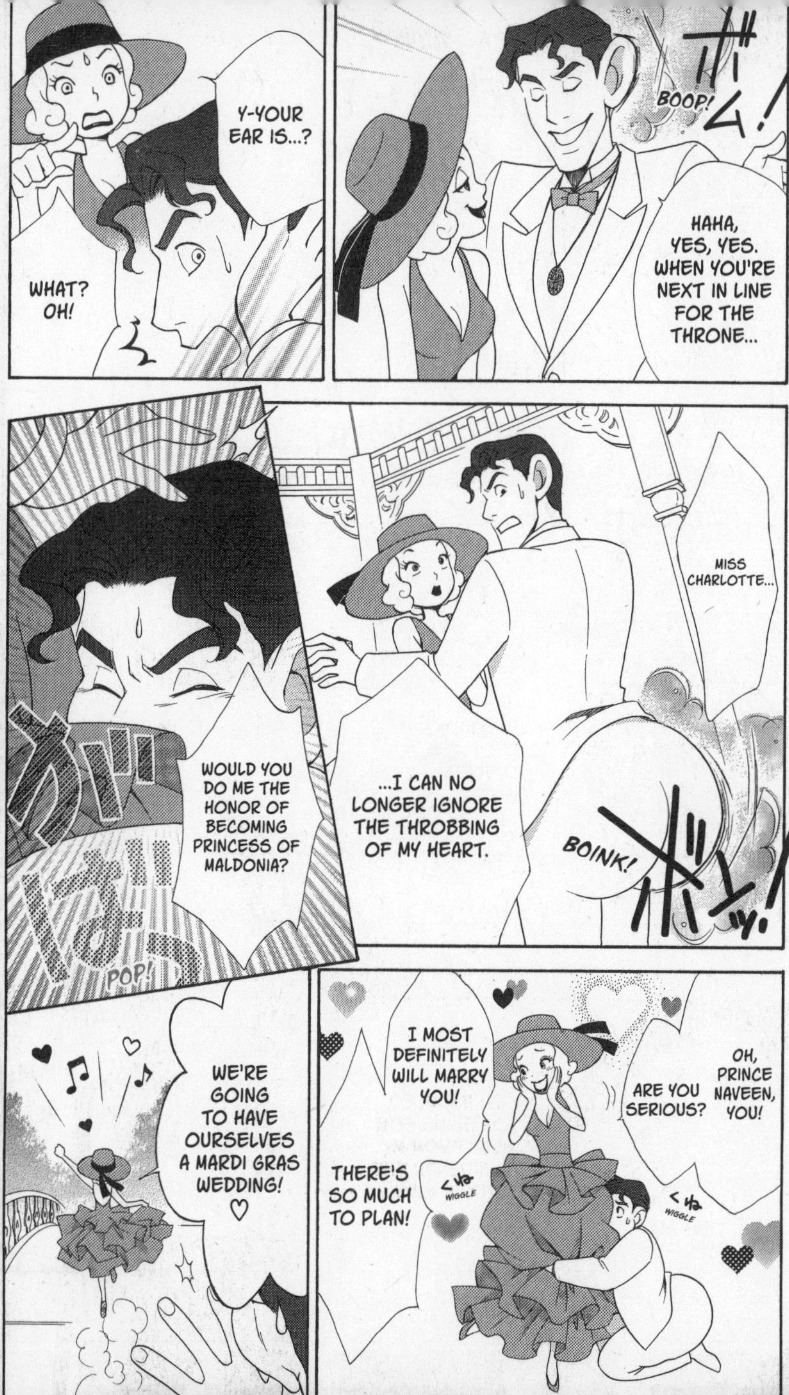
BOOP!
HAHA, YES, YES. WHEN YOU'RE NEXT IN LINE FOR THE THRONE...
Y-YOUR EAR IS...?
WHAT? OH!
MISS CHARLOTTE...
...I CAN NO LONGER IGNORE THE THROBBING OF MY HEART.
BOINK!
WOULD YOU DO ME THE HONOR OF BECOMING PRINCESS OF MALDONIA?
POP!
OH, PRINCE NAVEEN, YOU!
ARE YOU SERIOUS?
I MOST DEFINITELY WILL MARRY YOU!
WIGGLE
WIGGLE
THERE'S SO MUCH TO PLAN!
WE'RE GOING TO HAVE OURSELVES A MARDI GRAS WEDDING! ♡

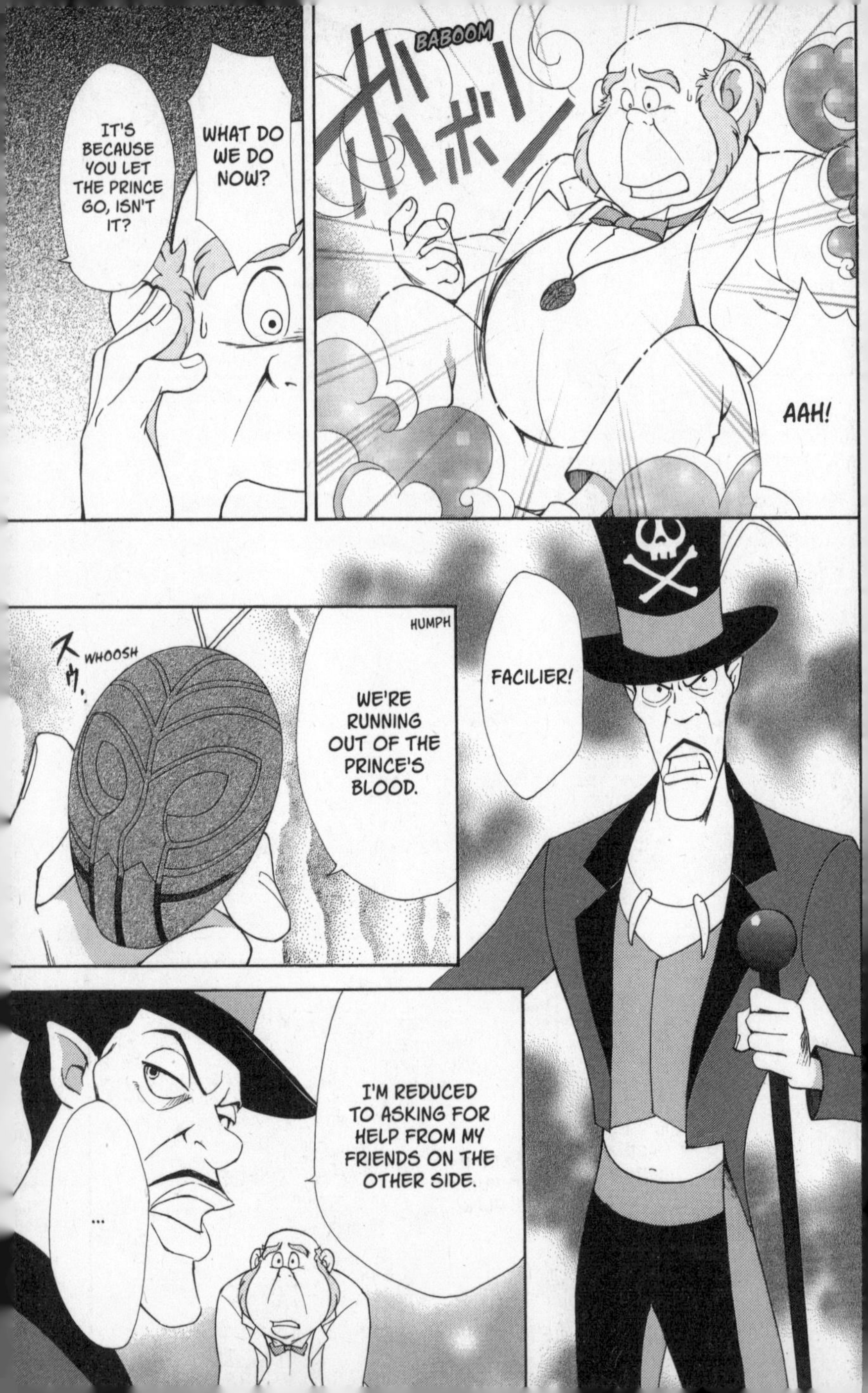
BABOOM
AAH!
WHAT DO WE DO NOW?
IT'S BECAUSE YOU LET THE PRINCE GO, ISN'T IT?
FACILIER!
HUMPH
WE'RE RUNNING OUT OF THE PRINCE'S BLOOD.
WHOOSH
I'M REDUCED TO ASKING FOR HELP FROM MY FRIENDS ON THE OTHER SIDE.
...

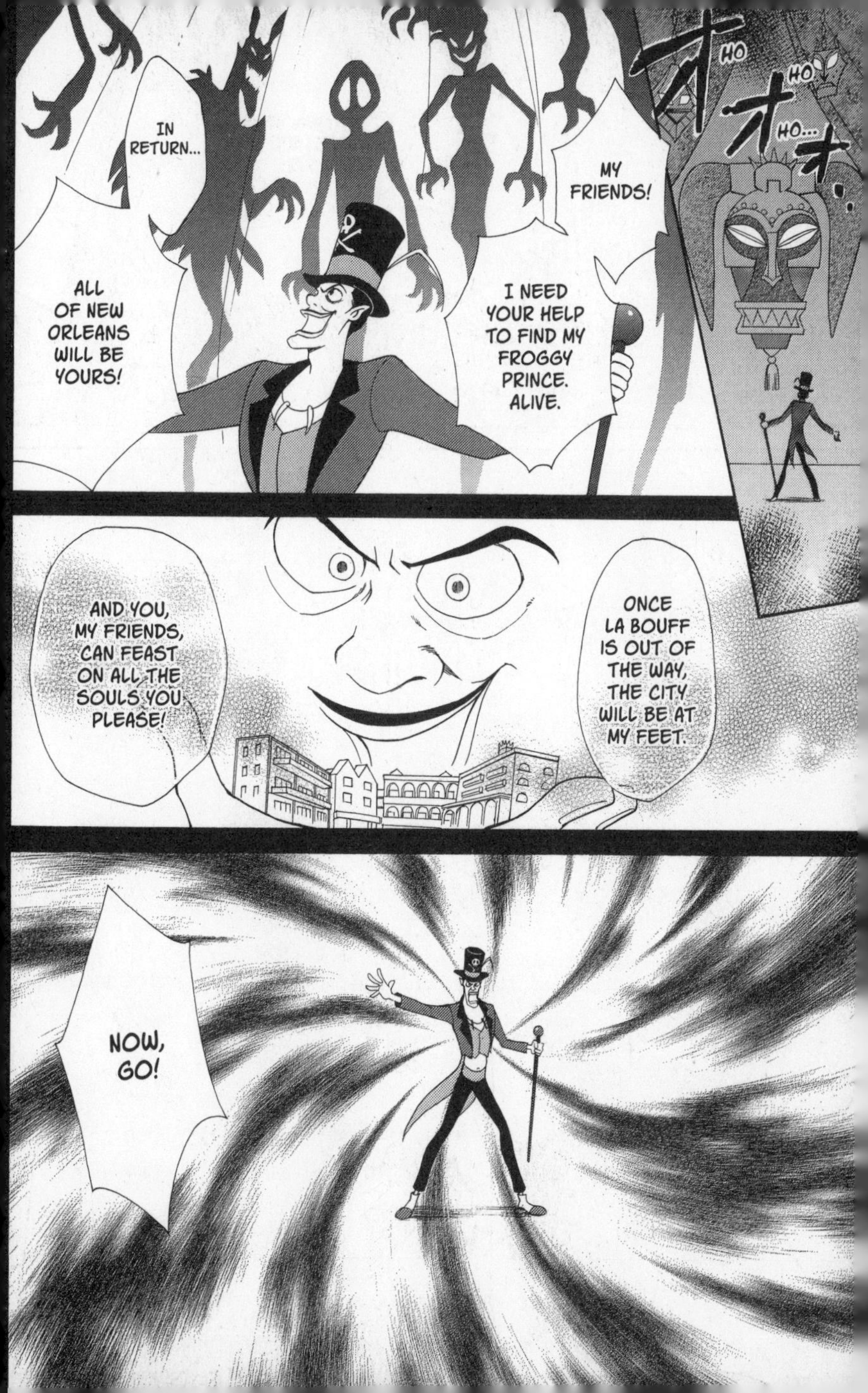
オオオ
HO HO HO...
MY FRIENDS!
I NEED YOUR HELP TO FIND MY FROGGY PRINCE. ALIVE.
IN RETURN...
ALL OF NEW ORLEANS WILL BE YOURS!
ONCE LA BOUFF IS OUT OF THE WAY, THE CITY WILL BE AT MY FEET.
AND YOU, MY FRIENDS, CAN FEAST ON ALL THE SOULS YOU PLEASE!
NOW, GO!

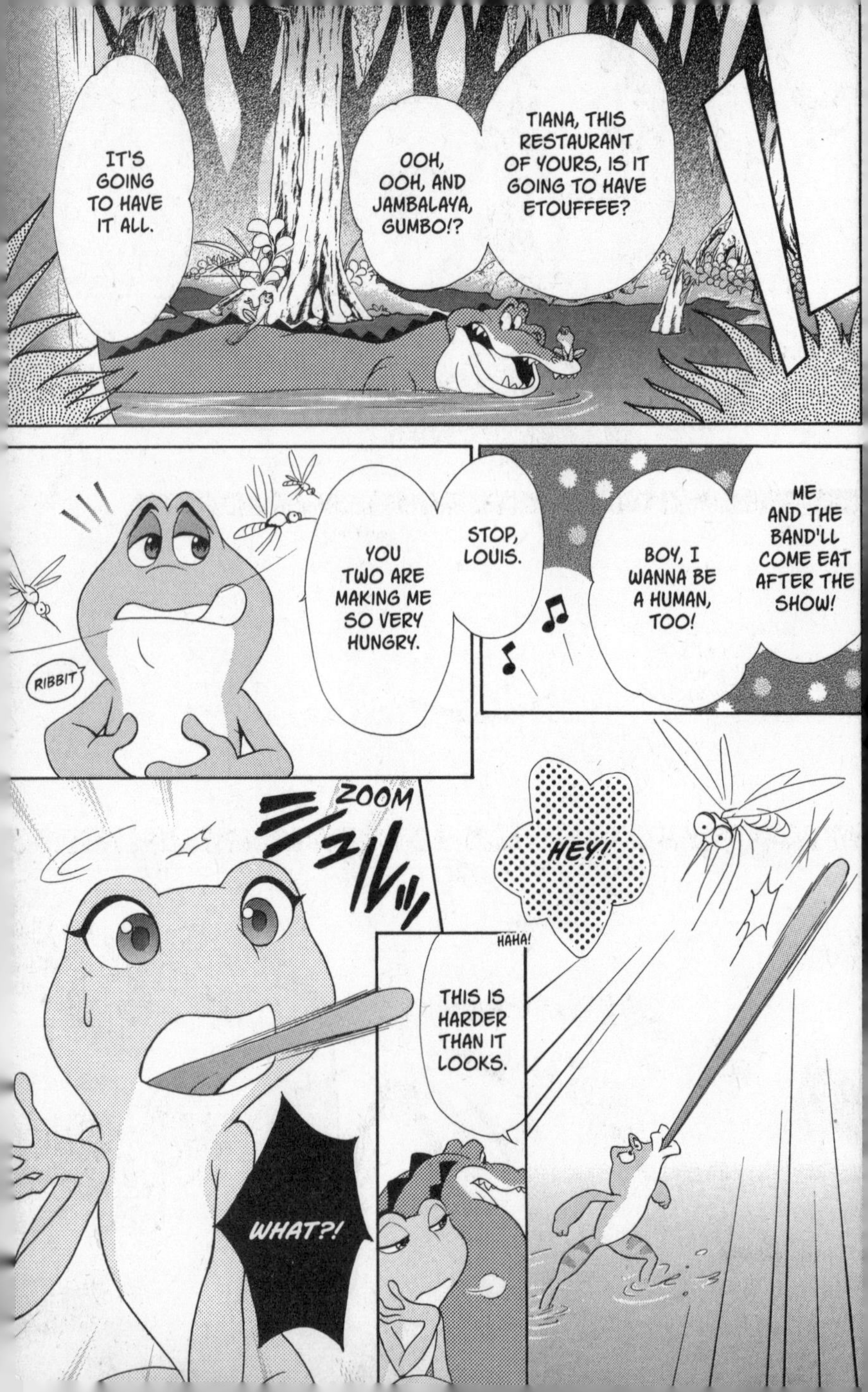
TIANA, THIS RESTAURANT OF YOURS, IS IT GOING TO HAVE ETOUFFEE?
OOH, OOH, AND JAMBALAYA, GUMBO!?
IT'S GOING TO HAVE IT ALL.
ME AND THE BAND'LL COME EAT AFTER THE SHOW!
BOY, I WANNA BE A HUMAN, TOO!
STOP, LOUIS.
YOU TWO ARE MAKING ME SO VERY HUNGRY.
RIBBIT
HEY!
HAHA!
THIS IS HARDER THAN IT LOOKS.
ZOOM
WHAT?!

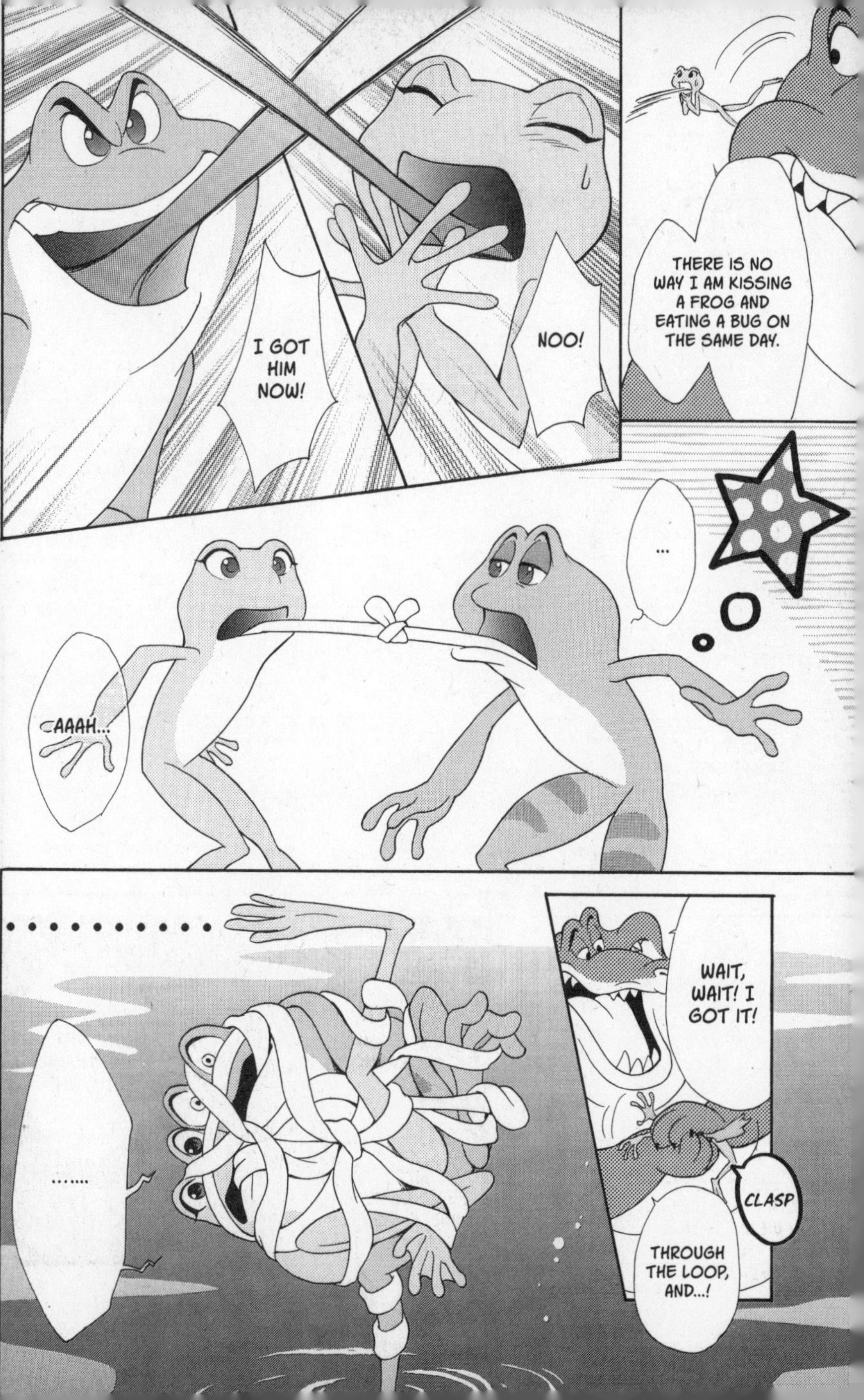
THERE IS NO WAY I AM KISSING A FROG AND EATING A BUG ON THE SAME DAY.
NOO!
I GOT HIM NOW!
...
AAAH...
WAIT, WAIT! I GOT IT!
CLASP
THROUGH THE LOOP, AND...!
....
....

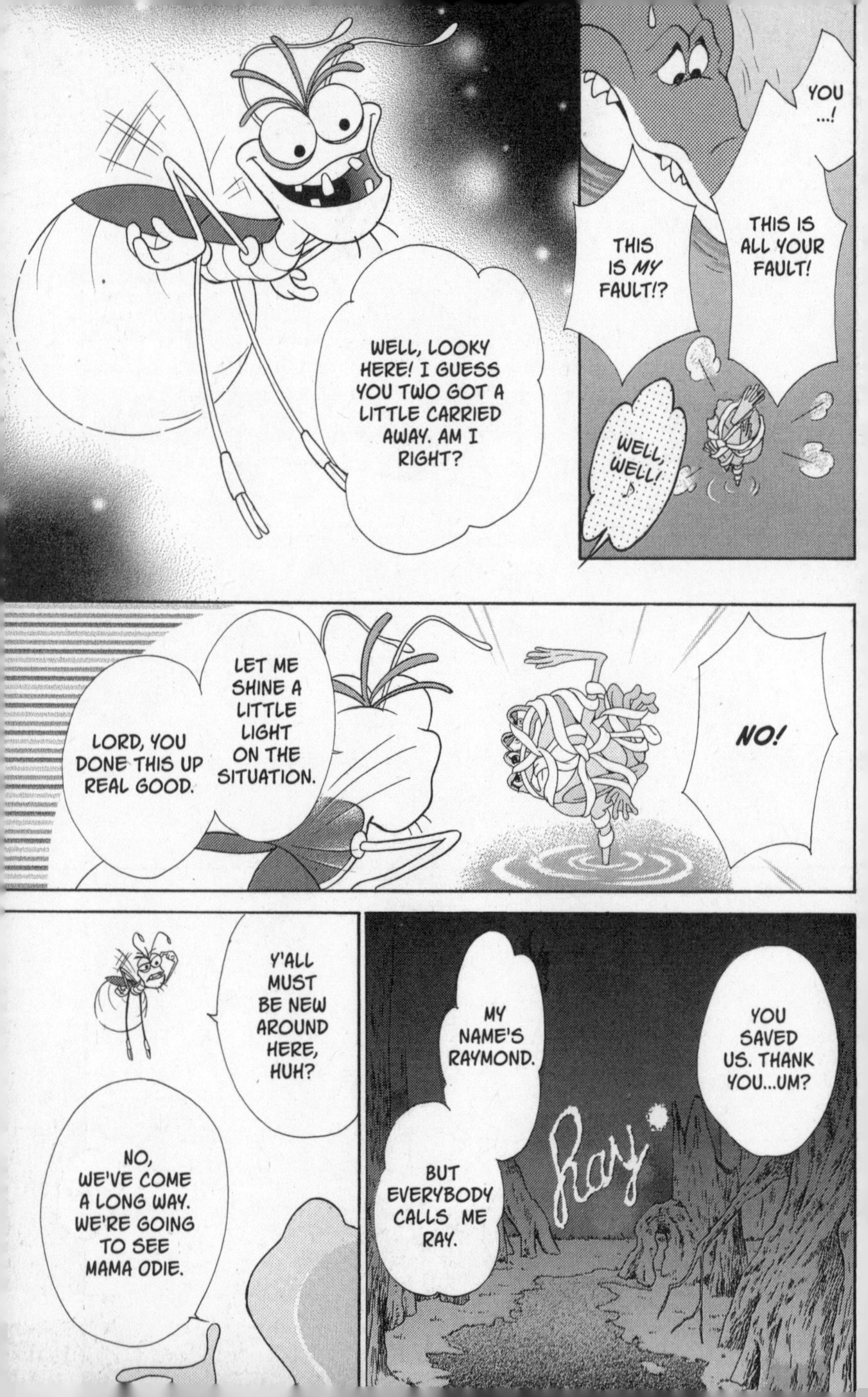
YOU ...!
THIS IS ALL YOUR FAULT!
THIS IS MY FAULT!?
WELL, WELL! ♪
WELL, LOOKY HERE! I GUESS YOU TWO GOT A LITTLE CARRIED AWAY. AM I RIGHT?
NO!
LET ME SHINE A LITTLE LIGHT ON THE SITUATION.
LORD, YOU DONE THIS UP REAL GOOD.
YOU SAVED US. THANK YOU...UM?
MY NAME'S RAYMOND.
BUT EVERYBODY CALLS ME RAY.
Ray
Y'ALL MUST BE NEW AROUND HERE, HUH?
NO, WE'VE COME A LONG WAY. WE'RE GOING TO SEE MAMA ODIE.

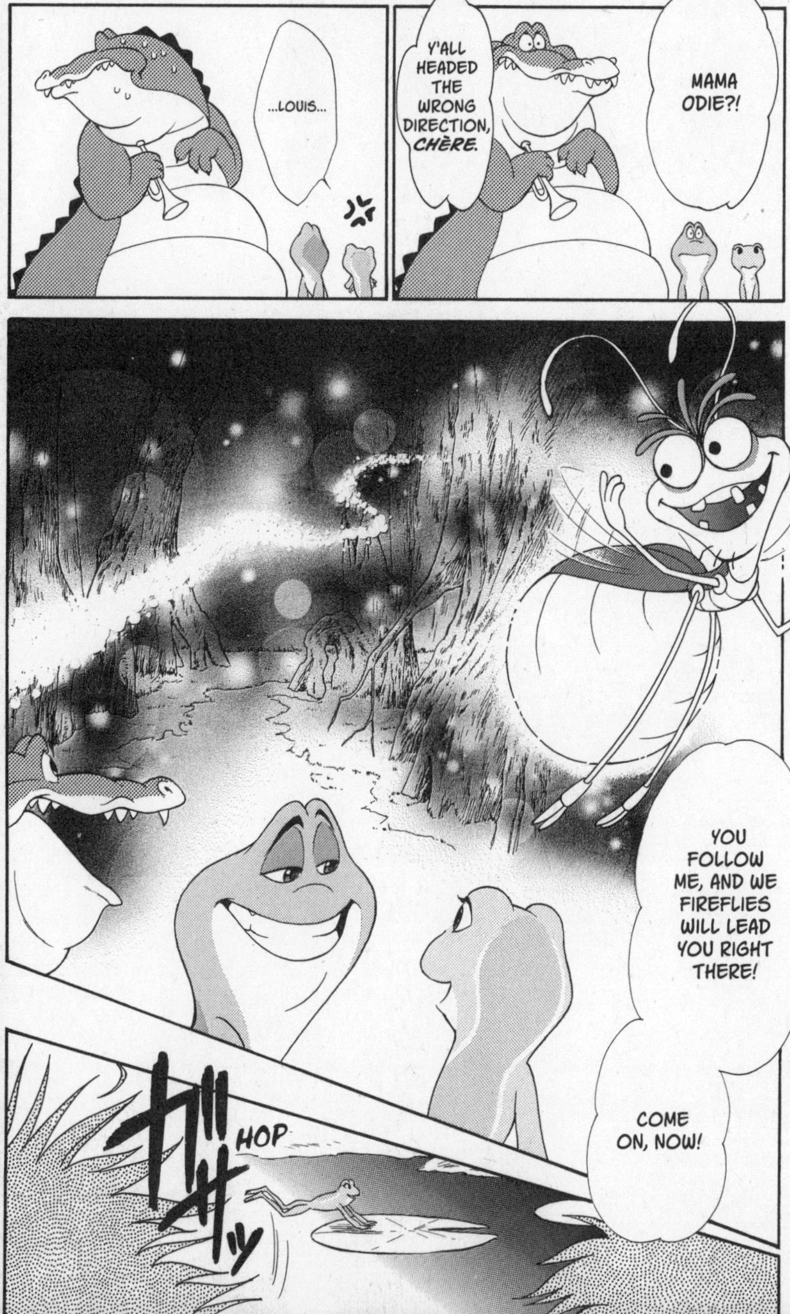
MAMA ODIE?!
Y'ALL HEADED THE WRONG DIRECTION, CHÈRE.
...LOUIS...
YOU FOLLOW ME, AND WE FIREFLIES WILL LEAD YOU RIGHT THERE!
COME ON, NOW!
HOP
ガサッ

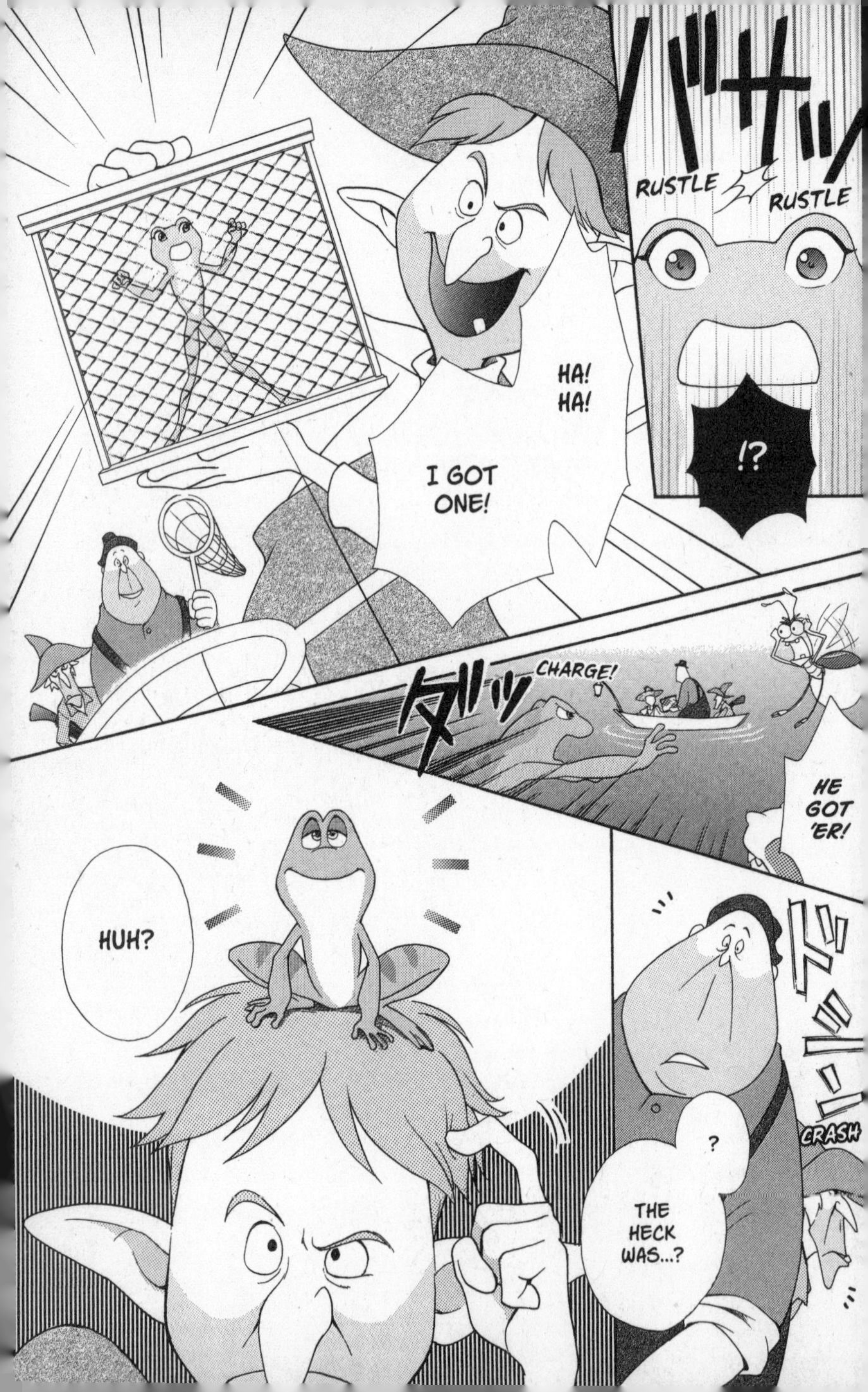
RUSTLE RUSTLE
!?
HA! HA!
I GOT ONE!
CHARGE!
HE GOT 'ER!
CRASH
?
THE HECK WAS...?
HUH?

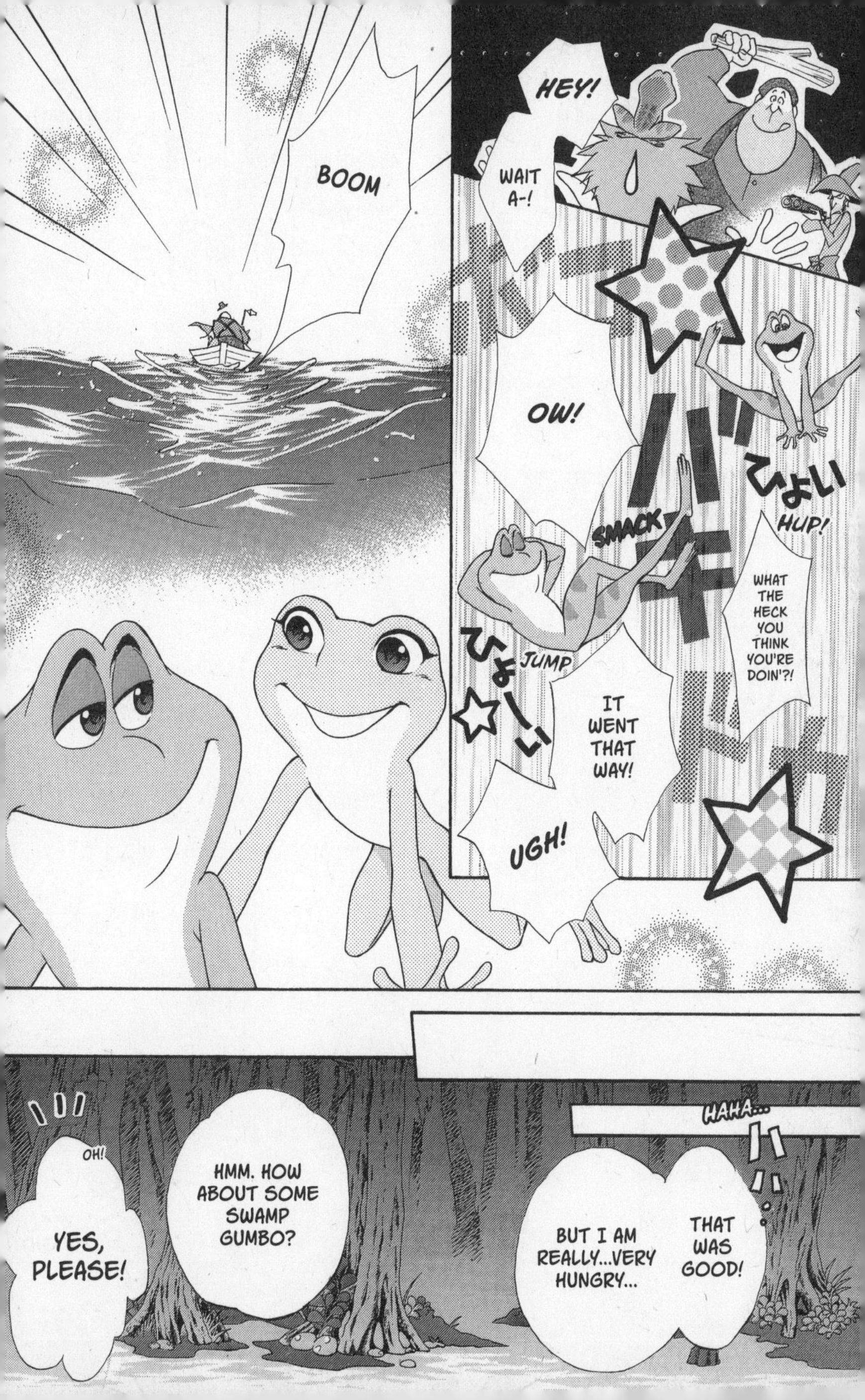

HEY!
WAIT A-!
ひょい
HUP!
WHAT THE HECK YOU THINK YOU'RE DOIN'?!
SMACK
OW!
ひょーい
JUMP
IT WENT THAT WAY!
UGH!
BOOM
HAHA...
THAT WAS GOOD!
BUT I AM REALLY...VERY HUNGRY...
HMM. HOW ABOUT SOME SWAMP GUMBO?
OH!
YES, PLEASE!

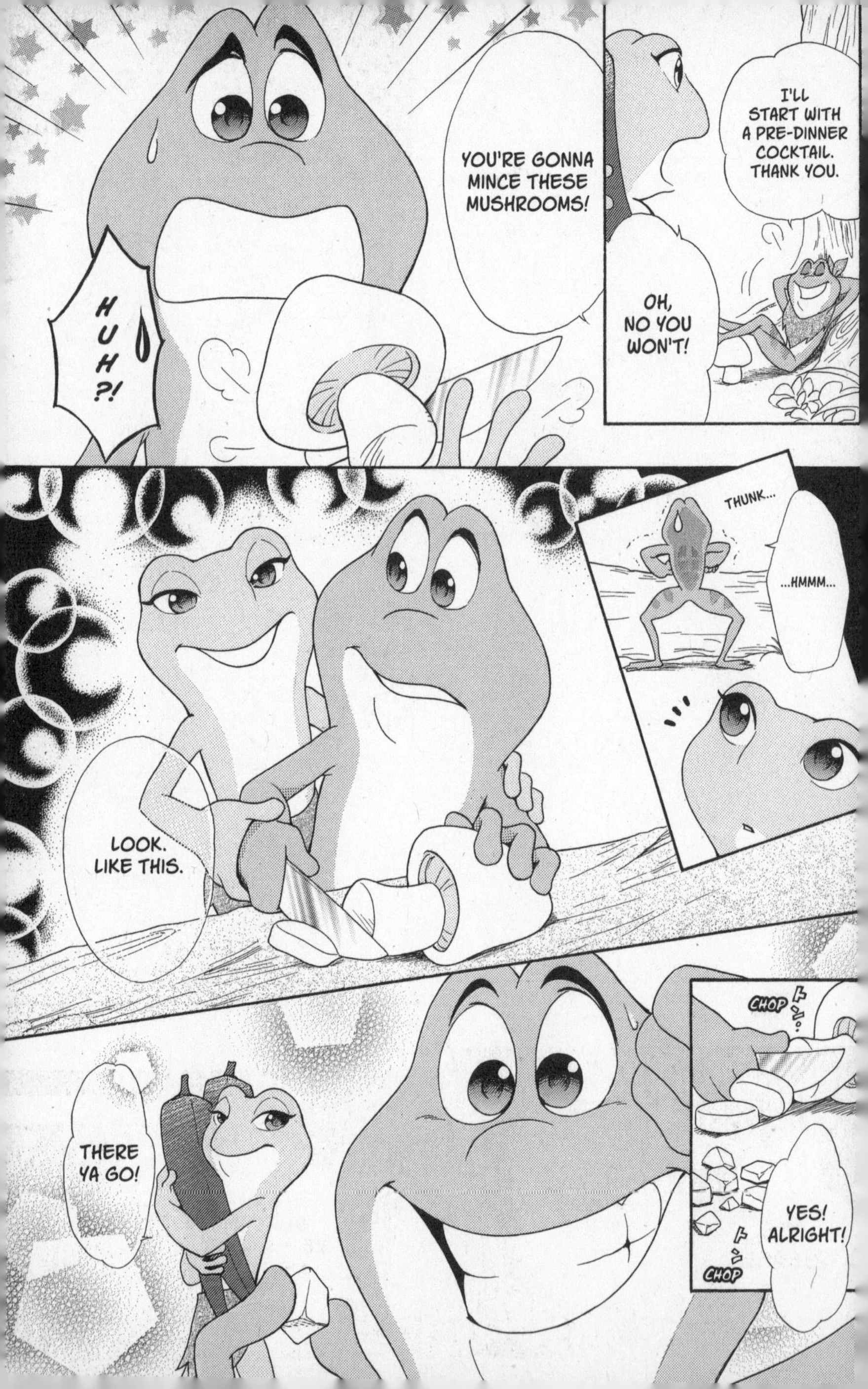
I'LL START WITH A PRE-DINNER COCKTAIL. THANK YOU.
OH, NO YOU WON'T!
YOU'RE GONNA MINCE THESE MUSHROOMS!
HUH?!
THUNK...
...HMMM...
LOOK. LIKE THIS.
CHOP
YES! ALRIGHT!
CHOP
THERE YA GO!

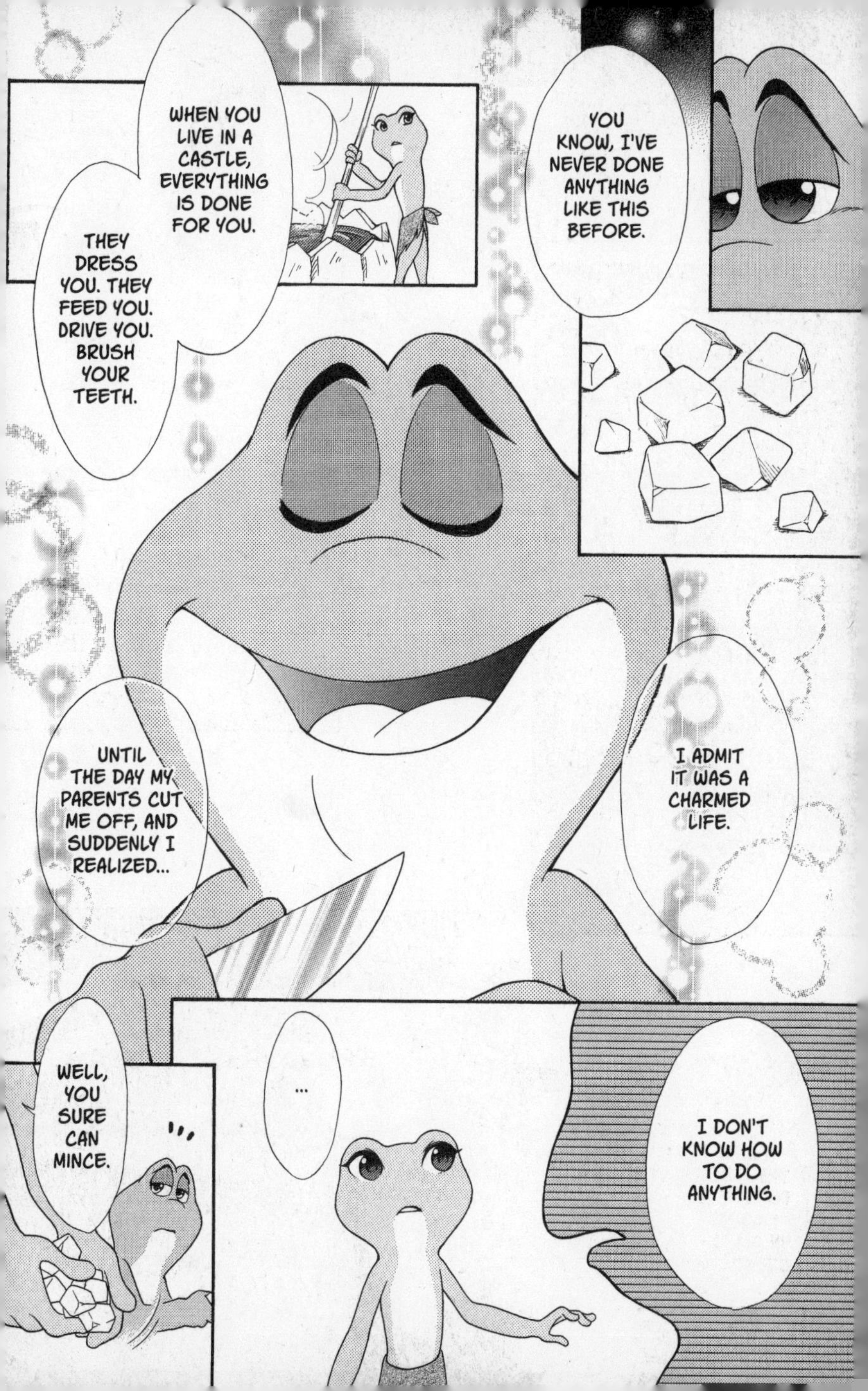
YOU KNOW, I'VE NEVER DONE ANYTHING LIKE THIS BEFORE.
WHEN YOU LIVE IN A CASTLE, EVERYTHING IS DONE FOR YOU.
THEY DRESS YOU. THEY FEED YOU. DRIVE YOU. BRUSH YOUR TEETH.
I ADMIT IT WAS A CHARMED LIFE.
UNTIL THE DAY MY PARENTS CUT ME OFF, AND SUDDENLY I REALIZED...
I DON'T KNOW HOW TO DO ANYTHING.
...
WELL, YOU SURE CAN MINCE.

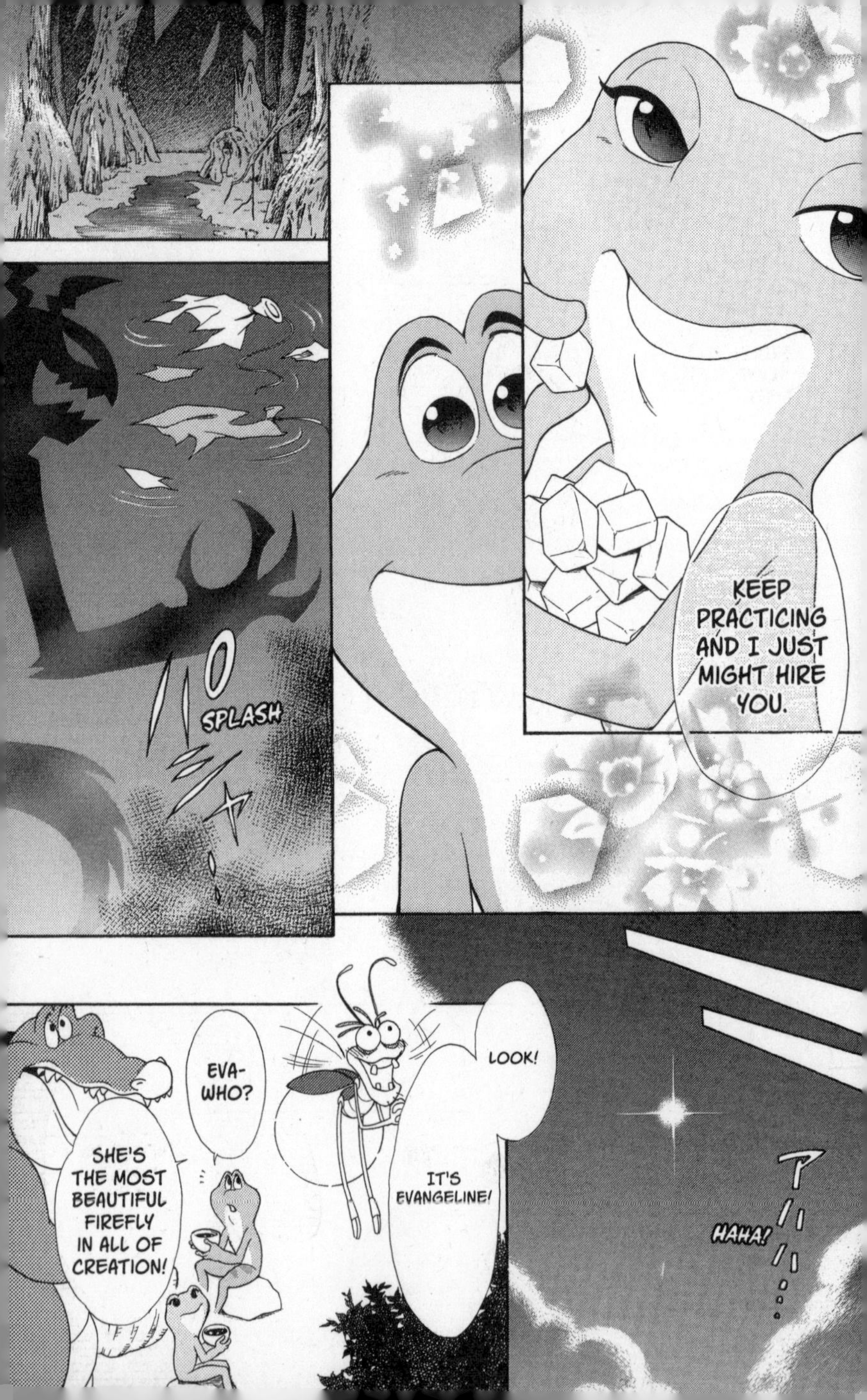
KEEP PRACTICING AND I JUST MIGHT HIRE YOU.
SPLASH
HAHA!
LOOK!
IT'S EVANGELINE!
EVA-WHO?
SHE'S THE MOST BEAUTIFUL FIREFLY IN ALL OF CREATION!

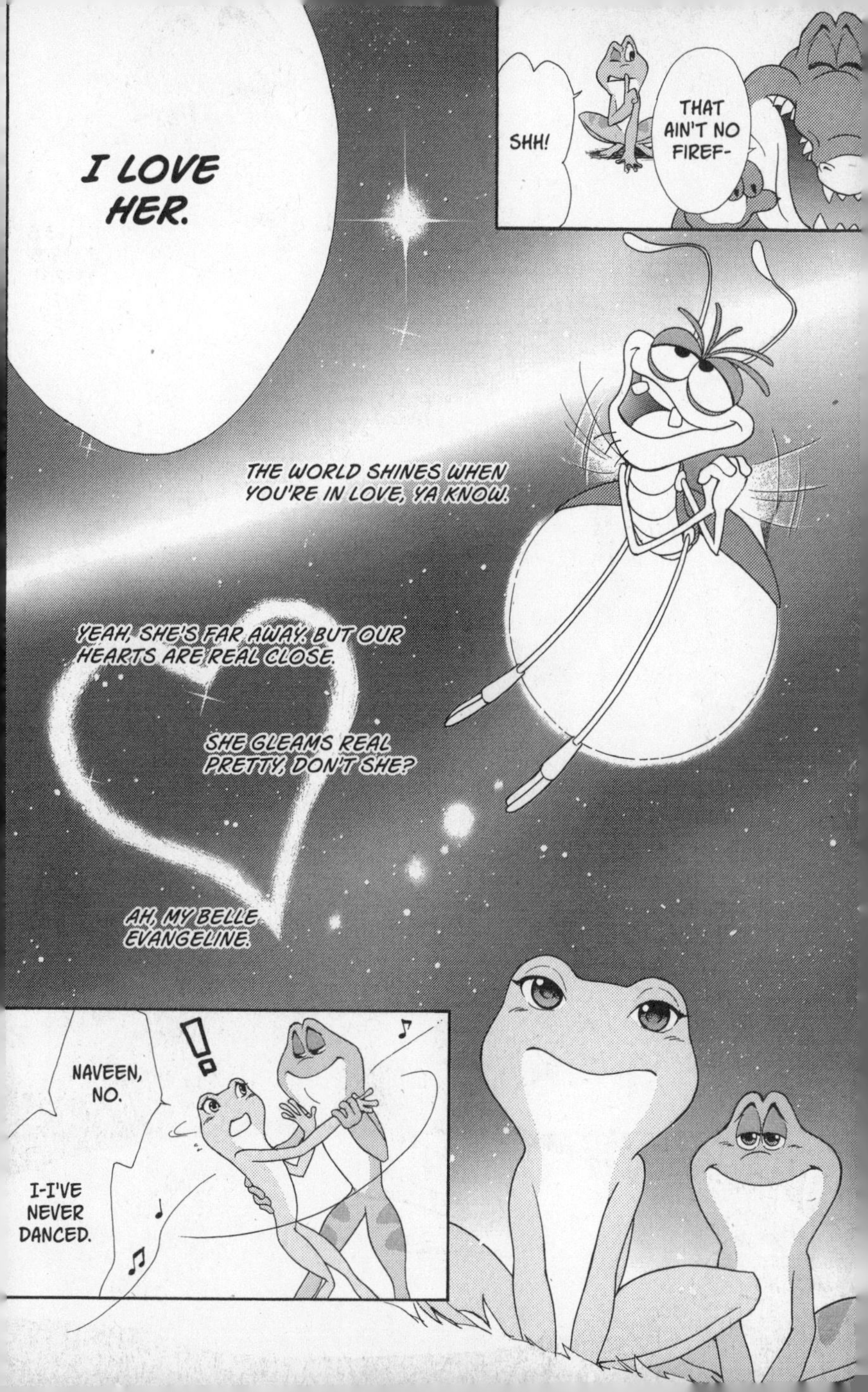
THAT AIN'T NO FIREF-
SHH!
I LOVE HER.
THE WORLD SHINES WHEN YOU'RE IN LOVE, YA KNOW.
YEAH, SHE'S FAR AWAY. BUT OUR HEARTS ARE REAL CLOSE.
SHE GLEAMS REAL PRETTY, DON'T SHE?
AH, MY BELLE EVANGELINE.
NAVEEN, NO.
I-I'VE NEVER DANCED.

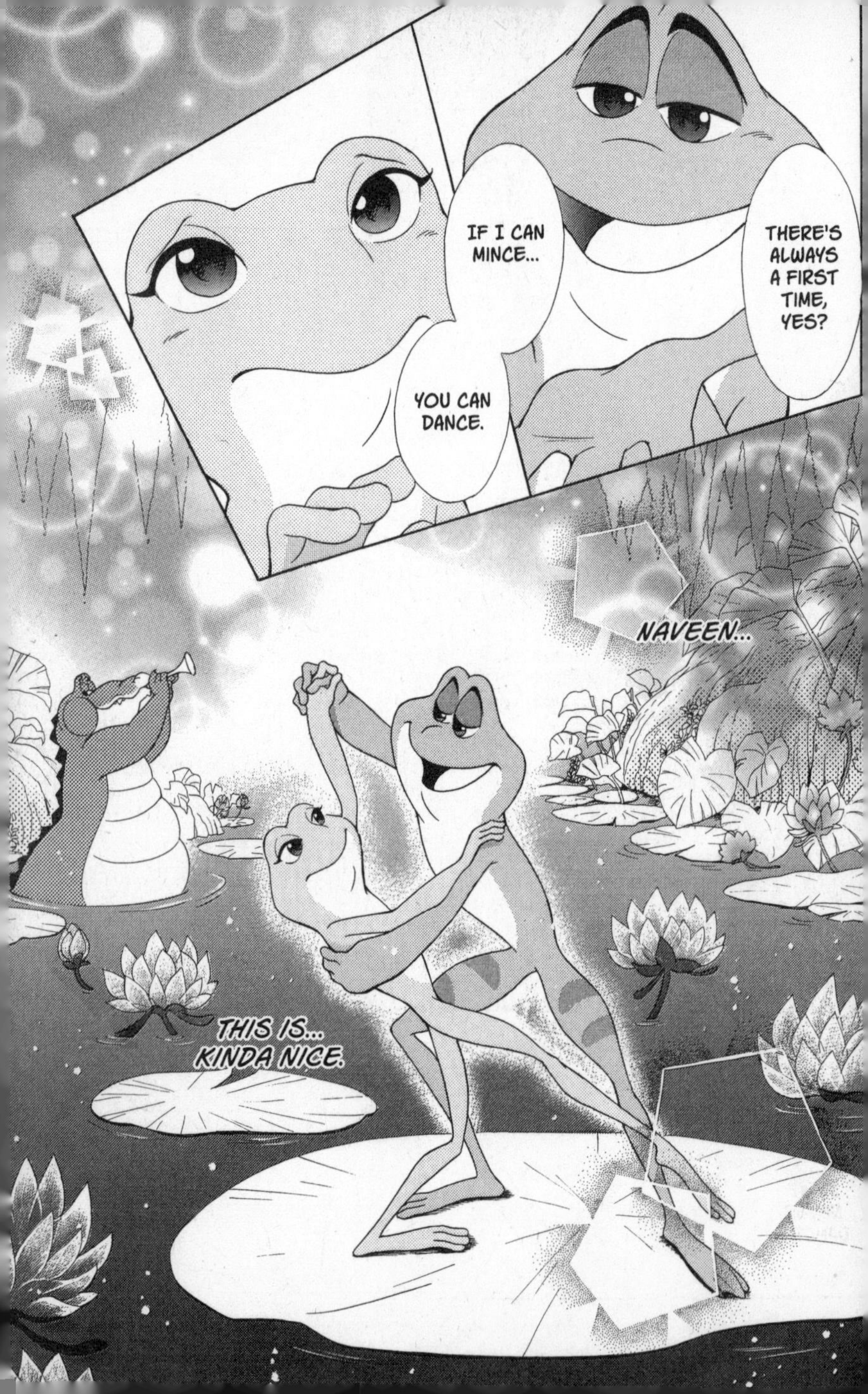
THERE'S ALWAYS A FIRST TIME, YES?
IF I CAN MINCE...
YOU CAN DANCE.
NAVEEN...
THIS IS... KINDA NICE.

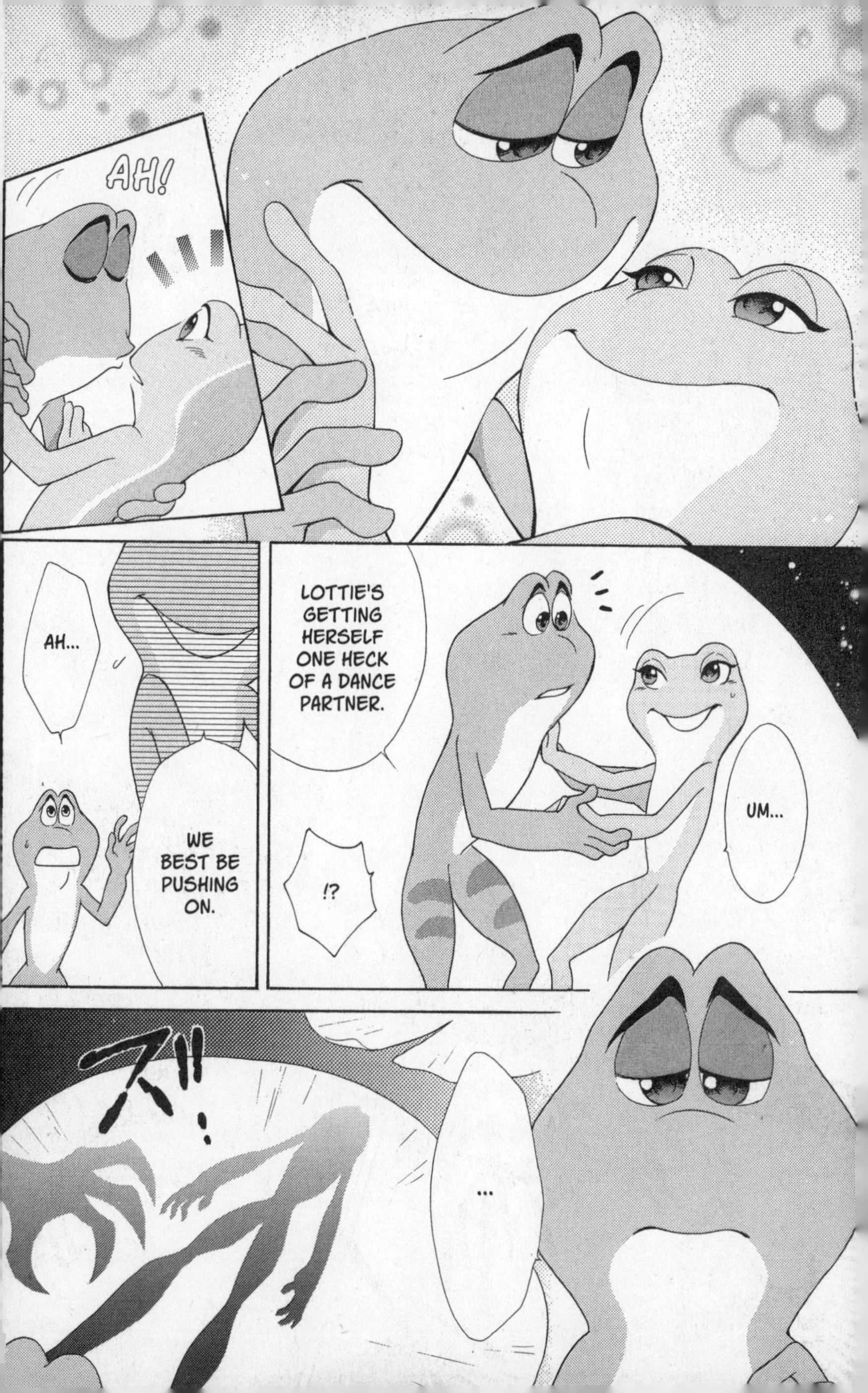
AH!
LOTTIE'S GETTING HERSELF ONE HECK OF A DANCE PARTNER.
UM...
!?
AH...
WE BEST BE PUSHING ON.
...

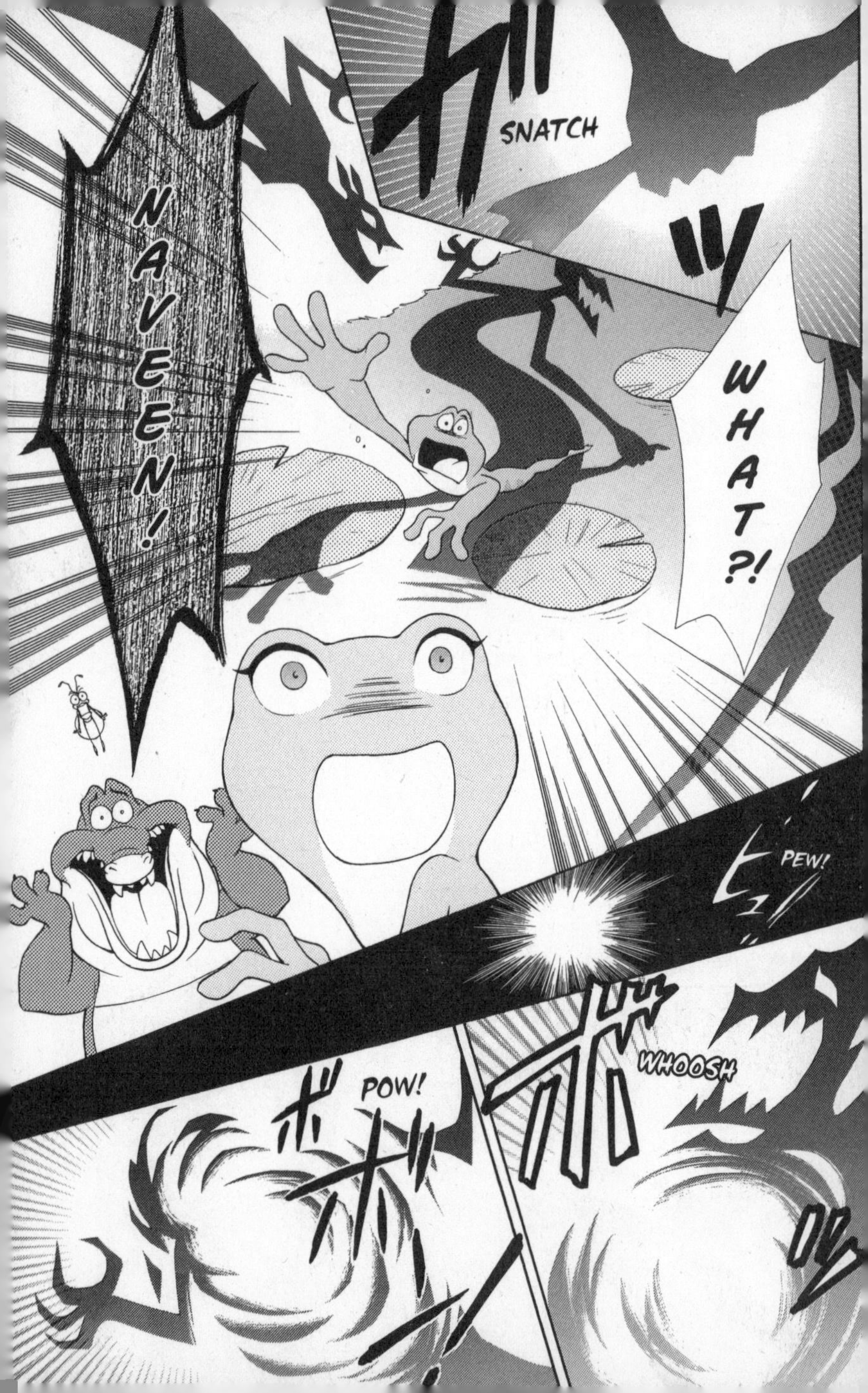
SNATCH
WHAT?!
NAVEEN!
PEW!
WHOOSH
POW!

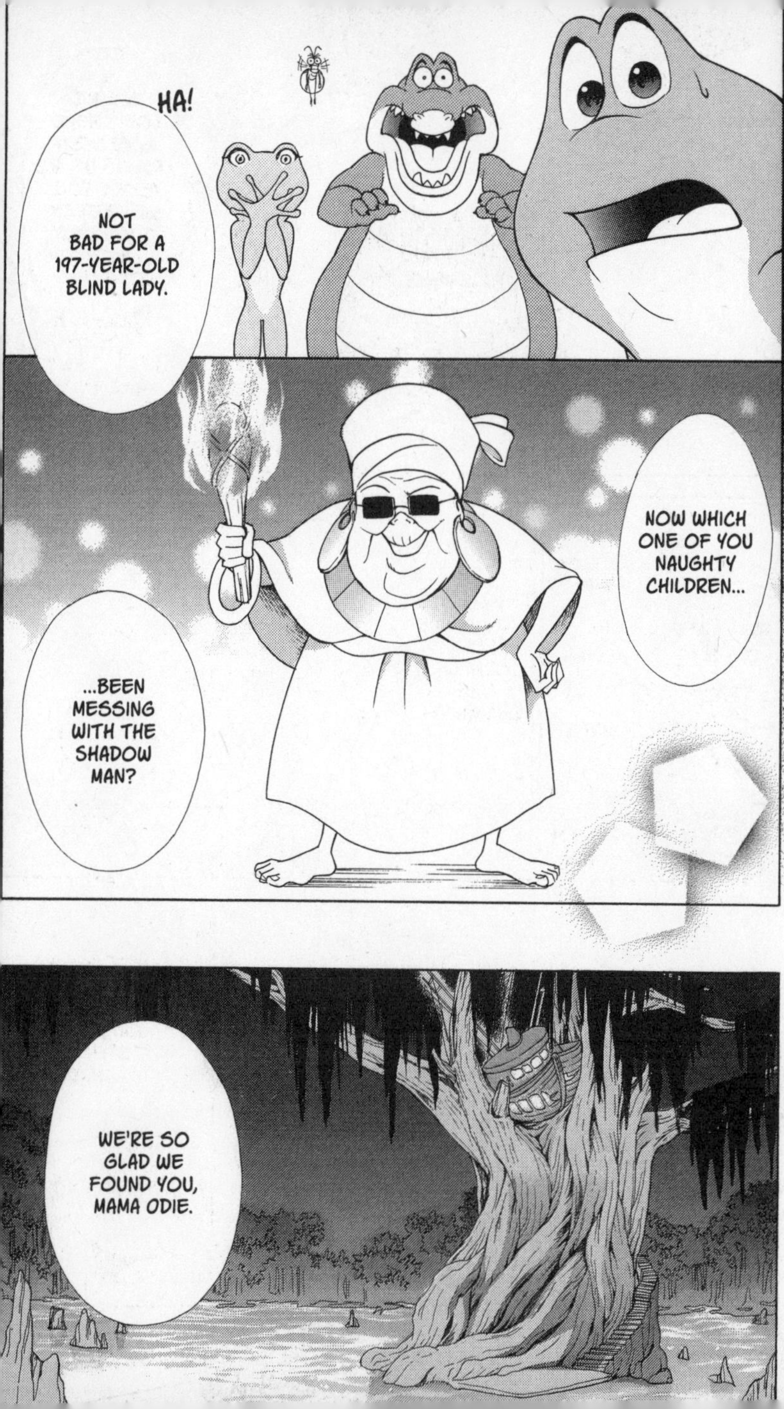
HA!
NOT BAD FOR A 197-YEAR-OLD BLIND LADY.
NOW WHICH ONE OF YOU NAUGHTY CHILDREN...
...BEEN MESSING WITH THE SHADOW MAN?
WE'RE SO GLAD WE FOUND YOU, MAMA ODIE.

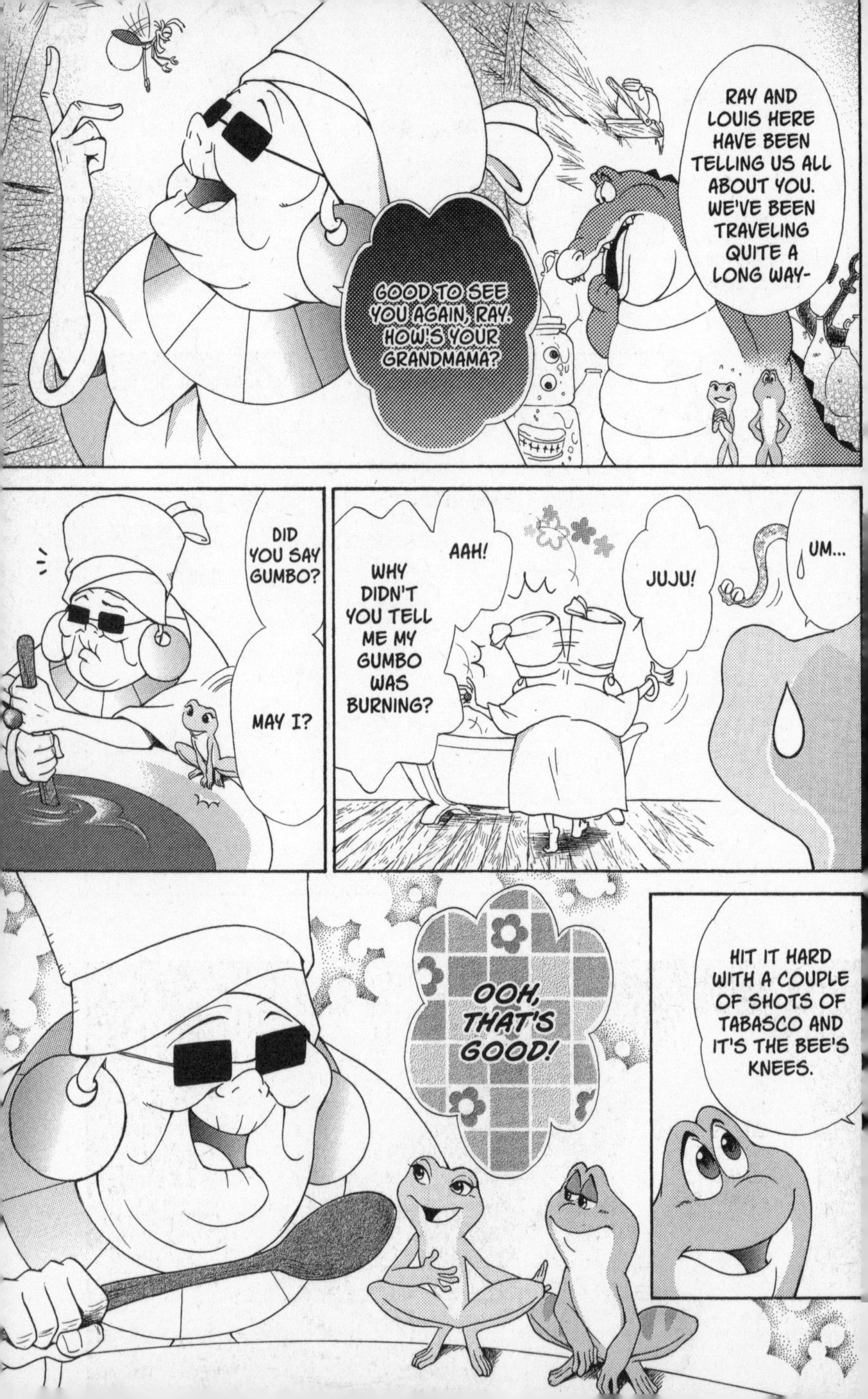
RAY AND LOUIS HERE HAVE BEEN TELLING US ALL ABOUT YOU. WE'VE BEEN TRAVELING QUITE A LONG WAY-
GOOD TO SEE YOU AGAIN, RAY. HOW'S YOUR GRANDMAMA?
UM...
JUJU!
AAH!
WHY DIDN'T YOU TELL ME MY GUMBO WAS BURNING?
DID YOU SAY GUMBO?
MAY I?
HIT IT HARD WITH A COUPLE OF SHOTS OF TABASCO AND IT'S THE BEE'S KNEES.
OOH, THAT'S GOOD!

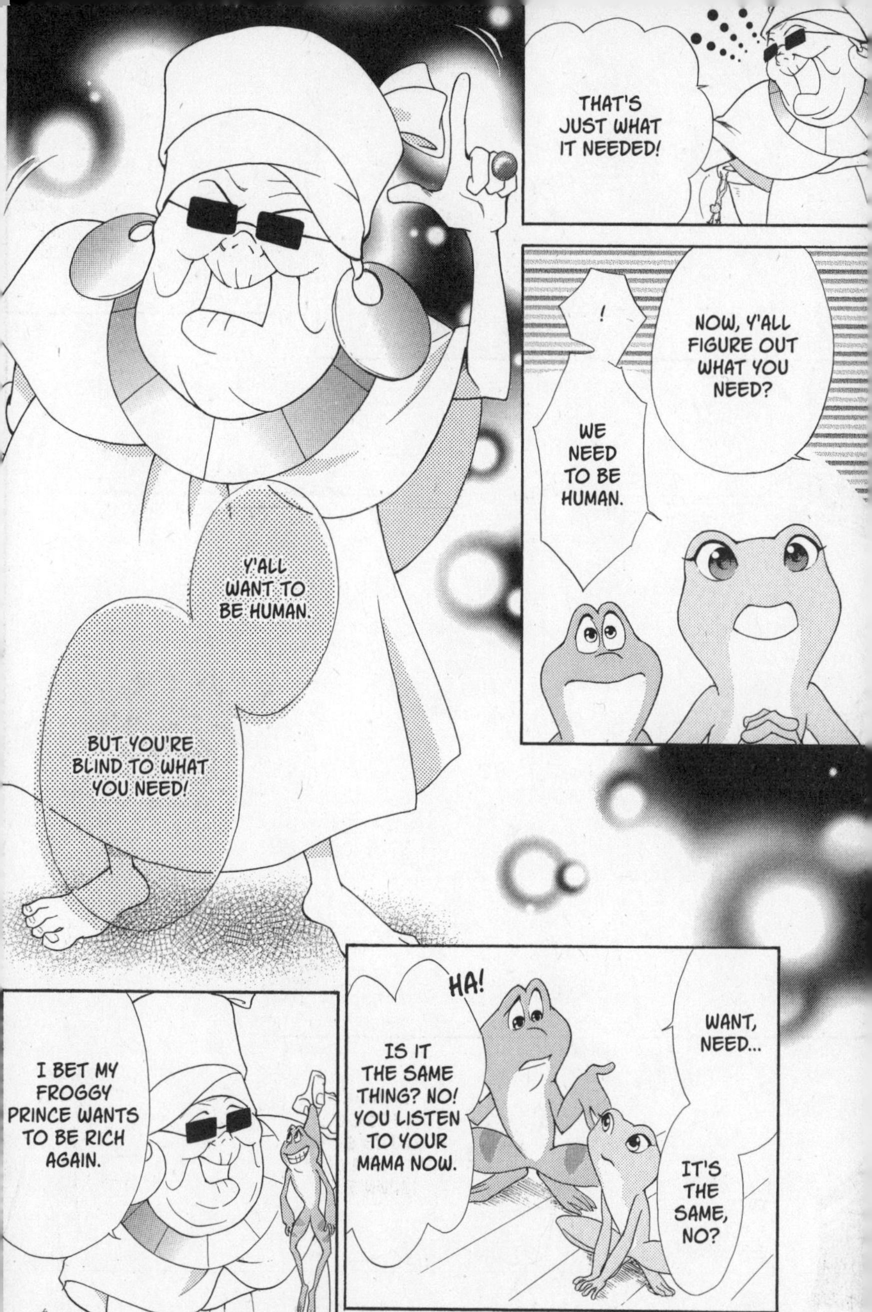
THAT'S JUST WHAT IT NEEDED!
NOW, Y'ALL FIGURE OUT WHAT YOU NEED?
!
WE NEED TO BE HUMAN.
Y'ALL WANT TO BE HUMAN.
BUT YOU'RE BLIND TO WHAT YOU NEED!
WANT, NEED...
IT'S THE SAME, NO?
HA!
IS IT THE SAME THING? NO! YOU LISTEN TO YOUR MAMA NOW.
I BET MY FROGGY PRINCE WANTS TO BE RICH AGAIN.

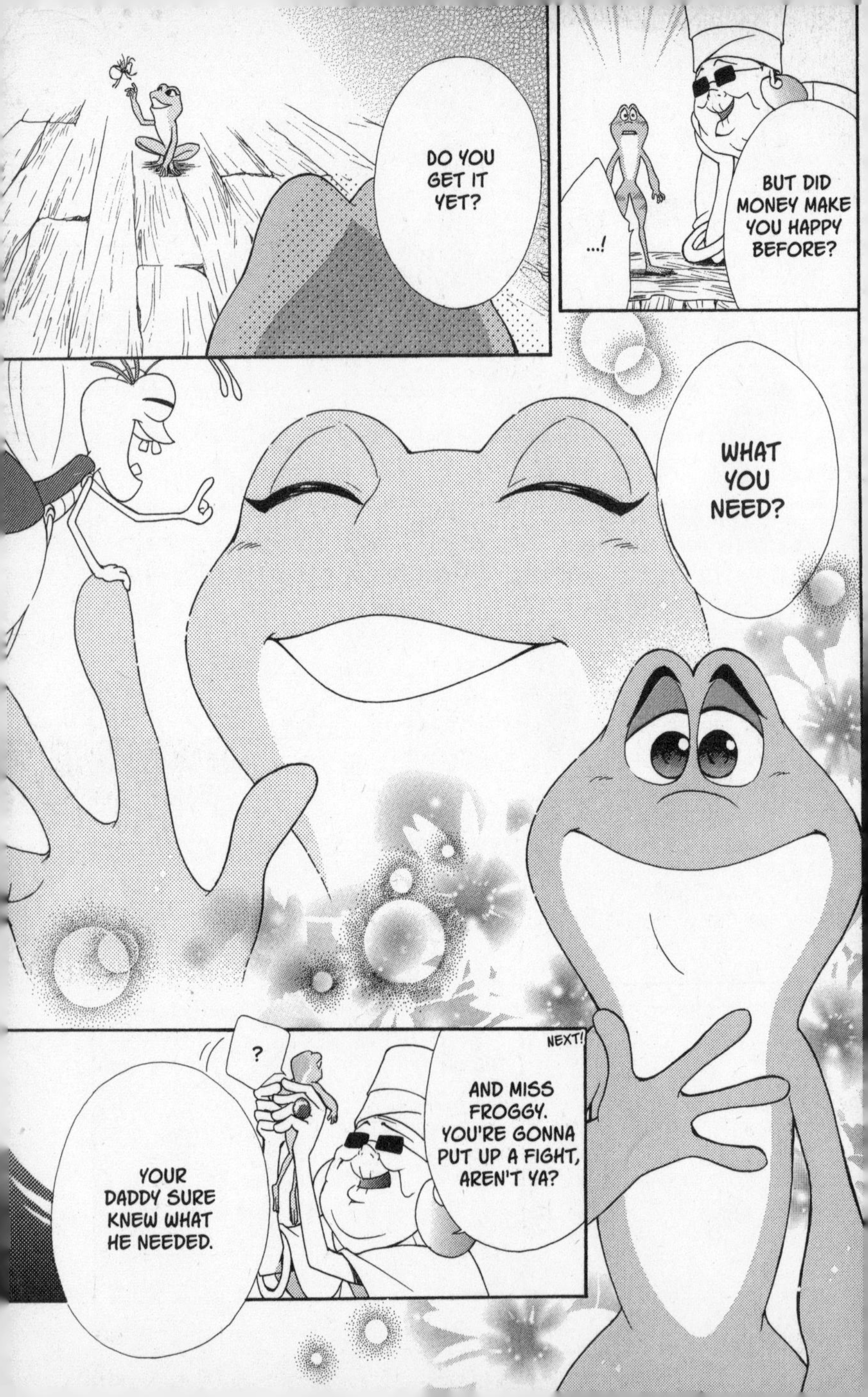
BUT DID MONEY MAKE YOU HAPPY BEFORE?
...!
DO YOU GET IT YET?
WHAT YOU NEED?
NEXT!
AND MISS FROGGY. YOU'RE GONNA PUT UP A FIGHT, AREN'T YA?
?
YOUR DADDY SURE KNEW WHAT HE NEEDED.

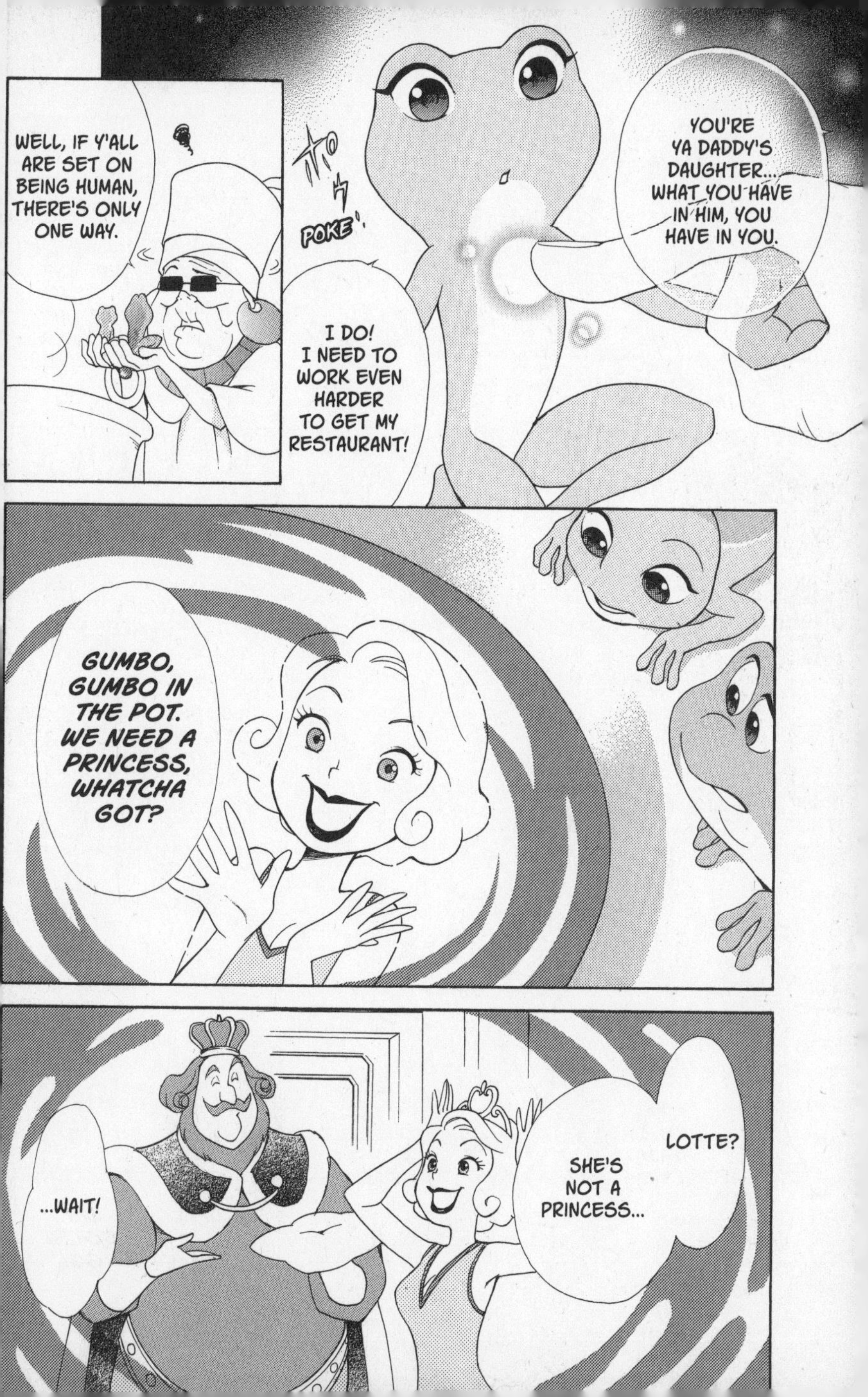
YOU'RE YA DADDY'S DAUGHTER... WHAT YOU HAVE IN HIM, YOU HAVE IN YOU.
POKE
I DO! I NEED TO WORK EVEN HARDER TO GET MY RESTAURANT!
WELL, IF Y'ALL ARE SET ON BEING HUMAN, THERE'S ONLY ONE WAY.
GUMBO, GUMBO IN THE POT. WE NEED A PRINCESS, WHATCHA GOT?
LOTTE?
SHE'S NOT A PRINCESS...
...WAIT!

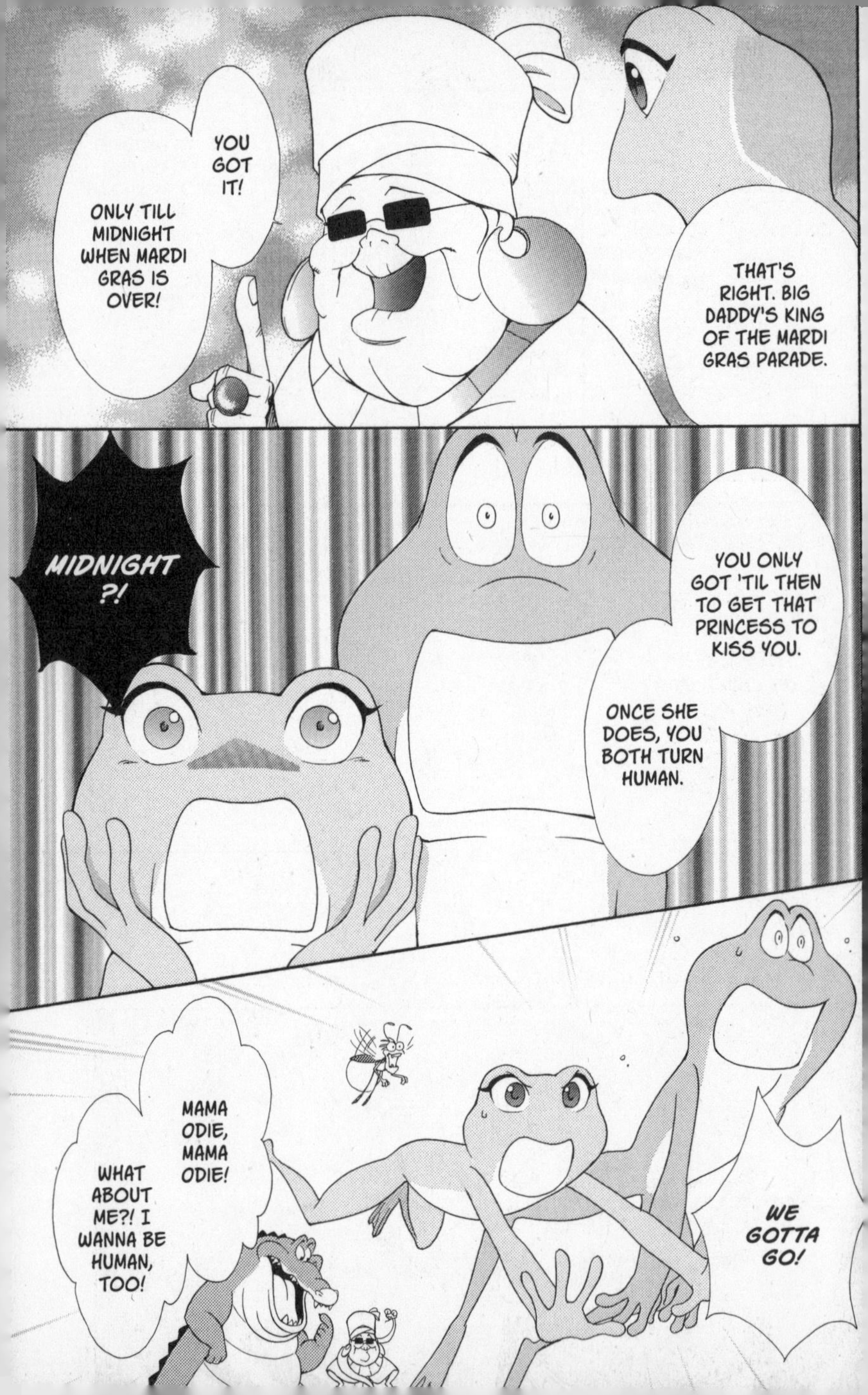
THAT'S RIGHT. BIG DADDY'S KING OF THE MARDI GRAS PARADE.
YOU GOT IT!
ONLY TILL MIDNIGHT WHEN MARDI GRAS IS OVER!
YOU ONLY GOT 'TIL THEN TO GET THAT PRINCESS TO KISS YOU.
ONCE SHE DOES, YOU BOTH TURN HUMAN.
MIDNIGHT ?!
WE GOTTA GO!
MAMA ODIE, MAMA ODIE!
WHAT ABOUT ME?! I WANNA BE HUMAN, TOO!

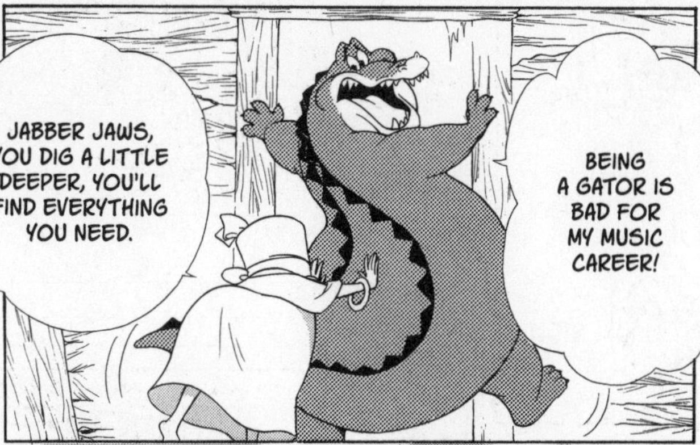
BEING A GATOR IS BAD FOR MY MUSIC CAREER!
JABBER JAWS, YOU DIG A LITTLE DEEPER, YOU'LL FIND EVERYTHING YOU NEED.
PHEW! MAMA'S GETTING TOO OLD FOR THIS.
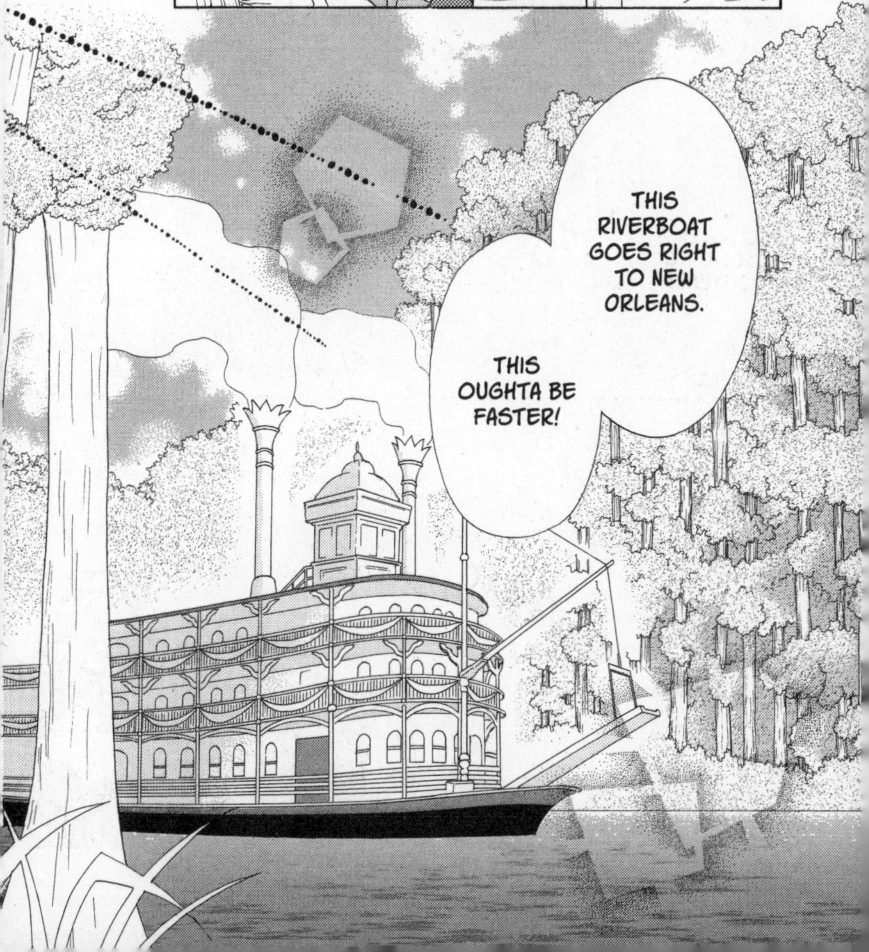
THIS RIVERBOAT GOES RIGHT TO NEW ORLEANS.
THIS OUGHTA BE FASTER!

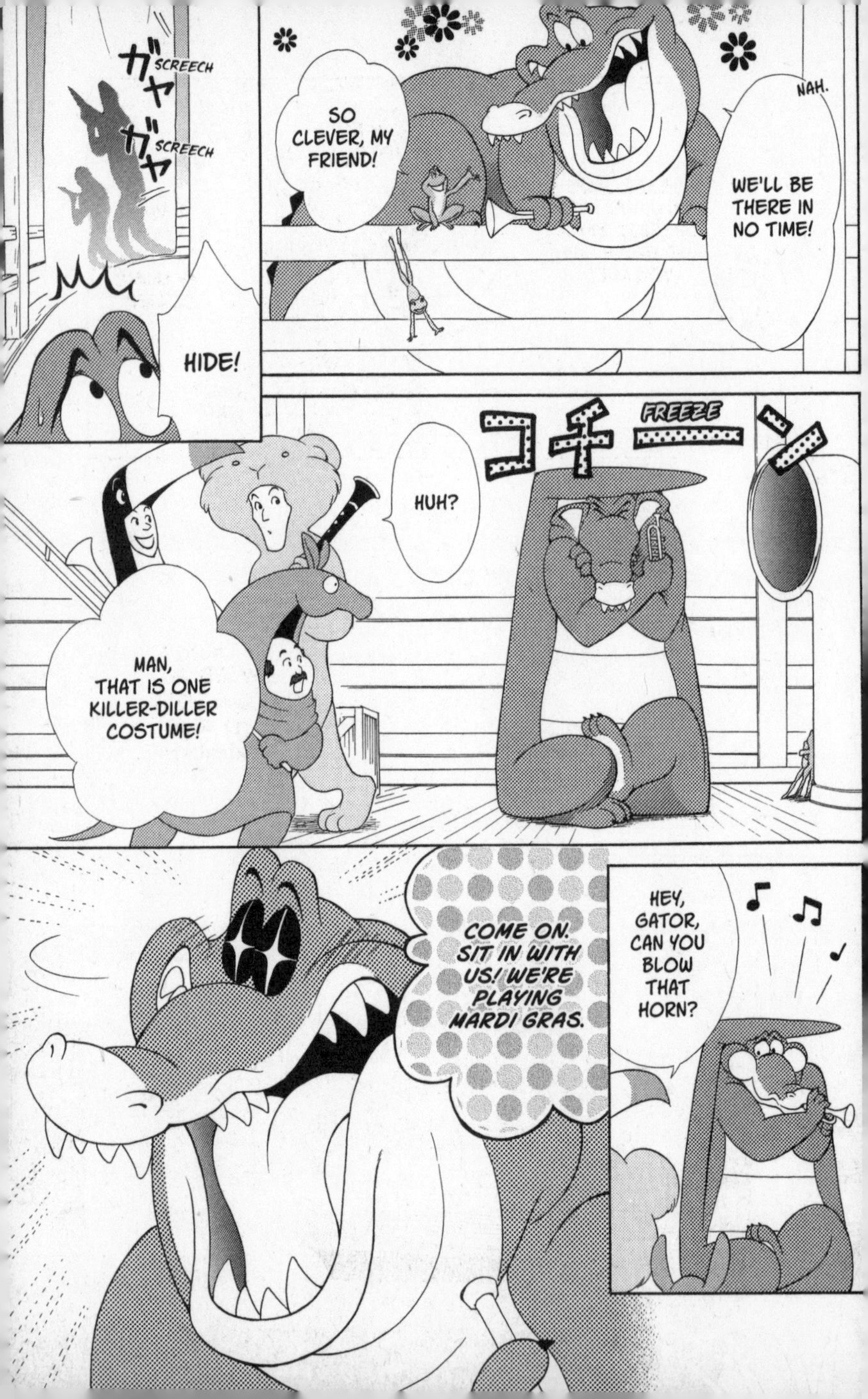
NAH.
WE'LL BE THERE IN NO TIME!
SO CLEVER, MY FRIEND!
ガ SCREECH ヤ ガ SCREECH ヤ
HIDE!
コチーン FREEZE
HUH?
MAN, THAT IS ONE KILLER-DILLER COSTUME!
HEY, GATOR, CAN YOU BLOW THAT HORN?
COME ON. SIT IN WITH US! WE'RE PLAYING MARDI GRAS.

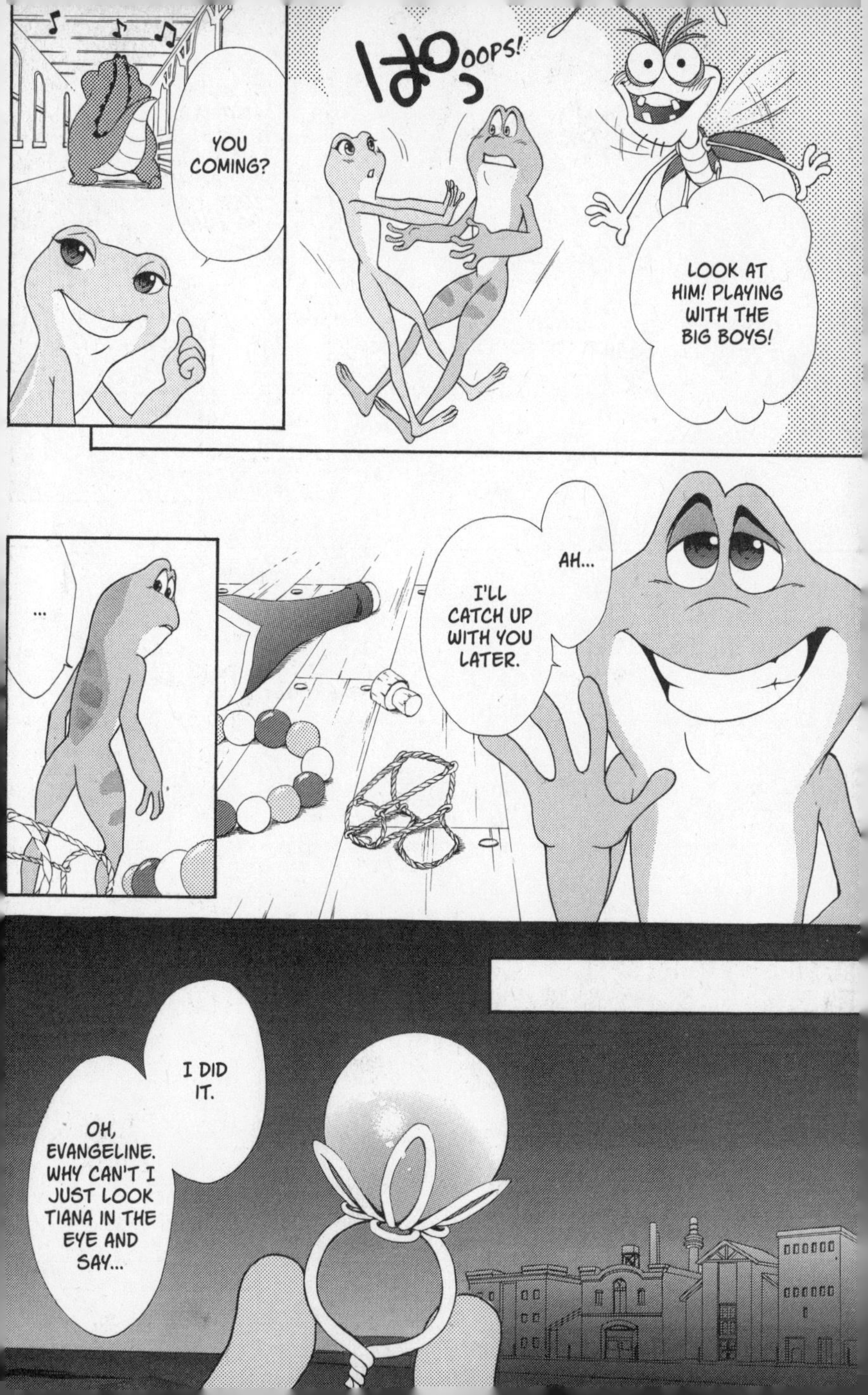
はっ OOPS!
LOOK AT HIM! PLAYING WITH THE BIG BOYS!
YOU COMING?
AH...
I'LL CATCH UP WITH YOU LATER.
...
I DID IT.
OH, EVANGELINE. WHY CAN'T I JUST LOOK TIANA IN THE EYE AND SAY...

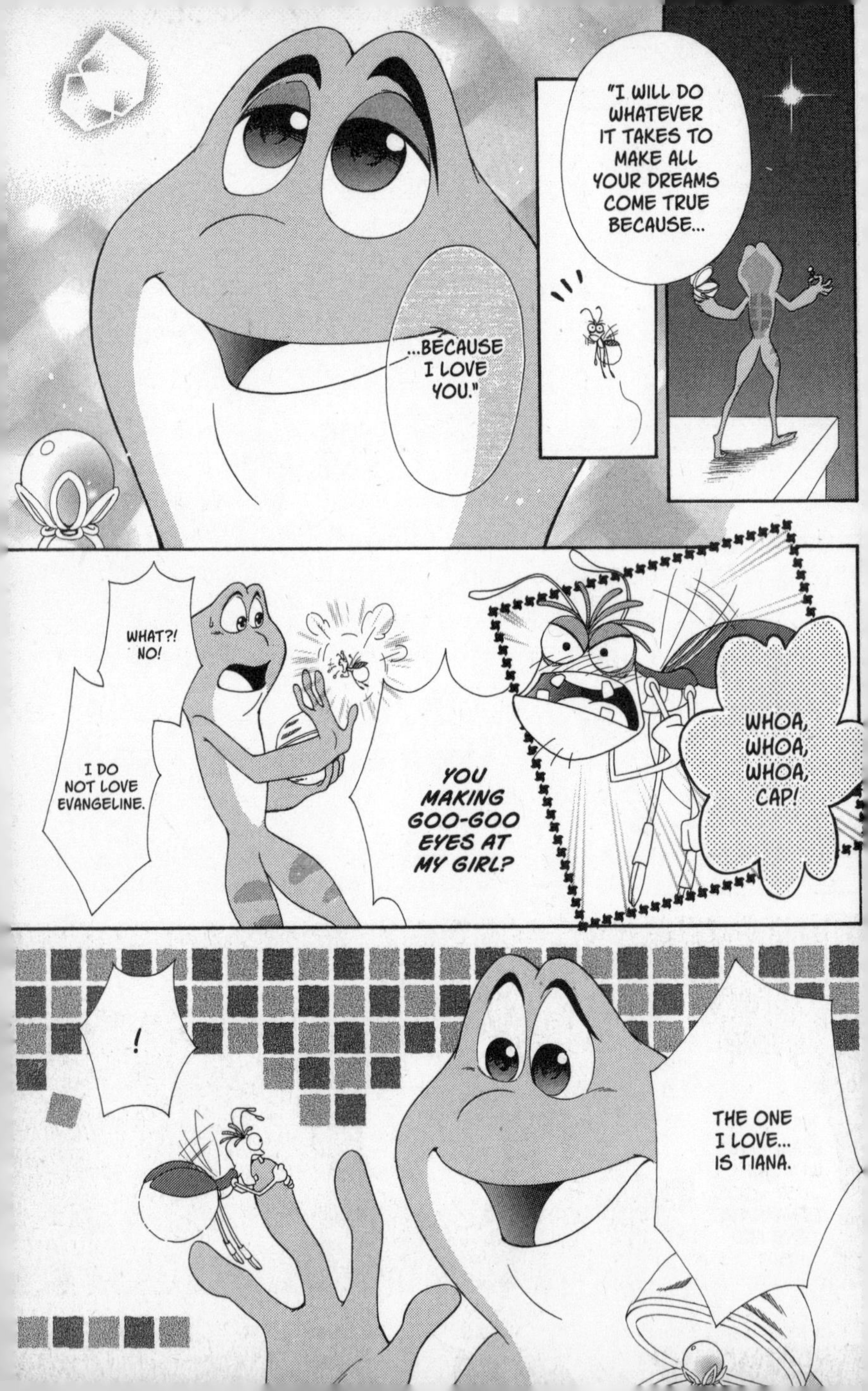
"I WILL DO WHATEVER IT TAKES TO MAKE ALL YOUR DREAMS COME TRUE BECAUSE...
...BECAUSE I LOVE YOU."
WHOA, WHOA, WHOA, CAP!
YOU MAKING GOO-GOO EYES AT MY GIRL?
WHAT?! NO!
I DO NOT LOVE EVANGELINE.
THE ONE I LOVE... IS TIANA.
!

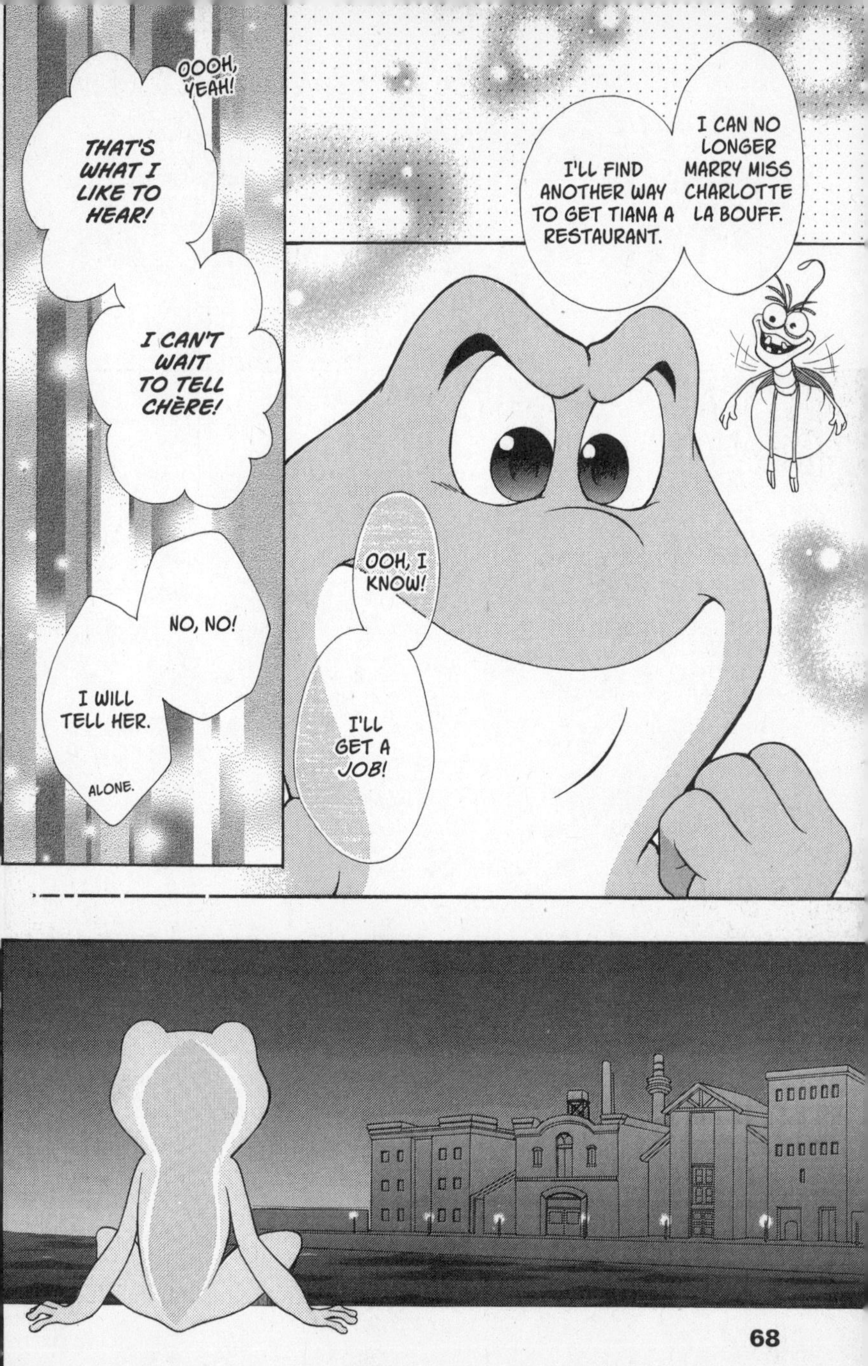
I CAN NO LONGER MARRY MISS CHARLOTTE LA BOUFF.
I'LL FIND ANOTHER WAY TO GET TIANA A RESTAURANT.
OOH, I KNOW!
I'LL GET A JOB!
OOOH, YEAH!
THAT'S WHAT I LIKE TO HEAR!
I CAN'T WAIT TO TELL CHÈRE!
NO, NO!
I WILL TELL HER.
ALONE.

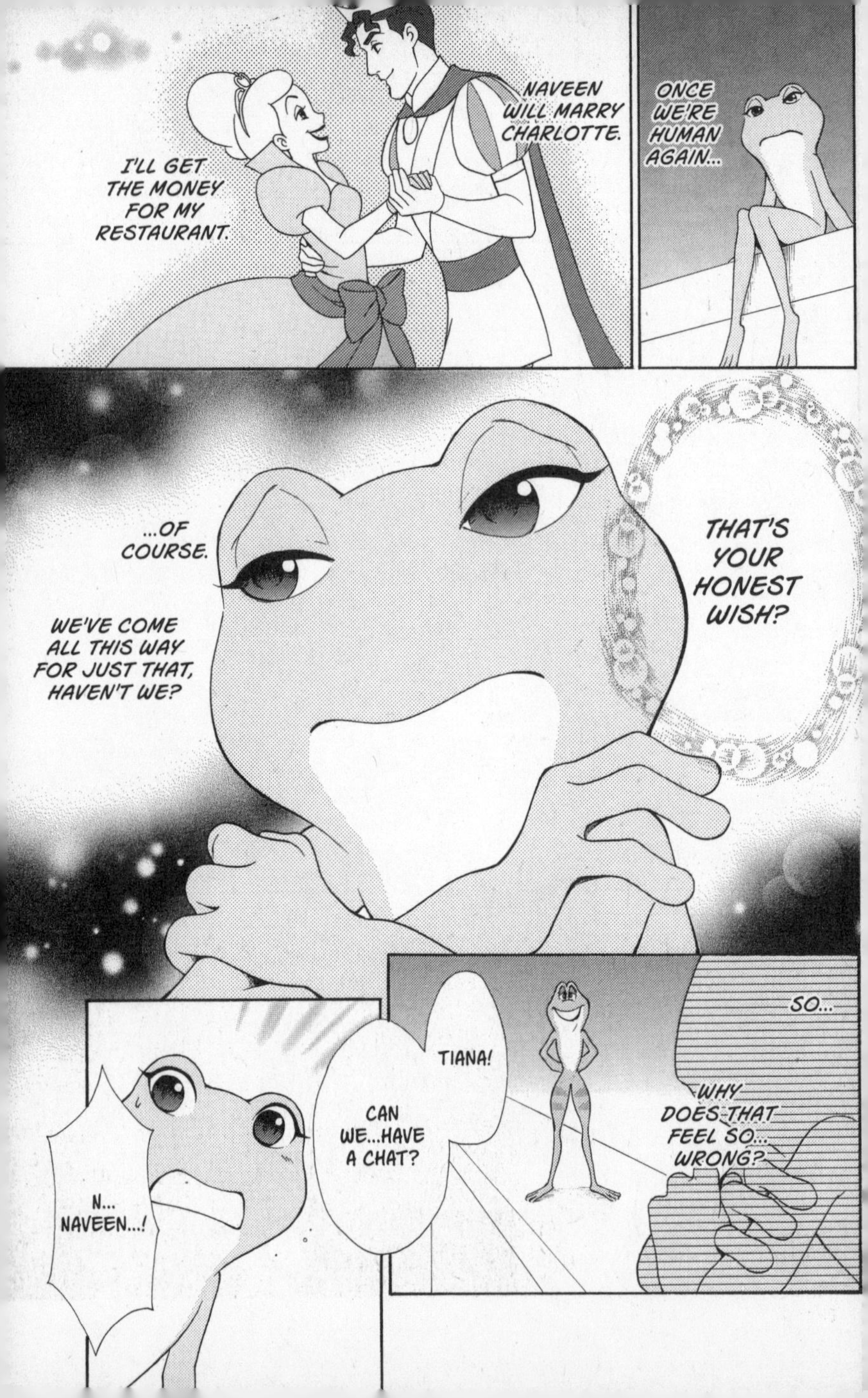
ONCE WE'RE HUMAN AGAIN...
NAVEEN WILL MARRY CHARLOTTE.
I'LL GET THE MONEY FOR MY RESTAURANT.
THAT'S YOUR HONEST WISH?
...OF COURSE.
WE'VE COME ALL THIS WAY FOR JUST THAT, HAVEN'T WE?
SO...
WHY DOES THAT FEEL SO... WRONG?
TIANA!
CAN WE...HAVE A CHAT?
N... NAVEEN...!

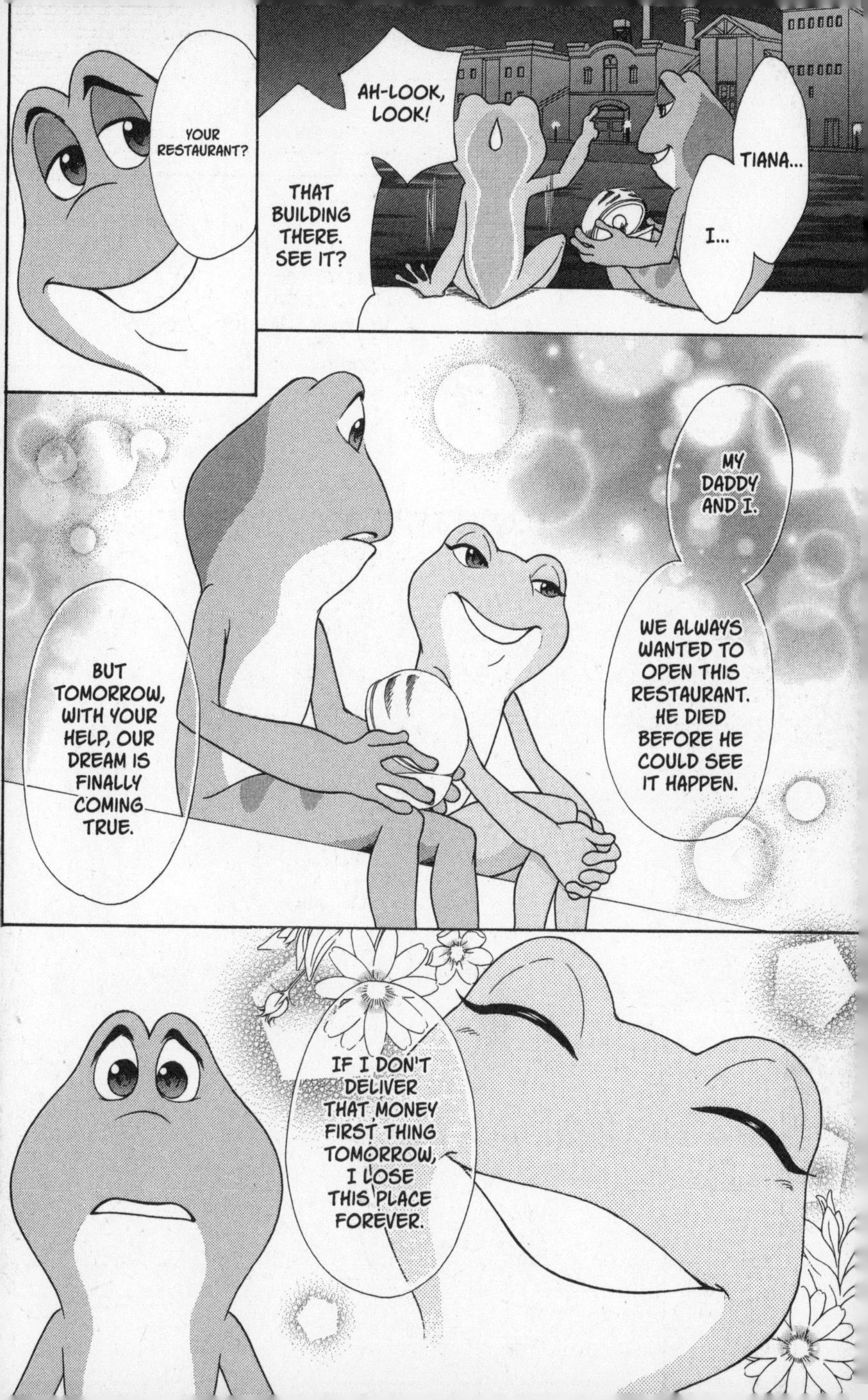
TIANA... I...
AH-LOOK, LOOK!
THAT BUILDING THERE. SEE IT?
YOUR RESTAURANT?
MY DADDY AND I.
WE ALWAYS WANTED TO OPEN THIS RESTAURANT. HE DIED BEFORE HE COULD SEE IT HAPPEN.
BUT TOMORROW, WITH YOUR HELP, OUR DREAM IS FINALLY COMING TRUE.
IF I DON'T DELIVER THAT MONEY FIRST THING TOMORROW, I LOSE THIS PLACE FOREVER.

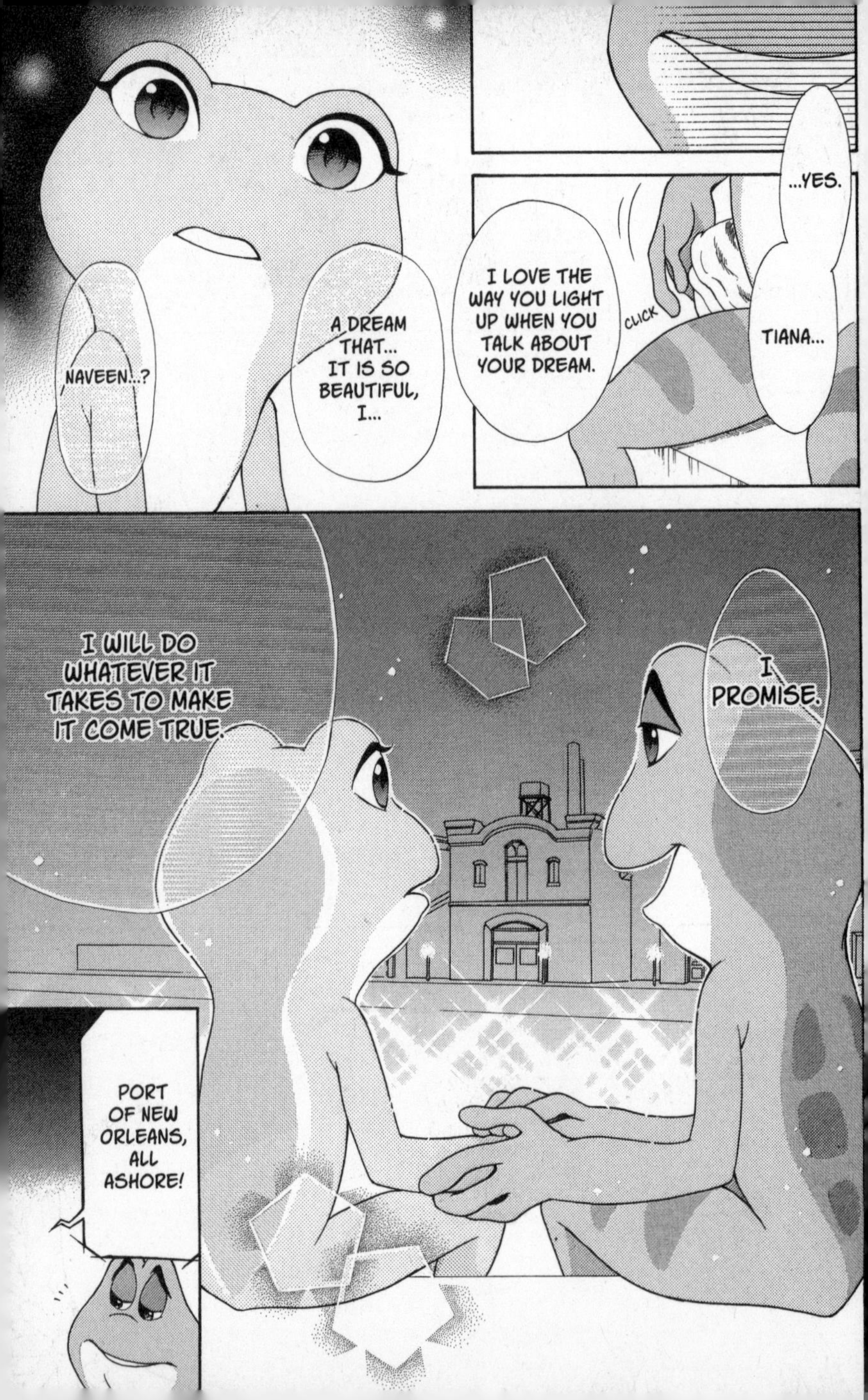
...YES.
TIANA...
CLICK
I LOVE THE WAY YOU LIGHT UP WHEN YOU TALK ABOUT YOUR DREAM.
A DREAM THAT... IT IS SO BEAUTIFUL, I...
NAVEEN...?
I PROMISE.
I WILL DO WHATEVER IT TAKES TO MAKE IT COME TRUE.
PORT OF NEW ORLEANS, ALL ASHORE!

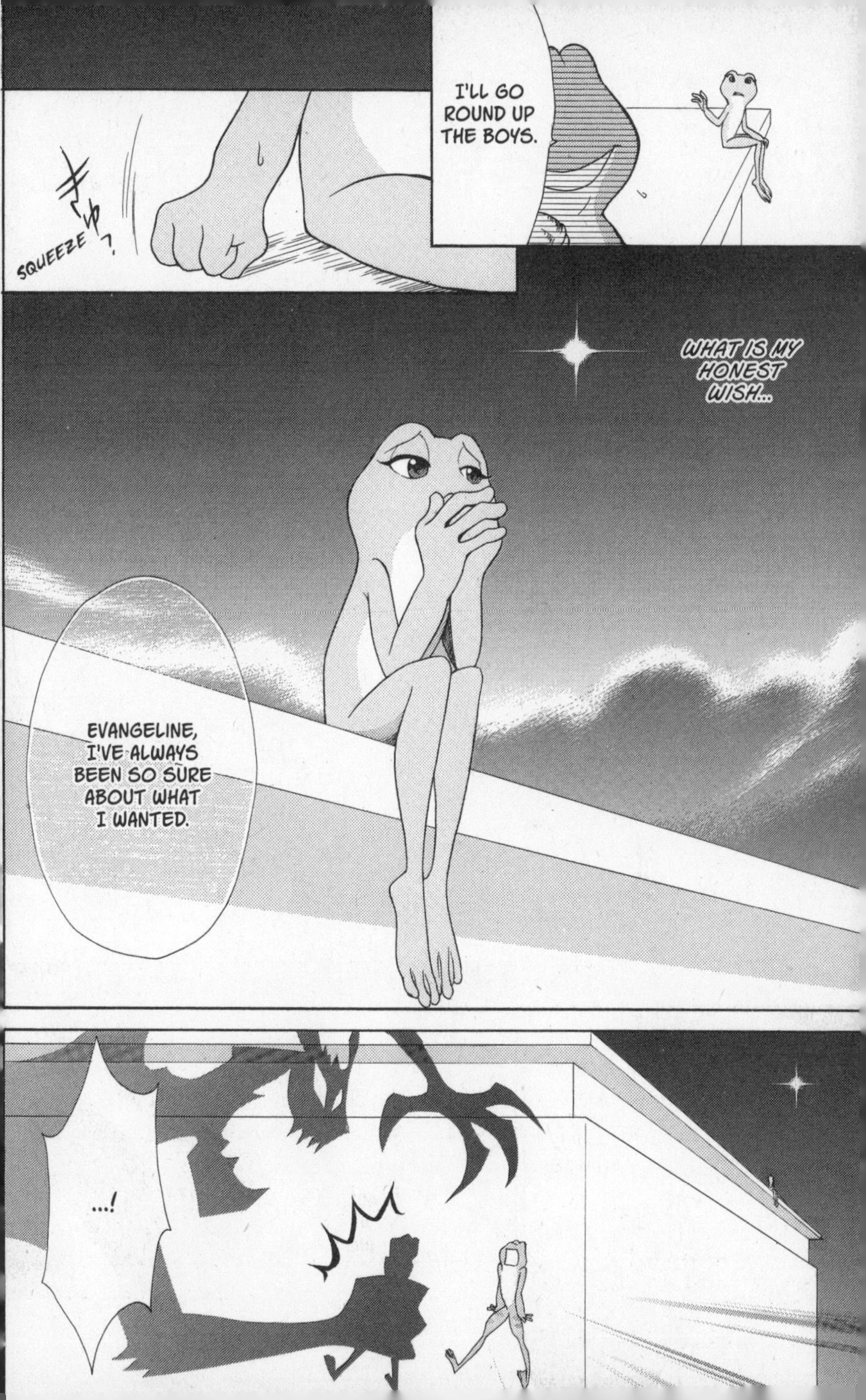
I'LL GO ROUND UP THE BOYS.
きゅ
SQUEEZE
WHAT IS MY HONEST WISH...
EVANGELINE, I'VE ALWAYS BEEN SO SURE ABOUT WHAT I WANTED.
...!

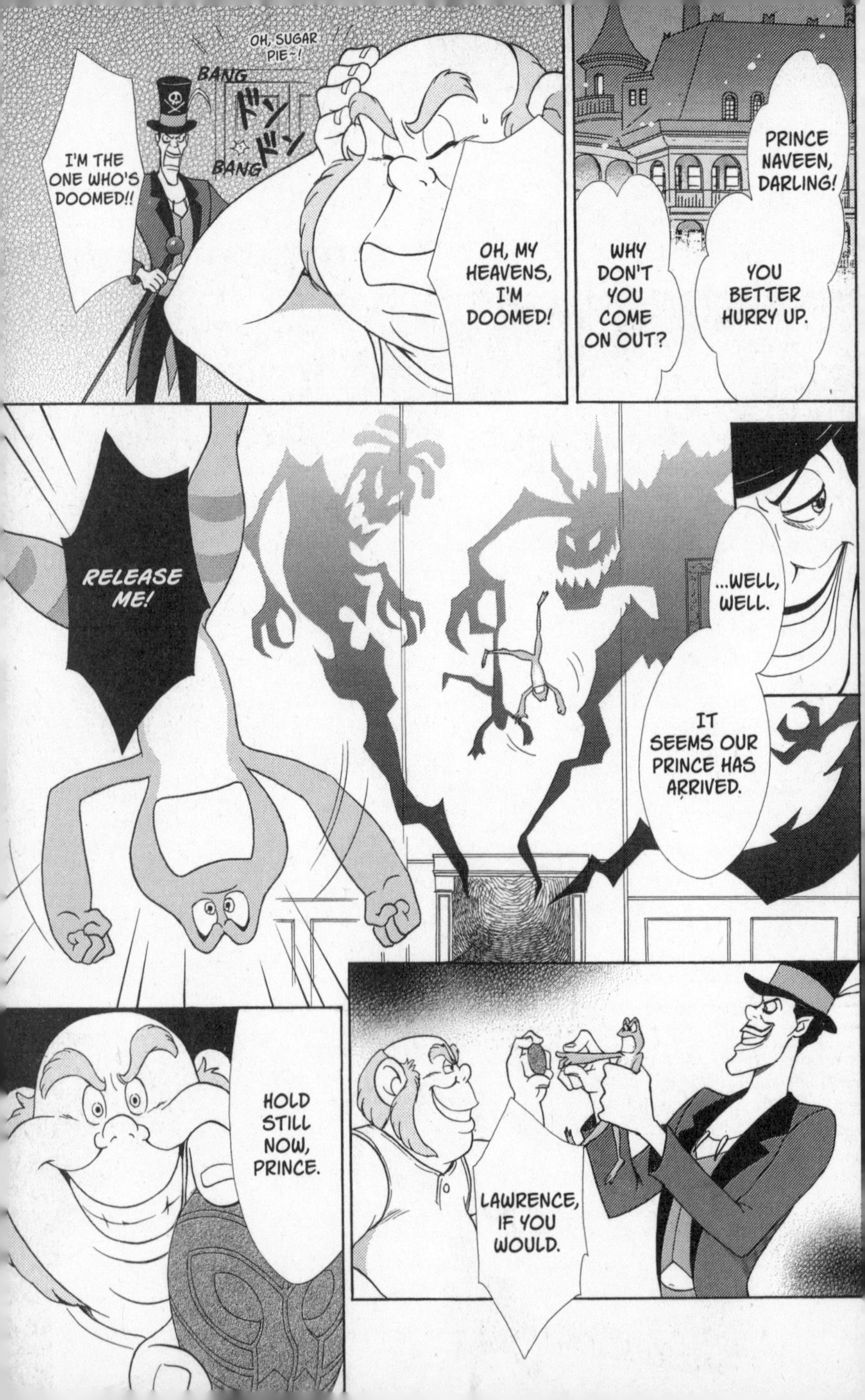
PRINCE NAVEEN, DARLING!
YOU BETTER HURRY UP.
WHY DON'T YOU COME ON OUT?
OH, SUGAR PIE~!
BANG
ドッ
BANG
ドッ
OH, MY HEAVENS, I'M DOOMED!
I'M THE ONE WHO'S DOOMED!!
...WELL, WELL.
IT SEEMS OUR PRINCE HAS ARRIVED.
RELEASE ME!
LAWRENCE, IF YOU WOULD.
HOLD STILL NOW, PRINCE.

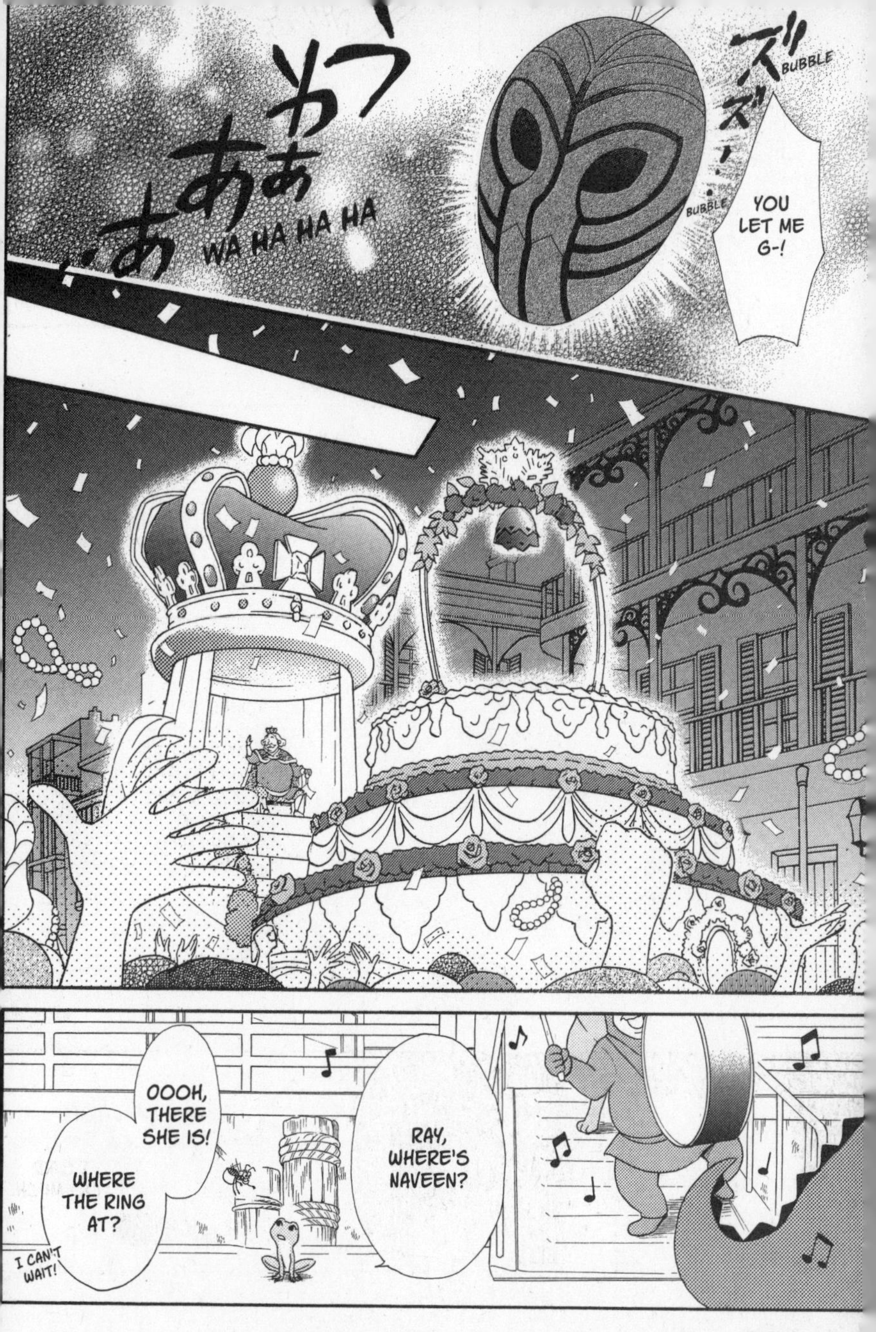
BUBBLE
BUBBLE
YOU LET ME G-!
WA HA HA HA
RAY, WHERE'S NAVEEN?
OOOH, THERE SHE IS!
WHERE THE RING AT?
I CAN'T WAIT!

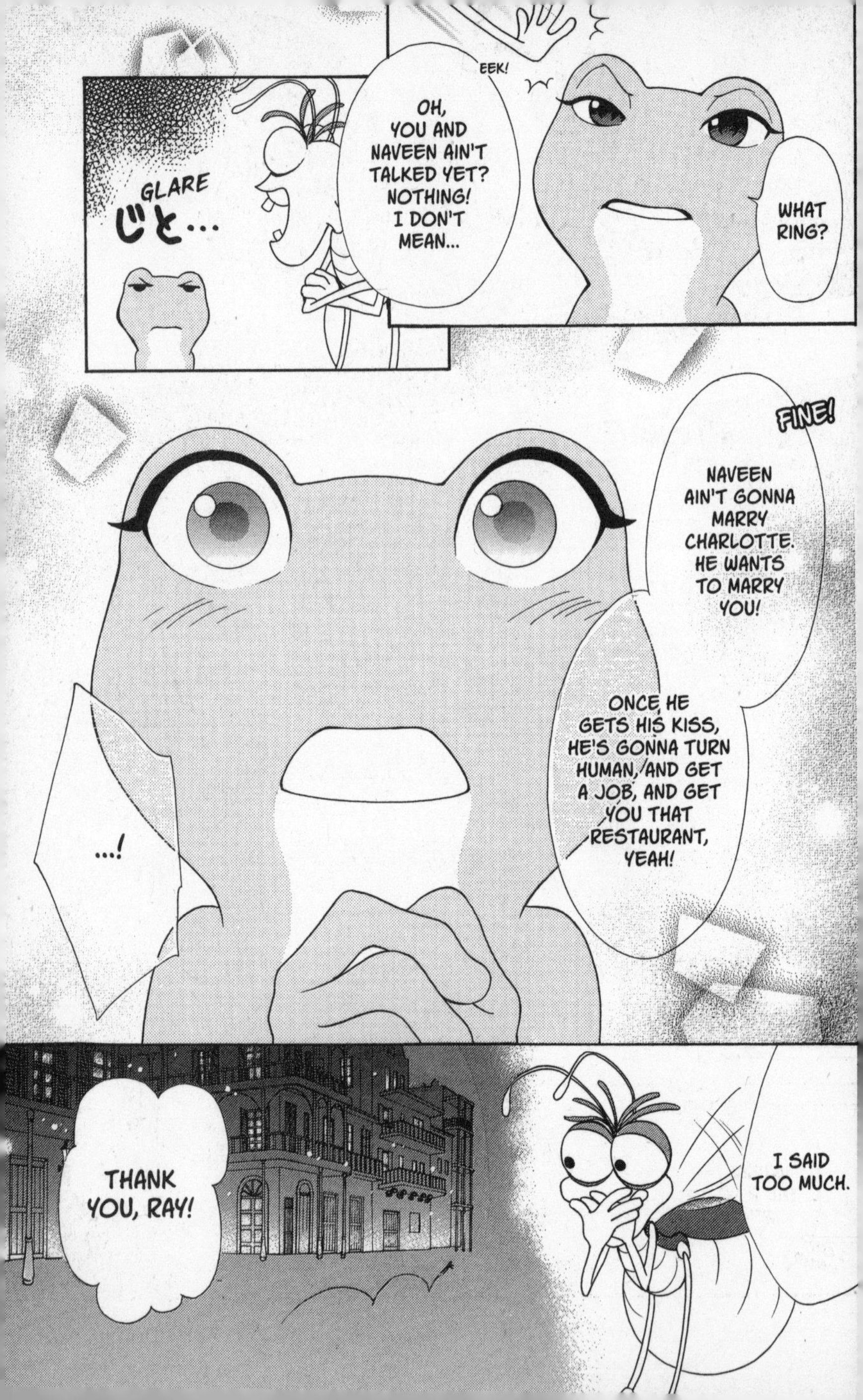
WHAT RING?
EEK!
OH, YOU AND NAVEEN AIN'T TALKED YET? NOTHING! I DON'T MEAN...
GLARE
じと…
FINE!
NAVEEN AIN'T GONNA MARRY CHARLOTTE. HE WANTS TO MARRY YOU!
ONCE HE GETS HIS KISS, HE'S GONNA TURN HUMAN, AND GET A JOB, AND GET YOU THAT RESTAURANT, YEAH!
...!
I SAID TOO MUCH.
THANK YOU, RAY!

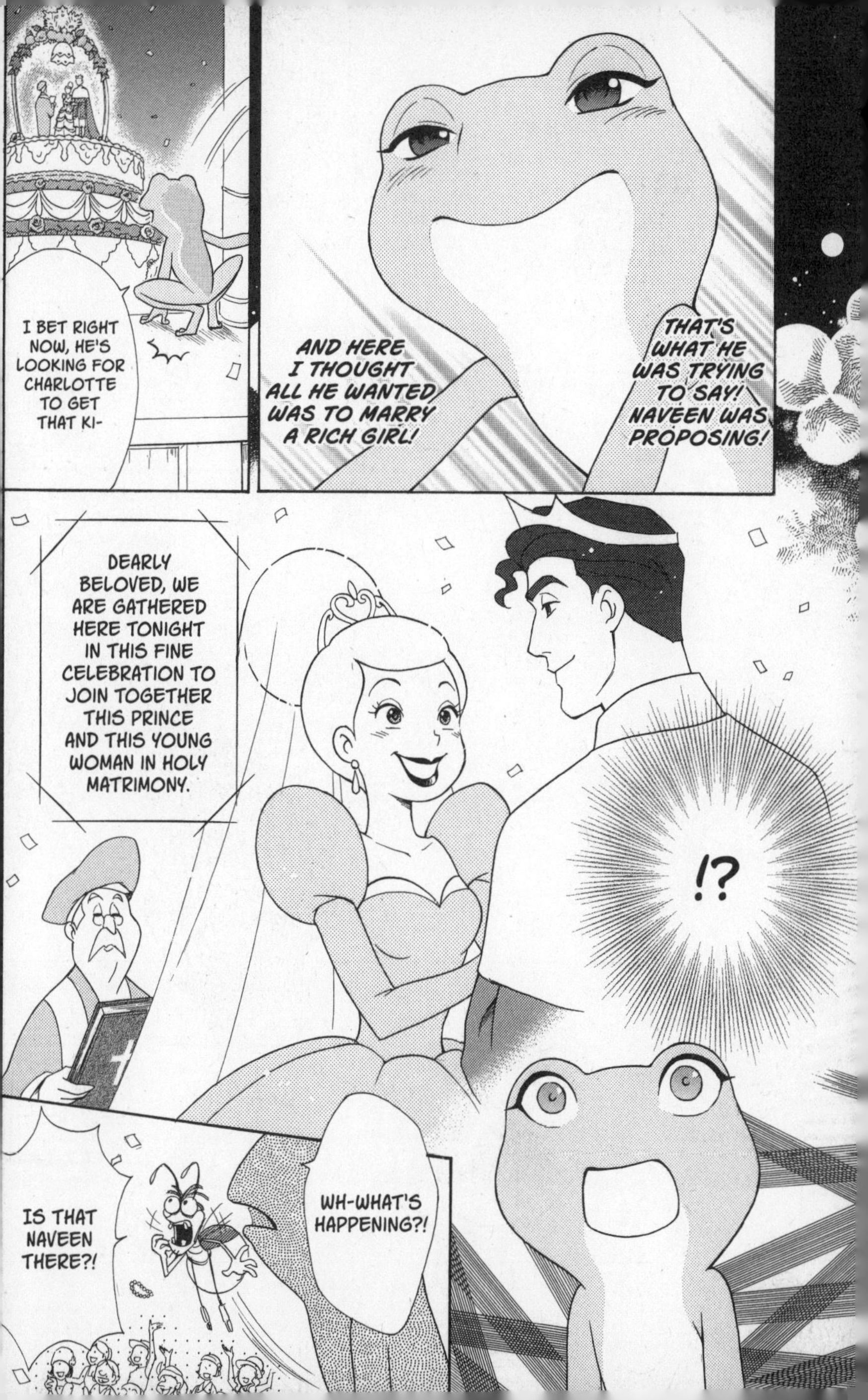
THAT'S WHAT HE WAS TRYING TO SAY! NAVEEN WAS PROPOSING!
AND HERE I THOUGHT ALL HE WANTED WAS TO MARRY A RICH GIRL!
I BET RIGHT NOW, HE'S LOOKING FOR CHARLOTTE TO GET THAT KI-
DEARLY BELOVED, WE ARE GATHERED HERE TONIGHT IN THIS FINE CELEBRATION TO JOIN TOGETHER THIS PRINCE AND THIS YOUNG WOMAN IN HOLY MATRIMONY.
!?
WH-WHAT'S HAPPENING?!
IS THAT NAVEEN THERE?!

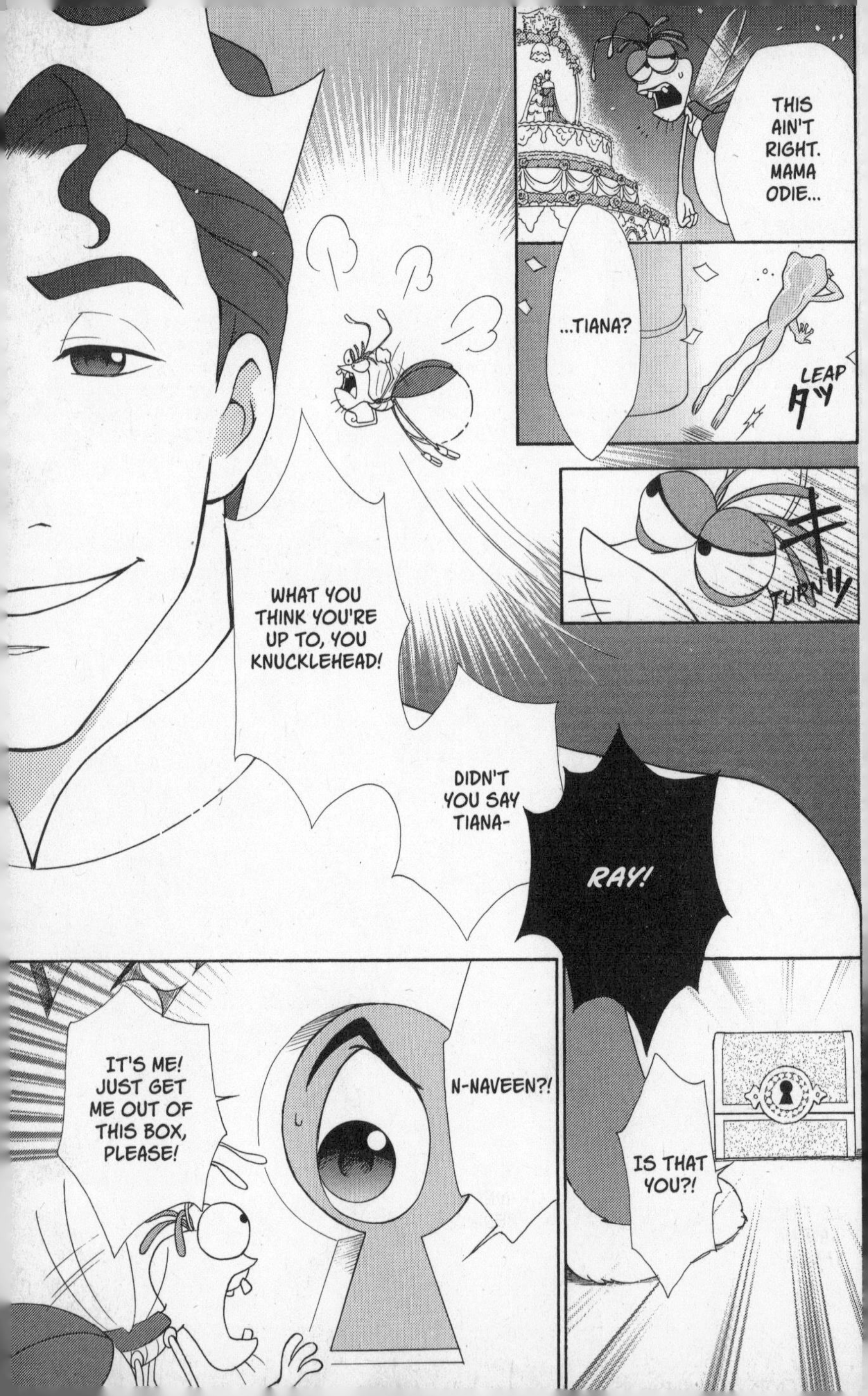
THIS AIN'T RIGHT. MAMA ODIE...
...TIANA?
LEAP タッ
TURN
WHAT YOU THINK YOU'RE UP TO, YOU KNUCKLEHEAD!
DIDN'T YOU SAY TIANA-
RAY!
IS THAT YOU?!
N-NAVEEN?!
IT'S ME! JUST GET ME OUT OF THIS BOX, PLEASE!

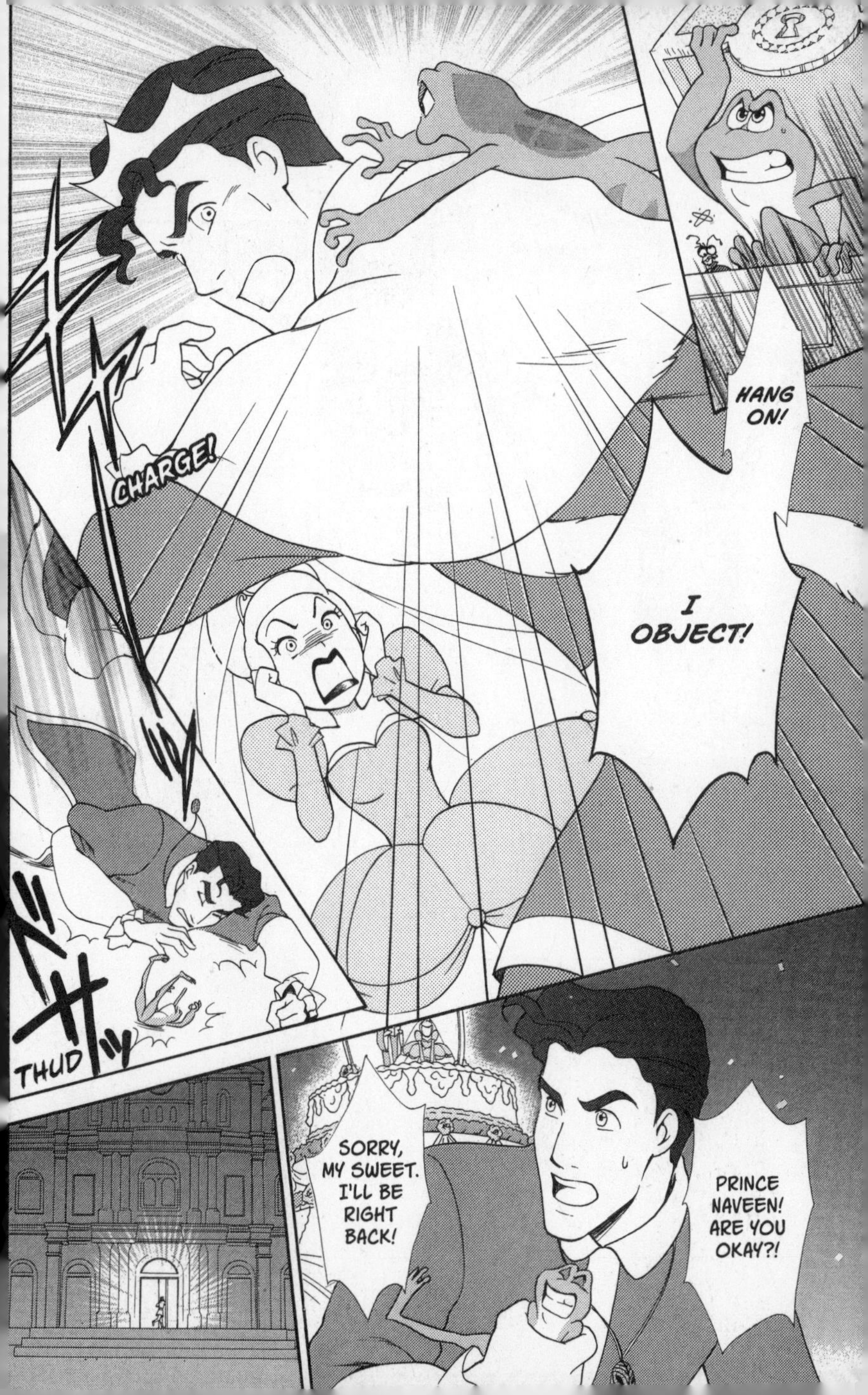
HANG ON!
CHARGE!
I OBJECT!
THUD
PRINCE NAVEEN! ARE YOU OKAY?!
SORRY, MY SWEET. I'LL BE RIGHT BACK!

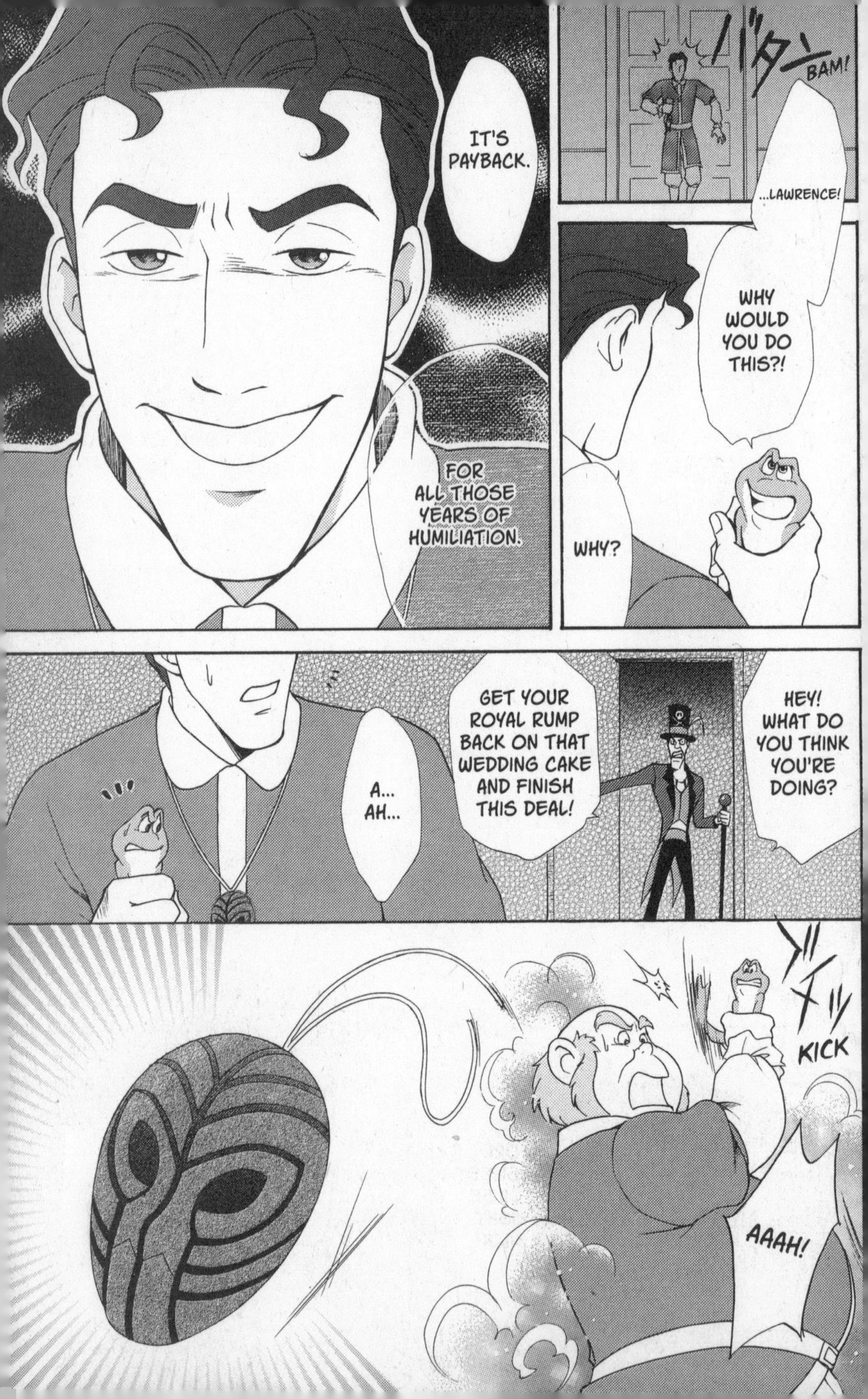
BAM!
...LAWRENCE!
WHY WOULD YOU DO THIS?!
WHY?
IT'S PAYBACK.
FOR ALL THOSE YEARS OF HUMILIATION.
HEY! WHAT DO YOU THINK YOU'RE DOING?
GET YOUR ROYAL RUMP BACK ON THAT WEDDING CAKE AND FINISH THIS DEAL!
A... AH...
KICK
AAAH!

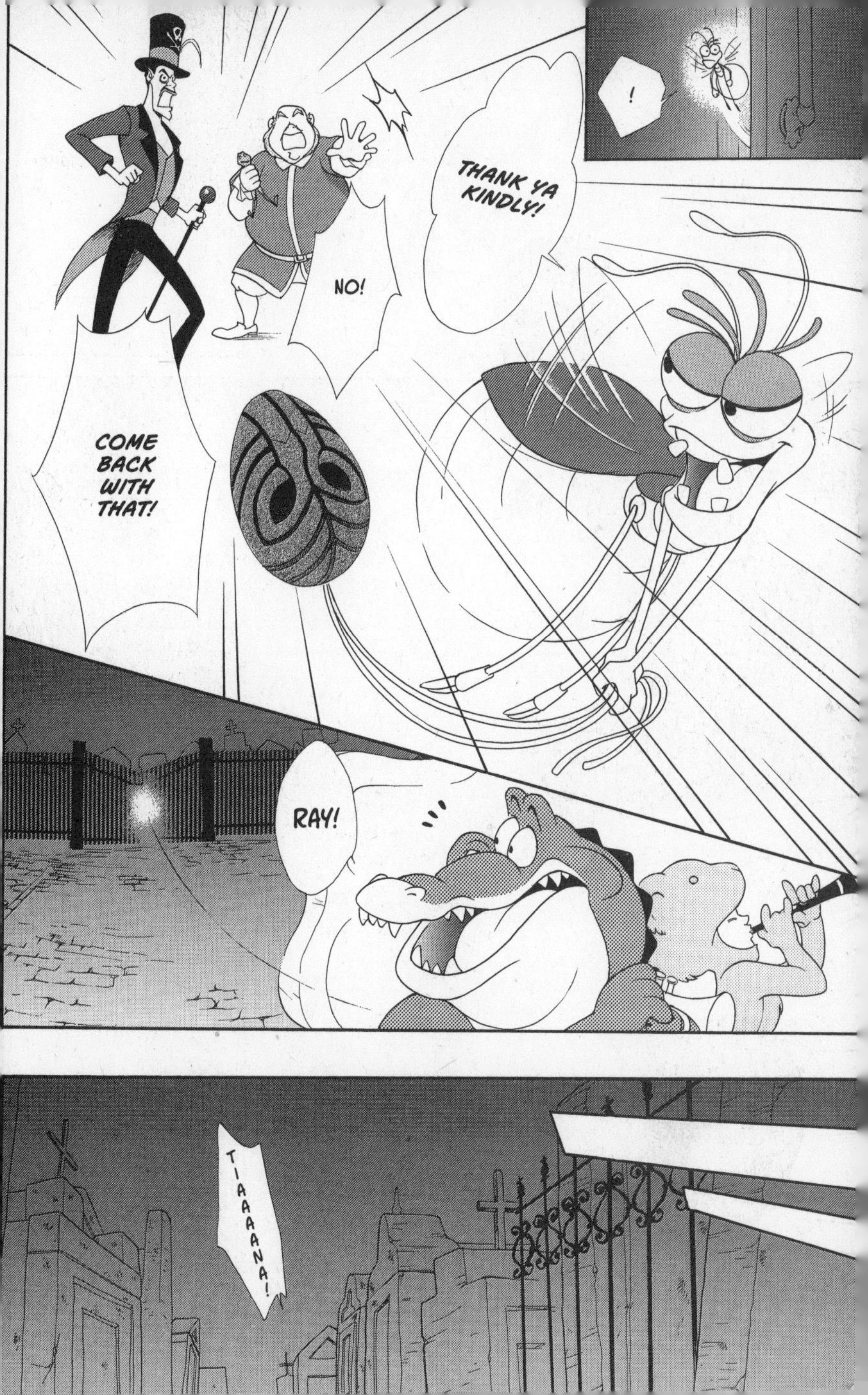
!
THANK YA KINDLY!
NO!
COME BACK WITH THAT!
RAY!
TIAAAANA!

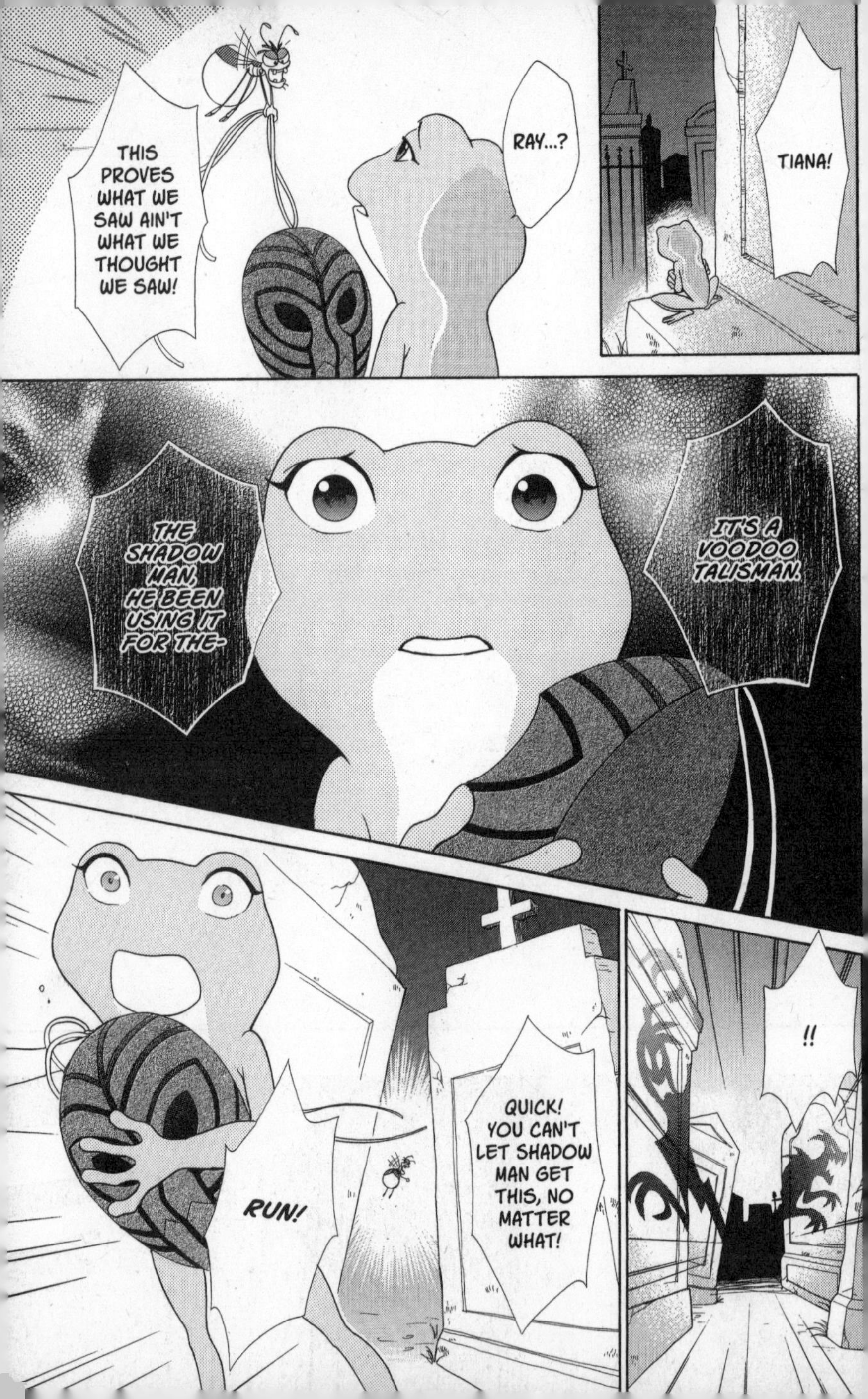
TIANA!
RAY...?
THIS PROVES WHAT WE SAW AIN'T WHAT WE THOUGHT WE SAW!
IT'S A VOODOO TALISMAN.
THE SHADOW MAN, HE BEEN USING IT FOR THE-
!!
QUICK! YOU CAN'T LET SHADOW MAN GET THIS, NO MATTER WHAT!
RUN!

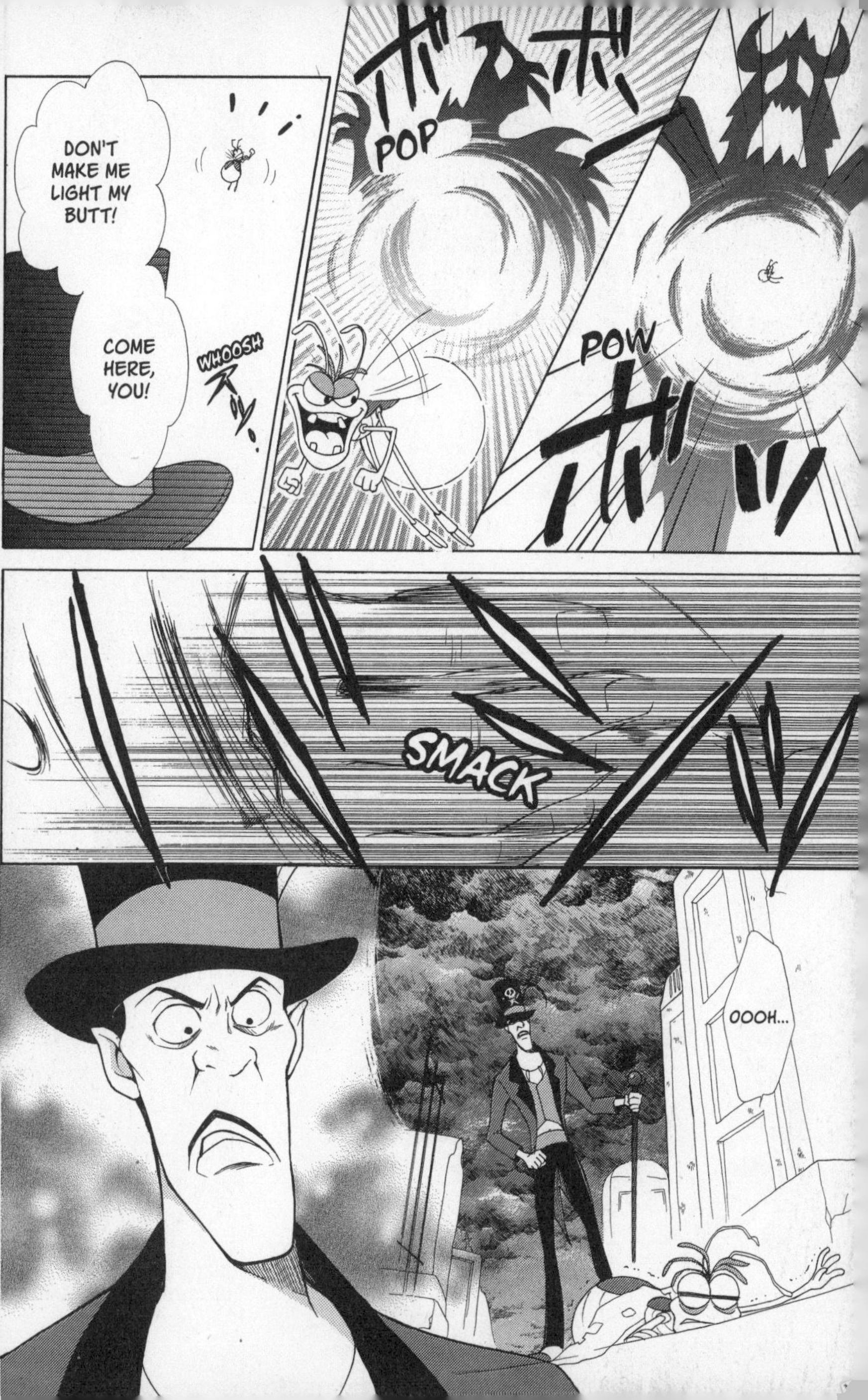
POW
POP
DON'T MAKE ME LIGHT MY BUTT!
COME HERE, YOU!
WHOOSH
SMACK
OOOH...

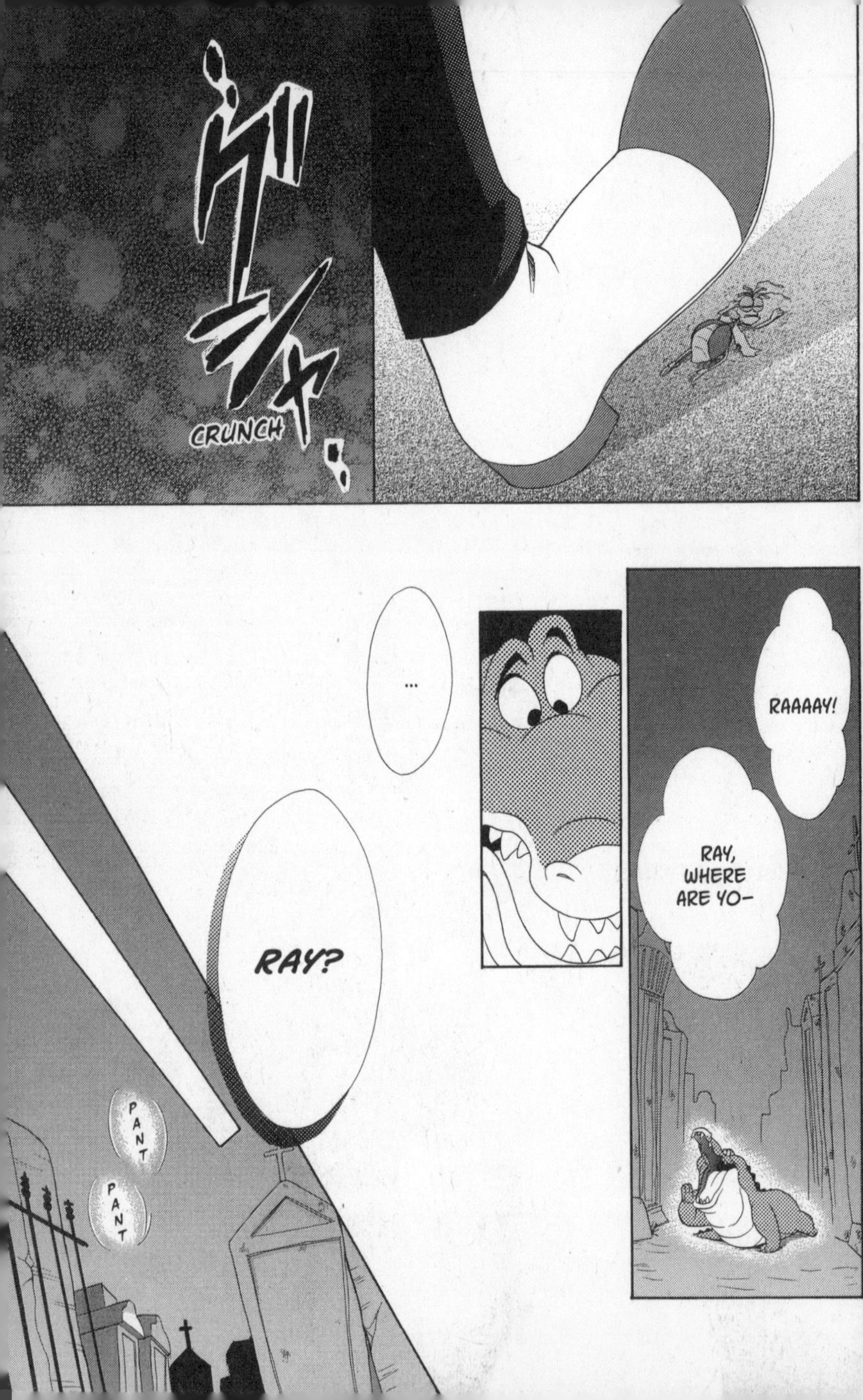
CRUNCH
RAAAAY!
RAY, WHERE ARE YO-
...
RAY?
PANT
PANT

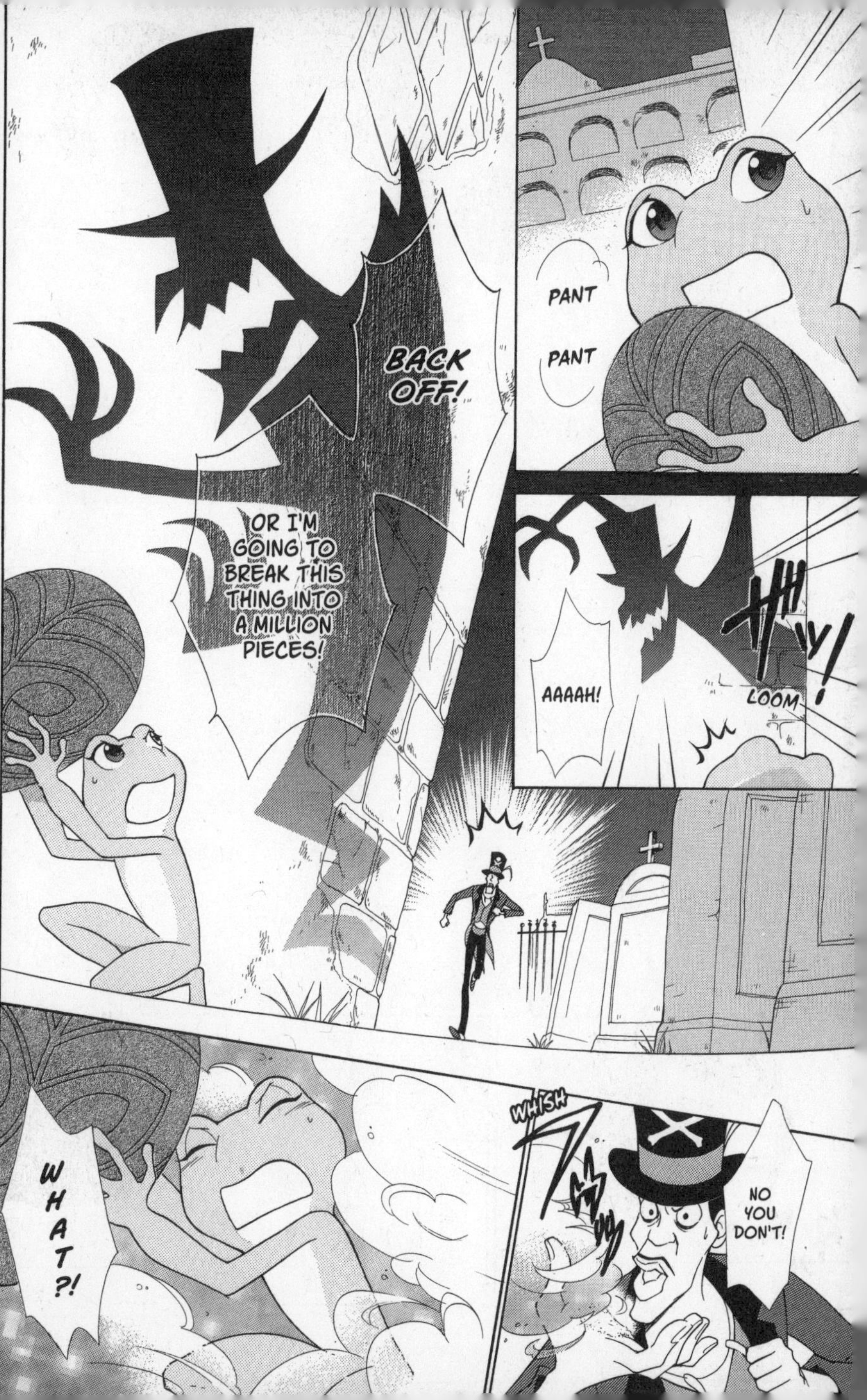
PANT
PANT
AAAAH!
LOOM
BACK OFF!
OR I'M GOING TO BREAK THIS THING INTO A MILLION PIECES!
NO YOU DON'T!
WHISH
WHAT?!

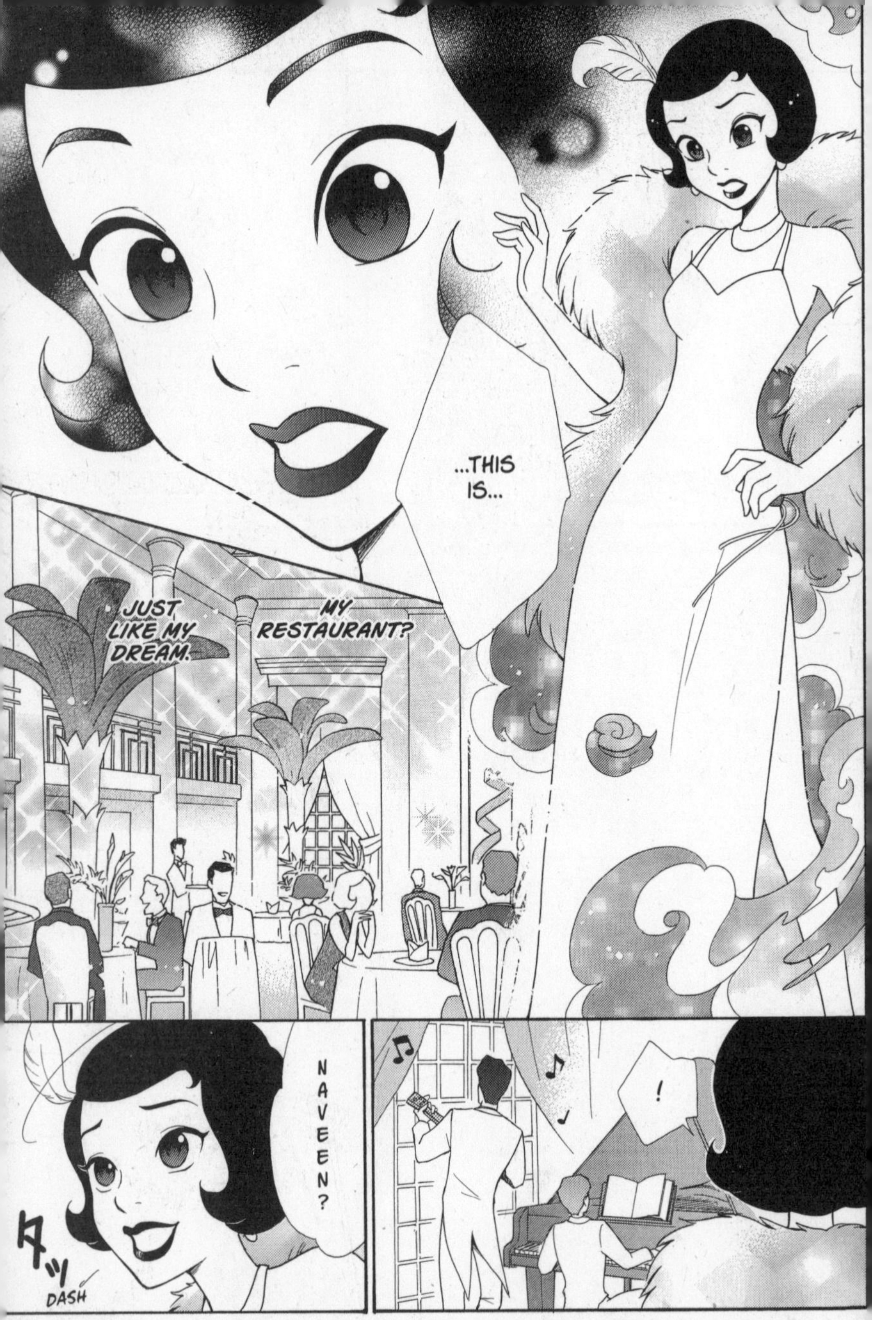
...THIS IS...
MY RESTAURANT?
JUST LIKE MY DREAM.
!
NAVEEN?
タッ
DASH

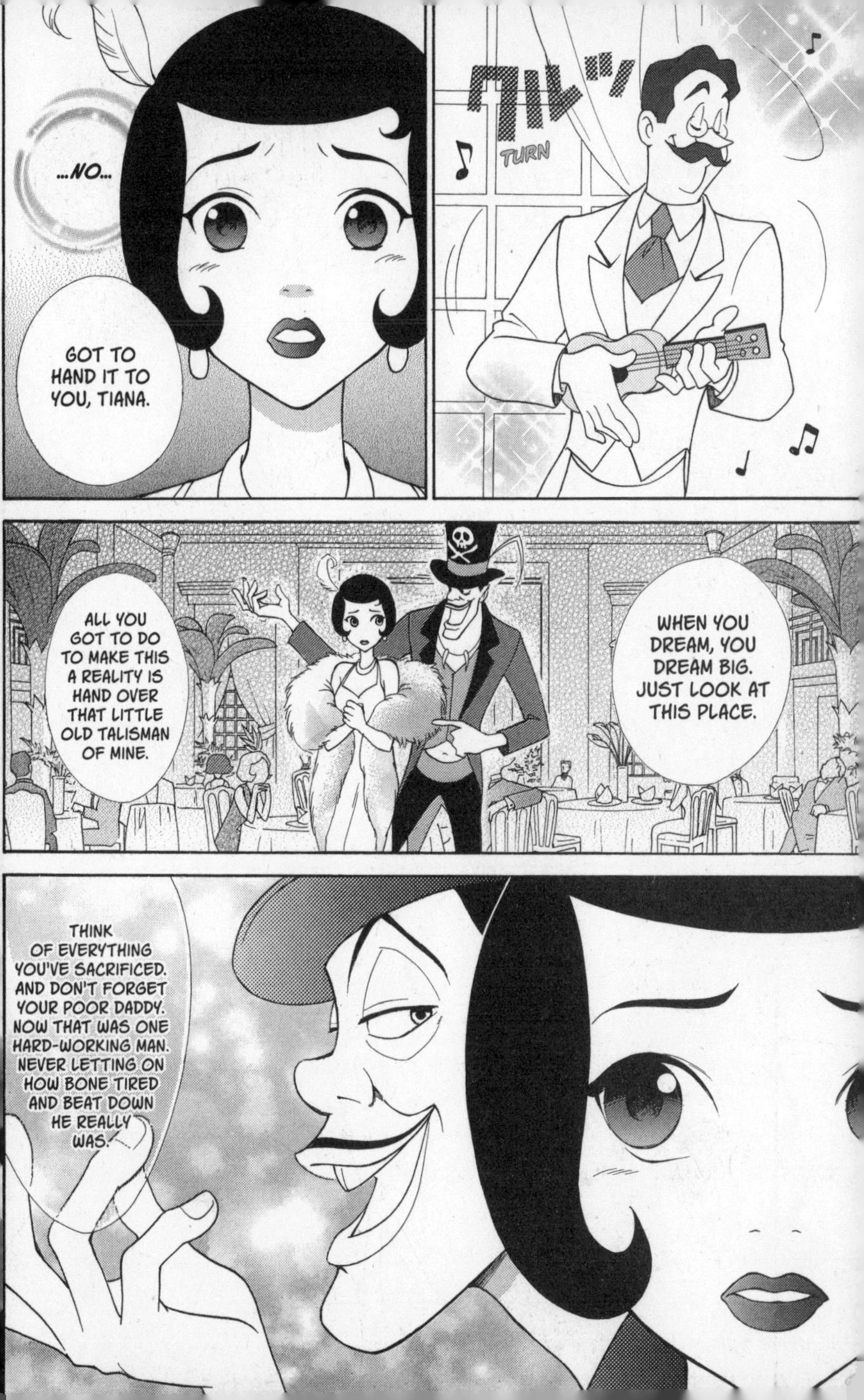
クルッ
TURN
...NO...
GOT TO HAND IT TO YOU, TIANA.
WHEN YOU DREAM, YOU DREAM BIG. JUST LOOK AT THIS PLACE.
ALL YOU GOT TO DO TO MAKE THIS A REALITY IS HAND OVER THAT LITTLE OLD TALISMAN OF MINE.
THINK OF EVERYTHING YOU'VE SACRIFICED. AND DON'T FORGET YOUR POOR DADDY. NOW THAT WAS ONE HARD-WORKING MAN. NEVER LETTING ON HOW BONE TIRED AND BEAT DOWN HE REALLY WAS.

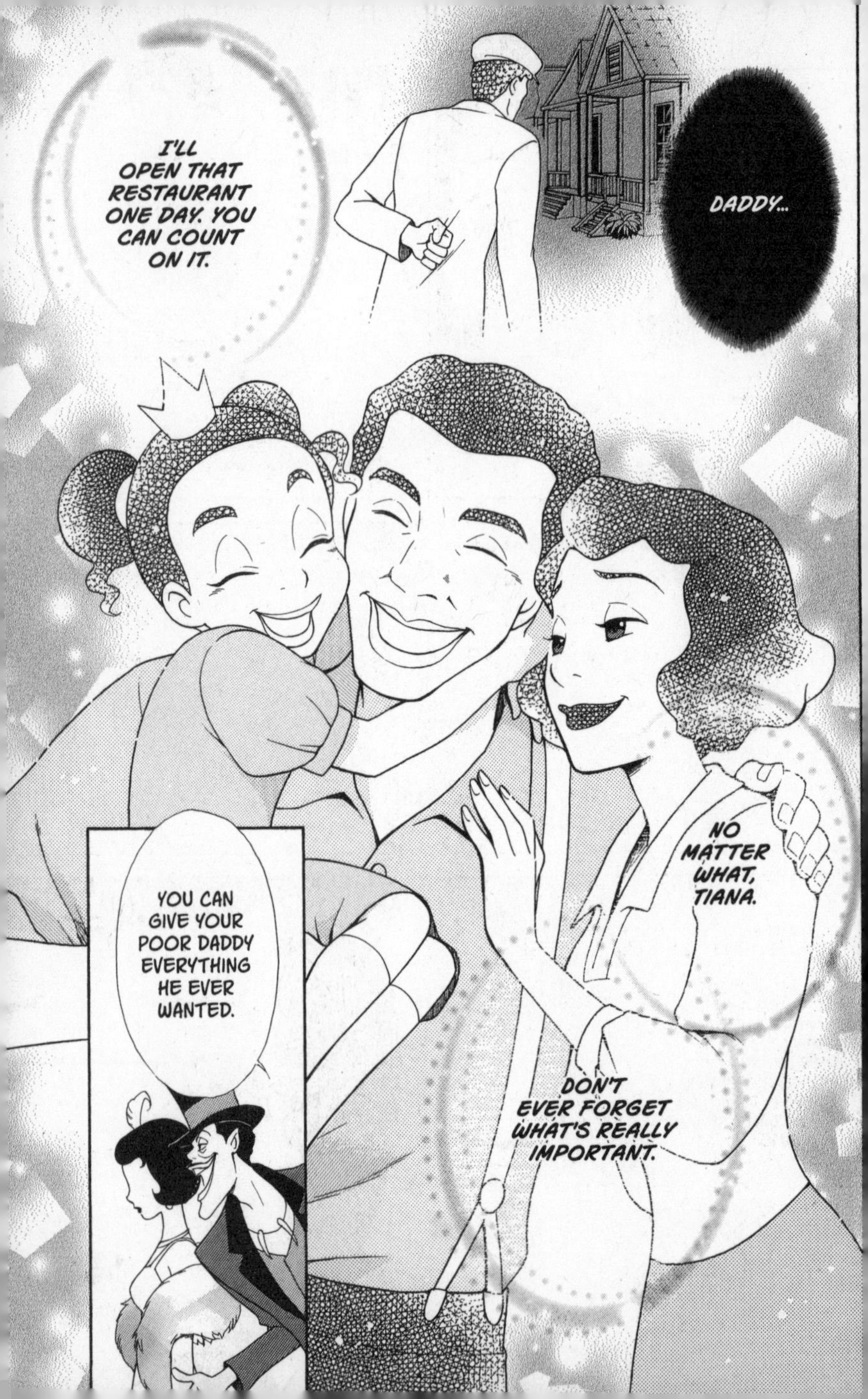
DADDY...
I'LL OPEN THAT RESTAURANT ONE DAY. YOU CAN COUNT ON IT.
NO MATTER WHAT, TIANA.
DON'T EVER FORGET WHAT'S REALLY IMPORTANT.
YOU CAN GIVE YOUR POOR DADDY EVERYTHING HE EVER WANTED.

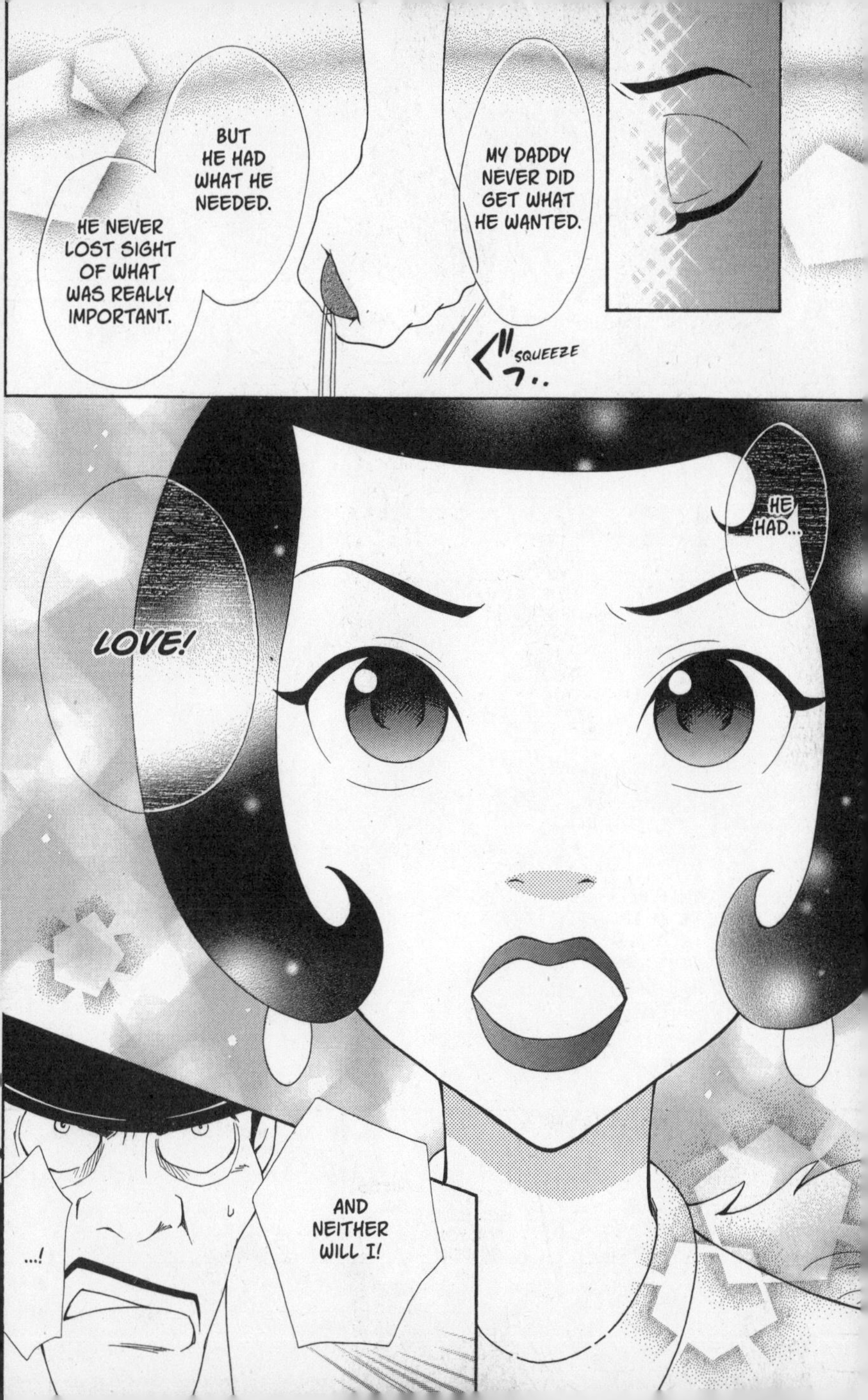
MY DADDY NEVER DID GET WHAT HE WANTED.
SQUEEZE
BUT HE HAD WHAT HE NEEDED.
HE NEVER LOST SIGHT OF WHAT WAS REALLY IMPORTANT.
HE HAD...
LOVE!
AND NEITHER WILL I!
...!

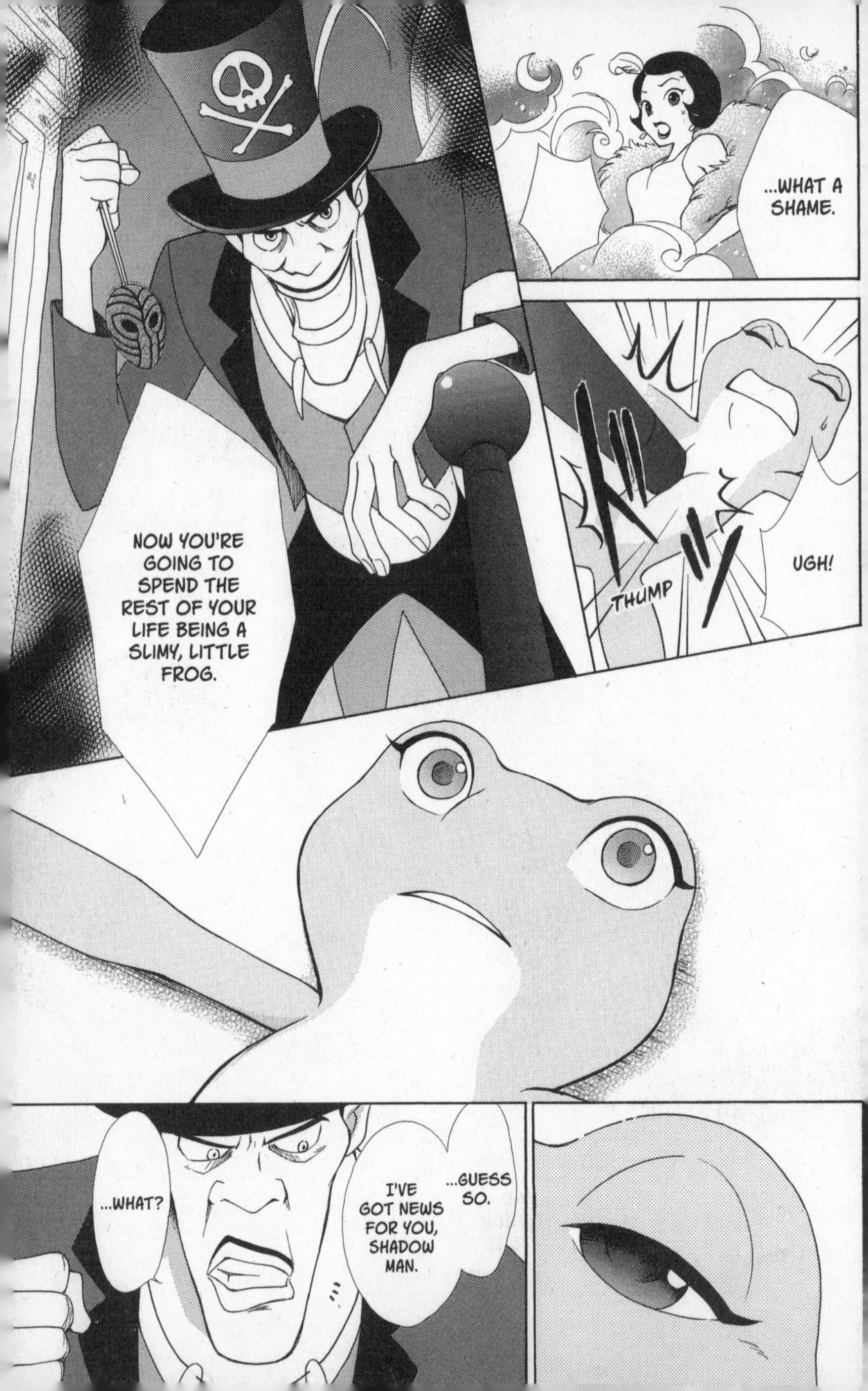
...WHAT A SHAME.
UGH!
THUMP
NOW YOU'RE GOING TO SPEND THE REST OF YOUR LIFE BEING A SLIMY, LITTLE FROG.
...GUESS SO.
I'VE GOT NEWS FOR YOU, SHADOW MAN.
...WHAT?

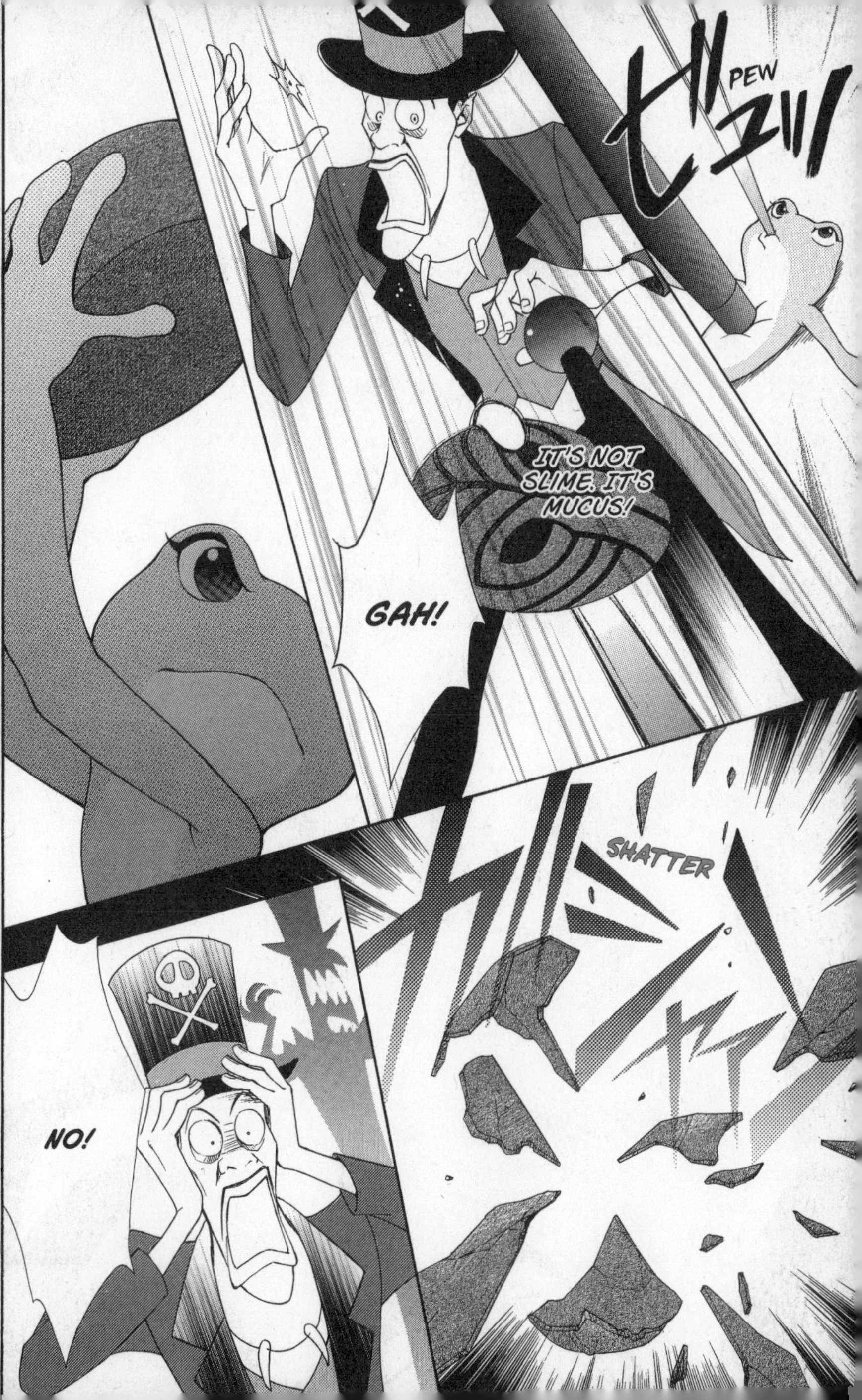
PEW
IT'S NOT SLIME. IT'S MUCUS!
GAH!
SHATTER
NO!

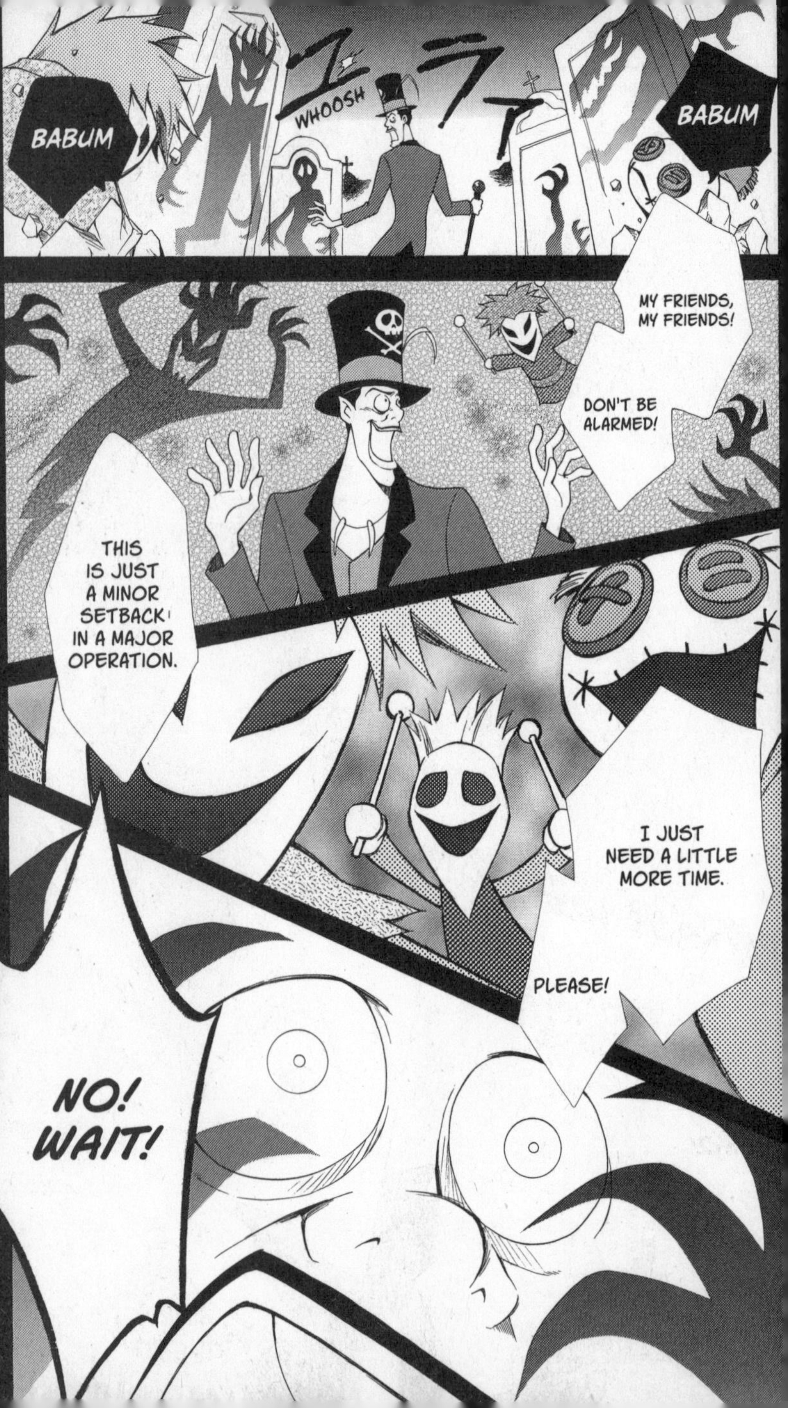
BABUM
WHOOSH
BABUM
MY FRIENDS, MY FRIENDS!
DON'T BE ALARMED!
THIS IS JUST A MINOR SETBACK IN A MAJOR OPERATION.
I JUST NEED A LITTLE MORE TIME.
PLEASE!
NO! WAIT!

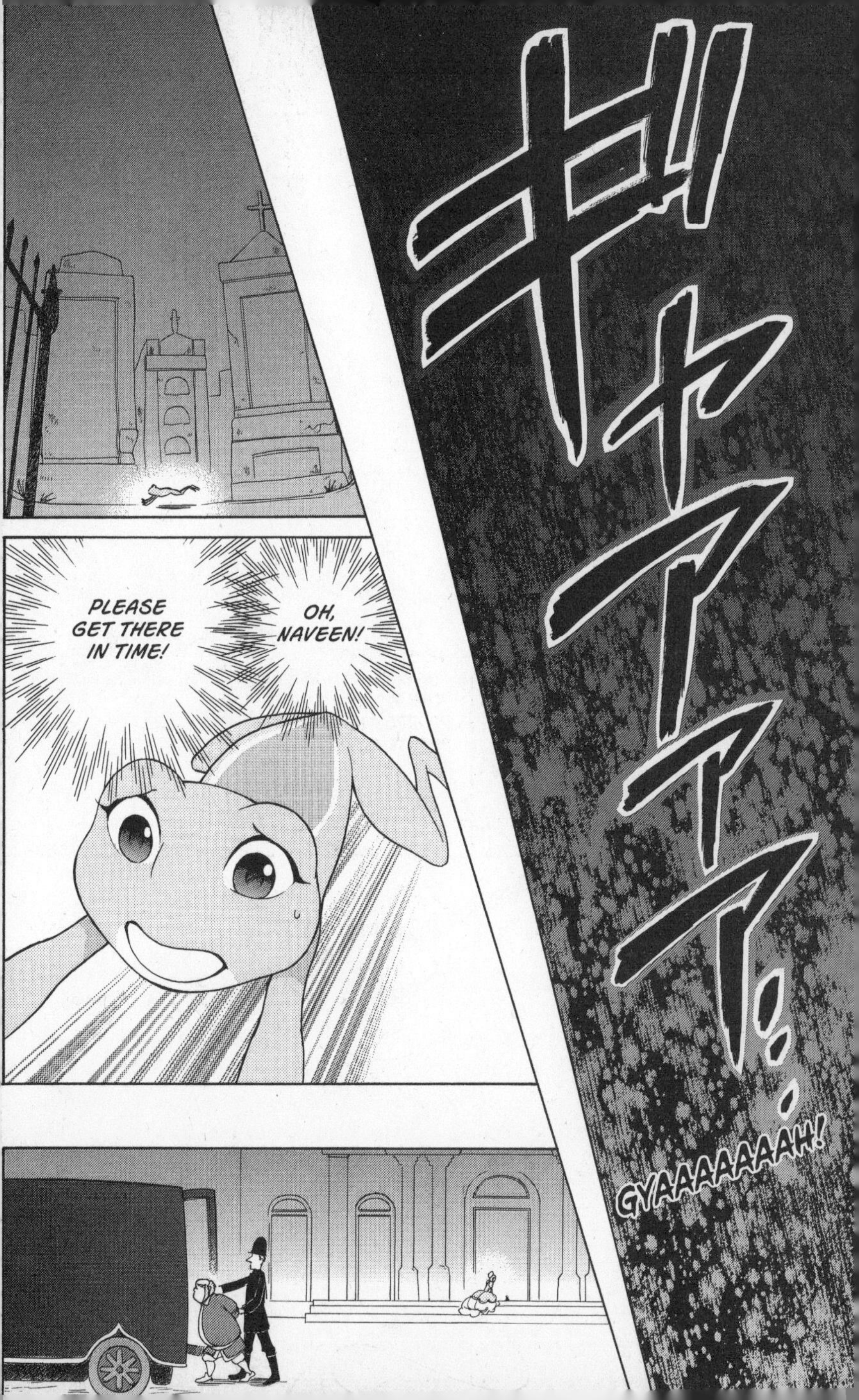
GYAAAAAAAH!
OH, NAVEEN!
PLEASE GET THERE IN TIME!

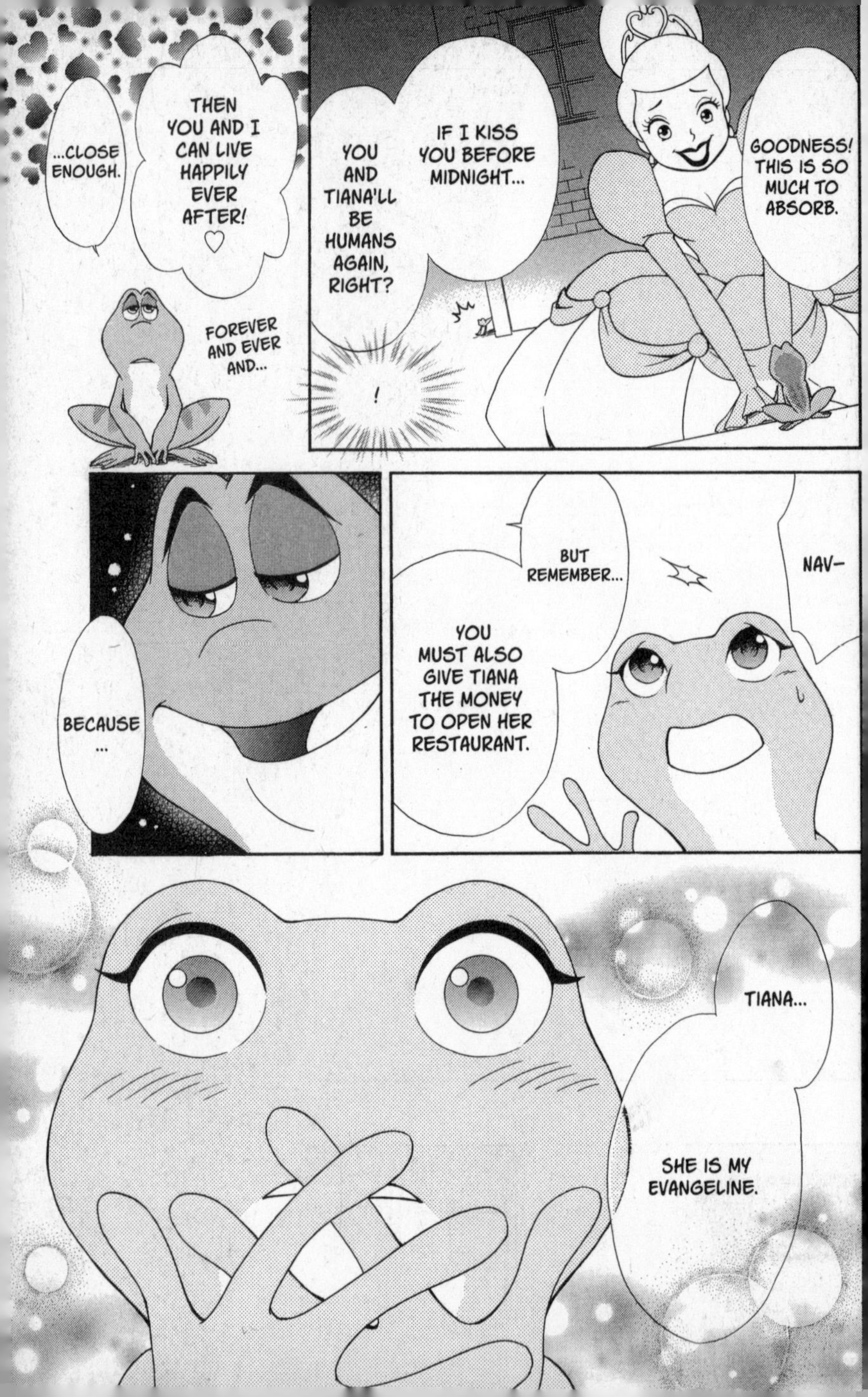
GOODNESS! THIS IS SO MUCH TO ABSORB.
IF I KISS YOU BEFORE MIDNIGHT...
YOU AND TIANA'LL BE HUMANS AGAIN, RIGHT?
!
THEN YOU AND I CAN LIVE HAPPILY EVER AFTER! ♡
...CLOSE ENOUGH.
FOREVER AND EVER AND...
NAV–
BUT REMEMBER...
YOU MUST ALSO GIVE TIANA THE MONEY TO OPEN HER RESTAURANT.
BECAUSE ...
TIANA...
SHE IS MY EVANGELINE.

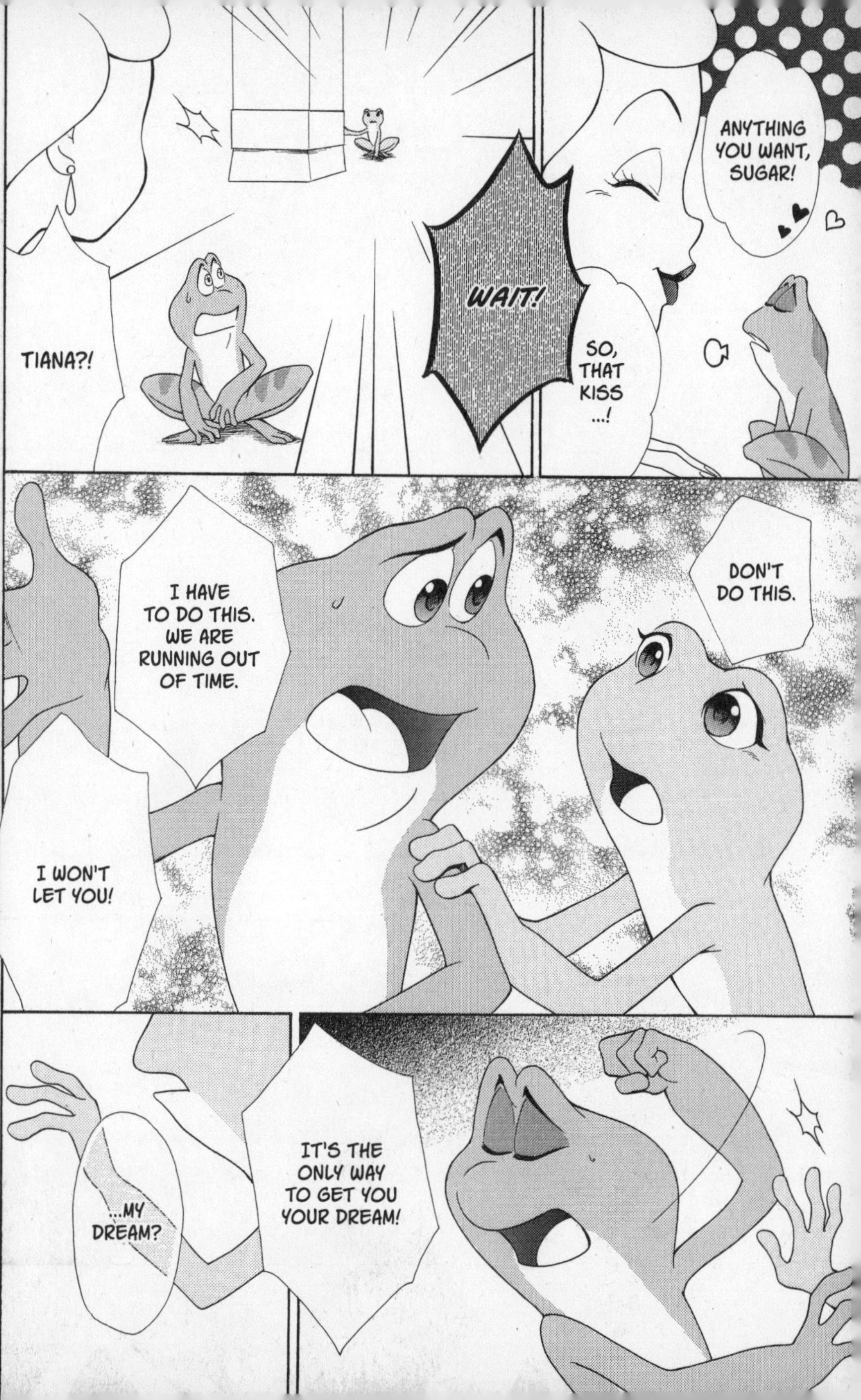
ANYTHING YOU WANT, SUGAR!
SO, THAT KISS ...!
WAIT!
TIANA?!
DON'T DO THIS.
I HAVE TO DO THIS. WE ARE RUNNING OUT OF TIME.
I WON'T LET YOU!
IT'S THE ONLY WAY TO GET YOU YOUR DREAM!
...MY DREAM?

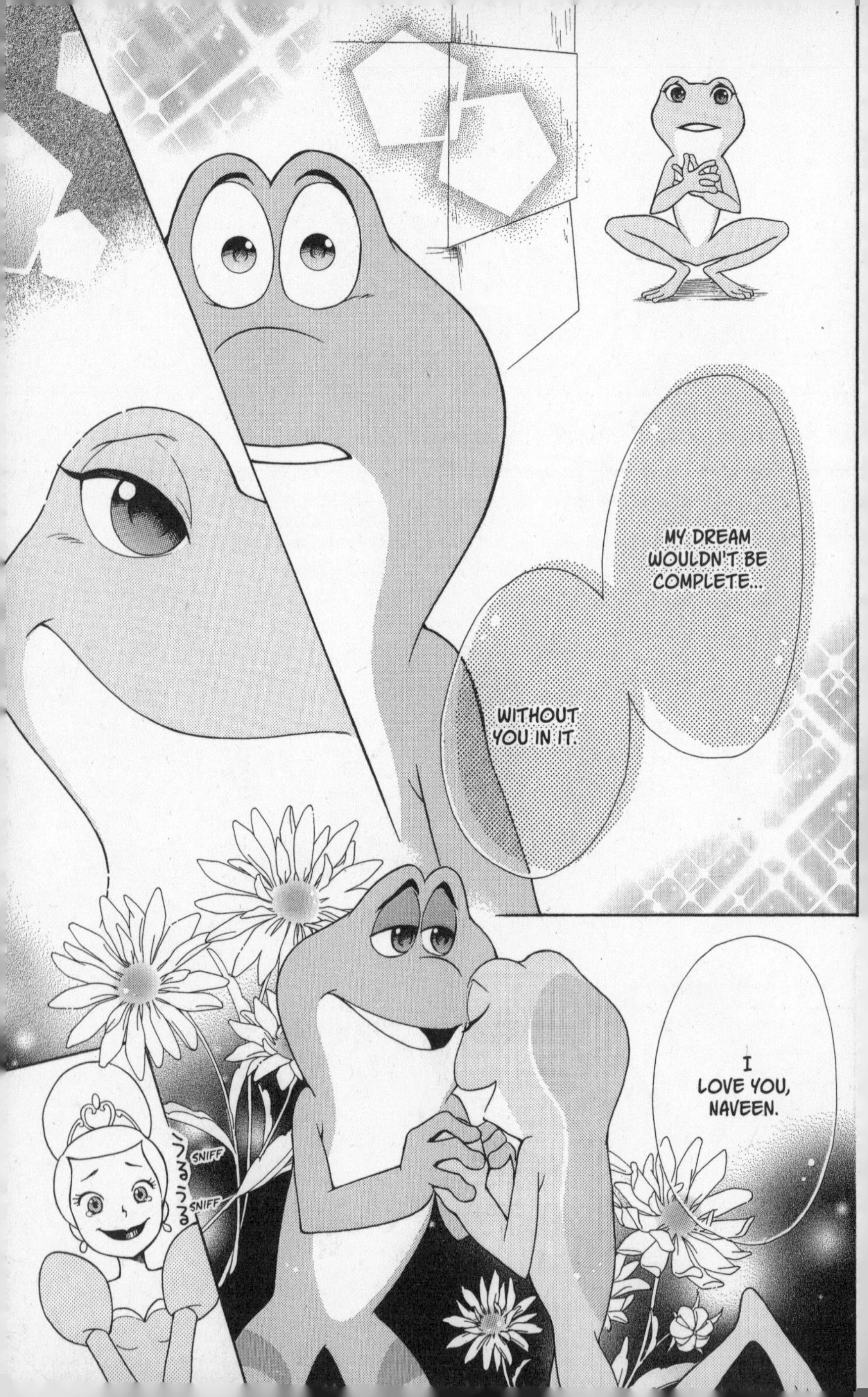
MY DREAM WOULDN'T BE COMPLETE...
WITHOUT YOU IN IT.
I LOVE YOU, NAVEEN.
SNIFF
SNIFF

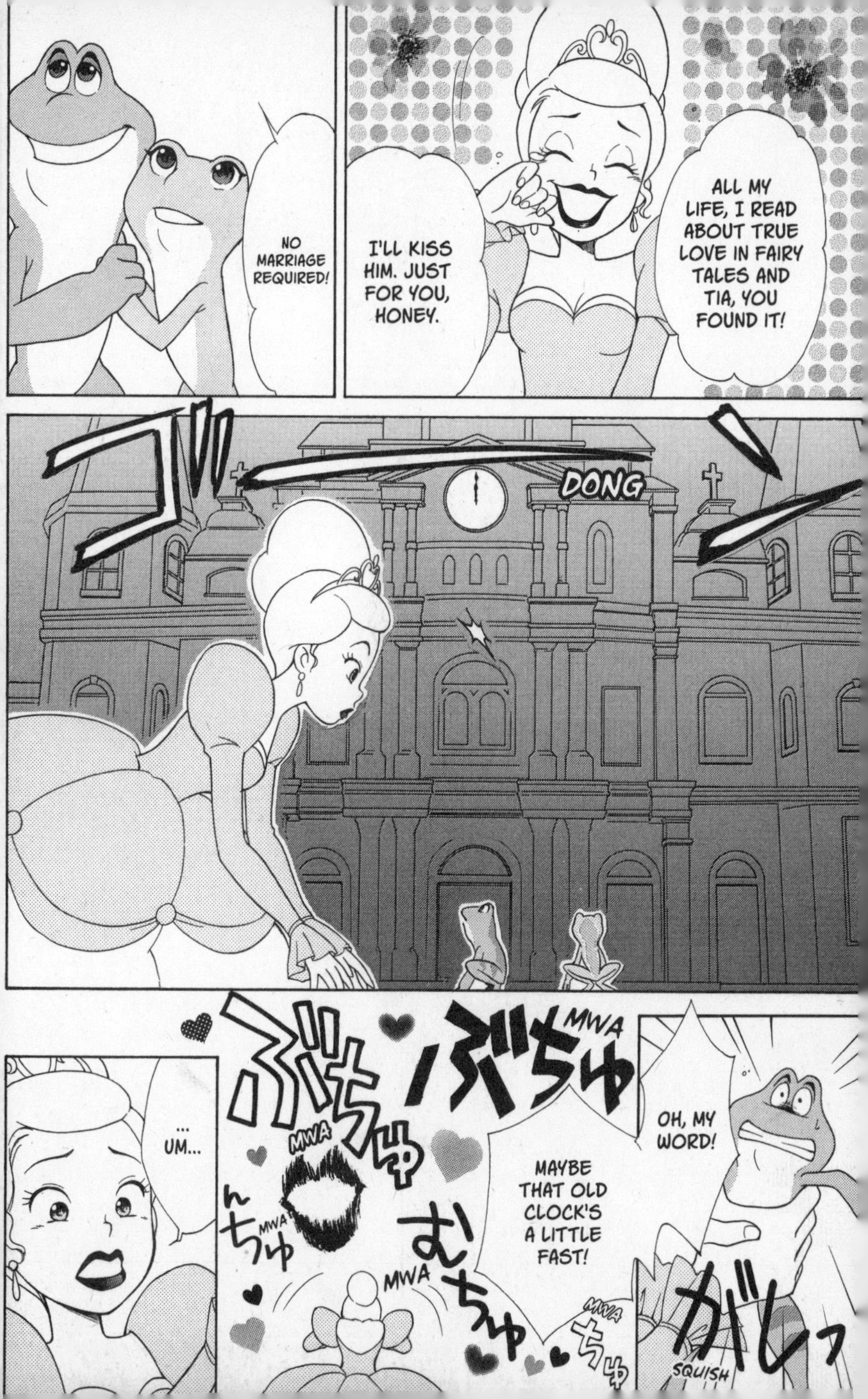
ALL MY LIFE, I READ ABOUT TRUE LOVE IN FAIRY TALES AND TIA, YOU FOUND IT!
I'LL KISS HIM. JUST FOR YOU, HONEY.
NO MARRIAGE REQUIRED!
ゴーン
DONG
OH, MY WORD!
MAYBE THAT OLD CLOCK'S A LITTLE FAST!
がしっ
SQUISH
ぶちゅ
MWA
ぶちゅ
MWA
んちゅ
MWA
むちゅ
MWA
ちゅ
MWA
... UM...

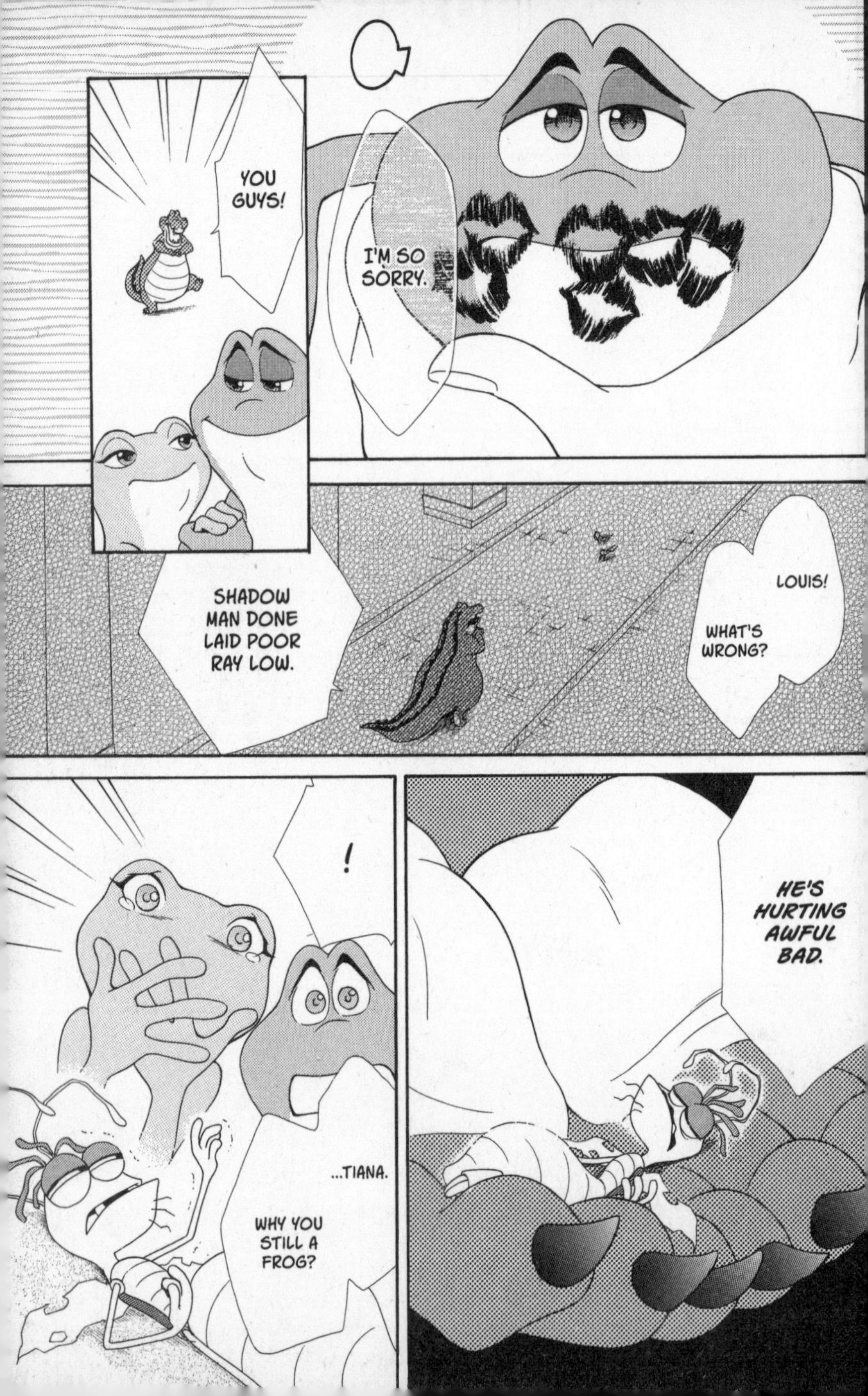
I'M SO SORRY.
YOU GUYS!
LOUIS!
WHAT'S WRONG?
SHADOW MAN DONE LAID POOR RAY LOW.
HE'S HURTING AWFUL BAD.
!
...TIANA.
WHY YOU STILL A FROG?

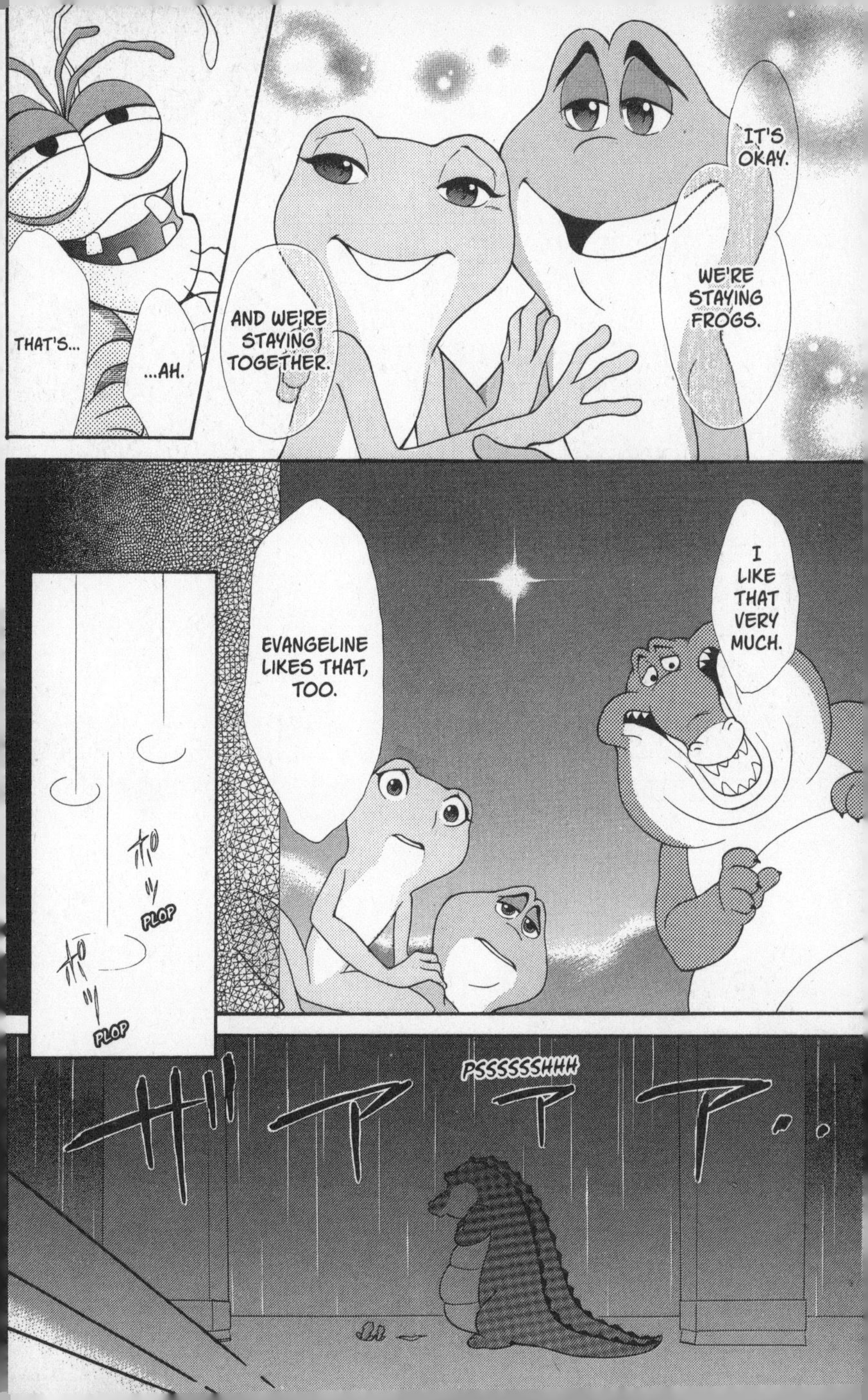
IT'S OKAY.
WE'RE STAYING FROGS.
AND WE'RE STAYING TOGETHER.
THAT'S...
...AH.
I LIKE THAT VERY MUCH.
EVANGELINE LIKES THAT, TOO.
PLOP
PLOP
PSSSSSSHHH

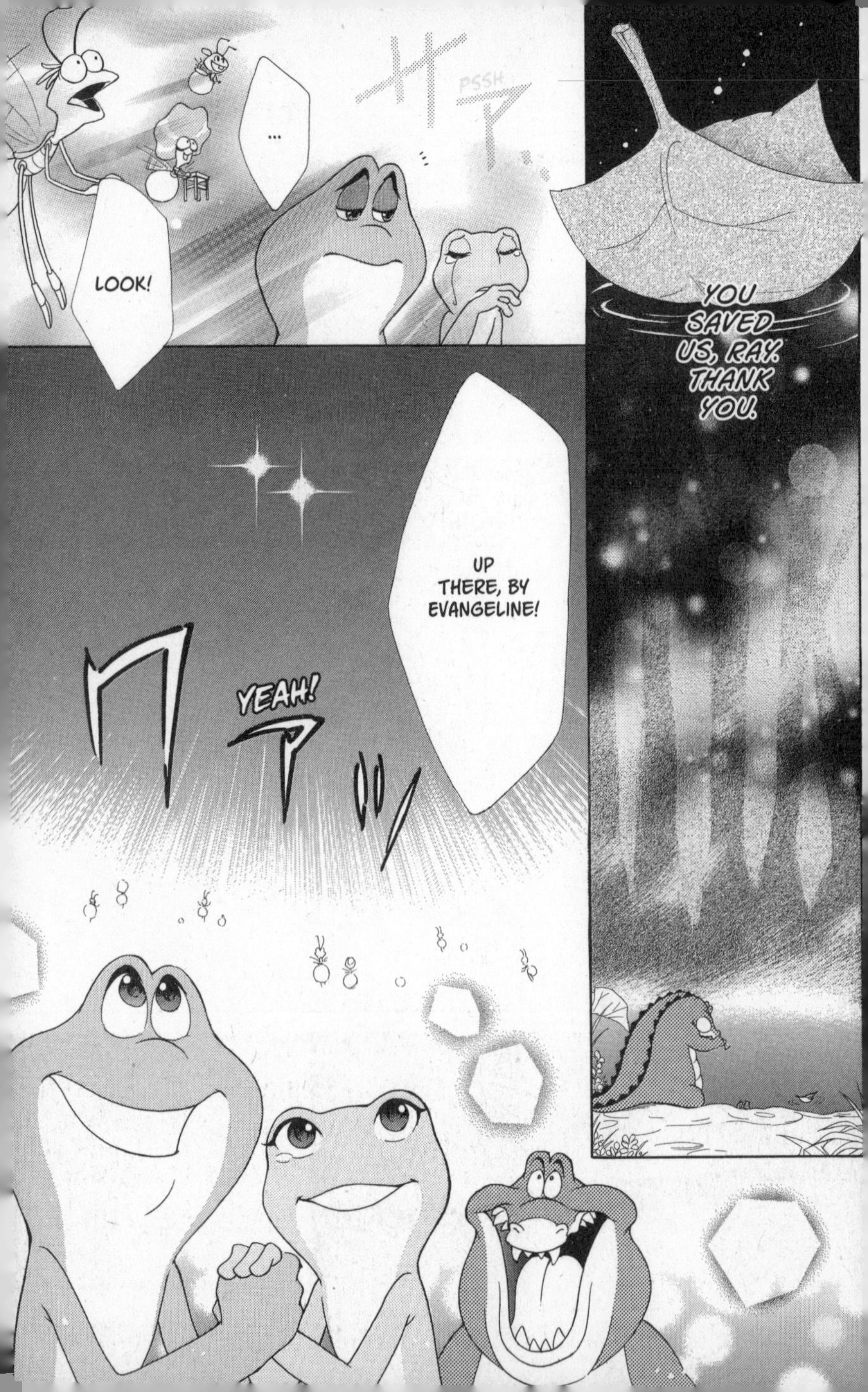
YOU SAVED US, RAY. THANK YOU.
PSSH
...
LOOK!
UP THERE, BY EVANGELINE!
YEAH!

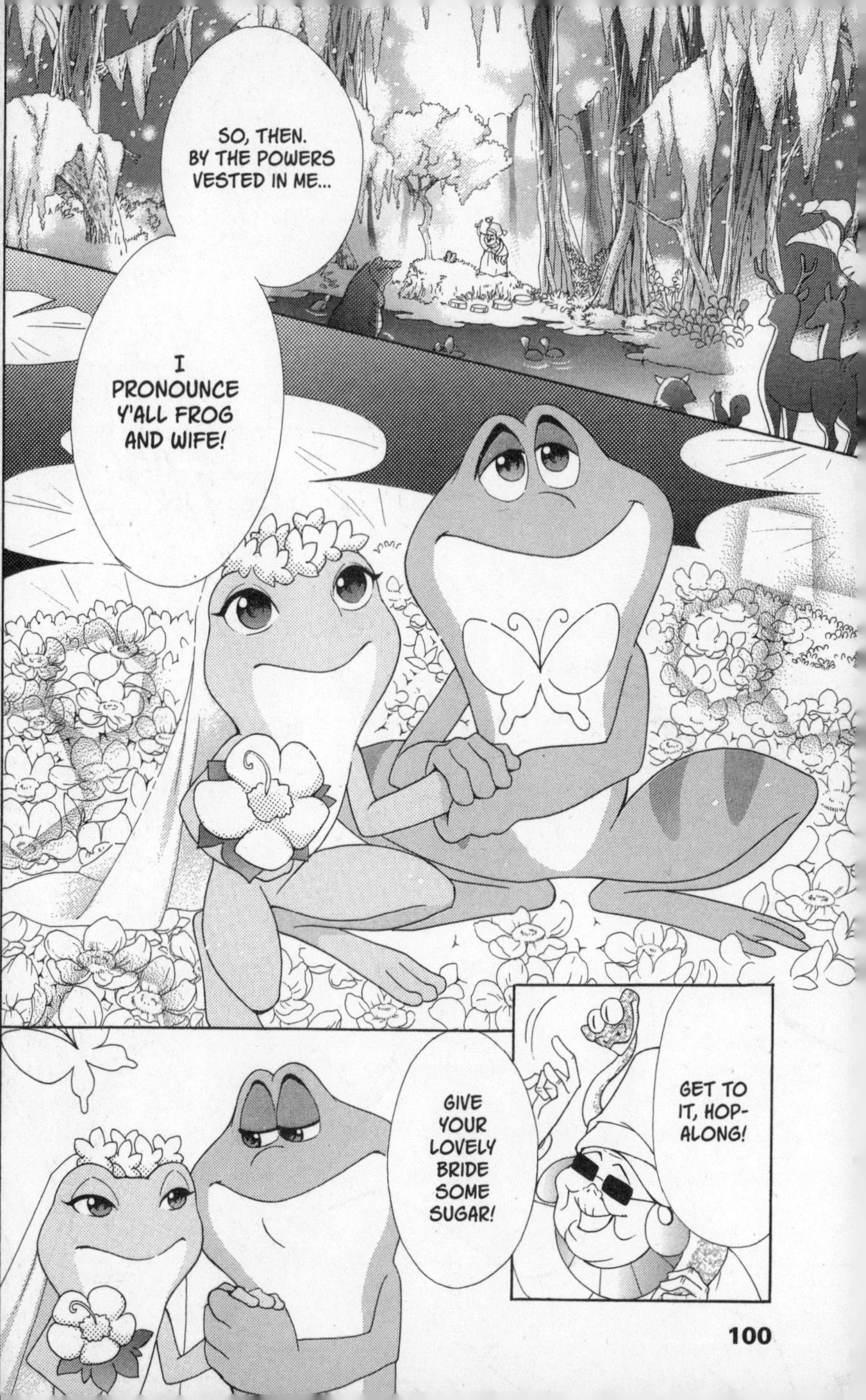
SO, THEN. BY THE POWERS VESTED IN ME...
I PRONOUNCE Y'ALL FROG AND WIFE!
GET TO IT, HOP-ALONG!
GIVE YOUR LOVELY BRIDE SOME SUGAR!

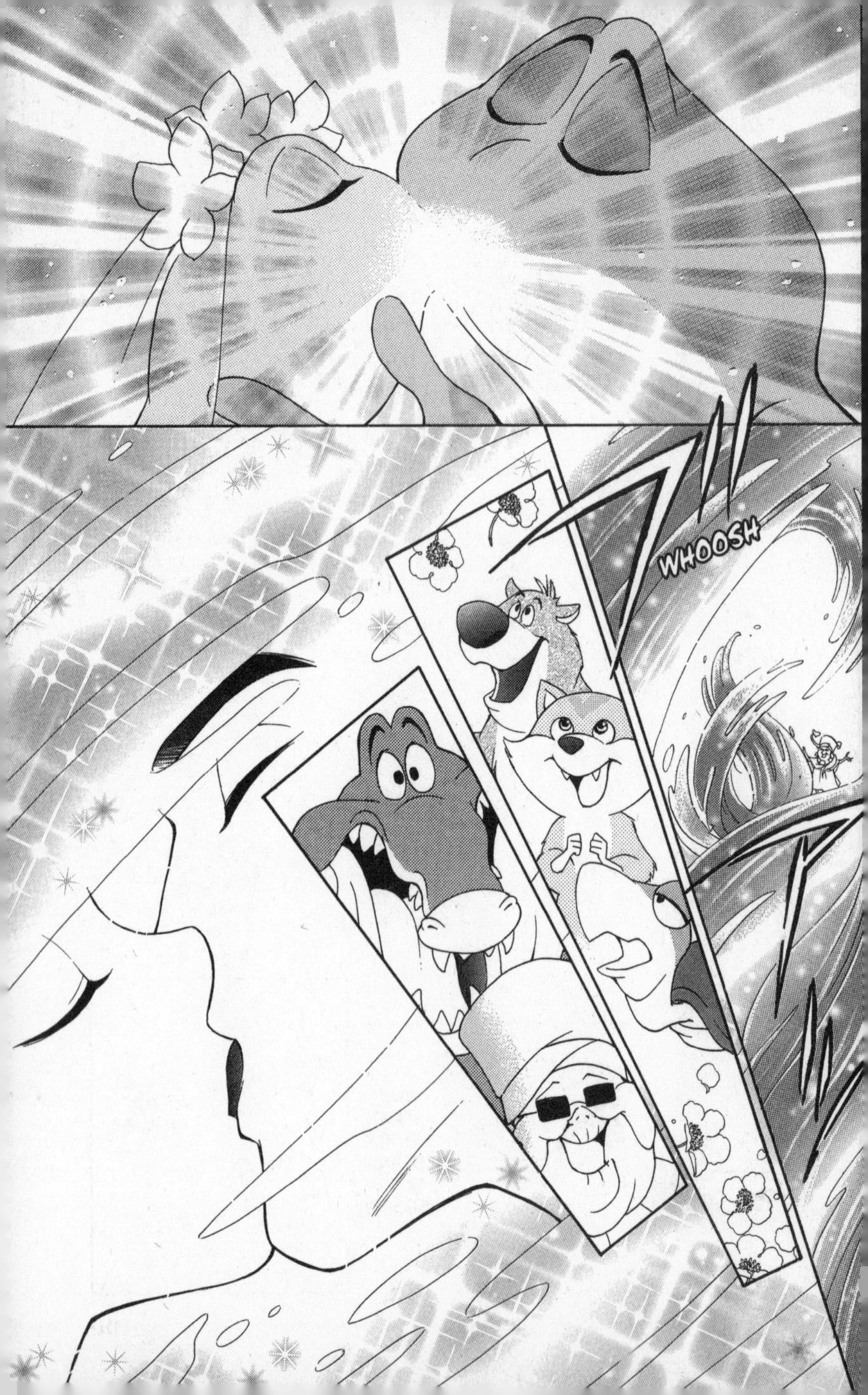
WHOOSH

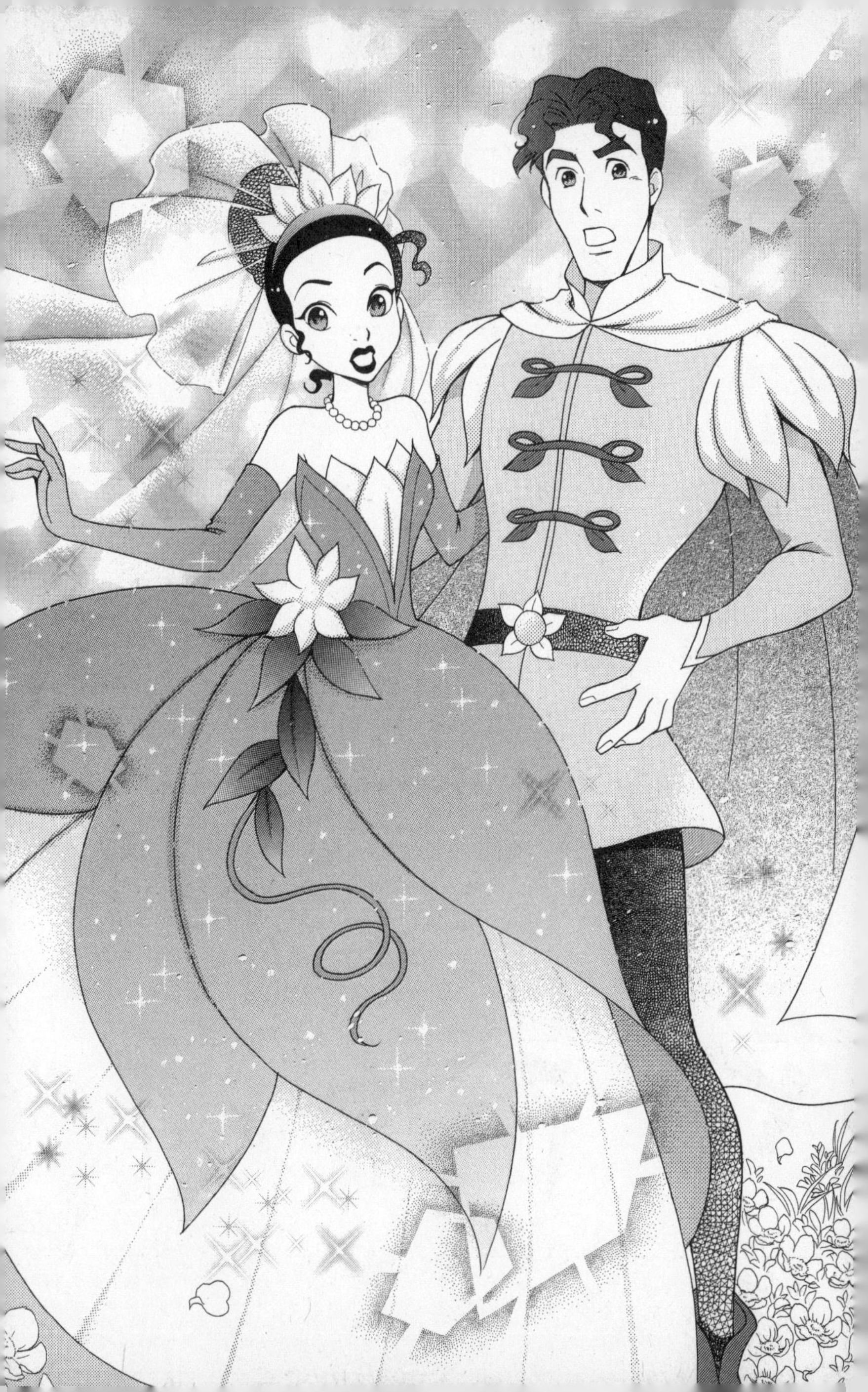

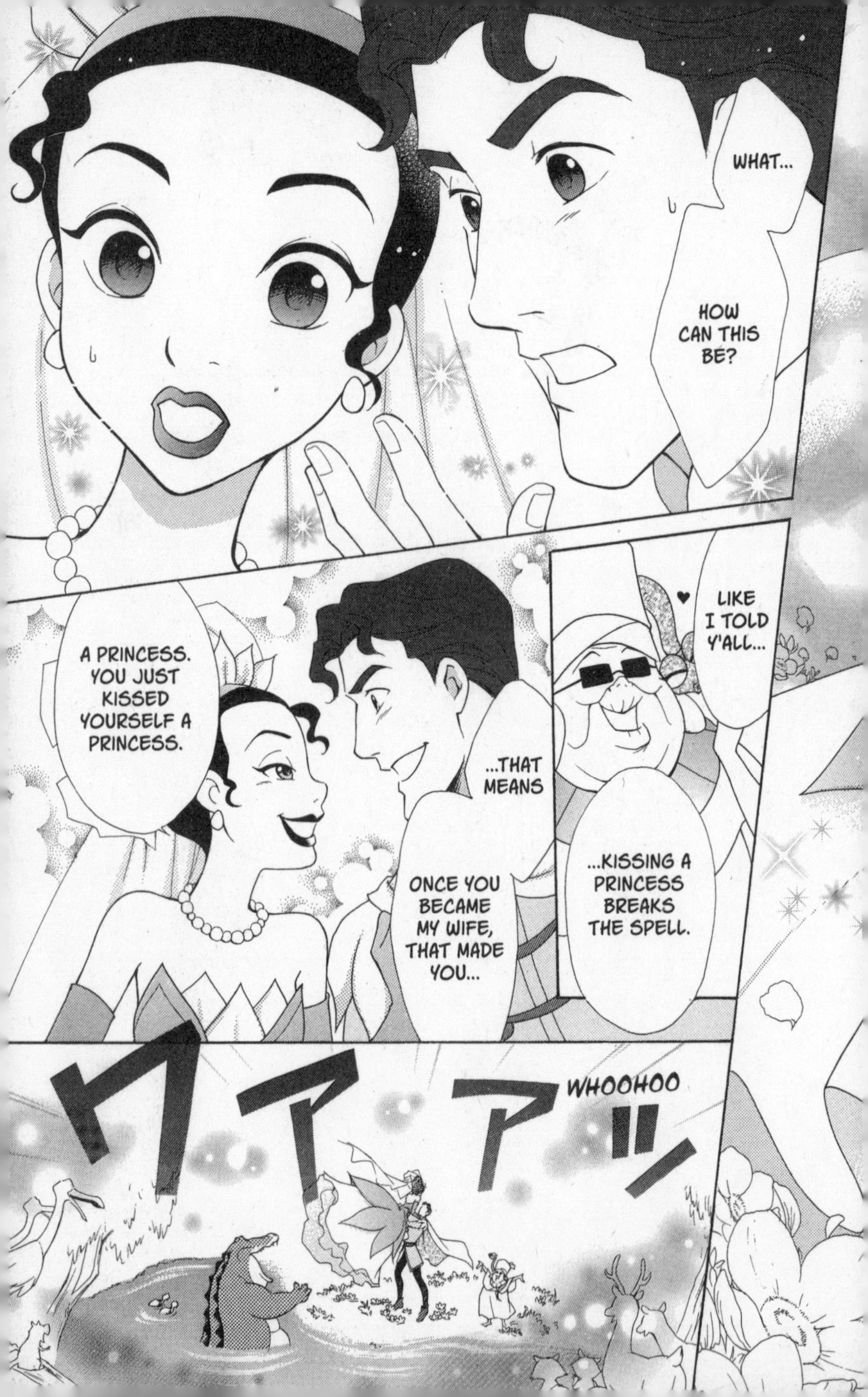
WHAT...
HOW CAN THIS BE?
LIKE I TOLD Y'ALL...
...KISSING A PRINCESS BREAKS THE SPELL.
...THAT MEANS
ONCE YOU BECAME MY WIFE, THAT MADE YOU...
A PRINCESS. YOU JUST KISSED YOURSELF A PRINCESS.
WHOOHOO

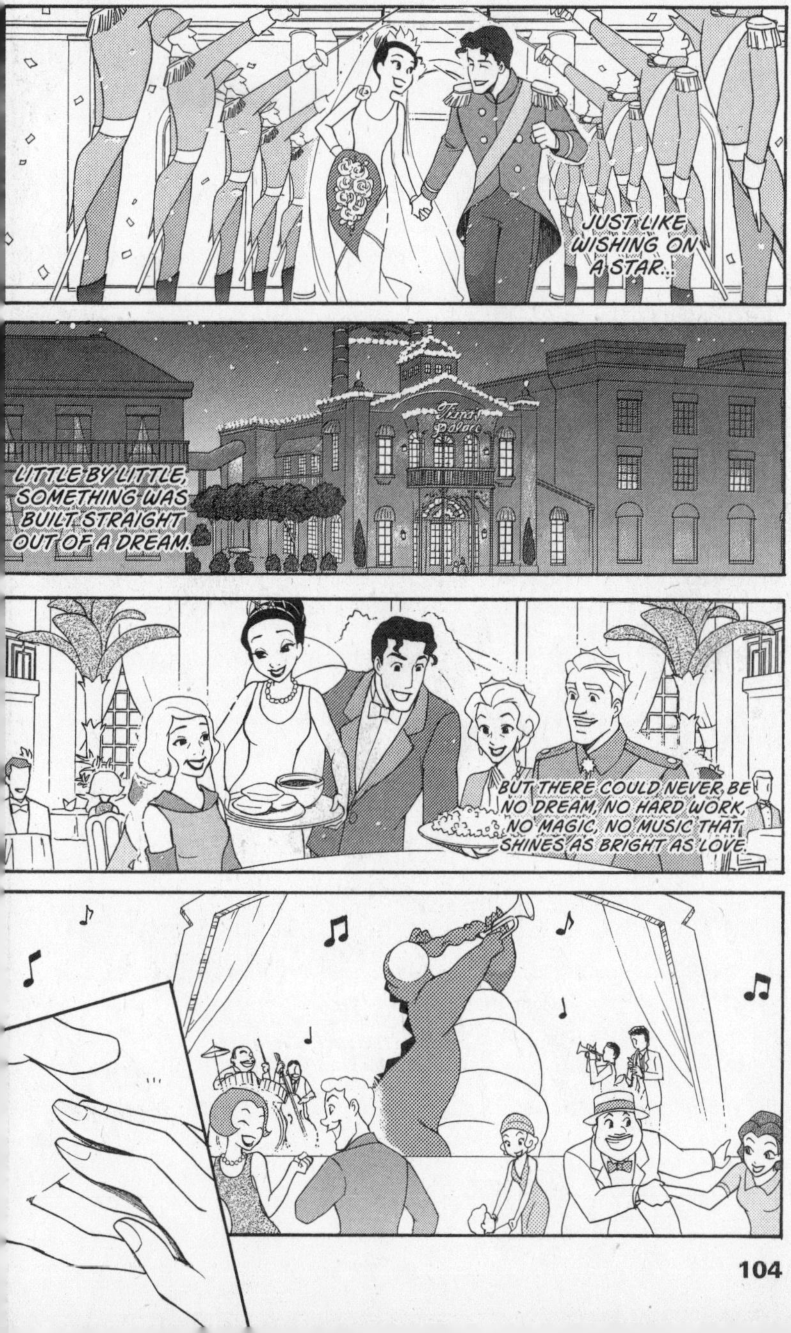
JUST LIKE WISHING ON A STAR...
LITTLE BY LITTLE, SOMETHING WAS BUILT STRAIGHT OUT OF A DREAM.
BUT THERE COULD NEVER BE NO DREAM, NO HARD WORK, NO MAGIC, NO MUSIC THAT SHINES AS BRIGHT AS LOVE.
...

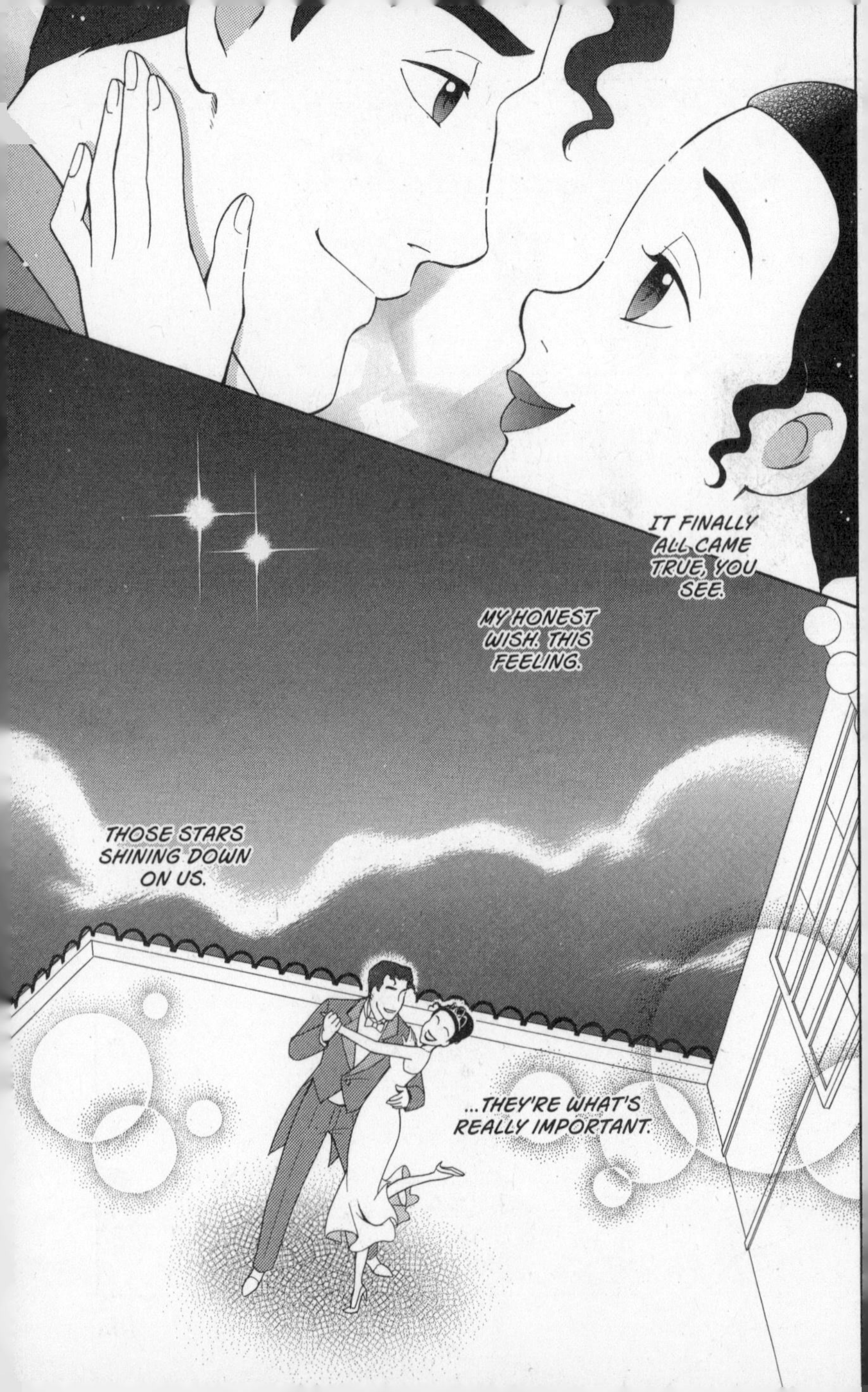
IT FINALLY ALL CAME TRUE, YOU SEE.
MY HONEST WISH. THIS FEELING.
THOSE STARS SHINING DOWN ON US.
...THEY'RE WHAT'S REALLY IMPORTANT.

Manga Cover Sketches
by Nao Kodaka

Sketch #1

Sketch #2

Manga Cover Sketches
by Nao Kodaka

Sketch #3

Sketch #4

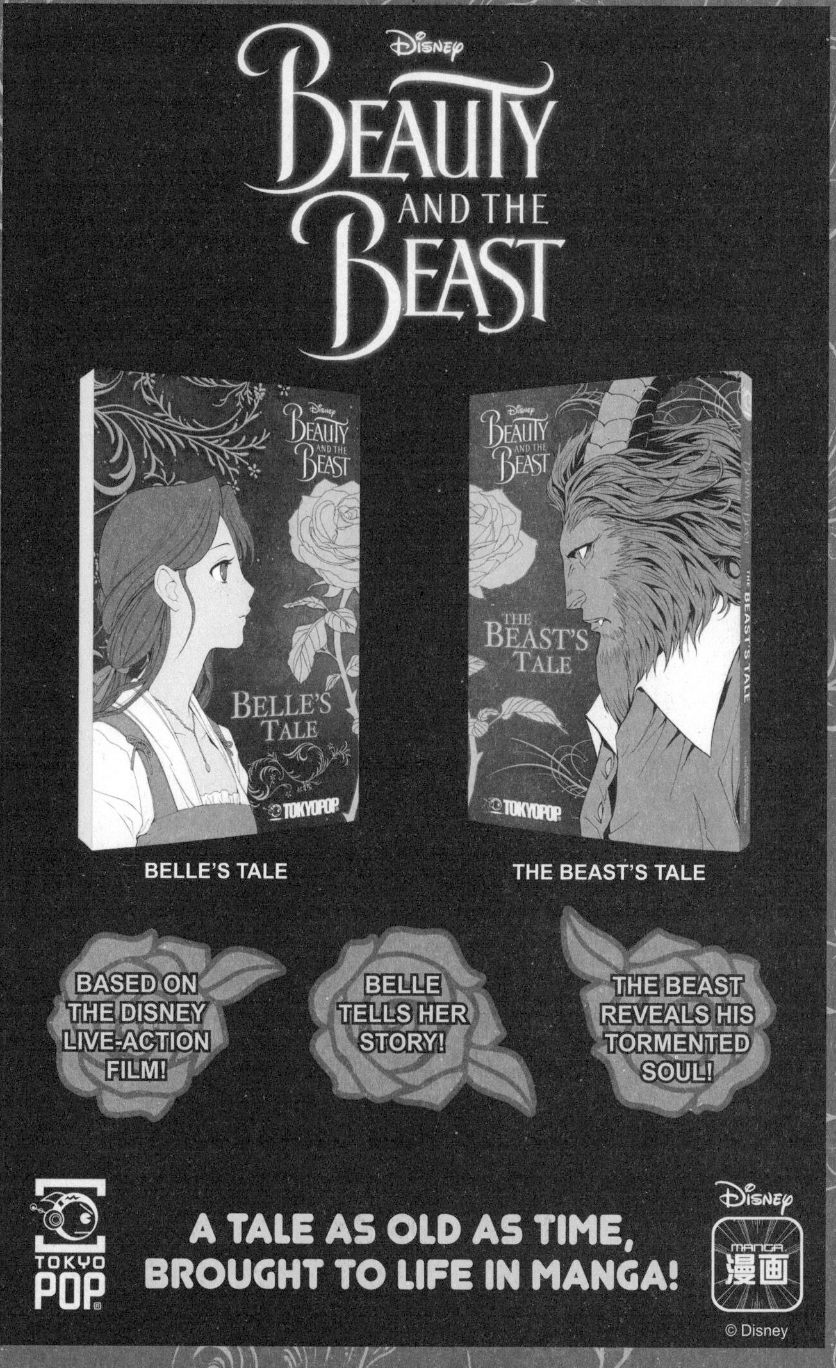
Disney
BEAUTY AND THE BEAST
Disney Beauty and the Beast
BELLE'S TALE
TOKYOPOP
Disney Beauty and the Beast
THE BEAST'S TALE
TOKYOPOP
BELLE'S TALE
THE BEAST'S TALE
BASED ON THE DISNEY LIVE-ACTION FILM!
BELLE TELLS HER STORY!
THE BEAST REVEALS HIS TORMENTED SOUL!
TOKYO POP
A TALE AS OLD AS TIME, BROUGHT TO LIFE IN MANGA!
Disney
MANGA
漫画
© Disney

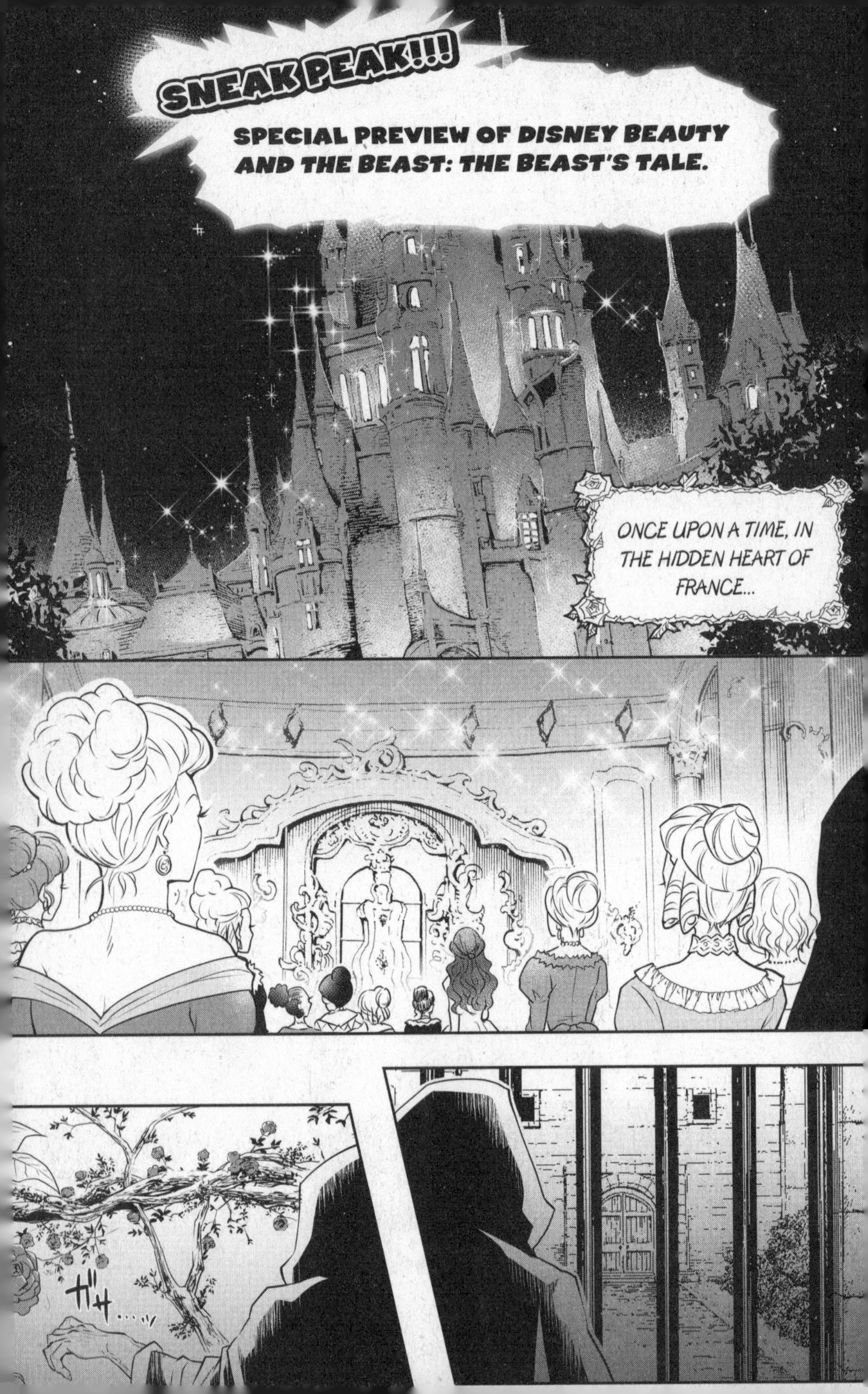
SNEAK PEAK!!!
SPECIAL PREVIEW OF DISNEY BEAUTY AND THE BEAST: THE BEAST'S TALE.
ONCE UPON A TIME, IN THE HIDDEN HEART OF FRANCE...
ガサ....ッ

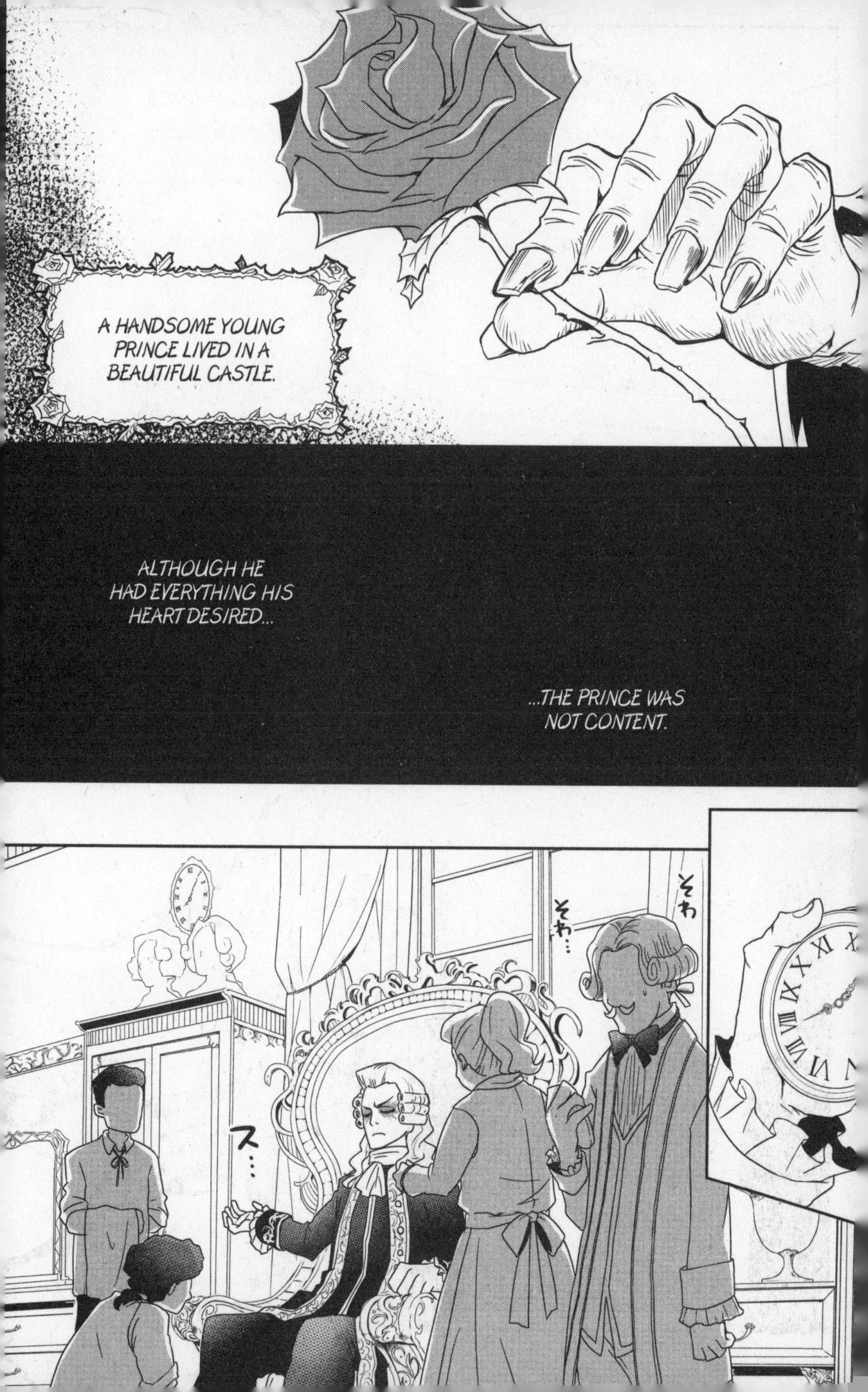
A HANDSOME YOUNG PRINCE LIVED IN A BEAUTIFUL CASTLE.
ALTHOUGH HE HAD EVERYTHING HIS HEART DESIRED...
...THE PRINCE WAS NOT CONTENT.
そわ
そわ…
ス…

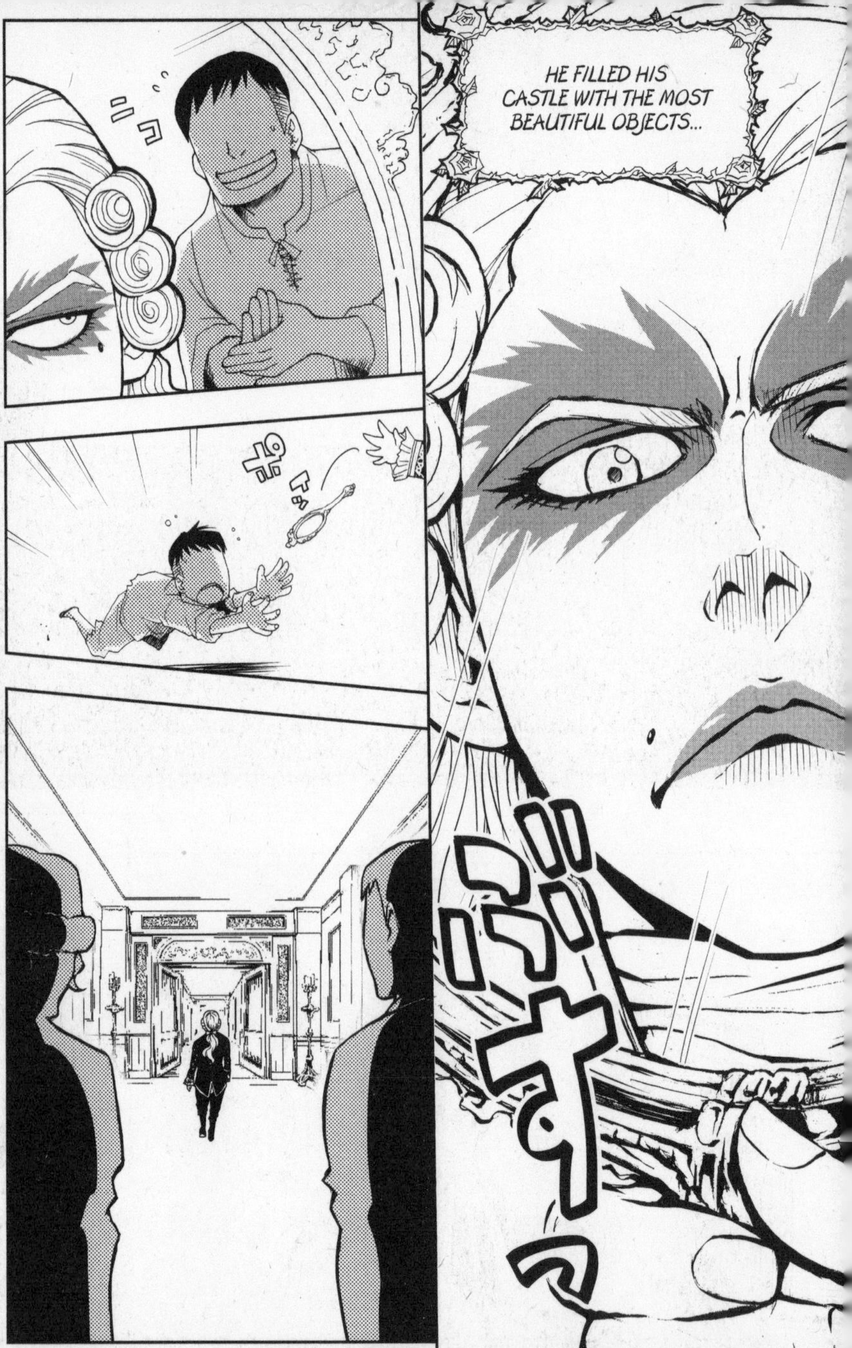
HE FILLED HIS CASTLE WITH THE MOST BEAUTIFUL OBJECTS...

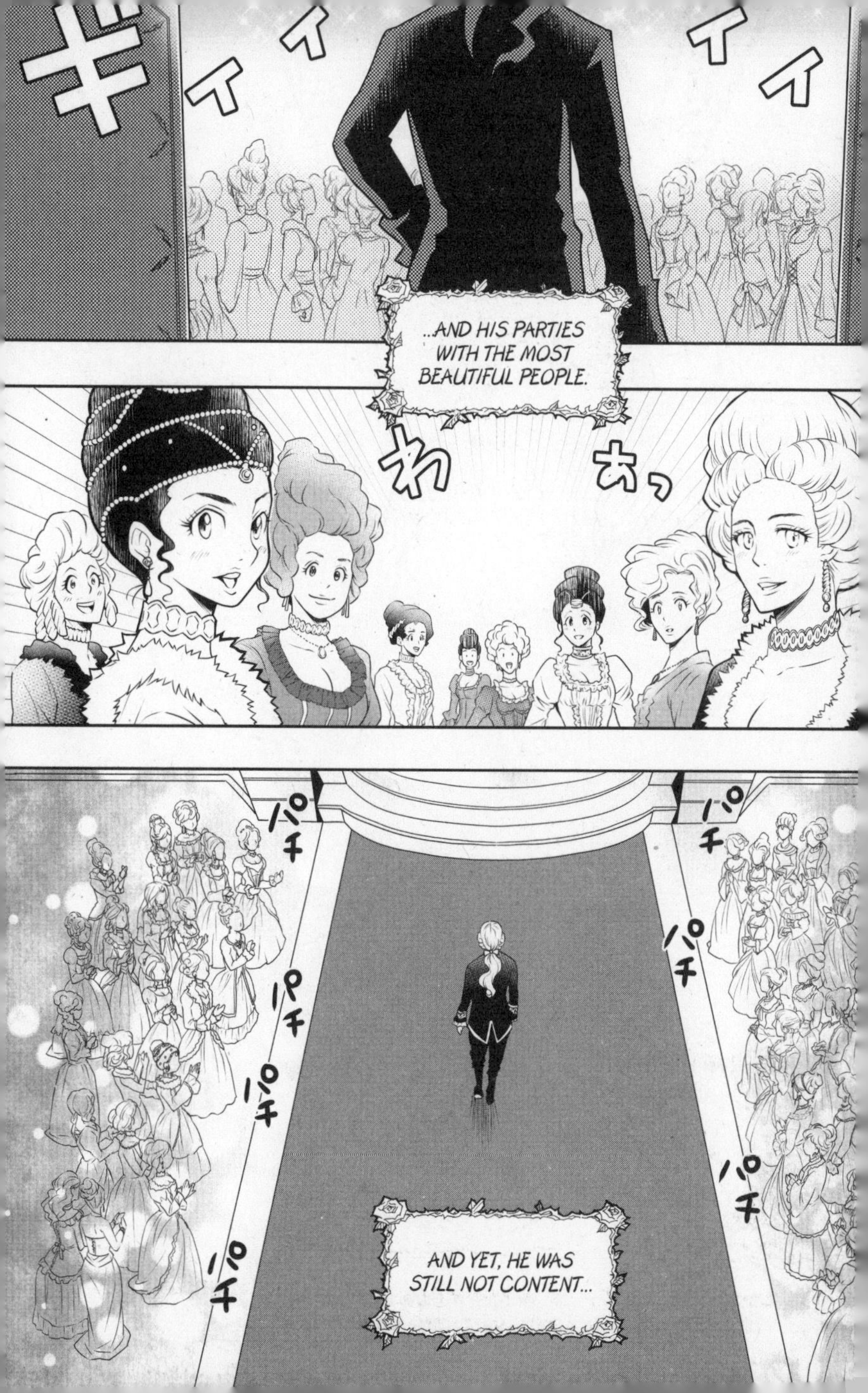
ギィィイイ
...AND HIS PARTIES WITH THE MOST BEAUTIFUL PEOPLE.
あっ
わ
パチ
パチ
パチ
パチ
パチ
パチ
AND YET, HE WAS STILL NOT CONTENT...

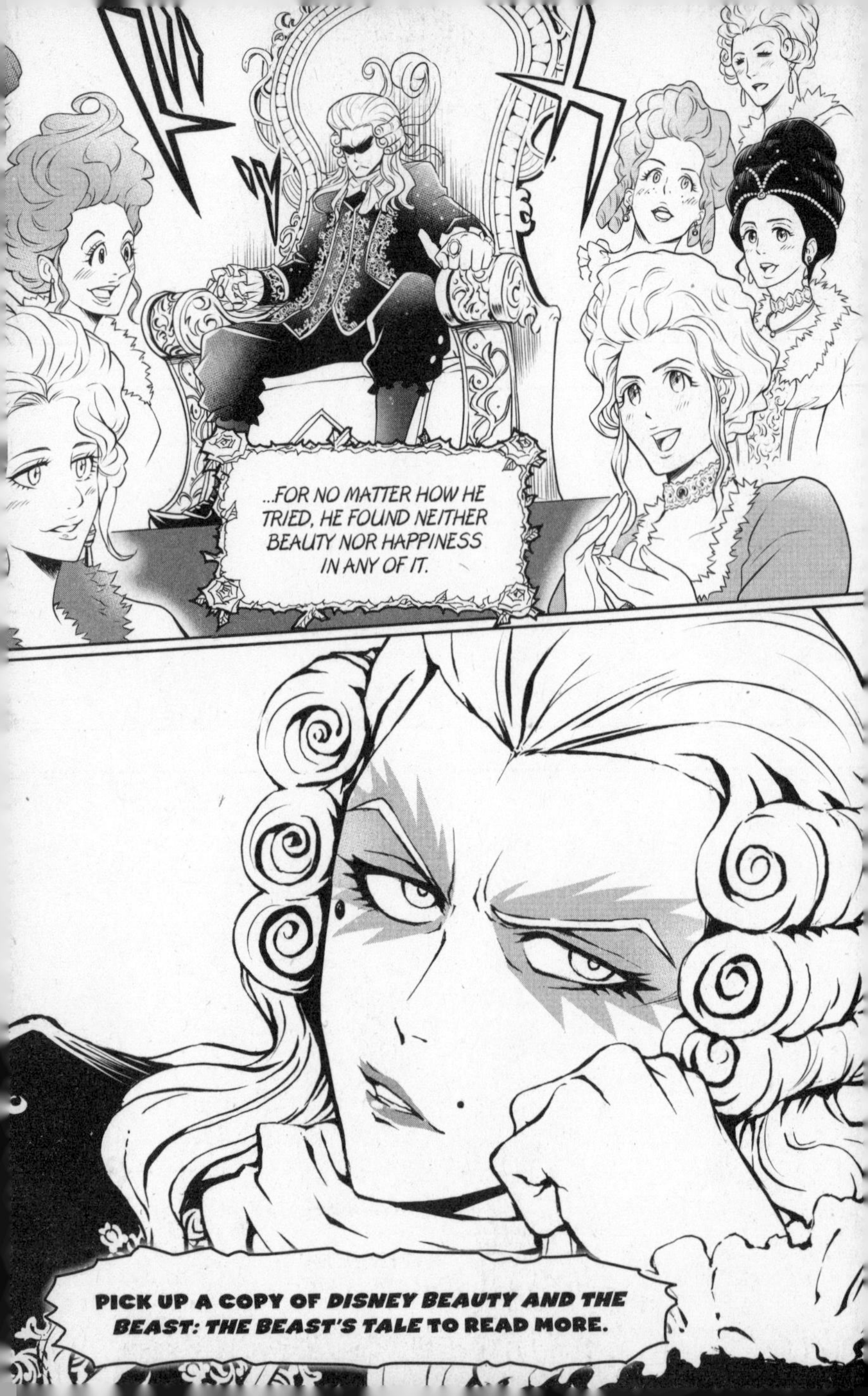
...FOR NO MATTER HOW HE TRIED, HE FOUND NEITHER BEAUTY NOR HAPPINESS IN ANY OF IT.
PICK UP A COPY OF *DISNEY BEAUTY AND THE BEAST: THE BEAST'S TALE* TO READ MORE.

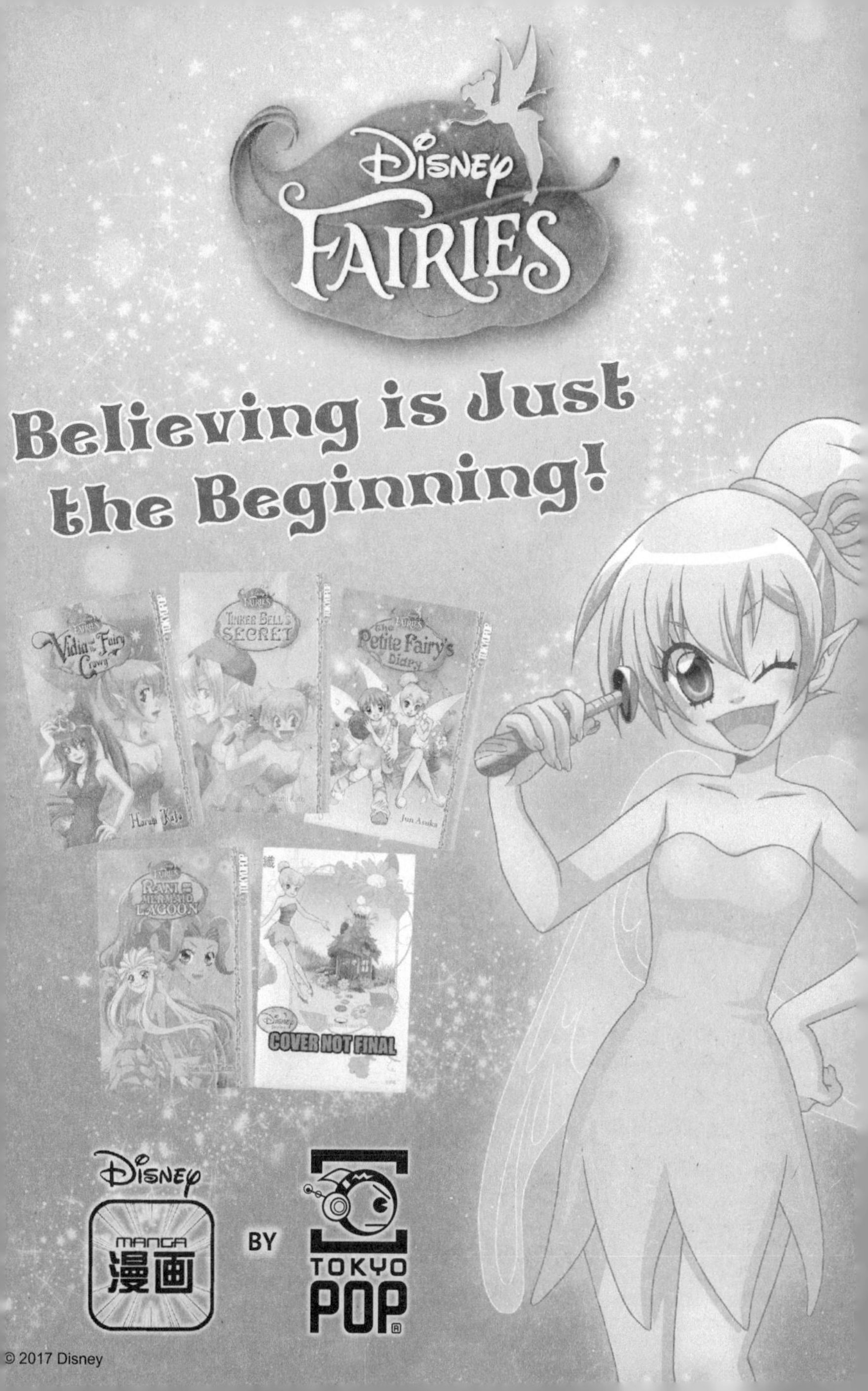
Disney
FAIRIES
Believing is Just the Beginning!
Tinker Bell's Secret
The Petite Fairy's Diary
Jun Asuka
COVER NOT FINAL
Disney
MANGA
漫画
BY
TOKYO POP
© 2017 Disney

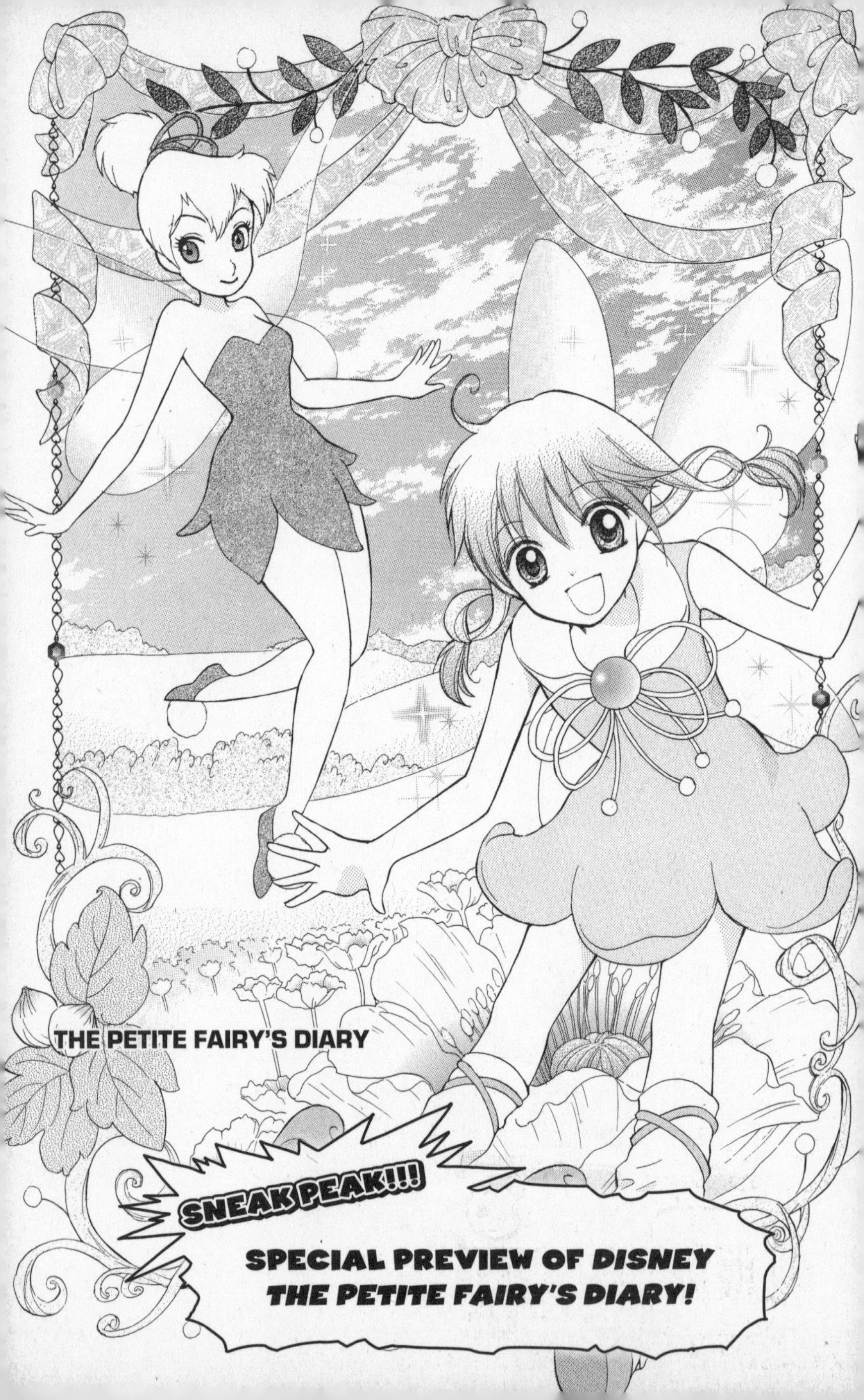
THE PETITE FAIRY'S DIARY
SNEAK PEAK!!!
SPECIAL PREVIEW OF *DISNEY THE PETITE FAIRY'S DIARY!*

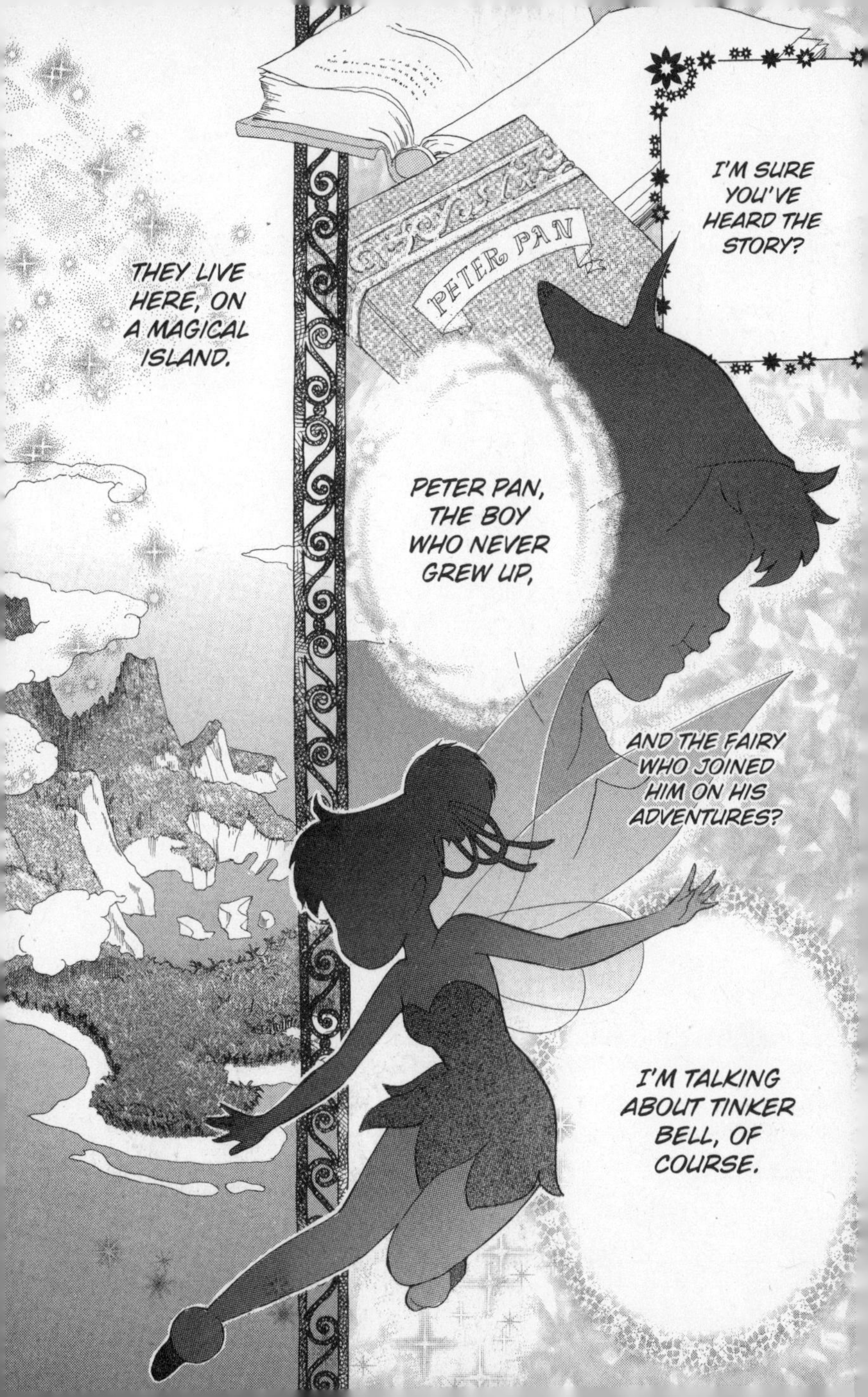

I'M SURE YOU'VE HEARD THE STORY?
PETER PAN
PETER PAN, THE BOY WHO NEVER GREW UP,
AND THE FAIRY WHO JOINED HIM ON HIS ADVENTURES?
I'M TALKING ABOUT TINKER BELL, OF COURSE.
THEY LIVE HERE, ON A MAGICAL ISLAND.

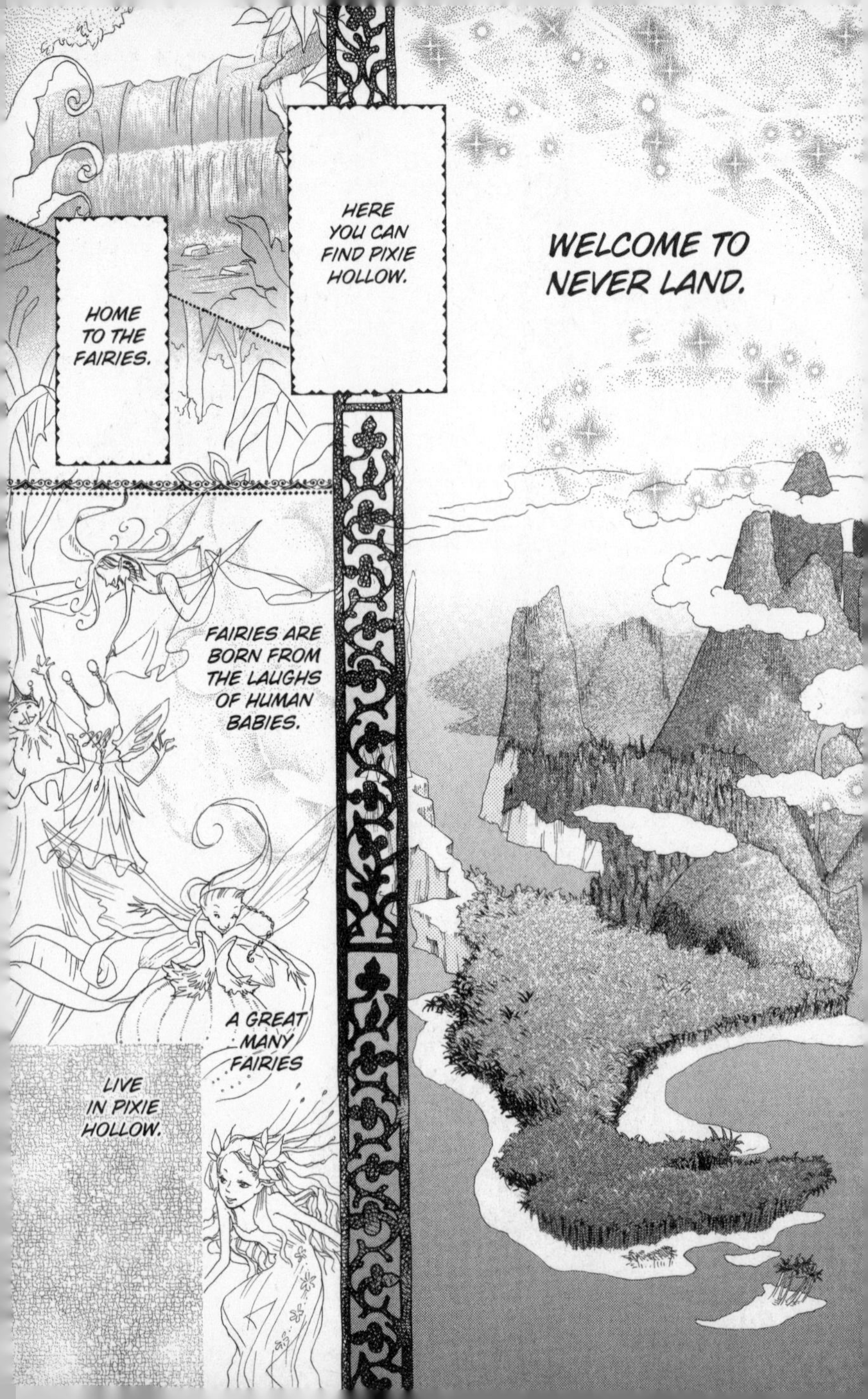
WELCOME TO NEVER LAND.
HERE YOU CAN FIND PIXIE HOLLOW.
HOME TO THE FAIRIES.
FAIRIES ARE BORN FROM THE LAUGHS OF HUMAN BABIES.
A GREAT MANY FAIRIES
LIVE IN PIXIE HOLLOW.

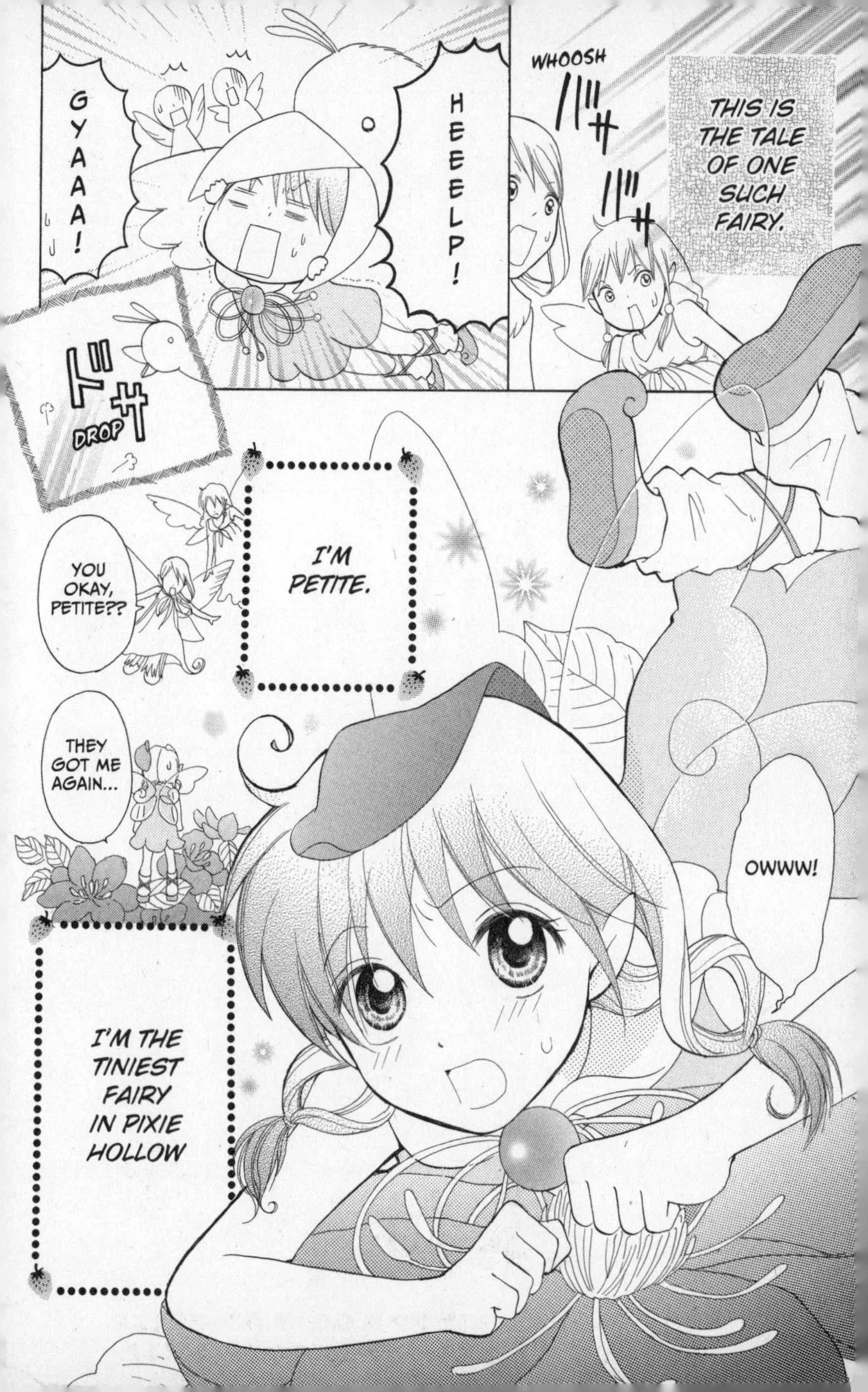
WHOOSH
THIS IS THE TALE OF ONE SUCH FAIRY.
HEEELP!
GYAAAA!
DROP
OWWW!
I'M PETITE.
YOU OKAY, PETITE??
THEY GOT ME AGAIN...
I'M THE TINIEST FAIRY IN PIXIE HOLLOW

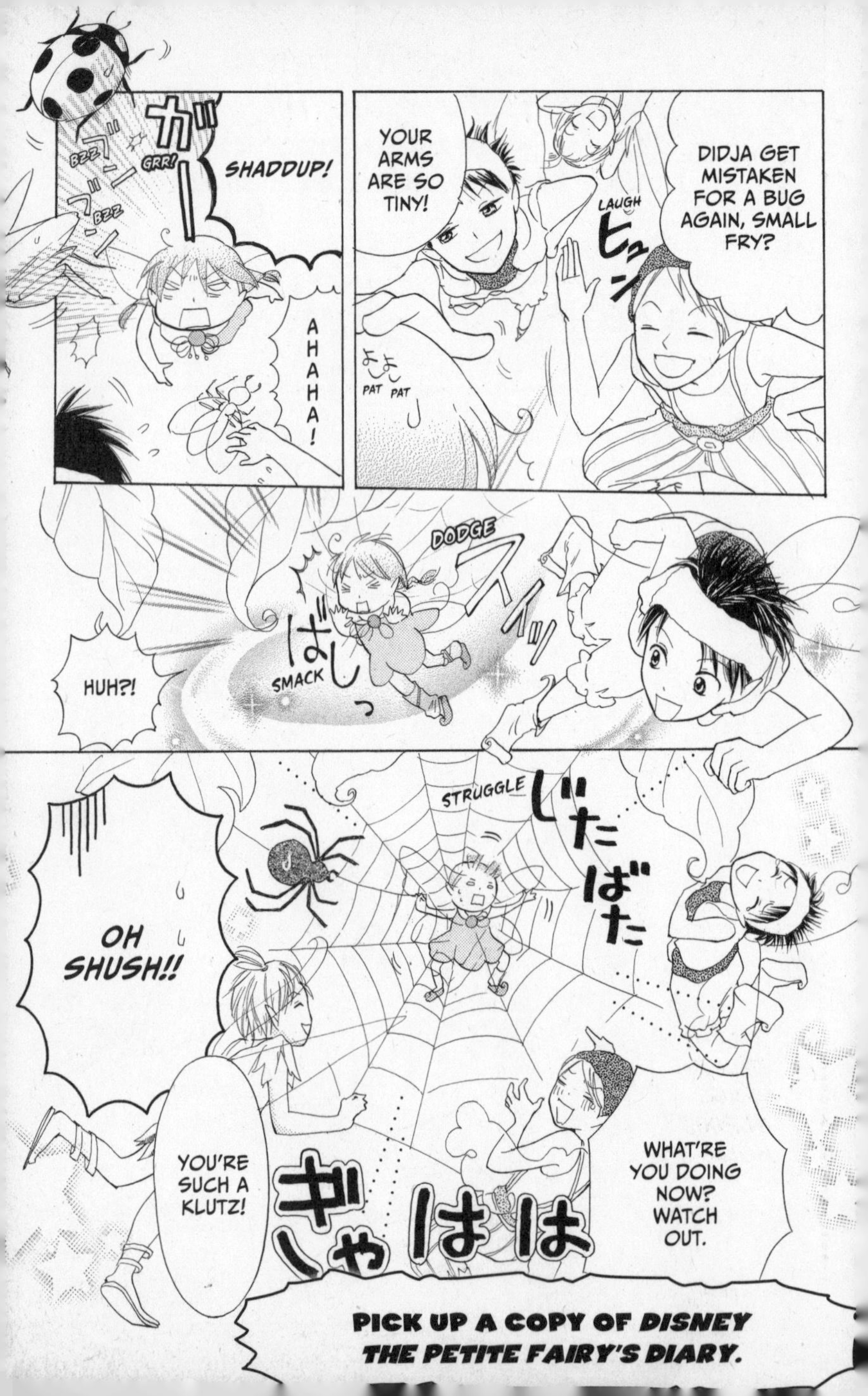

DIDJA GET MISTAKEN FOR A BUG AGAIN, SMALL FRY?
ヒュン
LAUGH
YOUR ARMS ARE SO TINY!
よしよし
PAT PAT
ガー
GRR!
SHADDUP!
ブーン ブーン
BZZ BZZ
AHAHA!
スイッ
DODGE
ばしっ
SMACK
HUH?!
じたばた
STRUGGLE
OH SHUSH!!
WHAT'RE YOU DOING NOW? WATCH OUT.
ぎゃははは
YOU'RE SUCH A KLUTZ!
PICK UP A COPY OF *DISNEY THE PETITE FAIRY'S DIARY.*

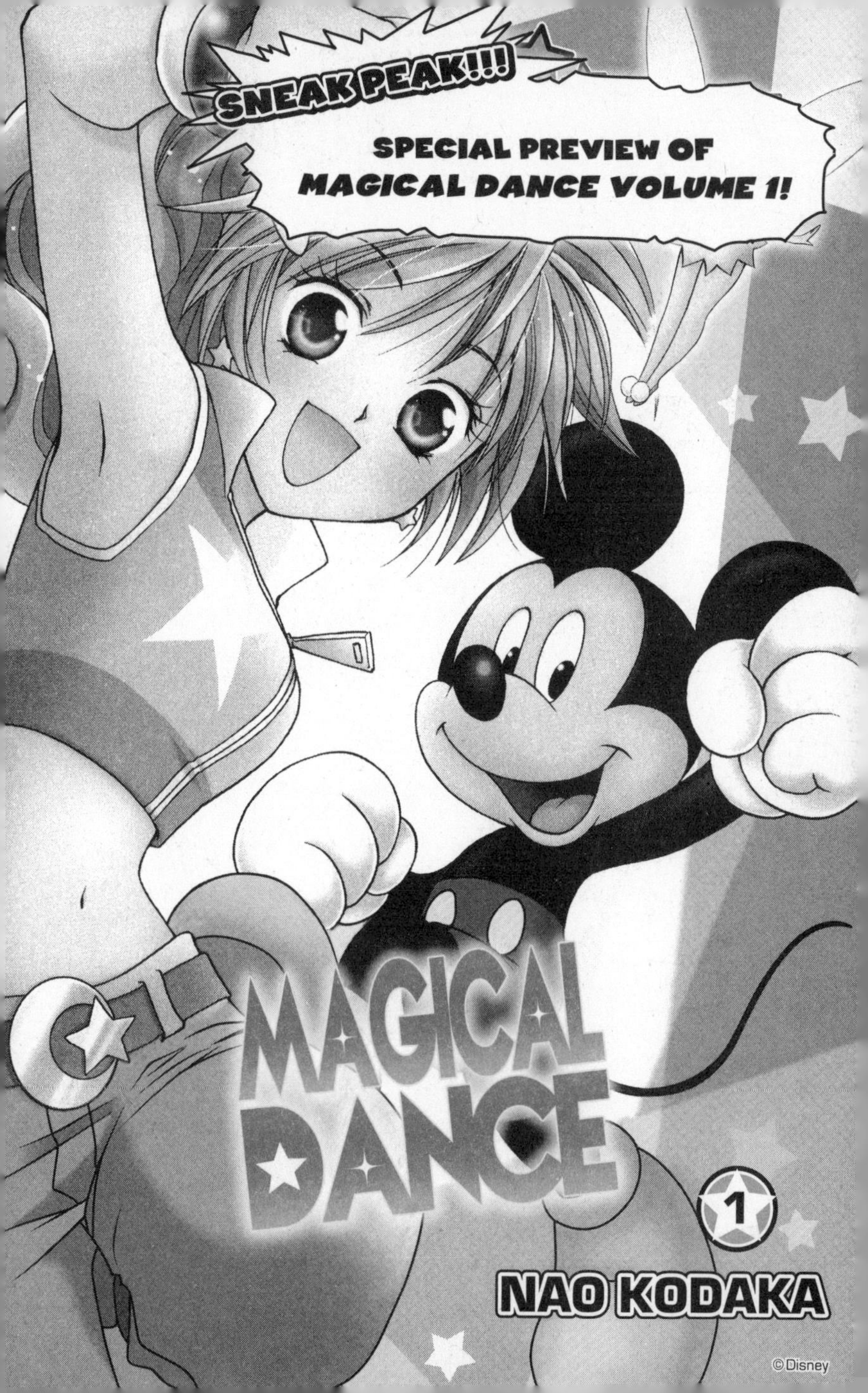
SNEAK PEAK!!!
SPECIAL PREVIEW OF
MAGICAL DANCE VOLUME 1!
MAGICAL DANCE
1
NAO KODAKA
© Disney

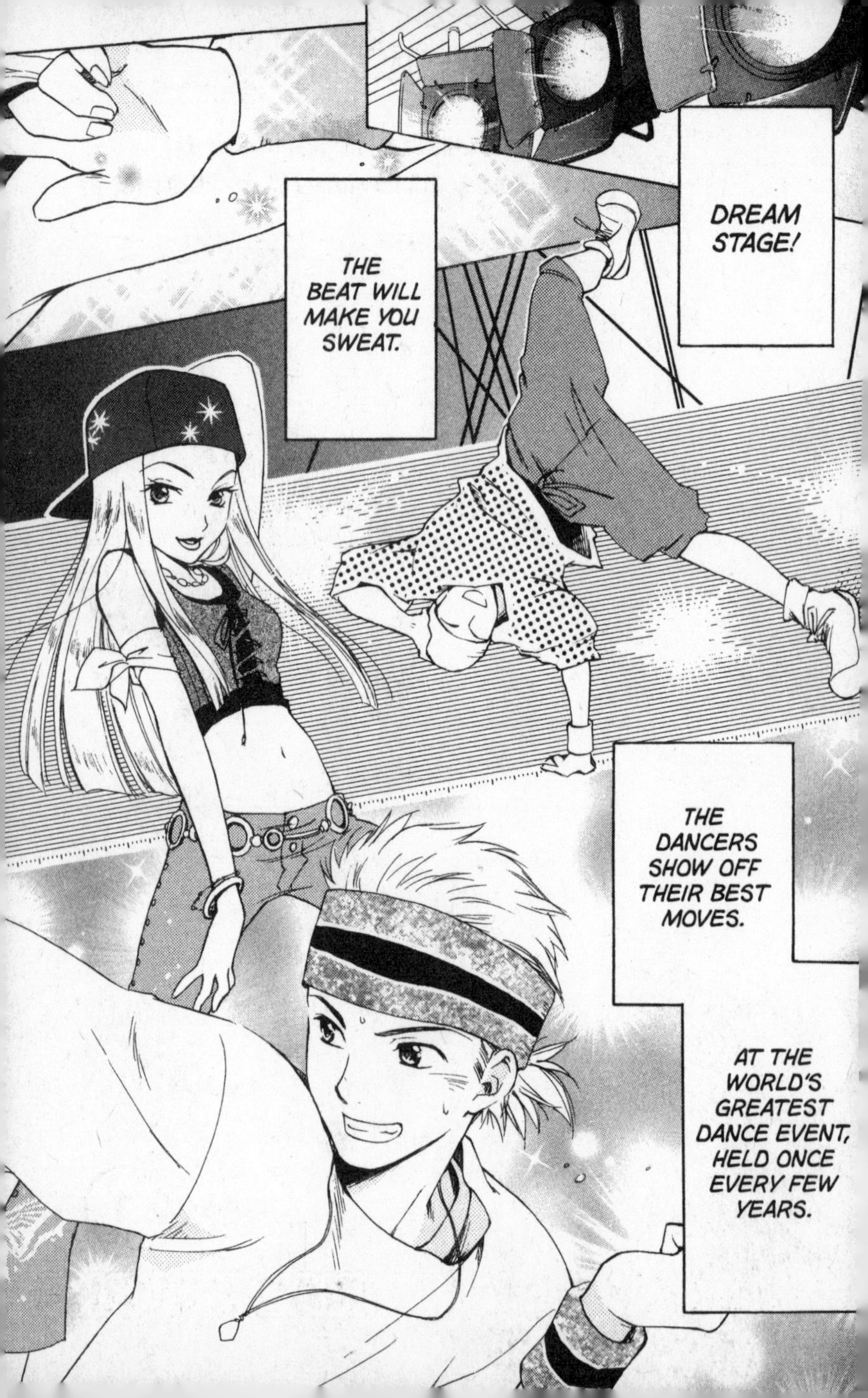
DREAM STAGE!
THE BEAT WILL MAKE YOU SWEAT.
THE DANCERS SHOW OFF THEIR BEST MOVES.
AT THE WORLD'S GREATEST DANCE EVENT, HELD ONCE EVERY FEW YEARS.

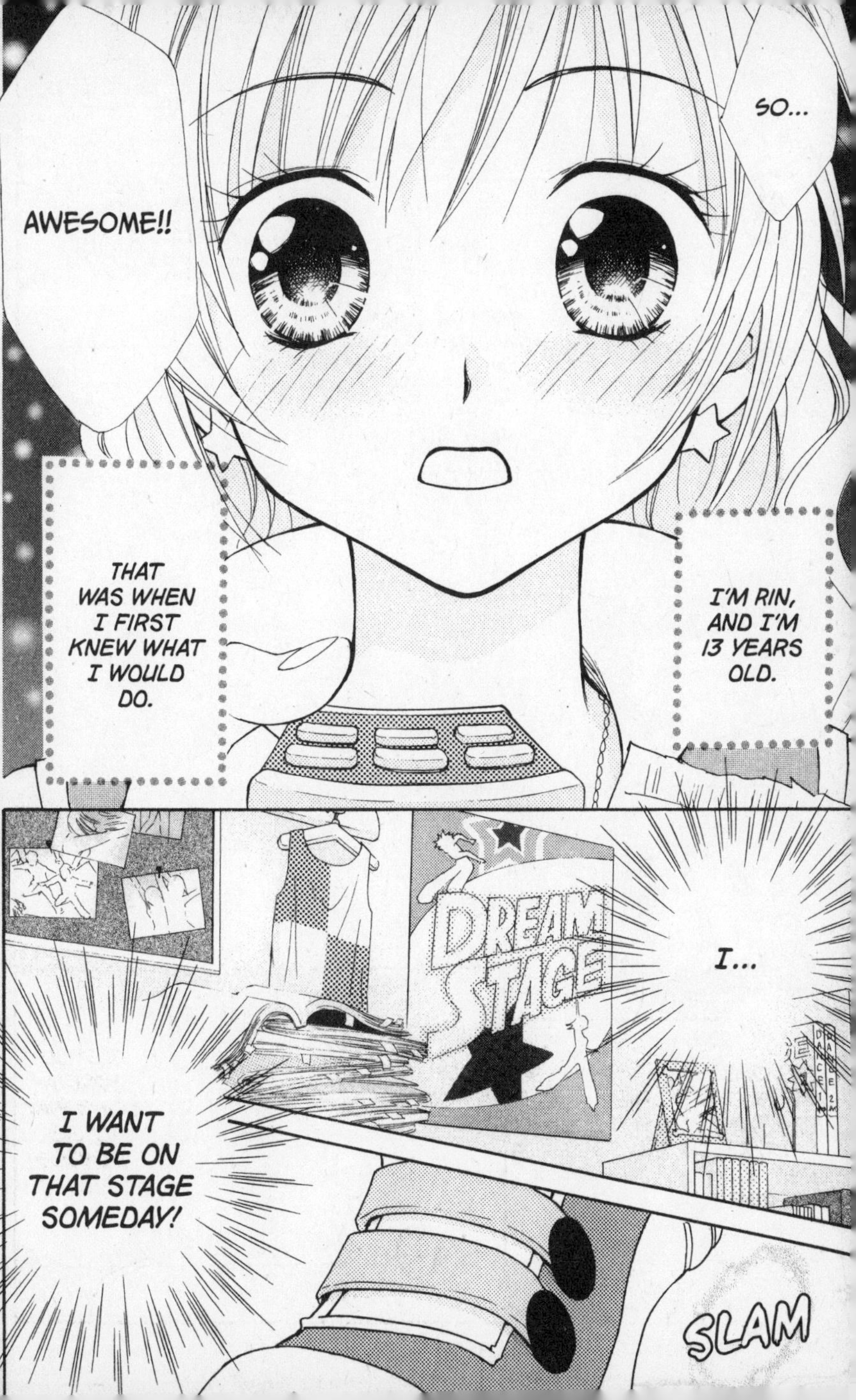

SO...
AWESOME!!
I'M RIN, AND I'M 13 YEARS OLD.
THAT WAS WHEN I FIRST KNEW WHAT I WOULD DO.
I...
DREAM STAGE
I WANT TO BE ON THAT STAGE SOMEDAY!
SLAM

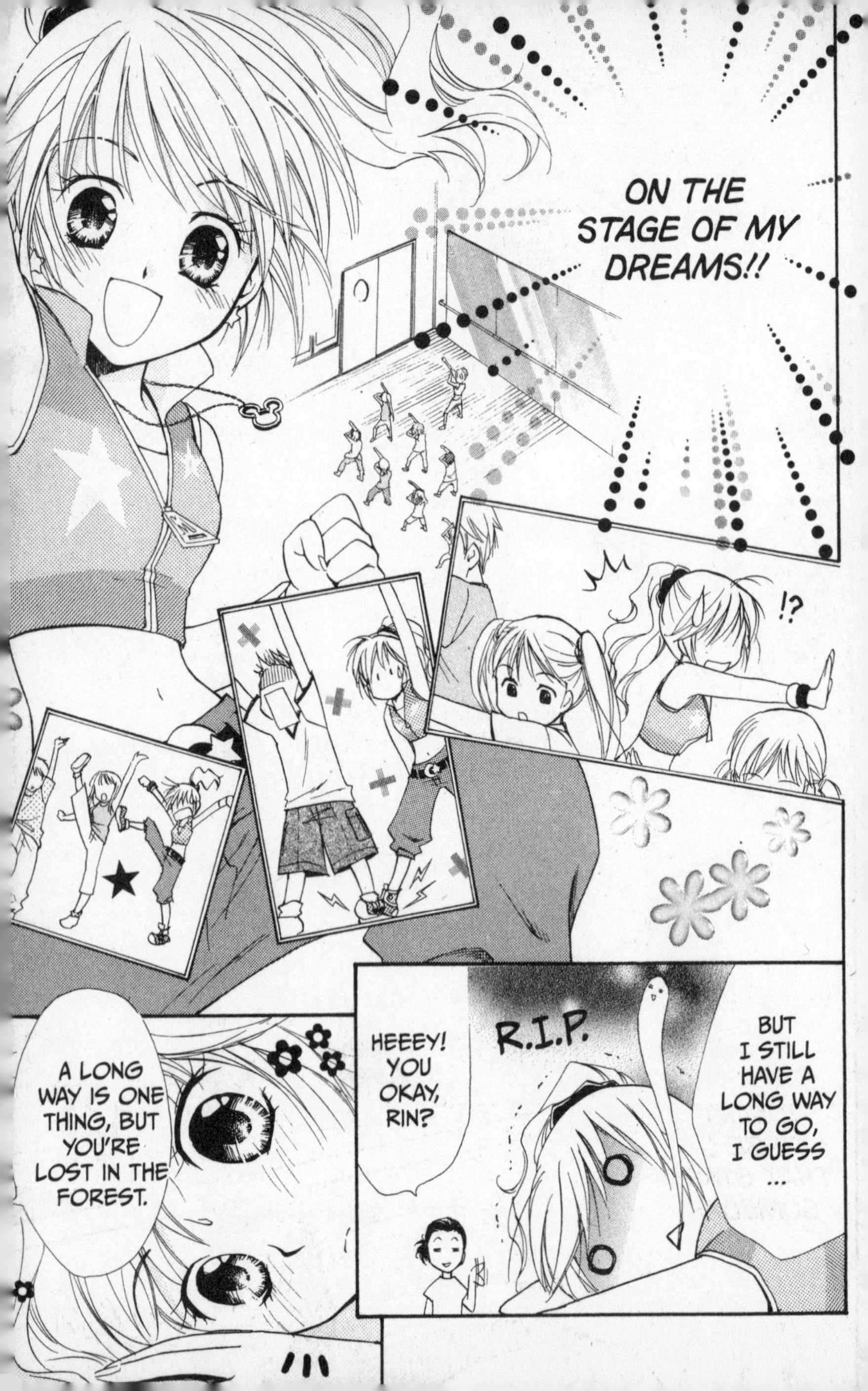
ON THE STAGE OF MY DREAMS!!
!?
BUT I STILL HAVE A LONG WAY TO GO, I GUESS ...
R.I.P.
HEEEY! YOU OKAY, RIN?
A LONG WAY IS ONE THING, BUT YOU'RE LOST IN THE FOREST.

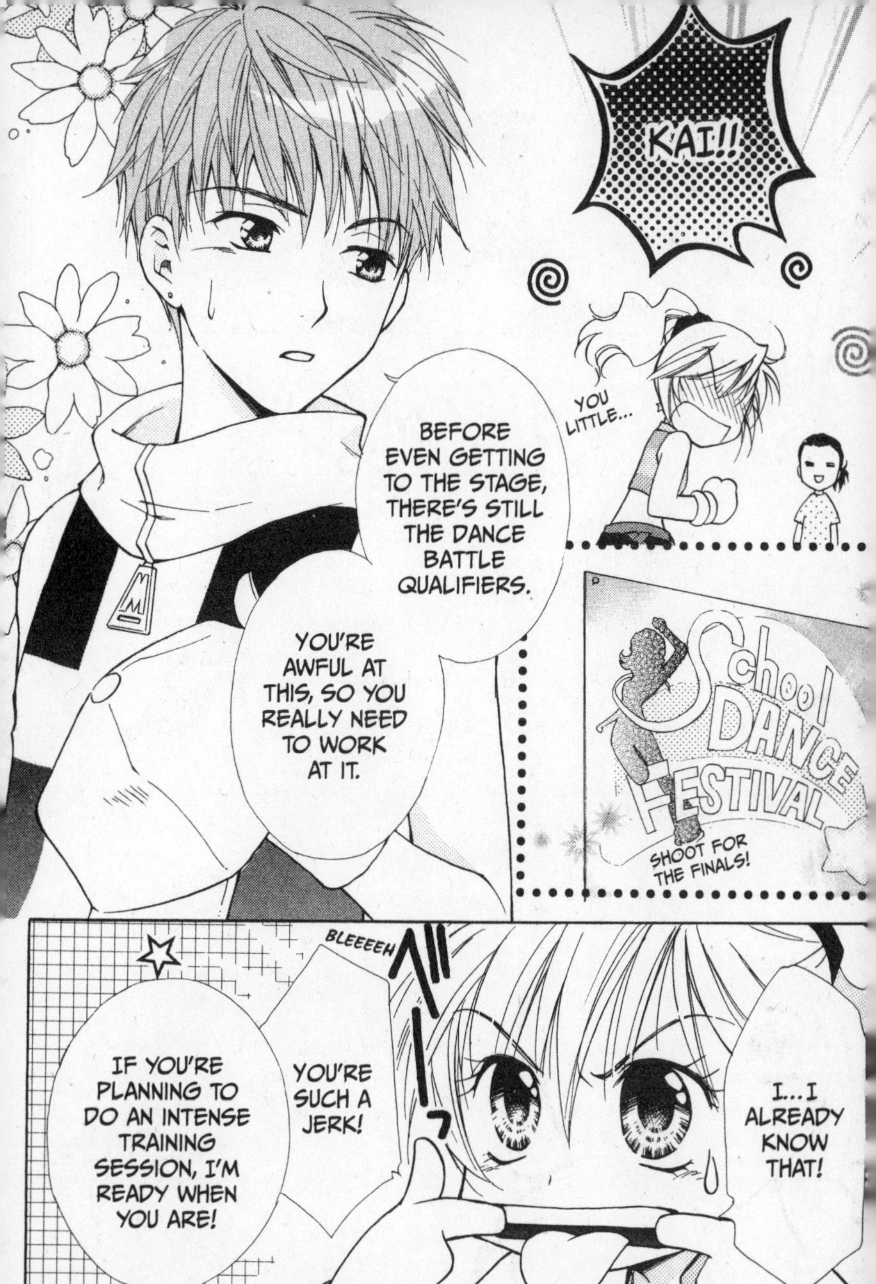
KAI!!
YOU LITTLE...
School DANCE FESTIVAL
SHOOT FOR THE FINALS!
BEFORE EVEN GETTING TO THE STAGE, THERE'S STILL THE DANCE BATTLE QUALIFIERS.
YOU'RE AWFUL AT THIS, SO YOU REALLY NEED TO WORK AT IT.
I...I ALREADY KNOW THAT!
BLEEEEH
YOU'RE SUCH A JERK!
IF YOU'RE PLANNING TO DO AN INTENSE TRAINING SESSION, I'M READY WHEN YOU ARE!

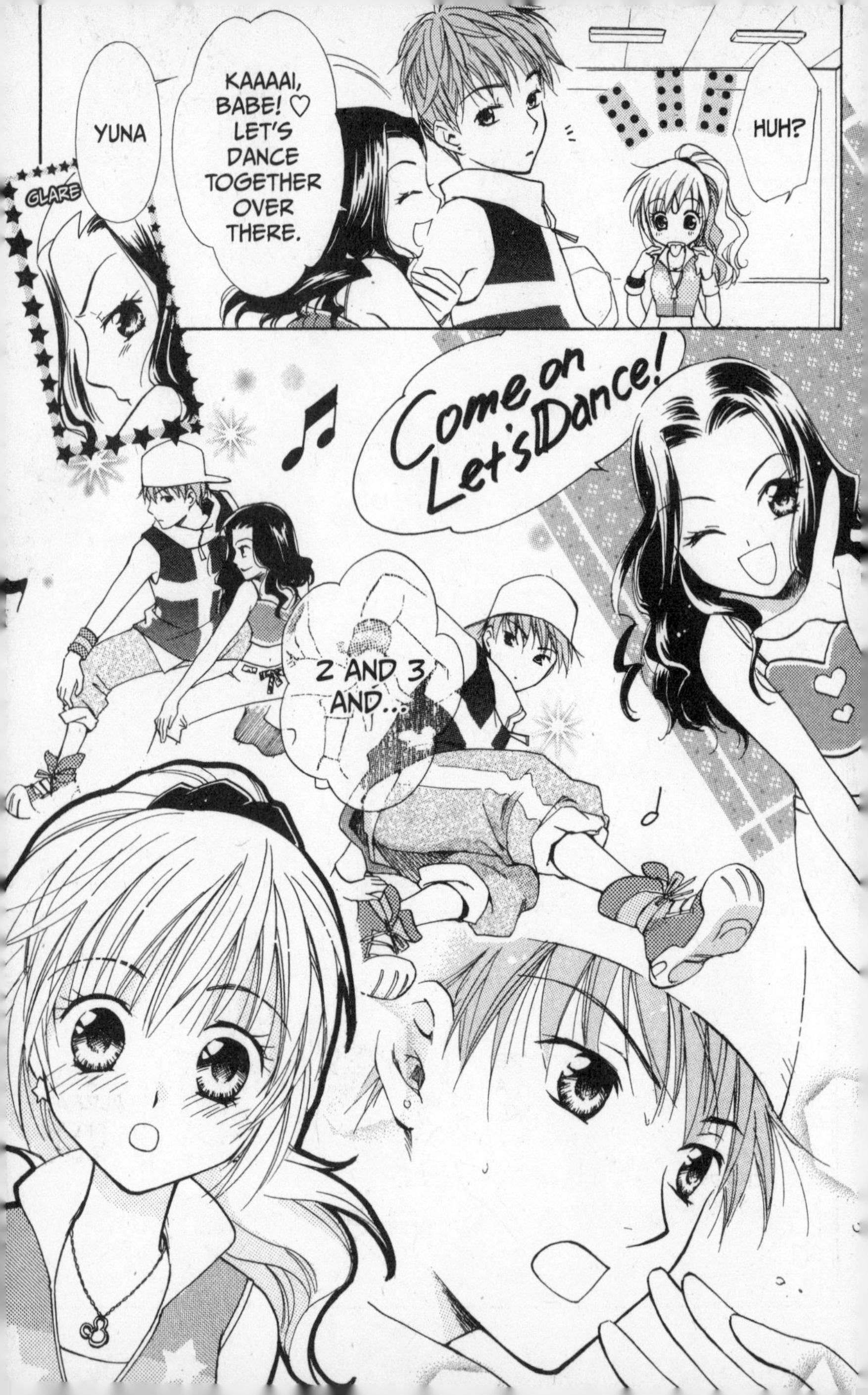
HUH?
KAAAAI, BABE! ♡ LET'S DANCE TOGETHER OVER THERE.
YUNA
GLARE
Come on Let's Dance!
2 AND 3 AND...

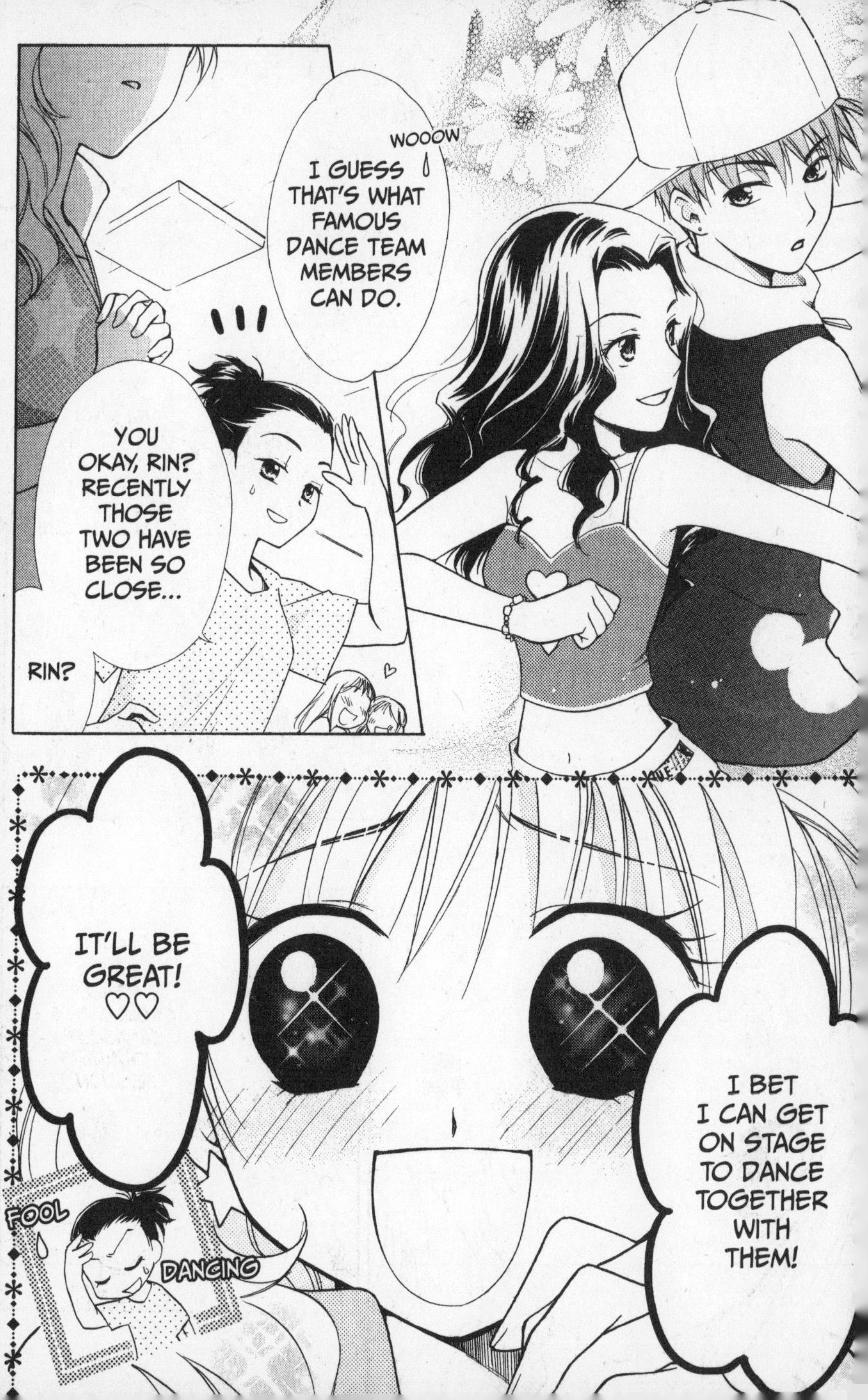
WOOOW
I GUESS THAT'S WHAT FAMOUS DANCE TEAM MEMBERS CAN DO.
YOU OKAY, RIN? RECENTLY THOSE TWO HAVE BEEN SO CLOSE...
RIN?
I BET I CAN GET ON STAGE TO DANCE TOGETHER WITH THEM!
IT'LL BE GREAT! ♡♡
FOOL
DANCING

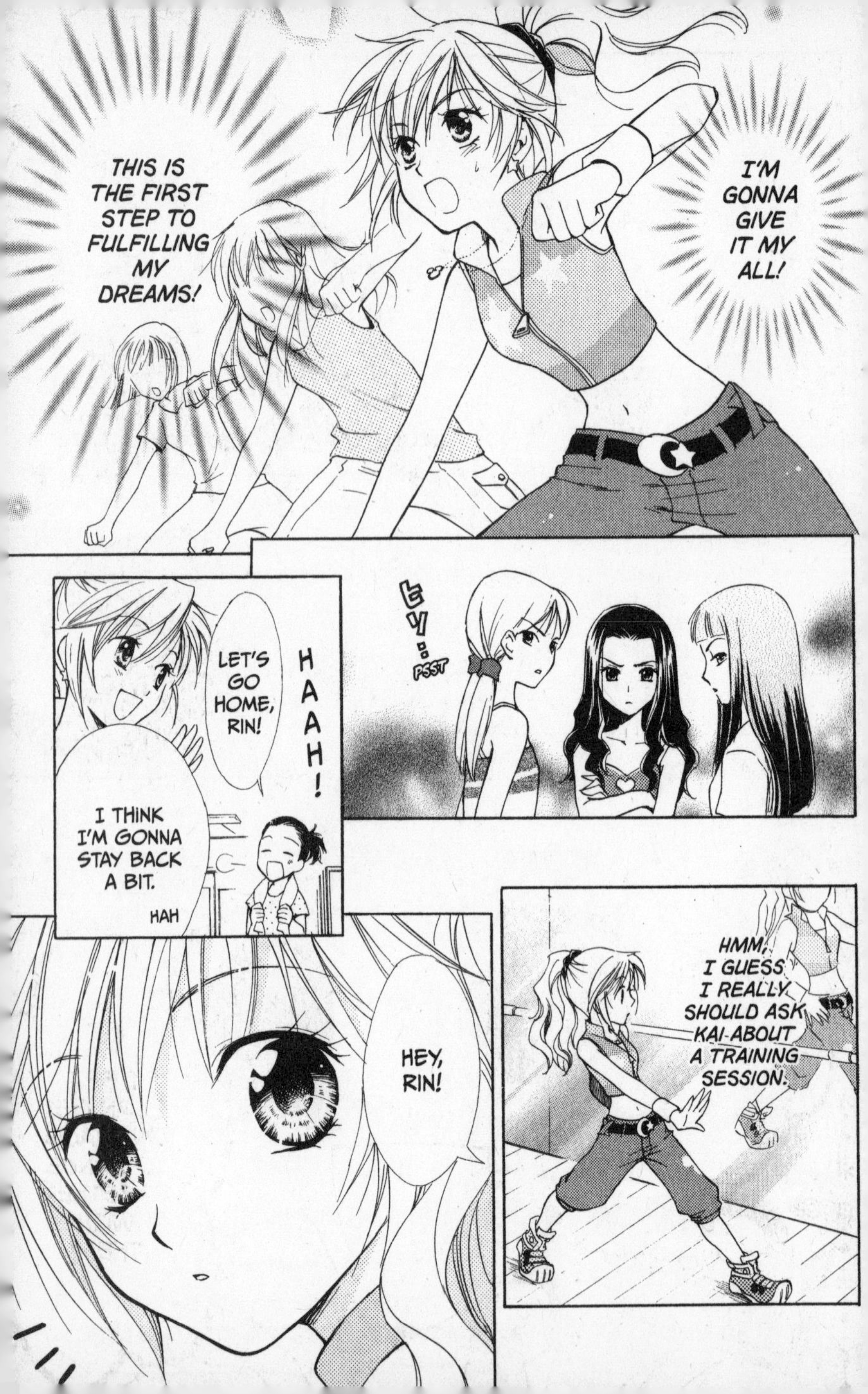
I'M GONNA GIVE IT MY ALL!
THIS IS THE FIRST STEP TO FULFILLING MY DREAMS!
ヒソ
PSST
HAAAH!
LET'S GO HOME, RIN!
I THINK I'M GONNA STAY BACK A BIT.
HAH
HMM, I GUESS I REALLY SHOULD ASK KAI ABOUT A TRAINING SESSION.
HEY, RIN!

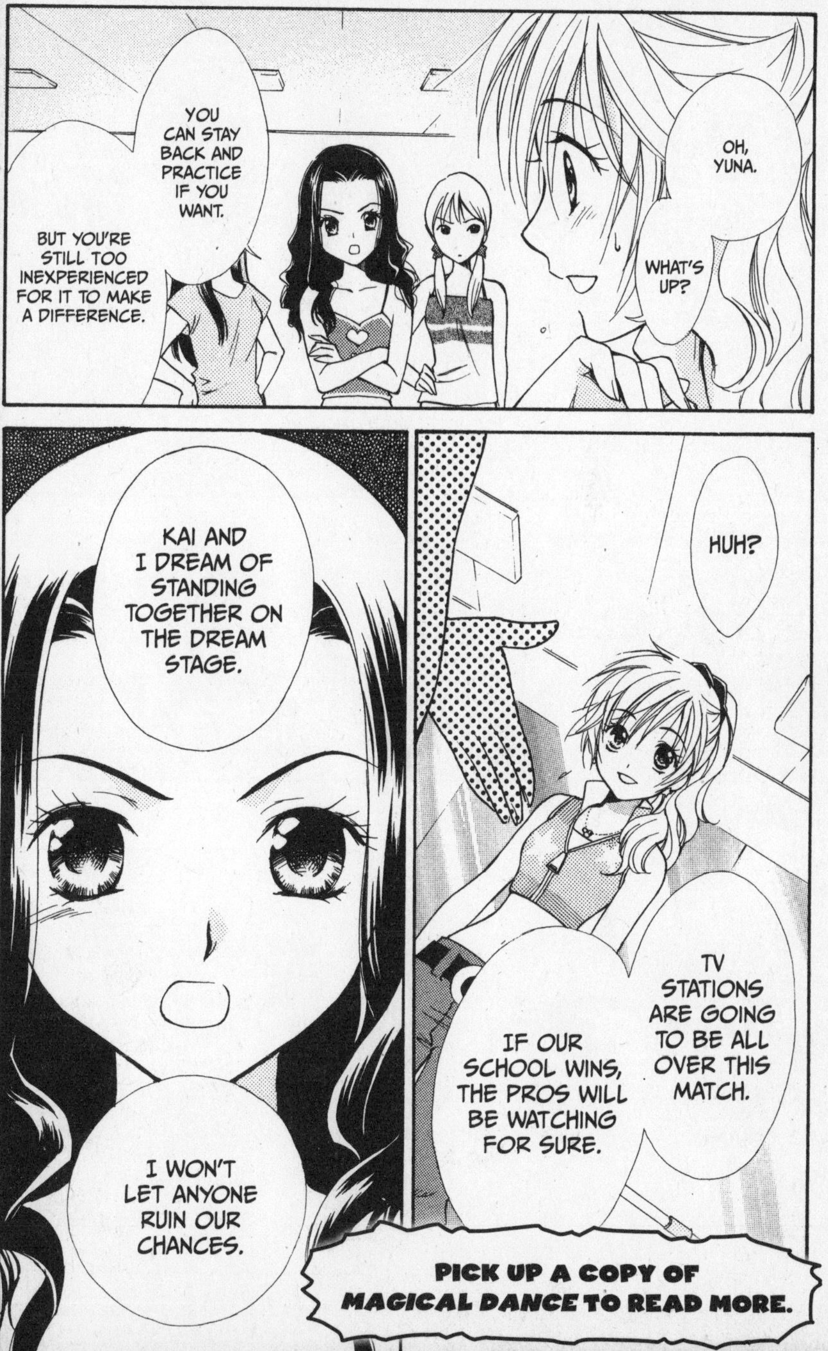
OH, YUNA.
WHAT'S UP?
YOU CAN STAY BACK AND PRACTICE IF YOU WANT.
BUT YOU'RE STILL TOO INEXPERIENCED FOR IT TO MAKE A DIFFERENCE.
HUH?
TV STATIONS ARE GOING TO BE ALL OVER THIS MATCH.
IF OUR SCHOOL WINS, THE PROS WILL BE WATCHING FOR SURE.
KAI AND I DREAM OF STANDING TOGETHER ON THE DREAM STAGE.
I WON'T LET ANYONE RUIN OUR CHANCES.
PICK UP A COPY OF *MAGICAL DANCE* TO READ MORE.

MAGICAL DANCE

Rin joins a troupe with her fellow students and soon realizes that she has two left feet. She practices day and night but is discouraged by the lack of results and almost gives up on her dreams. Impressed by her passion and dedication, Tinker Bell appears to give her a little encouragement in the form of Disney magic!

FROM THE CREATOR OF DISNEY KILALA PRINCESS!

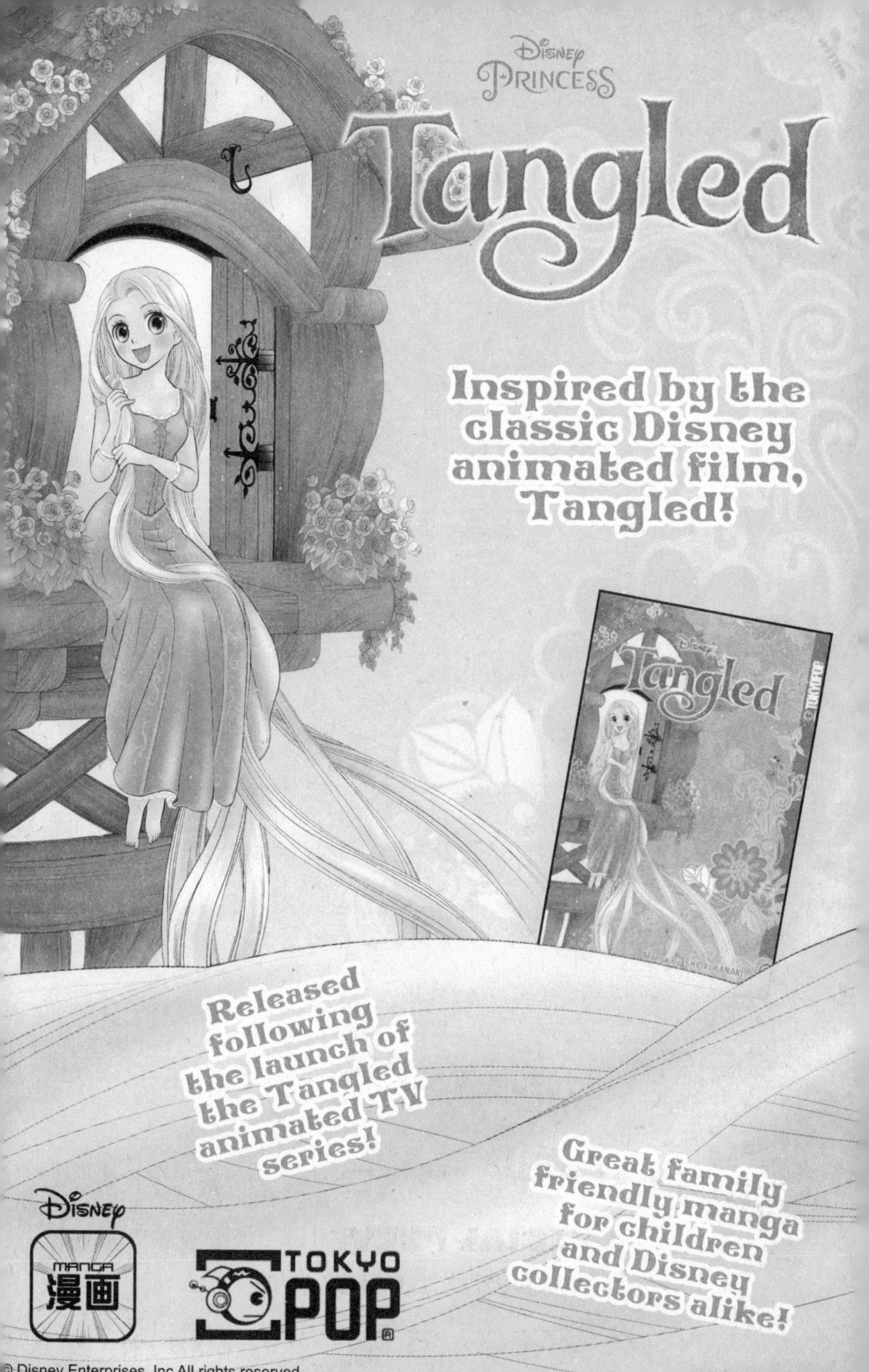
Disney Princess
Tangled
Inspired by the classic Disney animated film, Tangled!
Disney Tangled
TOKYOPOP
Manga by SHIORI KANAKI
Released following the launch of the Tangled the Tangled animated TV series!
Great family friendly manga for children and Disney collectors alike!
Disney
MANGA 漫画
TOKYO POP

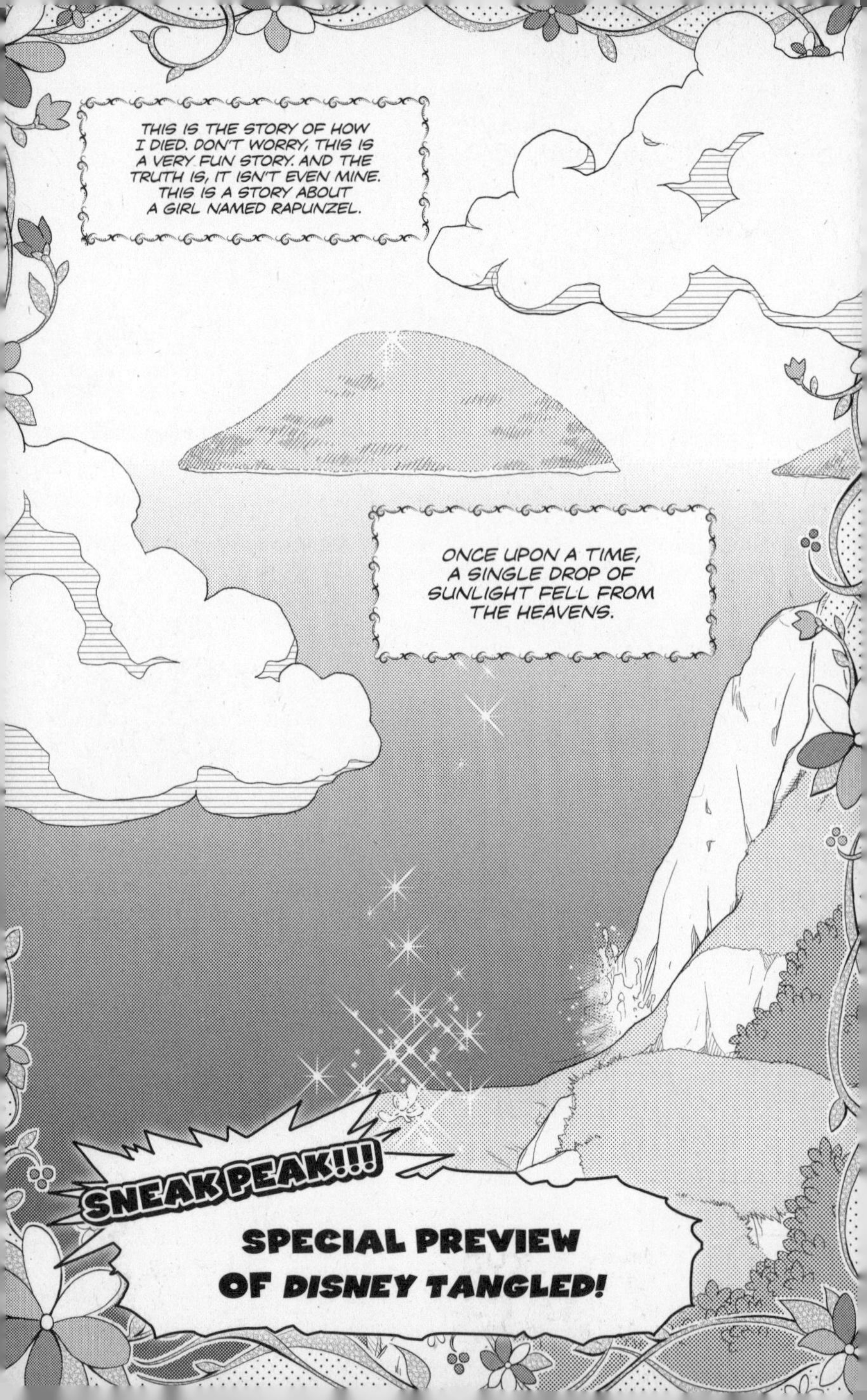
THIS IS THE STORY OF HOW I DIED. DON'T WORRY, THIS IS A VERY FUN STORY. AND THE TRUTH IS, IT ISN'T EVEN MINE. THIS IS A STORY ABOUT A GIRL NAMED RAPUNZEL.
ONCE UPON A TIME, A SINGLE DROP OF SUNLIGHT FELL FROM THE HEAVENS.
SNEAK PEAK!!!
SPECIAL PREVIEW OF DISNEY TANGLED!

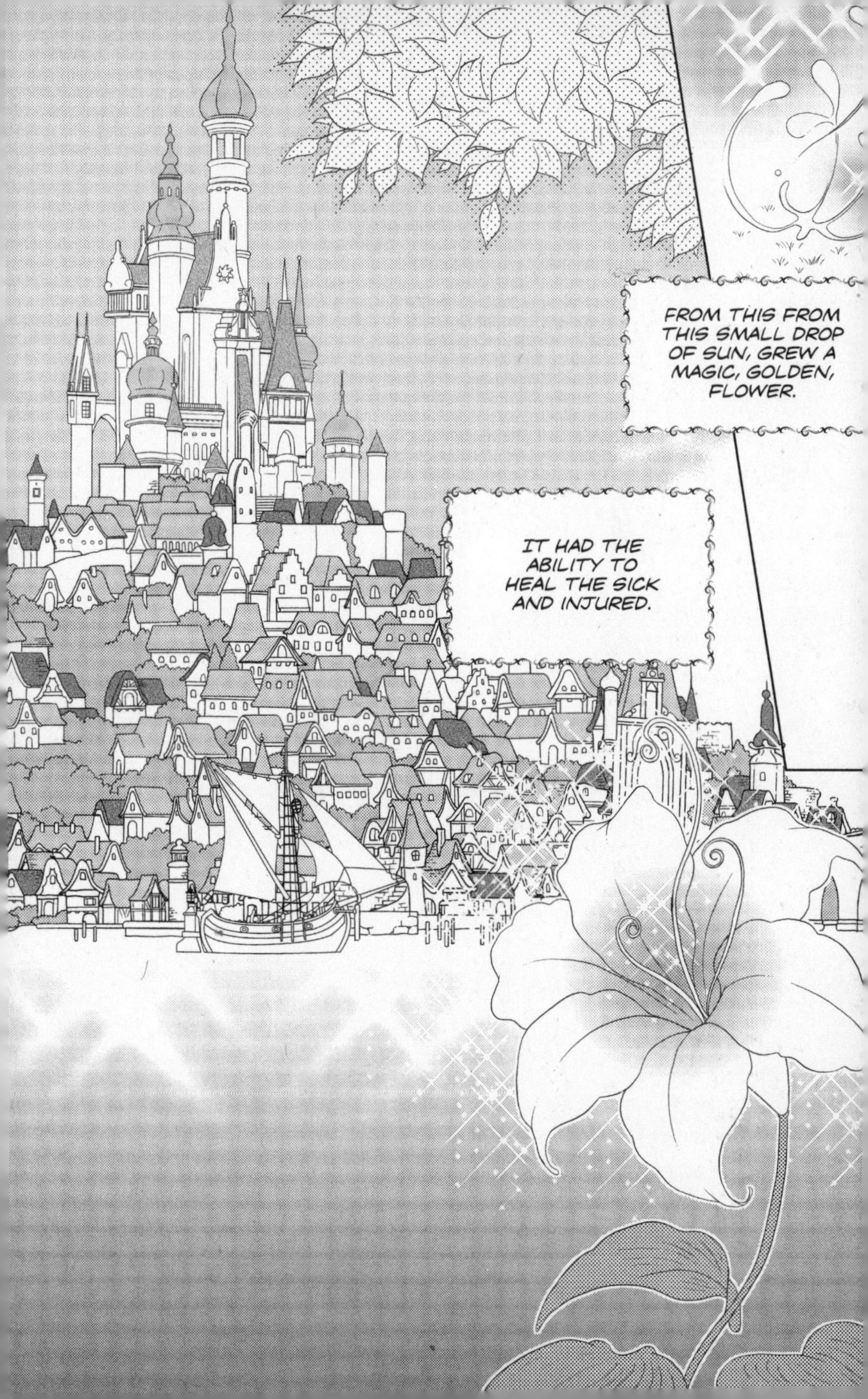
FROM THIS FROM THIS SMALL DROP OF SUN, GREW A MAGIC, GOLDEN, FLOWER.
IT HAD THE ABILITY TO HEAL THE SICK AND INJURED.

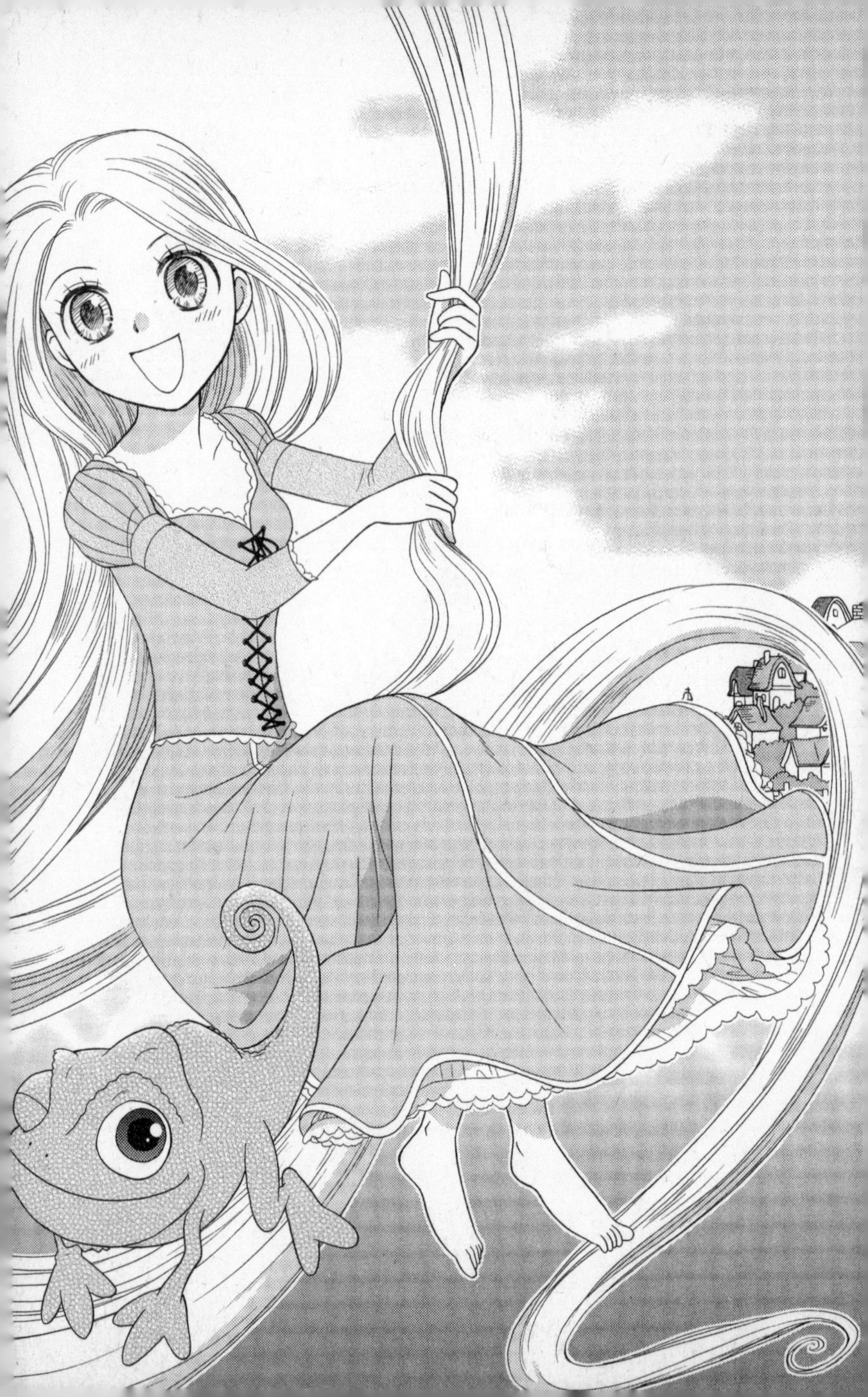

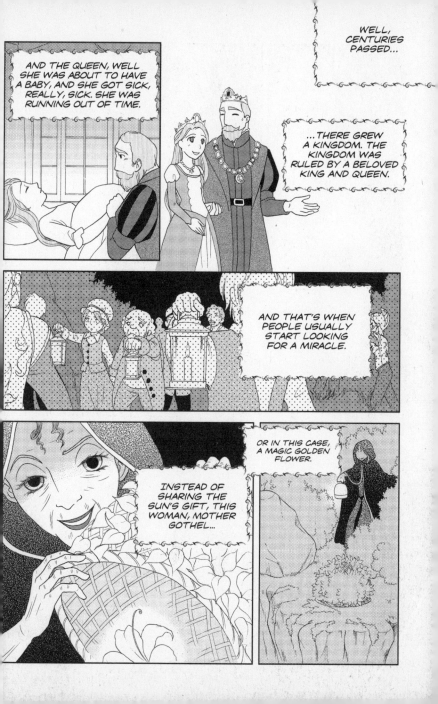

WELL, CENTURIES PASSED...
...THERE GREW A KINGDOM. THE KINGDOM WAS RULED BY A BELOVED KING AND QUEEN.
AND THE QUEEN, WELL SHE WAS ABOUT TO HAVE A BABY, AND SHE GOT SICK, REALLY, SICK. SHE WAS RUNNING OUT OF TIME.
AND THAT'S WHEN PEOPLE USUALLY START LOOKING FOR A MIRACLE.
OR IN THIS CASE, A MAGIC GOLDEN FLOWER.
INSTEAD OF SHARING THE SUN'S GIFT, THIS WOMAN, MOTHER GOTHEL...

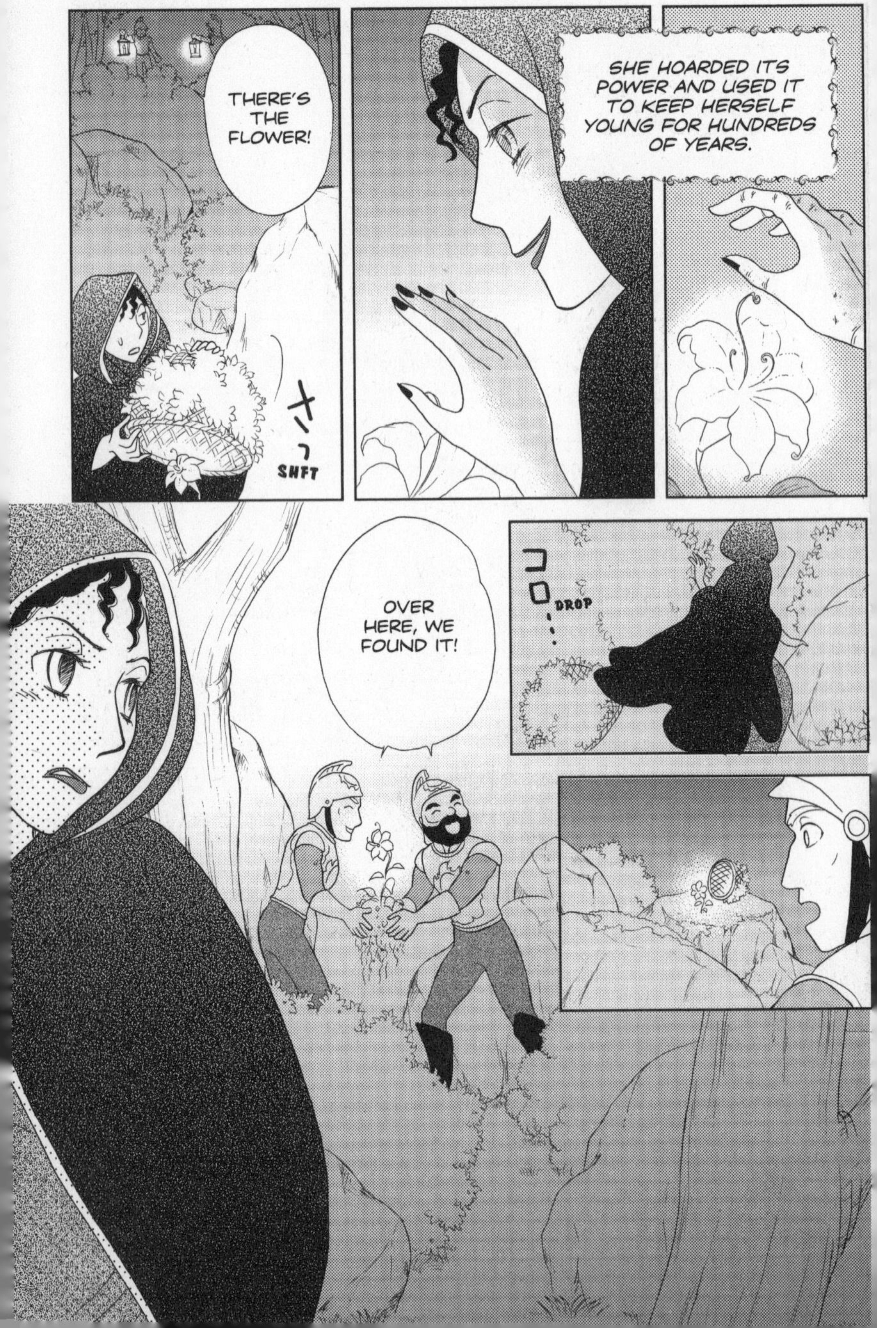
SHE HOARDED ITS POWER AND USED IT TO KEEP HERSELF YOUNG FOR HUNDREDS OF YEARS.
THERE'S THE FLOWER!
さっ
SHFT
コロ...
DROP
OVER HERE, WE FOUND IT!

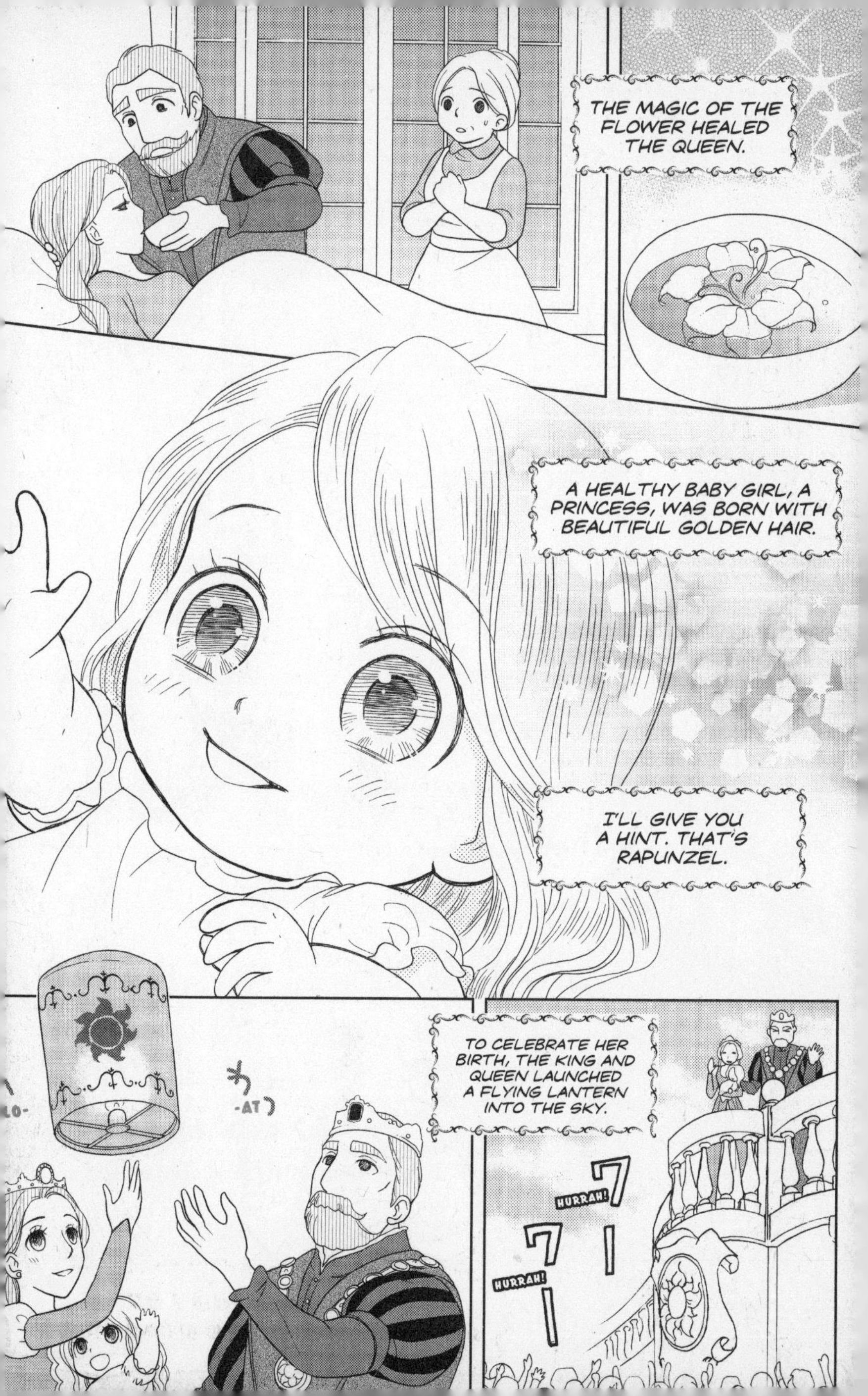

THE MAGIC OF THE FLOWER HEALED THE QUEEN.
A HEALTHY BABY GIRL, A PRINCESS, WAS BORN WITH BEAUTIFUL GOLDEN HAIR.
I'LL GIVE YOU A HINT. THAT'S RAPUNZEL.
TO CELEBRATE HER BIRTH, THE KING AND QUEEN LAUNCHED A FLYING LANTERN INTO THE SKY.
HURRAH!
HURRAH!

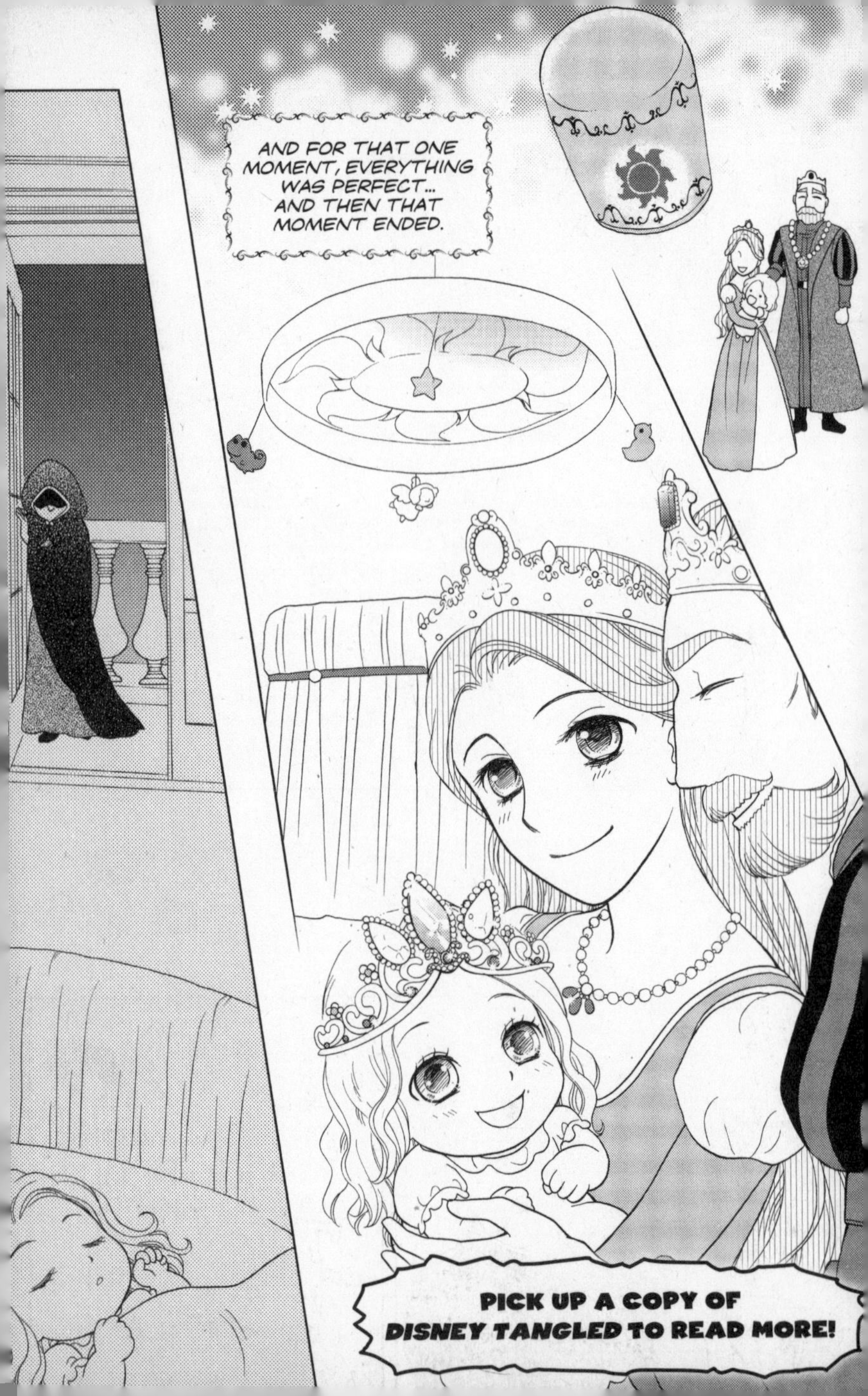
AND FOR THAT ONE MOMENT, EVERYTHING WAS PERFECT... AND THEN THAT MOMENT ENDED.
PICK UP A COPY OF *DISNEY TANGLED* TO READ MORE!

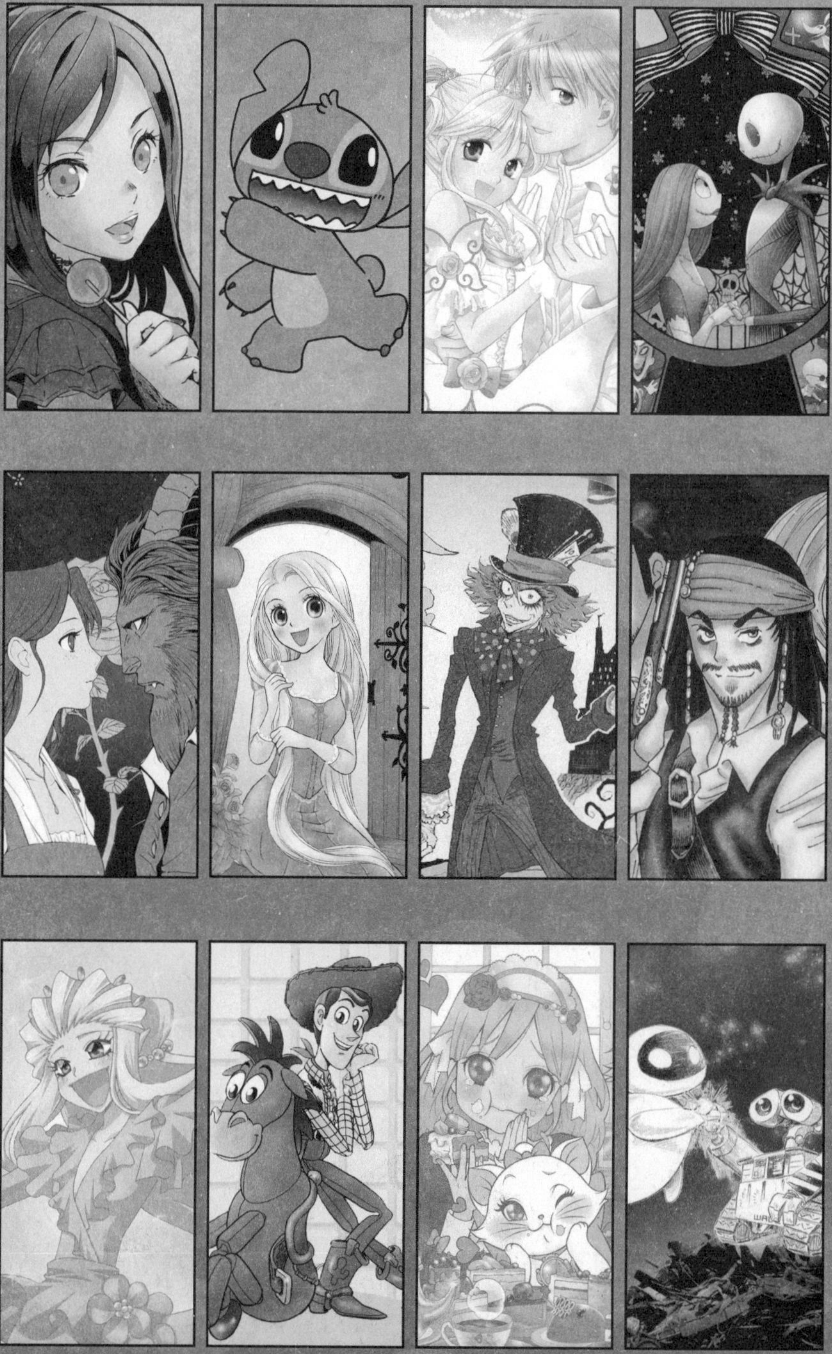

Add These Disney Manga to Your Collection Today!

SHOJO

- ☐ DISNEY BEAUTY AND THE BEAST
- ☐ DISNEY KILALA PRINCESS SERIES

FANTASY

- ☐ DISNEY DESCENDANTS SERIES
- ☐ DISNEY TANGLED
- ☐ DISNEY PRINCESS AND THE FROG
- ☐ DISNEY FAIRIES SERIES
- ☐ MIRIYA AND MARIE

KAWAII

- ☐ MAGICAL DANCE
- ☐ DISNEY STITCH! SERIES

PIXAR

- ☐ DISNEY • PIXAR TOY STORY
- ☐ DISNEY • PIXAR MONSTERS, INC.
- ☐ DISNEY • PIXAR WALL-E
- ☐ DISNEY • PIXAR FINDING NEMO

ADVENTURE

- ☐ DISNEY TIM BURTON'S THE NIGHTMARE BEFORE CHRISTMAS
- ☐ DISNEY ALICE IN WONDERLAND
- ☐ DISNEY PIRATES OF THE CARIBBEAN SERIES

TOKYO POP

Disney The Princess and the Frog Manga
Manga by Nao Kodaka

Publishing Assistant - Janae Young
Marketing Assistant - Kae Winters
Technology and Digital Media Assistant - Phillip Hong
Translator - Kelly Bergin
Copy Editor - Daniella Orihuela-Gruber
Graphic Designer - Phillip Hong
Retouching and Lettering - Vibrraant Publishing Studio
Editor-in-Chief & Publisher - Stu Levy

A  Manga

TOKYOPOP and 🐸 are trademarks or registered trademarks of TOKYOPOP Inc.

TOKYOPOP inc.
5200 W Century Blvd
Suite 705
Los Angeles, CA 90045 USA

E-mail: info@TOKYOPOP.com
Come visit us online at www.TOKYOPOP.com

f www.facebook.com/TOKYOPOP
y www.twitter.com/TOKYOPOP
▶ www.youtube.com/TOKYOPOPTV
p www.pinterest.com/TOKYOPOP
◉ www.instagram.com/TOKYOPOP
t. TOKYOPOP.tumblr.com

ISBN: 978-1-4278-5805-4
First TOKYOPOP Printing: December 2017
10 9 8 7 6 5 4 3 2 1
Printed in CANADA

STOP

THIS IS THE BACK OF THE BOOK!

How do you read manga-style? It's simple! To learn,
just start in the top right panel and follow the numbers: